THIS TIME IT WAS FOR REAL. . . .

"Look at me," Dominick said with urgency. When Mercy hesitated, he caught her chin in his fingers and tipped up her face.

Slowly he bent his dark head and brushed one corner of her mouth with his. Mercy opened her lips in invitation. His breath caressed her softly.

She closed her eyes, suspended, wanting to absorb his touch so badly, but afraid to. Afraid he would vanish again and this would all be a dream, another fantasy that would leave her inconsolably empty.

But he did not vanish. He buried his hands in her hair, pulling her head back. "I want you," he whispered again and again. "I want you. . . ."

Love's Illusion

Katherine Sutcliffe

A TOPAZ BOOK

TOPAZ
Published by the Penguin Group
Penguin Putnam Inc., 375 Hudson Street,
New York, New York 10014, U.S.A.
Penguin Books Ltd, 27 Wrights Lane,
London W8 5TZ, England
Penguin Books Australia Ltd, Ringwood,
Victoria, Australia
Penguin Books Canada Ltd, 10 Alcorn Avenue,
Toronto, Ontario, Canada M4V 3B2
Penguin Books (N.Z.) Ltd, 182–190 Wairau Road,
Auckland 10, New Zealand

Penguin Books Ltd, Registered Offices:
Harmondsworth, Middlesex, England

Published by Topaz, an imprint of Dutton NAL,
a member of Penguin Putnam Inc.
Previously published in an Onyx edition.

First Topaz Printing, May, 1998
10 9 8 7 6 5 4 3 2 1

 REGISTERED TRADEMARK—MARCA REGISTRADA

Printed in the United States of America

This book is dedicated to several very special people:

First and foremost, Jacqueline Cantor, my editor, whose wonderful enthusiasm and appreciation for my writing inspire me to drive that much harder for perfection.

To my agent, Ruth Cohen, who is always there when I need her.

To numerous people in the business who have done what they can to help: Kathryn Falk, Kathe Robin, and Carol Stacy of *Romantic Times* magazine; John Nelson of National Books; Denise Favor of Martin News; Pam Huddleston of Trinity News; Frances Perine, Louise Laumb, Jason Simms, and Nancy Gray of Waldenbooks; Carole Williams of the Book Rack; and Denise Little and Susan Heimann of B. Dalton.

And to those individuals who strive and survive right along with me: Phoebe Stell, Jillian Hunter, Laura Kinsale, Rebecca George, and Carol Bolin (who brought me the wonderful research book all the way from London!)—special friends, wonderful writers. I love you all.

There are more things in heaven and earth, Horatio,
Than are dreamt of in your philosophy.
                    —William Shakespeare, *Hamlet*

PROLOGUE

London, 31 August, 1888

Had Mercy Dansing still possessed any belief, any fear of God whatsoever on that sweltering August night, she might have considered that what had just transpired between her and George Balfour, junior politician of Balliol College, crusader for the socialist cause, had been an unpardonable sin.

"Dear God," she whispered, "what have I done?"

Mercy buried her face in her hands, felt the hot betrayal of her shame run from her eyes and down her cheeks. Her mother would have said, "You made yer bed, Mercy, now lie in it," but somehow that was a little too apropos in this circumstance. Much too apropos.

Now what?

She looked again toward the sleeping man. His soft snores disgusted her; the coins gleaming from the tabletop made her feel ill. He had offered her money. Money! As if there was any fortune on earth worth her chastity.

Her hand tightened on the chair arm as she tried to stand. She might manage it if she were careful. The pain wasn't so bad now. She thought the bleeding had stopped. But the burning was there. There was a difference. There was a part of her missing that never, never could be replaced. And she had given it away for what? Some slim hope that the clean-shaven student from Balliol College would marry her, would save her from the very thing that had just taken place?

George Balfour tossed in bed. His narrow white chest looked repugnant to Mercy now. It shone with sweat, and the hair beneath his arm was matted and wet. He groaned, rolled his head, and called softly, "Elaine . . ."

Mercy closed her eyes, swallowed back her disgust, then left her chair.

The coins. They were there still, taunting her. More coins than she could make in a week of selling watercress or groundsel or chickweed. It would buy her a used coat from Rosemary Lane. Though August was not yet finished, winter was just around the corner. More important, it would buy her food. Enough food to last her a fortnight. She was so hungry. So very hungry.

She walked cautiously toward the table, her eyes on the coins, her stomach knotting as much from starvation as from the war her conscience was waging in her mind. She glanced at George Balfour, then back at the coins. She glanced toward the door, then back at the coins. He had thought her worth it, or he wouldn't have offered it. He *was* sympathetic to the people's plight, or he wouldn't have come to London's East End in the first place. He wasn't a dislikable man. Perhaps a little pompous and unrealistic in his ideas, but . . .

Only this once.

This once.

After all, she had made a mistake, and she knew it. She would never do it again, not, at least, until she married. She didn't think much of the act anyway. She couldn't imagine what it was that made the other girls giggle and roll their eyes. It was painful and humiliating and somehow violating, and . . . Only this once. He owed her, after all. He had led her on, made her feel like someone special. He had told her once that she was one of the most intelligent women he had ever met, that if she had been born a man, with title of course, she might have been accepted by any university in England.

Oh, yes. He owed her. Because of him she had given up the last remaining dignity she could call her own. Why not take the bloody money? She had whored herself for a dream, a dream that had vanished the moment he informed her he was marrying a young woman who was his peer. That was *after* he had taken Mercy's virginity, even while he was still inside her.

She reached for the coins.

Just this once.

No one would know.

Except me.

Except me.

Except me.

With all the will she could muster, she drew her trembling hands away from the money, turned her back on the sleeping man, and walked out the door.

The hot silence of the night hit her with a palpable force, somehow intensifying the shame in her body. The air seemed thick, hard to breathe, as Mercy moved woodenly down one street after another, ducking in and out of the shadows. The moon overhead was clear of cloud and white against the deep blackness of the night, reflecting off her pale hair and skin. Something had died inside her tonight. Self-respect. Nothing would ever be the same again.

She shied as a figure stumbled out of an alley, the stink of ale heavy enough to repulse Mercy until she recognized the drunkard. The woman, all of five feet, two inches tall, turned her round face and bright eyes up to Mercy and said, "Gum, but y' give me ole 'eart a stop, Mercy. Yer out late, lass. Been keepin' time with ole Georgie agin?"

"Aye," Mercy responded.

"An' where's yer handsome brother? 'E'll be cofferin' me money if I ain't careful."

"I have not seen Oliver, Polly," she replied.

Shambling closer, Polly Nichols smiled, revealing a mouth missing five front teeth. With her gray-streaked brown hair tumbling from beneath her hat, she looked much older than her forty-two years. "Could ye loan me a sixpence, Mercy, till tomorrow night? The Fryin' Pan 'as turned me out of me bed agin 'cause I ain't got fourpence."

"I'm sorry, Polly, I don't have any money."

"No?" She waved a hand in dismissal. "No bother. I'll soon get me doss money. See wot a jolly bonnet I've got now?"

"It's very pretty," Mercy told her. "I'll see you to mine and Ollie's apartment if you'd like to stay there for the night."

"Naw, I ain't goin' there, luv. Never you mind. I've 'ad me lodgin' money three times today but I spent it.

I'll earn it back soon enough. As Ollie says, 'is easy enough sailin' along on our bottoms.' I'll make it, lass, never you fear!''

Polly Nichols swayed off down the street, her brown linsey-woolsey dress swinging limply from side to side, her black-ribbed wool stockings bunched about her ankles. Mercy watched her until she rounded the corner of Whitechapel Road, where she disappeared in the dark.

By the time Mercy arrived back at Sultan Street and the tenement apartment she shared with her half-brother, the bone-grubbers were already scavenging the walks and alleys, their greasy bags tossed on their backs as they moved about the refuse searching for bits of bones with shreds of meat still clinging to them. She felt her stomach rumble and thought again of the coins she had left behind.

Turning down the street, she was met with the familiar sight of a dozen or so women lined up against the walls, sleeping, or trying to sleep. Several children and babies were lying asleep on the hard walk, with neither pillow nor covering. Several men slept standing upright or leaning against one another. Farther from the group, a man held his wife in his arms while she slept. Still another man, his clothing caked with gutter mud, slept with his head in the lap of a woman, who was also asleep. And beyond him . . .

Mercy turned her eyes from the coupled man and woman. She wasn't shocked. She had seen it all since moving to Sultan Street. She didn't even feel disgusted, not considering what she had just done.

"Where you been, Mercy?"

She looked around into her half-brother's dark eyes. The moon reflected off his golden hair in swatches of yellow.

"Yer out late," he said to Mercy.

She ignored him and started for the door.

"I wouldn't," came his voice behind her. "Occupied."

She slowly turned to face him. "It wouldn't be the first time," she replied flatly.

He flipped a coin in the air. "I've got my ha'penny for breakfast. Where's yours?" As she started back toward the room, he called out, "I may have found you a job, Mercy. Won't know for certain for another two, three weeks."

She stopped and asked silkily, "Whoring for whom?"

He smiled charmingly and approached her, ran one long finger down her face before saying, "I'd hate to think of anyone else havin' ya, Mercy darlin'."

She backed away, shivering from his touch, then turned and hurried to their apartment. Luckily there were no lights burning. The muffled moans and shifting of bodies were the only evidence that the cramped chamber was occupied by anyone other than herself.

Sinking to her pallet on the floor, she faced the wall, praying for sleep, praying that in the morning she would awaken and this night would have been nothing but a bad dream. It wasn't much to ask of God, not so much as asking that the past seven months had never happened, or that her mother and father were not really dead. Just tonight. Just this one small favor . . . *if* He was still listening. Tonight never happened.

Please, she thought, let it never have happened.

1

20 September, 1888

Mercy stood at the edge of the walk, her eyes on the black coach as she waited for the door of the town house to open. Finally it did, and her heart turned over as the young woman exited the house on George Balfour's arm. A man and woman of some forty years followed. Mercy suspected they were George's parents.

Gripping her reticule, Mercy fought back the dizziness that had plagued her for the last week. Her face felt cold despite the heat of the day. Her fingers trembled. It had been her damnable anger and bitterness that had forced her to come here, and her desperation. She didn't know what else to do.

She was about to step forward when George looked up. The smile on his face vanished, and he hesitated in his stride toward the carriage. As he spoke softly to his fiancée, Mercy saw the girl's doelike eyes shift toward her. The young woman frowned, her disapproval obvious. Yet Mercy did not look away until the girl turned once more for the carriage.

George Balfour approached her, his slender shoulders stiff, his hands clenched at his side.

Mercy smiled.

"Good morning," he said.

She smiled again, doing her best to ignore the nausea that was crawling up the back of her throat.

"Well." He stopped before her. "You are looking very pretty," he said. "Is that a new hat?"

She nodded, unable to speak, unable, even, to think. The long speech she had rehearsed the weeks before was scattering around in her head like leaves in a gale.

George glanced back at the coach before saying, "I'm

14

getting married tomorrow. I hope you haven't come here to make a mess of things. She's a very sheltered young lady and I would hate for her feelings to be hurt in any way.''

Her courage having fled her, Mercy stared at her hands, feeling the shame of that night as keenly as if it had just happened. For the second time in her life she had made a fool of herself by coming here.

He touched her arm. ''Mercy, I should apologize. I didn't mean for things to go so far. You know I am very fond of you.''

''Oh?'' She turned her eyes up to his, her own overflowing with tears.

He looked away.

''Are you still volunteering at the hospital?'' he asked.

She nodded.

''I had hoped that night that you would take the money and put it toward your tuition to that nursing school you were interested in.''

''I don't want your money,'' she responded. ''Not for that. I shall make it my own way, or not at all.''

''I see. Perhaps you've found other employment? A man was by asking after you one day last week. I didn't know what to tell him.''

''Who was he?''

''He wouldn't tell me his name, but he was rather personal. I thought at first he was planning to blackmail me or something like that. I thought perhaps Oliver had sent him.''

''Oliver doesn't know about us. I saw no reason to tell him. It would only make matters worse.''

He smiled kindly, if not sadly. ''I read in the *Times* about poor Polly Nichols being murdered, and more recently, Annie Chapman. It seems you have a fiend about Whitechapel. I hope you'll be careful.''

''Are you coming?'' the young woman in the distance called out. The entire group was staring curiously at Mercy and George.

''A moment!'' he called back. Then, to Mercy, he asked more softly, ''Was there some reason why you came here today?''

She opened and closed her mouth. The feeling of dizziness had left her speechless. Finally she shook her head.

"Then I must be going. Ta-ra, Mercy, and good luck."

She watched as he spun on his heel and rejoined his future bride. Then she turned her back on them all and walked back to Sultan Street.

Mercy closed her eyes as the heat and noise pounded against her head with brutal force. It had been the hottest summer in a hundred years, and the wettest. Even now, as phaeton and hansom and bus jousted amid the London streets for position, the sky was turning dark again to the west. Tempers grew short with impatience as the humidity soared, shorter as the *Star*-crier's voice carried clearly over the throng of traffic and the frantic cajoling and whistling of drivers.

"Depression escalates as foreign competition rises! Unemployment expected to soar!"

She did her best to tune out the shrill, constant crying, to concentrate on the crowds moving in swarms up and down the walks. Impossible. The air, thick with sulfurous fog, made breathing and seeing an accomplishment. It exaggerated the sickness in her stomach until she was forced to lean against a lamppost or collapse to the walk. She gripped it tightly, pressed her face against the smooth cool metal, hoping for relief, praying someone would see her and care enough to stop, if only for a moment, and ask about her welfare. Of course no one did; she wasn't surprised. The struggle for existence in London during the past year had daily become more and more severe, and the feverish excitement and reckless expenditure were not only encroaching on the repose and leisure of the upper class but also hitting all others with as much impact. As the wear and tear of life grew greater, the vitality of young and old was sooner exhausted. Mercy saw it in all of their faces. As the wealthy saw their fortunes depleted, the poor watched their already paltry existence grow bleaker. Two years before, Tennyson had written in his *Locksley Hall Sixty Years After:* "There among the glooming alleys Progress halts on palsied feet, Crime and Hunger cast our maidens by the thousand on the street."

The pain gripped her, as it had earlier when rising from

her bed, bending her double, driving her nearly to her knees. Still she gripped the lamppost, holding on for her life. If she fell to the ground, she would never get up. These dispassionate men and women would walk across her as if she were dirt to be trod on.

"Never," she said through her teeth.

"Wot the bloody hell kept ya?" came Oliver's voice behind her.

Looking back, she saw him draw one hand through his blond hair before looking down at her. He cut a handsome figure to the feminine passersby. His stout boots were shined and his cable-cord trousers fit him smartly. His corduroy jacket had a back and sleeves of fustian, and there was a red silk kingsman about his throat. The clothing was used, of course, all bought from Petticoat Lane with the money he had made off his whores.

"You'd think me sister would be happy I've found her a respectable position. You'd think she'd want to show up for her interview on time for impression's sake, but no. She leaves me hangin' about some bloody street corner as if I were a bleedin' costermonger at Covent Garden."

"I'm sick," she replied.

"Yer always bloody sick. Y' make me sick, for all that, with yer whinin' and daydreamin' about how it used to be. Get up, for bleedin' sake, before I give y' somethin' to whimper about."

She tried but she couldn't. The dizziness that had plagued her for the last week had set in with a vengeance. Perhaps it was the heat. Or perhaps the hunger she had hoped to overcome since arriving in London those many months ago was finally defeating her . . . but she doubted it.

"I said get up, Mercy, or you'll be late for yer appointment. You don't know to wot lengths I had to go to to get Forbes to interview ya. It's a choice position, I vow, and he's willing to pay in advance." Going down on his knees before her, he tipped up her chin with his finger and smiled. "Look at it this way, darlin'. Get this position and be rid of me for a while."

"Sounds too good to be true." She somehow managed a smile in return, noting that his eyes took on a hard glint of anger that might have frightened her were they back in the privacy of their apartment. Here he was less likely to retaliate verbally or physically than when they were alone. This made her brave, but not stupid. She turned her face away and struggled to her feet.

The heat bore in on them as they moved down the sidewalks. Occasionally they would detour through alleys, and she would take that opportunity to breathe deeply of the cool and quiet. She had ceased asking herself why fate had taken such a cruel twist, robbing her of a comfortable, albeit simple life, altering it to one of poverty. What good would it do? No reasoning would make her understand because there was no reason behind it. She had tried praying for a while, but no longer. The vicar's ''God helps those who help themselves'' had struck a note of truth in her consciousness some three or four weeks ago, and since that day she had refused to enter a church again. If the biting and scratching for survival were to be totally on her shoulders, then, by God, she had only herself to thank for the rewards.

They arrived at Buckingham Street as the first rumble of thunder broke across the sky. Mercy stared across the bustling street at the closed double iron gates, barely hearing the disturbance overhead or the traffic noise or her brother's voice droning on and on in her ear.

''Are y' listenin' to me, Mercy?''

Mercy shifted her attention to Oliver's fierce grip on her arm and nodded.

''Forbes has promised a month's wage in advance if yer hired. I'll be around soon to collect it. Are y' hearin' me, gal?''

''Aye,'' she said, ''I hear you.''

Catching her face in his fingers, he lowered his head over hers and grinned. ''Will y' be givin' yer lovin' brother a proper good-bye, darlin'? After all, I've managed to land you the most enviable position in London.''

''That remains to be seen.''

''You are an ungrateful little bitch. You would rather volunteer all yer time to a bunch of half-dead beggars in a hospital charity ward than see to yer own brother's welfare.''

Mercy said nothing.

He shoved her away. "Remember," he said, "you'll be hearin' from me."

There was no denying that, Mercy knew. So, stepping into the street, she fixed her eyes on the distant gates and rallied forth, looking neither left nor right. She walked with purpose, head up and shoulders back, concentrating away the dizziness that made the world tip and sway around her. Only once did she hesitate, slowing as a pair of ragamuffins darted from behind a carriage post, upsetting a dustman, who shook his fist and cursed them for the beggars they were. Then, as if he sensed her standing there watching, he looked sheepishly her way, ducked his head, and returned to his business, but not before she saw his eyes come briefly back to hers. There was curiosity in the glance. Perhaps surprise. Lifting a pale hand to her bonnet, she tugged it more closely over her features and continued toward the gates.

The shrubbery was motionless around her and overhead. Odd. From the moment she stepped off Buckingham Street, in through the towering gilded gates of Greystone Manor, it seemed as if she had stepped into a sort of vacuum. Standing in a dark green shade surrounded by high elms and firs, Mercy threw a curious glance about her, noting the vivid green clumps of grass dotted with eyebright and anemones. Turning then, she looked back out the gates. Sun reflected off the street's granite sets in hazy shafts of light. Stately carriages moved up and down the streets. Dapper gentlemen and genteel women sauntered along the walks; yet even as she watched them, the image grew vague and distant. For an instant she imagined she was dreaming it all.

Hearing a noise, she turned again. There before her were several mastiffs blocking her passage up the drive. Her heartbeat quickened, for she knew that should the fierce-looking animals attack, she would stand little chance against them.

They did not move.

A sound filled her ears then, like the rushing of wings. She looked to the treetops and saw them move, stirred by such a scant breeze that she deemed it unlikely that it was the cause of the sound. Then music, like tiny chimes, surrounded her. She looked to both left and right, again to the trees, for, strangely, the light tinkling seemed to be coming from there. She listened hard, for the music entranced her, filled her with a longing she had never before experienced. She felt like weeping.

An oppression overcame her then. Something seemed near her, and with a sense of panic she looked around, again to the trees, toward the strangely unmoving dogs. An odd expectation overcame her, and she spun back toward the gates.

For a fraction of an instant she was blinded by light. So white was the intensity of it that she stumbled backward and threw up her hand to shield her eyes. A moment passed; then slowly she lowered her arm. The light was gone. In its place was only a man.

Only a man?

An oblique shaft of sunlight found its way through the trees and lit his face, his figure in a halo so uncannily beautiful that Mercy caught her breath. What strange joy filled her as she looked into his unequaled face. What happiness surged through her heart as she gazed into his caressing eyes. She dared not breathe or blink, for fear that he would disappear as swiftly as he had appeared.

He watched her intently, his eyes a startling blue, his hair far blacker than mere black. Finally he said simply, "Hello."

The dizziness assailed her again. The world slowly tilted and began its slow, undulating spin around her, dragging her down into a vortex of darkness. Suddenly devoid of all strength, she collapsed toward the ground.

His arms came around her, sweeping her up so effortlessly she might have floated to the marble bench hidden by the tangled lair of ivy and bramble to one side of the road.

"Here, now," she heard him whisper. "I'm sorry I startled you."

She shook her head, unable to speak while slightly pressing her face into his chest. The pungent smell of freshly cut grass clung to him, and for a moment she pictured Huntingdon, her home, with its rolling pastures glistening with dew. With his arms about her she felt safe again, and secure—more secure than she had felt since being forced to London by Oliver.

When he at last deposited her on the bench, part of her white-blond hair had become loose and had fallen from her bonnet, half-covering her face. As he swept it back with his fingers, she was forced to raise her eyes to his again.

"Better?" he asked.

She was unable to do anything beyond nod, entranced as she was by his appearance. It seemed to Mercy that she must be dreaming it all; his skin seemed very brown in contrast to his billowy white shirt. He had a strong nose and heavy black eyebrows.

"Who are you?" he asked. Resting on one knee, he sat back from her and openly regarded her features.

She took a breath, then replied, "Mercy."

"Mercy." He smiled. "As in Angel of . . . ?"

She looked away, feeling her cold cheeks turn warm. "As in Dansing, sir."

He caught her chin with the tip of his finger and tilted her face back toward his. "Mercy Dansing, why are you here?"

"To see Roger Forbes about a position with D'Abanville."

"Ah."

Looking beyond him to the wheelbarrow and hoe at the edge of the trees, she said, "I suppose you work here as well?"

He followed her gaze before smiling and responding, "I suppose."

"Is he a hard taskmaster, then?"

"D'Abanville?" Helping her from the bench, he responded, "I think you will have to be the judge of that, Mercy Dansing." He pointed up the drive. "The house is some two hundred yards up this road. You'll find Roger Forbes there."

"And D'Abanville?"

He gave her a swift sideways look before smiling. "Perhaps. He's a bit of an eccentric, prone to bouts of brooding, and very reclusive. But don't let him intimidate you."

"I am not easily intimidated." Then, noticing the dogs in her path, she was about to reconsider, when the man lifted his hand and without a word sent the animals trotting into the dark wood lining the drive. Relieved and feeling stronger, Mercy walked to the middle of the road and was about to begin the trek to the house when she recalled she had not thanked the gentleman for his help. She stopped and turned.

He was gone.

A spiral of wind whipped up the leaves where he had stood and scattered them around her skirt hem. The limbs overhead shifted, rustled like a gentlewoman's petticoats. Then came the chimes, so soft and distant and sorrowful she wondered if she imagined them . . . wondered remotely if she had imagined him as well.

His departure left her feeling strangely alone in the dim roadway. She walked fast toward her destination, or as fast as her weakened condition would allow, taking in her surroundings, yet thinking only of the man who had befriended her. She would never forget his eyes or his kindness. It was the first true kindness she had experienced since her arrival in London.

Leaving the tunneled causeway, she stepped into the sunlight. She saw the house in the distance, its limestone walls grown black with soot and age. Towering spires rose up against the sky, and the windows' leaded glass winked in the afternoon light. The house and grounds were not what she might have expected to find in London, but perhaps sprawled over some English countryside.

If a breath of air stirred here, it made no sound. Only an occasional bird flew in and out of her line of vision, and as she shielded her eyes and looked to the heavens, she saw a great black jackdaw swoop through a flock of sparrows and glide soundlessly toward the towerhouse on the far end of Greystone Manor.

As the lane inclined uphill, Mercy grew warmer from her exertions. As she neared the house, she could hear the sharp rapping of hammers. Could smell the heady fragrance of fresh-cut cedar and the almost stifling scent of paint. The front door stood open. Men moved in and out of the house, carrying tools and buckets and ladders. Somewhat nervously she approached.

Entering the open double doors, she found an enormous marble-floored vestibule under renovation. Men

were intent on putting the last touches of pale blue paint
to the walls. Others were rolling an Oriental rug out over
the floor. Among all this was a pale gentleman in a violent hurry, who, with his gray hair standing up in great
disorder all over his head, looked as if he were about to
suffer an attack of the vapors over the workers' apparent
slothfulness.

D'Abanville? she wondered. Mercy experienced a
slight twinge of unease at the thought.

He said, "Gentlemen—and I use the term loosely—
guests are due to arrive here at six. I trust you will be
finished by then?"

"Of course," someone replied.

"Of course!" He jabbed his wire-rimmed spectacles
back on his nose before turning and spotting Mercy.

"D'Abanville?" she asked.

"Are you a guest come early?" he replied in a panicky
voice.

"I am here to interview," she responded.

"And you are . . . ?"

As he approached, Mercy noted he was no taller than
her own five feet and seven inches.

"Mercy Dansing. I believe my brother made the appointment. I am to see Roger Forbes."

Stopping before her, he held out his hand. "I am Roger
Forbes." After she shook his hand, he explained, "I am
D'Abanville's manager. I oversee his business as well as
his house. If you will just continue down this gallery to
my offices, we'll talk in privacy."

She carefully picked her way through the mess strewn
about the floor as, much impressed by her richly ap-
pointed surroundings, she regarded the twin staircases
winding to the left and right of the high-ceilinged vestibule. The balustrades were of rich, glowing mahogany,
and along the ceilings high overhead were molded carv-
ings like garlands.

However, as Forbes stepped by her and they continued
down the gallery, they left the new manor behind and
entered a much darker and danker part of the house. The
air smelled musty with mold. Wallpaper had begun
crumbling to dust, and occasionally a spider's web would

flutter like a silver streamer from some high, dim corner of the corridor.

Arriving at his well-lit chambers, Forbes asked Mercy to be seated. She sank thankfully into an upholstered armchair.

Apparently not one to dally in frivolous conversation, Forbes sat behind his desk, peered at Mercy over the top of his spectacles, and said straightforwardly, "Do you have any experience, my dear?"

Mercy looked with some discomfiture into Roger's intense gray eyes. There was an element of shrewdness about him, and Mercy had no doubts that he ran D'Abanville's business and house with all the austerity of a navy admiral.

She replied, "I have done some sewing, sir, in George's-in-the-East."

"What sort?"

"I finished trousers for the gentlemen, sir. I made the button holes and stitched on the buttons as well—that is, until the job ran out."

"And what were you paid?"

"A ha'penny a pair, sir, but I had to buy my own cotton."

"What else?"

"For a while I sewed men's shorts. I was paid tenpence a dozen for those. I also sewed lawn-tennis aprons for the ladies and was paid threepence a dozen. For a short time I was employed as a sackmaker, earning a farthing for each."

"Anything besides sewing?"

"My first week in London I shelled peas for twopence a peck."

"And besides all that, what have you been doing?"

Starving, she thought.

"Have you any sort of reference at all?"

"I have volunteered my services these past months to London Hospital."

"Do you fancy yourself a Florence Nightingale, Miss Dansing?"

"I had hoped . . ." Looking at her hands, she bit her lip.

"Yes?"

"I had hoped to one day earn enough for tuition to the Florence Nightingale School of Nursing at St. Thomas Hospital."

His eyebrows went up. "How very commendable of you, Miss Dansing. But you hardly seem the sort to waste her life on mopping feverish brows and emptying chamber pots."

Mercy looked at him in surprise and anger. "Sir, I hardly believe that doing what one can to help those in need during a time of ill health and trouble should be determined a waste."

"Of course, you are right. I only meant that you are a lovely young lady. I'm certain any young man would see you fit to marry. Is it not my understanding that these 'Florence Nightingales' are to be unmarried? And are to remain unmarried for the duration of their employment?"

"That is correct."

"Then you are not bothered about marriage and children?"

"Not in the least."

"Then it is safe to say that should I decide to hire you for this position, you will not be exchanging your resignation for a wedding ring anytime soon?"

"Certainly not."

He sat back in his chair. "Tell me of your background, Miss Dansing."

"I come from Huntingdon. My father was a farmer of wheat until the fall in grain prices forced him to bankruptcy. My father died three months after losing the farm and my mother died within six months of him. Then I came to London with my half-brother, whom you have met, I think."

"Indeed. Your brother was most complimentary when speaking of you."

"He would be," she said.

A long silence ensued. Finally Roger Forbes leaned forward in his chair and asked, "Do you wish this position, Miss Dansing?"

"Perhaps . . . if I knew what the position entailed, sir."

"Your brother did not inform you?" He appeared surprised.

"No, sir, he did not, other than to say it was to assist D'Abanville."

"Well, then, there you have it. What more is there to say?"

"Perhaps if you outlined the duties . . . ?"

"There will be the usual attention paid to his animals. There are numerous rabbits, mice, and birds, not to mention those ghastly dogs," he added. "There is the boa constrictor, although he may or may not ask you to feed the mice to the serpent. He usually does that himself. There will be the occasional levitation and, of course, the routine disappearances."

Speechless, Mercy sat on the edge of the chair and tried to decide whether she should laugh at this man's apparent humor.

"Is something wrong?" he asked. "Don't tell me you are disinclined toward snakes?" His eyes widened then as he finally noted her confusion. "Miss Dansing, did your brother not inform you of what sort of position this is?"

"He did not."

"You have heard of the Great D'Abanville?"

"No."

He adjusted his glasses. "Madam, D'Abanville is world-renowned. Why, he is the descendant of the Great Faust of Germany."

"That is very well, but I do not know him, nor have I ever heard his name until my brother informed me that I would be assisting him—if you approved of me, of course. I assumed I would be his secretary."

"Miss Dansing, Dominick D'Abanville is a magician."

She said nothing, just fixed him with a look of shock and bewilderment. At last gathering her wits about her, she said, "Do you mean he is a practitioner of sorcery?"

"Sorcery? Good heavens, no! He is only a magician, a sleight-of-hand artist—and very good at it, I must confess. He makes people believe in the unbelievable, in the impossible. Why, I once watched him make a horse disappear with a snap of his fingers."

"Sorcery!" she exclaimed. Leaving her chair, she said, "I'm sorry, but I must turn down the position, Mr. Forbes. In good conscience, I cannot abide such chicanery."

As she turned for the door, his voice stopped her.

"Your brother will be upset, Miss Dansing." He left his chair and came up behind her. "Oliver explained to me his indebtedness. Suffice it to say, without the rather sizable income D'Abanville is willing to pay, you will doubtless lose your apartment. Forgive me if I sound cruel. I know the problem you've had in finding employment. This wretched depression has brought meager times to us all. If you refuse this position, what chance have you of finding another? Would you rather sell chestnuts or hot potatoes on street corners . . . or worse?"

She looked at him.

"Desperate means bring desperate measures, Miss Dansing. I offer you a respectable position, a comfortable existence, and a salary of five pounds a month."

"Five pounds!"

He nodded.

Her pride struggled futilely against her better judgment, and as another spasm of hunger knotted her stomach, her judgment won out. "Five pounds," she repeated.

"And room and food. All that you can eat, Miss Dansing."

She could hardly contain her eagerness as she asked, "My brother asks that my first month's wage be paid in advance. Will you do it?"

"Certainly. But understand that you will then be obligated to remain here for the month, to provide D'Abanville with your services . . . no matter what."

The alternative tumbled through her mind: her brother's temper should she return to their apartment unemployed. At five pounds a month, even turning over half the wage to her brother, she would soon be able to save enough to leave London or pay her tuition to nursing school.

"I understand," she told him.

The door opened then. Mercy came face-to-face with a woman of an estimated forty years. Her dark brown hair had begun graying at the temples, and it was drawn back severely from her face. She too wore glasses, and a dress of brown taffeta, as prim as Mercy's calico but more fitted in the bodice. Unsmiling, she returned Mercy's perusal, openly regarding her silver-blond hair, mostly hidden beneath her bonnet, noting her brown eyes, and finally her face.

"Miriam," Forbes said, "meet D'Abanville's new assistant. Have you seen him, by chance?"

"Not since breakfast. He retired to his quarters, I believe, in preparation for tonight."

"Very well." Forbes stepped around Mercy toward the door. "I've business to attend. Miriam, show Mercy to her room and make certain she is comfortable. Explain, too, that she is to hostess this evening's affair."

Startled, Mercy looked from Miriam to Forbes and said, "Hostess? But, sir, I am not prepared—"

"See to it, Miriam!" he ordered. "In the meantime I will have Micah collect your things, Miss Dansing, and bring them to Greystone." Then he disappeared out the door.

Miriam turned away and said, "Come along."

They walked in silence down the dreary corridor, passing from compartment to compartment, from passage to passage, until they reached a narrow, steep staircase that wound into the darkness high above their heads. A heavy silence pervaded this portion of the house, and as Miriam turned to face Mercy again, her eyes were cold.

She said, "Employees come and go by this staircase until the renovation of the other is complete."

Mercy followed her up the stairway to the second floor. Instead of the gas lamps that had brightened the lower corridors, oil lamps dotted the long hallways with flickering orange light. Walking at Miriam's side, Mercy asked, "What exactly do my duties of assistant and hostess entail?"

Miriam responded without looking her way. "As D'Abanville's assistant, should he perform publicly you will stand at his side and try your best to look attractive. As his hostess, you will be expected to project the bearing and deportment of a lady at all times."

"When do I meet him?"

"When he is ready to be met, Miss Dansing." Miriam shoved open the last door in the long hallway before turning back to face her. Her eyes, large behind her glass lenses, reflected the light from the lamp on the wall. "I will give you fair warning. Dominick expects certain qualities from his people. Loyalty above all else. Do not expect to be his friend. He has no room in his life for friends." Her mouth pursed slightly; then she turned toward the room.

"You are free to decorate as you wish. I think you'll be comfortable here. If you have a need for anything, you'll let us know. Dominick likes his employees to be comfortable at all times."

Mercy stopped inside the threshold, her eyes taking in the simply furnished but comfortable apartment. To her it seemed like a castle. "It shall suit me perfectly," she replied.

Getting no response, Mercy looked back at her companion. The disdain gone from her eyes, Miriam watched her now with curiosity.

"Have you been ill?" Miriam asked. "You are so very pale and thin."

"No."

There was silence then, as if Miriam were waiting for further explanation. When there was none, she said, "I'm certain you'll want to freshen up and change before you meet our guests."

"But I'm not prepared—"

"I imagine I have something suitable that might fit you. No doubt D'Abanville will want to see that you are dressed properly as soon as possible. I believe his first scheduled appearance is next week."

"Am I to understand that these performances will be on a stage? Before an audience?"

"Certainly."

Miriam closed the door between them, and Mercy turned back to the room. There was a fireplace faced with a pale gray Georgian mantel. Inside the hearth an iron coal-burning stove had been placed, and beside it a hod to hold the coal. Atop the stove was placed a blackened teakettle, a blue-and-white glazed cup and saucer, a matching pot, and a tin of tea. Beside it was a container of biscuits. Mercy hurried to the stove, wasted no time in lighting a fire and preparing the tea. She ate a handful of the buttery biscuits, savoring each delectable mouthful before swallowing. She could hardly believe that Oliver had accomplished this. Laughing to herself, she thought it might be his only honorable accomplishment.

Only when her hunger had been temporarily sated did she turn to survey the room at length.

Mercy tore off her bonnet and shook her hair loose. The hair breezed about her hips as she walked to the mahogany chest of drawers and put down her purse. She looked first at the walls, papered in a pattern of fading pink rosebuds, then at the murrey curtains, drawn open to expose a grime-coated window. A scrap of worn green carpet decorated the otherwise bare floor at the foot of the bed. All the comforts of home, she thought, still unable to believe that the nightmare of the last six months was over. Then the kettle began to whistle.

After measuring the water into the china pot, Mercy moved to the window. From here she could see the tower perfectly, and though daylight had not entirely waned, she noted a dim yellow light shining from the tower's row of tiny rectangular windows. She looked then to the garden below, fixed her eyes on a distorted fir tree, and near it, a gray wooden tub that, left to the elements, had crumbled piecemeal to the ground. Along the buckled brick walk grew withered vegetation; creepers and ivy and knee-high weeds sprouted among broken flowerpots and mounds of decaying leaves.

She tried opening her window, and found that it gave with little resistance, offering the musty quarters a much-needed draft of fresh air. She took a deep draw of it, allowing the twilight's coolness to soothe her state of dizziness and nausea. As soon as she drank her tea and her biscuits were given time to digest, she was certain both of the annoying discomforts would leave her forever. She turned back to regard her new home.

It was comfortable. And quiet. The tenement quarters on Sultan Street that she shared with Oliver would fit nicely between these four walls. She could very easily become contented here, should the position of assistant to D'Abanville prove acceptable.

Hearing a noise outside the window, she turned and found upon her windowsill a jackdaw—no doubt the very one she had noticed circling the tower on her arrival. Somewhat startled, she stared at the bird, expecting him to take flight at the sight of her. He didn't, but lifted and stretched his wings while he pranced back and forth along the sill. Something glittered in his beak, then fell to the floor at Mercy's feet.

A ring.

Stunned, she picked it up, held it in the light spilling through the window, and studied the delicate gold scroll that housed a ruby of significant size. A woman's ring, and very beautiful, not to mention expensive. "Naughty bird," she said to the jackdaw. "Where have you found this?"

He fluttered his wings, cocked his head at the sound of her voice. Then he leapt from the sill and flew away. He soared directly to the tower, dropped gracefully from the sky and into an open window.

Frowning, she studied the ring again, turning it over and over in her hands. She had never examined such an expensive object so closely, and considering its great value, Mercy grew anxious. She knew, by listening to Oliver, that there were as many dishonest jewelers in London as there were reputable ones. Finding one who would be willing to fence such a piece would not be difficult, and the money she would receive from such a transaction would see her far away from this wretched city and back to Huntingdon.

She shook her head. It wasn't in her. She knew what she would do: turn it over to Forbes, for very possibly it belonged to someone on the estate. Dropping it into her dress pocket, she eagerly returned to her tea.

The pain had started an hour ago, fierce and grinding deep in her belly. She felt better now, but only slightly. The occasional whiff of food wasn't helping, however. For a while, a short while, after eating the biscuits, the queasiness had subsided, but it was back so strong her skin had grown clammy with sweat.

Mercy stood by the entrance of the ballroom, watching D'Abanville's guests as they chatted to each other. She had been nervous and apprehensive about meeting these people, not at all comfortable in the dress Miriam had offered her to wear. Unaccustomed to wearing so elaborate a costume, she had at first refused to don it, only to be reminded by Miriam in a dictatorial voice that she would do as she was instructed or risk being dismissed on the spot.

The dress was not altogether unappealing to Mercy. Of amethyst silk, it fit snugly through the bodice and flared ever so gently over the several silver-gray petticoats she wore beneath it. But the bodice was far too daring, exposing too much of her breasts. Numerous times as she greeted the guests, she found herself under the scrutiny of both gentleman and gentlewoman, and not being accustomed to such attentions, she became greatly flustered.

She had been ordered to wear her hair down. D'Abanville preferred it that way. The silver-white skeins flowed in waves over her back to her waist, and as she stood to one side of the open French doors, the breeze occasionally billowed the hair like a cloud around her shoulders.

Eight o'clock had come and gone and still there was no sign of D'Abanville. With each half-hour that passed, the guests became more and more curious about their host. As did Mercy. As she stood attentively behind the table of refreshments, she learned by listening to the guests' conversations that no one here actually knew D'Abanville personally, although they knew of him. He was very well-known on the Continent, and though he was not titled, he was accepted by the highest social order because of the notoriety he had attained.

Where had he come from? No one knew. He had suddenly appeared in Paris three years before, had demanded an audience of President Jules Grévy, then proceeded to flabbergast the President with his wizardry. He had been asked back twice since to perform for President Carnot, and each time had succeeded in mystifying all concerned. Rumor had it that he had been summoned to London by Her Majesty. Seemingly Victoria had met him on her tour earlier in the year to Charlottenburg, Germany. In temporary residence at Charlottenburg Castle, he had been employed to entertain the aging and ill

Empress Augusta. Speculation was that even Victoria had become slightly smitten by him, and had been heard warning her ladies-in-waiting not to look him in the eye, for to do so would certainly be the undoing of their innocence.

Spellbound, Mercy continued to eavesdrop, doing her best to concentrate her thoughts on something other than the luscious display of food spread out before her. Caviar, pâté with bits of truffles, cold sliced ham and turkey, and exquisite slices of almond cake with layers of raspberry paste covered the table in glittering trays of crystal and silver. It seemed ironic that before her was all the food she had ever dreamed of eating while living on Sultan Street, and she couldn't tolerate the sight or smell of it now, no matter how her stomach ached with the need for it.

She had poured herself a punch, hoping the fruity beverage would assuage the heat from her skin, when the guests' conversation took an unexpected twist. A buxom woman dressed in a cinnamon-colored satin gown spangled in silver turned her sleekly coiffed head toward her gentleman companion and asked, "Have you heard the dreadful news? Another murder has taken place, and not very far from here. I've heard the young woman was of a respected family. God forbid that the maniac killer from Whitechapel begin murdering decent women."

A gust of wind through the door billowed Mercy's gown and hair and rattled the crystal stemware on the table. Sickened by what she had heard, she moved as inconspicuously as possible out the door, onto the veranda.

Lightning danced on the distant treetops, great jagged spears of light that turned the night into day. Clouds boiled just above the trees and rumbled, and behind her, women screamed as wind barreled though the open doors and windows. The lights along the walls, as well as the chandelier swinging high above the ballroom floor, flickered then went out, leaving the startled guests in total darkness.

A stunned silence befell the crowd. As the storm filled the air, Mercy experienced the same peculiar sensation that had gripped her upon her arrival on the estate that morning. Someone was watching her. She sensed it. Knew it.

A curious chill crept over her as, standing alone on the veranda, the darkness engulfed her. Anticipation flooded her. Then, just as suddenly, it left her. The ballroom exploded with brilliant light, causing several women to swoon and others to scream.

Mercy ran to the door and stared disbelieving as the gas fixtures suddenly flickered to life once again. On the stage, where the violinist had only moments before serenaded the audience with ''The Blue Danube,'' swirled a luminescent cloud of smoke. Within it stood a man with hair far blacker than black and eyes of startling blue. He looked over the crowd to where she stood trembling in the door and said:

''Hello.''

2

Mercy did not realize that the rain was driving against her back. Suddenly Miriam broke through the guests crowding around their host, grabbed her arm, and pulled her so roughly out of the downpour that Mercy nearly lost her balance.

"What do you think you're doing?" Miriam demanded.

Mercy shook her head, slowly coming to her senses. What had happened in that fraction of an instant that her eyes met his? She could not explain it. Suddenly she had lost all sense of time and space. The ability to breathe, to move, even to blink, had deserted her completely. Even now she felt numb. But for the aching flutter of her heart she felt nothing at all.

Until she looked at him again.

Mercy stared at Dominick D'Abanville, thinking he looked very different from the man who had befriended her that morning. He was very tall, taller than she remembered, with a lean, muscular build enhanced by the finely tailored black suit he wore. He smiled pleasantly at the tittering women surrounding him, lowering his dark head occasionally toward this one or that one while making some flattering remark that, more often than not, made the lady blush shamelessly and laugh aloud. Something turned over inside Mercy that felt disconcertingly like jealousy. She was chagrined at such a response.

"Miss Dansing," came Miriam's voice again. Then she stepped before Mercy, blocking her line of vision so Mercy had no choice but to focus on her face. Only then did Mercy become totally aware that her hair and dress had begun dripping rainwater onto the floor. "Miss Dansing, go upstairs immediately and change. When D'Abanville has performed, he will expect you to accompany him while he meets his guests, and you certainly shan't do so looking like that. Quickly!'' she stressed, then, turning Mercy toward the door, gave her a push.

Mercy hurried from the room, made her way through the dim passageways until arriving at the winding stairway. Out of breath, she dropped onto the bottom stair, closed her eyes, and did her best to rationalize her behavior. She was not a young woman to overrespond to dilemma, being neither superstitious nor delicate in feelings, so why was she shaken with the impulse to leave Greystone that very instant?

Yet she did not leave, but stared up and down the empty corridor, realizing only then how quiet, how still her surroundings were.

Mercy continued to her room, where she changed out of Miriam's dress and redonned her own calico frock with its modest white collar. She brushed out her hair and was turning back toward the door when she was stopped by a noise outside her window. She approached the window and looked down into the courtyard.

The rain had stopped as suddenly as it had started, although clouds continued to roll wildly over the ground and around the towerhouse, flashing with light occasionally and rumbling with thunder. Along the walkway, puddles of water reflected the orange glow of lantern light from some near or distant window. It was there that Mercy noted a movement within the patches of bleak mist. She looked harder, leaning slightly over the windowsill, feeling the drizzle brush her face. What was there?

A dog moved into the patch of light, then another, their wet, yellow coats clinging to their muscular bodies. As if they sensed her presence at the window, they turned their black faces up and stared at her with glittering yellow eyes. The sight caused her to shiver. Then the sensation of being watched came over her again, and she spun toward the door.

D'Abanville stood in the doorway, leaning against the doorframe, his arms folded across his chest as he regarded her. Mercy stared at him a long moment, paralyzed by fear and the same fascination she had experienced the last two times they had met. Then the dizziness struck her again, and the pain. Had there been a chair at hand, she might have dropped into it. There wasn't, so she clung to her consciousness with all her strength and prayed she did not collapse at his feet again.

He continued to regard her in silence, blue eyes never moving from her face. Tranced by his hard smile and easy air, she stood unable to do anything but return his stare.

"Sir," she said, "may I be so bold as to ask that you discontinue sneaking up on me in such a way?"

A long moment of silence passed; then he replied, "You may not."

She closed her mouth and waited, feeling her face turn from cold to hot in the moment it took D'Abanville to push away from the door and approach her. She backed away until, pressed up against the windowsill, she could retreat no farther.

The dogs in the courtyard began to bark. Thunder trembled the walls and the floor beneath her feet. Still he came on until he stood nearly against her, and she had the ridiculous notion that he was about to take her in his arms, to crush her against his chest . . .

He stepped by her and looked out the window. She heard the whisper of his satin-lined jacket against his silk shirt, so close was he standing. The dogs' barking immediately stopped, and as she peered around him into the courtyard, she saw them streak out of the yard as if the devil were in hot pursuit. She moved away.

D'Abanville straightened, and though she sensed he was looking down at her, she refused to look up.

"The dogs shouldn't be out," he said. "I'll have to speak to Micah about that. They can be dangerous if left unattended. Should you decide to walk the grounds, Miss Dansing, make certain they are penned before doing so."

"Why do you keep them?" she asked, moving farther from him toward the door. "They are obviously vicious."

"Because it amuses me," he replied. He sat upon the windowsill, just slightly, so one long leg was barely off the floor and swinging from side to side. He folded his arms again over his chest and looked at Mercy directly. "One has to keep up appearances, you know. I have my reputation to consider."

"You enjoy frightening people?"

"I enjoy entertaining them. There are times in this profession when the two go hand in hand."

She glanced at him sideways. "I don't care for being frightened."

"Then I shan't frighten you. Look at me, Mercy. Does merely looking at me frighten you?"

Mercy forced herself to do so, focusing on his mouth and not his eyes.

"*Are* you frightened of me?" he asked.

She shook her head no.

"Then look at me."

Hesitantly she did so, meeting his dark-lashed eyes with her own.

"Have you enjoyed the party?" he asked softly.

"No."

"Why?"

She raised her hand and brushed away an errant hair from her cheek. "I am not comfortable with those people."

"Perhaps you prefer the company of indigent children?"

Mercy frowned. "How do you know that? Did Roger tell you about London Hospital?"

He looked away briefly, caught the curtain's edge between his fingers before responding. "I saw you there once."

She was surprised. "You are certain it was me?"

"Oh, yes. It was a Tuesday three weeks ago. You were standing at the far end of the ward reading a book to a young boy with bright red hair."

Mercy looked away. With a sinking in her heart, she said, "That would have been Tom. He died soon after."

"I'm sorry."

"Are you? Why? Did you know him?"

"Must I know him to feel pity over his passing?"

"Your pity comes too late, I think. But that is always the case with socialists such as yourself."

"Am I a socialist?"

"It is a very popular way to think among your class. Or perhaps you are a Social Darwinian, in which case you are probably not sorry over Tom's passing at all, but see it as a fitting solution to the overpopulation of the unfit."

"I abhor Francis Galton and his eugenics. Any man who would offer cash bonuses to encourage marriage and births among the 'fit' and segregation and sterilization for the 'unfit,' in my opinion, should be burned at the stake."

Strong words, but Mercy somehow found it hard to believe him. George Balfour had made many similar statements, as had the other undergraduates from Balliol or Toynbee College who thought their "cultured" presence in the East End would somehow make a difference to the poor's plight.

"You look doubtful," he said. "I take it you've heard those words before."

"And others. I wonder what your class knows about the East End's situation? You know only what you read in the papers, and have no doubt never ventured forth yourself into that filthy pit."

He smiled.

Mercy frowned. She had begun sweating again, a certain sign that her illness was about to resurface. Not in front of him, she thought. Those blue eyes were too shrewd. She could feel them taking in her every detail, assessing her pallor, her frailty, perhaps even the dampness of her skin. He would know. And then what?

Lifting her chin and forcing herself to meet his eyes directly, she said, "You think I exaggerate. How often have you reflected on what it must be like to have no home at all except the common kitchen of a low lodging house; to sit there, sick and weak and bruised and wretched, for lack of fourpence with which to pay for the right of a doss; to be turned out after midnight to earn the requisite pence, anywhere and in any way, and in the course of earning it to come across your murderer and to caress your butchering assassin. That is what it is like for the women in the East End these days, Mr. D'Abanville. They must take the chance of meeting some killing fiend or else starve. I am not certain what is worse: the lingering death of starvation or to have your life ended in just a few short seconds of pain.''

Realizing her eyes were wet with suppressed tears, Mercy turned away, struggling to keep some semblance of calm within her. In a lower voice she added, ''I do not judge you for your ignorance, sir, so please take no offense. I was as ignorant as the rest of the world once. Although my family was far from wealthy, I did have a comfortable house to call home, and three meals a day. If my dinner was an hour late, I thought I would starve. I promise you, that feeling of emptiness is so very pale in comparison to real hunger, not only of the stomach, but of the soul.''

Having walked toward the stove, Mercy grabbed the back of her chair and looked around at D'Abanville. His eyes were still on her, intense, penetrating. Was it too much to hope that she had stirred some honest sentiment within him? ''There is nothing so hungry as the soul without love, Mr. D'Abanville, without compassion and kindness. It is no wonder so many women turn to prostitution. Aside from the reward of money, they are also allowed, for a few minutes anyway, to imagine—fantasize, if you will—that someone cares.''

He must have heard something in her tone that she had not meant to be there, for suddenly he was moving toward her, hesitantly, his countenance worried. She backed away, not daring to let him too near. If he touched her, as he had earlier that day—oh, dear God, how often these last hours she had recalled the gentleness of that hand . . . No, no! she thought with panic. Don't touch me or I will crumble. Genuine caring was all she wanted, not pity.

''Mercy,'' he said softly, ''are you ill?''

She raised her icy hands to her cheeks.

''Will you let me help you into the chair?''

''No. It is only a momentary weakness. It will pass.''

He raised his hand anyway, brushed her forehead with the backs of his fingers. ''You have a fever, lass.''

She wet her lips. ''I think not. 'Tis only overexcitement. I tell you it shall pass.'' She raised her eyes to his then; there was a long pause. No matter how she willed herself to look away, she could not, though she could not bear his looking at her that way. His look seemed to reach inside her and acknowledge the truth of her lie.

Finally he dropped his hand and began, "You are excused—"

"Sir?" Her eyes flew open wide and her hand reached out and clasped his coat. "Pray, do not dismiss me from this job so soon. The illness will pass. It is passing already."

He looked down at her hand. Only then did she realize where she had placed it. His heart beat strongly against her palm. She felt hopelessly abashed by her move. But as she withdrew her hand, he gently caught her narrow wrist in his fingers and finished, smiling, "I would hardly have you believing that I am some . . . 'hard taskmaster'?" He laughed softly as she lowered her eyes in bemusement. "You are excused from your hostess duties for the evening only, Mercy Dansing. I suspect it was too much to ask on your first day at work. Rest tonight. You'll feel stronger tomorrow."

"But I feel stronger already." She smiled at him brightly, for it was true. The dizziness and pain had subsided somewhat and she was eager to get on with her duties.

"Are you certain? You are under no obligation—"

"I am very certain."

He studied her a moment longer. "Very well. But I will keep a close eye on you throughout the evening. If I see that becoming blush on your face become pale again, I will order you to bed in a moment and will abide no further rebuke."

Not until he had moved away was she able to recover her sensibilities enough to recognize the effect his presence was having on her. She did not look at him again until he stopped at the door. As he held his hand out to her, she gaped at it like a frightened child before forcing herself to move, to lift her own hand and place it in his. As his gentle fingers wrapped around hers, he lifted her hand to his mouth and said:

"I'm glad you're here. Welcome to Greystone, Miss Dansing."

* * *

Even before they entered the foyer, Mercy sensed a sudden wariness in D'Abanville. He had held her arm gently all the way from her room. They had made small talk about the house and his profession, D'Abanville revealing very little about either. He had surprised her by informing her that they would be leaving London soon for a short stay in Liverpool, where they would be performing at the Empire Theater. Then suddenly his grip tightened so forcefully she gasped. He quickly dropped his hand from her arm, squared his shoulders, and almost reluctantly entered the vestibule. New guests had arrived. Two men stood just inside the door, water dripping off their mackintoshes onto the floor.

The taller of the pair spotted D'Abanville first. Sweeping his bowler hat from his head, he approached Dominick, his hand extended but his smile not quite reaching his eyes as he greeted Mercy's employer.

"D'Abanville, it is a pleasure, sir. How do you do?"

"Very well," she heard him reply.

"I am Chief Inspector Chesterton from the Criminal Investigation Department of the Metropolitan Police. Might we talk somewhere privately, sir?"

A moment passed before Dominick responded, "I think not."

"Very well, then, I shall say what I've come to say here." Chesterton's eyes widened as he noticed Mercy standing in the shadows. When she remained where she was, he disregarded her and pursued his interest in D'Abanville. "Are you acquainted, sir, with a Miss Abigail Russell?"

"Yes."

"And when did you last see her, Mr. D'Abanville?"

A long silence ensued, punctuated by the staccato waltz from the next room.

Finally he said, "Last evening."

"Last evening," Chesterton repeated. "At what time, sir?"

"Early."

"*How* early, Mr. D'Abanville?"

"Why does it matter, Inspector?"

"How well were you and Miss Russell acquainted, Mr. D'Abanville? Was she your mistress?"

Again the silence. Mercy watched Dominick's hands clench, then unclench at his sides. Finally he responded, "I think that is none of your business."

"Ah, well." Chesterton pursed his lips, then said, "She is dead, Mr. D'Abanville."

For a moment the orchestra hesitated in its serenade, or perhaps it just seemed that way. Moving further into the vestibule, Mercy focused her eyes on D'Abanville's back, doing her best to see if he had been shaken by the news. He did not move, and when he spoke again she heard no grief or surprise caused by the disclosure.

"How did it happen?"

"Murdered, sir. And not very far from here. In truth, her body was found just outside Greystone's boundaries. We fear that her murder might somehow be tied to the Whitechapel murders, sir."

Mercy caught her breath. D'Abanville too seemed affected by the ghastly news. Turning away from the inspector, he raked his long fingers through his hair as he paced the floor. When he looked up, it was into Mercy's eyes, but it was to Chesterton that he spoke.

"I was under the impression that the recent murders were always women from the Whitechapel area."

"True."

"They were prostitutes."

"True as well."

Angrily Dominick turned back to face Chesterton. "Then why in hell do you believe Abby was murdered by the same maniac?"

"It was the method of murder, sir. She was . . ." He looked toward Mercy, bowed his head apologetically, then finished, "Her throat was slashed and she was disemboweled."

Mercy was certain D'Abanville paled; his eyes closed. When he opened them again, however, he seemed not in the least distraught, whereas she could but cling to the doorframe and pray the horror she felt throughout her senses would not overcome her.

Chesterton continued. "I have spoken with her employees. I am told she was looking forward to seeing you at the opera."

"What are you getting at?" D'Abanville snapped.

When Chesterton's only response was a lift of one narrow brow, he exploded, "Out with it, sir! Have you come here to accuse me of something?"

"Accuse you?" Chesterton appeared thoughtful, staring at some point above D'Abanville's head. Finally he shook his head. "I have no evidence to prove that you were involved in Miss Russell's death. . . . You *were* at the opera last evening?"

A cold smile twisted Dominick's mouth. "I have the feeling you already know I was at the opera last evening."

"It was *Faust,* I believe—a rather tragic French opera by Gounod. Faust is an old man, weary of books and learning, and rather disappointed with his life. The devil, Mephistopheles, appears to him and shows him a vision of a beautiful woman. Faust is persuaded to sign a contract with the devil, and the old man becomes young again, giving himself up to the pleasures of youth and love. It has a rather tragic ending, I think, as the young woman dies and the devil drags Faust into hell with him. . . . You sat with Lord Rosenberry through the first half, then you left. And afterward?"

"I returned home."

"Ah, yes. Home." The inspector looked about the newly painted vestibule. "There has been a great deal of speculation about your moving into Greystone. It has a rather ghastly history, but I'm certain you are well aware of that. I wonder why you would wish to live here when there are plenty of pleasant estates to buy throughout London, throughout England for that matter."

When Dominick did not respond, Chesterton smiled. "You have done a great deal of renovation. One would hardly recognize the old place. Let me see, you've been in London . . . how long?"

"Six months."

Chesterton's assistant scribbled on a notepad.

"Six months," the inspector repeated. "I do believe that was just about the time the first mutilation took place in Whitechapel. Am I right, Lawton?" he asked without turning.

The assistant nodded. "That would be Emma Smith,

sir. She was assaulted with a knife on second April. She died of peritonitis soon after, at London Hospital.''

"Six months ago?'' Chesterton reiterated.

"Precisely six months,'' Lawton said.

Replacing his hat on his head, Chesterton said, "We've taken up too much of your time, Mr. D'Abanville. We will be keeping in touch, sir.'' He turned back to the door, then stopped. "By the way, you may be interested to know that at the time of Miss Russell's brutal murder she was wearing a gift from you. A . . .'' He lifted his hand toward his assistant.

Lawton flipped through his notebook and said, "Jewels, sir.''

"Ah! A necklace and bracelet, I believe?''

Lawton shut the book and said, "Rubies, sir.''

"Ah, yes. According to her lady's maid, there was also a ring. However, I am sorry to say it seems to be missing.''

The words came at Mercy like an unexpected blow. She stumbled backward, feeling consciousness evaporate like a mist.

The next thing she knew, there were hands touching her face. Gentle, warm hands, cradling her cheek, brushing her pale hair over her shoulders. A bright yellow light shone in her eyes so she was forced to blink and turn her head to avoid it. The pain was back, excruciating this time, drawing her body in on itself against her will.

"Mercy,'' came the voice. "Miss Dansing, are you all right?''

Inspector Chesterton's narrow features came into focus first. He was peering down over D'Abanville's shoulder. Closing her eyes, she tried to recall what had caused her such shock, tried to force down the pain. It was washing over her in dark waves, rippling down her legs and gnawing at her back.

"Mercy?''

Her eyes flew open at the sound of Dominick's voice. She must have looked terrified, for he responded, "Hush. There is nothing to be frightened of, Mercy, I assure you.''

"Can you tell us what happened, Miss Dansing?'' It was Chesterton again.

She looked from Chesterton to D'Abanville. He sat on the edge of the settee, leaning slightly over her, his dark head bent over hers. His eyes were on her, waiting, watching, holding her against her will until she forgot the pain she was feeling, forgot even Chesterton's awful disclosure, forgot there was a purpose for anything but having Dominick touch her again; it was all she could think of at that moment. She didn't even realize that she had lifted her hand with every intention of reaching out for him, until he wrapped his own fingers about her wrist and pressed it down into the settee beside him.

"If you have something to say to Chesterton," he said mildly, "I suggest that you say it so we might get you upstairs."

Without taking her eyes from his, Mercy shook her head, remotely wondering what spell he had cast upon her, so that, against her better judgment, she remained silent about the ring in her pocket.

He left the settee then and faced Chesterton. "I fear the young lady has been overly excited. You will excuse us?"

Chesterton looked at Mercy, his features dubious. "Very well," he said. "Miss Dansing, I wish you a rapid recovery. Perhaps we shall meet again when you feel more like conversing." Tipping his hat to D'Abanville, he quit the room, followed by his assistant.

Dominick stood away from Mercy, a dark figure in a halo of lamplight.

"Sir," she heard herself saying, "I'm sorry about your friend . . . Miss Russell."

"So am I," he responded quietly. Running his hands through his slightly curling black hair, then down his face, he closed his eyes and repeated, "So am I." A moment of silence passed before he looked at her again. "I highly suspect you need a bed as soon as possible, Miss Dansing. I'll see you back to your room, then I'm fetching a doctor."

Before she could refuse, he crossed the room and lifted her from the settee. Cradled in his arms, she rested her head against his shoulder as they moved back through the house, up the stairs, and to her room.

The rain was falling harder as he laid her on the bed.

With a strange lethargy she stared at the ceiling, remotely regarding the blackened patches caused by fumes from the oil lamps. D'Abanville returned to the door and closed it. She thought he had gone, but he hadn't. He was soon back, standing by her bed, smoothing her damp hair off her brow.

"Is there pain?" he asked gently.

She looked away from his eyes and stared toward the door, gripping her skirt in her hands. Oh, yes, she thought, there is pain. Frightening pain made more frightening because her mind and body were two separate entities, one unable to control the other.

"Mercy? How far along are you?" He took her hand.

She jerked it away. "I don't know what you mean," she said tightly.

"You are about to lose your baby, I think. It would help me to know how far along you are."

Great hot tears welled from her eyes and spilled down her cheeks. Her shoulders began to shake. As he sat down beside her, she covered her face with one hand and wept. "Oh, God, I am so ashamed!"

"Do you know who the father is?"

"Yes." She wept harder.

"Does he know?"

She rocked her head back and forth.

A soft knock at the door interrupted. Mercy closed her eyes and turned her face away, doing her best to quiet her sobs before D'Abanville opened the door an inch or two.

"What is going on in there?" came Miriam's voice from the corridor. "Your guests are wondering where you are."

Mercy held her breath.

"Miss Dansing is not feeling well," D'Abanville responded. "I would like you to check our guest list. I'm quite certain there are one or two physicians in attendance. Send one up to me immediately."

"Is it serious?" Miriam asked.

"Nothing that should alarm you."

No sooner had D'Abanville closed the door than Mercy was gripped again with pain, bowing her back and drawing her knees into her stomach. D'Abanville was beside her in an instant, shucking his black suit coat and rolling his white lawn sleeves up to his elbows. Odd that she should notice in such a mind-splitting moment how clean his hands were. How long-fingered, how gentle. Finally the pain passed and she relaxed.

"You are a strange man," she said groggily, and saw him smile.

The wind through the open window made the lamplight quiver, casting light and shadows over the walls and floors of the chamber. Mercy shivered, cold, suddenly, without his closeness to warm her. It was instinct that raised her hand to grip his shirt. She was afraid of being alone now; he was her sanctuary.

She whispered, "I'm so afraid."

"I'm right here."

"I'm so ashamed."

"Don't be. We all make mistakes. God knows I've made a few."

She tried to smile.

"Did he seduce you?"

She could have lied, but she didn't. "No, sir, he did not. If anything, I seduced him."

Silence. Wetting her dry lips, she turned her head and looked at his face. More silence. An angry flurry of rain spattered against the panes of the window behind him as she waited for his response. His eyes were fixed on her. The whiteness of his shirt shimmered gold in the lamplight.

"It seems I've shocked you, sir. No more than I shocked myself, I trust. I hardly thought it in me to do such a wicked, whorelike thing, but, as Roger said this morning, desperate means bring desperate measures. I was afraid of becoming a whore—a prostitute—so what did I do? I prostituted myself for a marriage proposal. No doubt I deserve this trial of agony. I am only sorry the child inside me will suffer so tragically now for it."

"He would have suffered either way," he surprised her by admitting. He bent more closely to her, regarding her intently. His soft black hair spilled over his brow, and a faint hint of woodsy cologne swirled lazily between them. "Tell me," he said. "Did you do or take anything to bring this miscarriage about?"

"No."

He looked relieved.

She closed her eyes and rested, wondering when the pain would wash over her again, dreading it, praying for it. That shamed her too. But what could she offer the child, after all? Home and hearth were a dream even for her. Was it fair to thrust it out into the East End like the other tens of thousands more to die of the elements or murder or starvation? There were children of ten years selling themselves on the streets while their mothers worked the back alleys for a pence. Oh, yes, she was glad for the pain.

Another two minutes of silence passed between them before it started again. It was happening now. No more false cramps. Squeezing her eyes closed, she gripped the sheet beneath her.

"Get out," she heard herself cry. "Please, let me alone. I am shamed enough. Get out and let it die with some sort of dignity. Let me die, for all that. I am so tired, so damnably tired!"

There was movement around her, but the words made no sense.

"Get out. Get out, damn you. You have no right to see this!"

"Stop fighting it."

"Please!"

"Take my hand."

"No, no."

"Hold my hand."

Somehow she reached out. She was aware her dress had been pulled up around her waist, but she did not care.

It was over quickly.

A knock sounded at the door. D'Abanville released her hand and left the bed, though she did not watch him do so. She had turned her face away and closed her eyes. He pulled her dress down nearly to her knees before moving toward the door. She opened her eyes a little, saw him reach for the door, then stop. He made a visibly difficult effort to control himself as the stranger's voice called out:

"Mr. D'Abanville? It is Dr. Alderman. You have a need for me, sir?" A moment passed. "D'Abanville?"

Finally he opened the door enough to see out. "Are you alone?" he asked.

"I am. Your secretary mentioned a young lady is ill?"

D'Abanville stepped back, allowing the doctor entrance. Seeing Mercy, he immediately became concerned and hurried to the bed. "Good Lord, what has happened here?"

Leaning back against the door, Dominick closed his eyes. "She has miscarried," he said softly.

"Mis . . ." The physician raised her skirt. He looked back at D'Abanville. "Why wasn't I summoned sooner? The fetus might have been saved."

There was a flash of guilt in Dominick's eyes as he looked at Mercy. Silence flowed back into the room as the doctor looked from one to the other, their eyes locked in the shared knowledge and acceptance of what they both had allowed to happen.

"I see," the doctor said more softly. Looking at D'Abanville directly, he asked, "I take it then that you are the father?"

Mercy closed her eyes, waiting. When no response came, she looked at D'Abanville again anxiously. The appeal must have shown in her eyes, for almost angrily he righted his shoulders and met the doctor's scrutiny.

"Yes," he said, "I am—was—the father."

"But you are not her husband."

"No." He walked to the window.

The doctor placed his bag on the floor and in a short time had removed all trace of the incident from the bed, wrapping it in the white sheet on which it had spilled. He then examined Mercy and found her condition to be satisfactory, under the circumstances.

"Her bleeding is normal," he said. "But I would watch her carefully. She is to be abed for the next forty-eight hours. If no problems have arisen by then, she is no doubt free of any complications." Snapping his bag shut, he glared at D'Abanville's back and said, "There are certain devices available to you both if you desire to avoid this unpleasantness again. I suggest you look into one of them if you plan to continue this relationship."

D'Abanville turned very slowly from the window and looked, not at the doctor, but at Mercy. Was there the faintest hint of a smile in his eyes?

"We shall endeavor to remember," he said dryly, perhaps chagrined at such a dressing-down when none of this was of his making.

The doctor then picked up the wadded sheet. "Have you some back stairs? I shall deposit this in my carriage as I leave."

D'Abanville walked to the door, grabbing up the coat he had earlier tossed aside, then showed Dr. Alderman out. Mercy watched him in the hall as he slid a purse from inside his coat, withdrew several crisp bills from within it, and gave them to the doctor. She heard him say softly, "I would appreciate your discretion concerning this matter."

"Of course." Alderman said more quietly, "For your peace of mind, Mr. D'Abanville, I doubt if I could have saved the fetus. The young lady is obviously malnourished and has been under severe stress, by the looks of her. Had the young woman remained in such straits and the fetus grown to full term, the birth could have killed them both."

D'Abanville reentered the room, closing the door gently behind him.

So it was ended, Mercy thought. She had thought to feel relieved, yet she felt sad. And tired. She longed now for sleep. How long since she had last spent an uninterrupted night?

She struggled to sit up. Suddenly *his* hands were on her, gently righting her. "What are you about?" he asked.

"I would like to change."

"Where is your nightdress?"

She pointed to the dresser.

He moved swiftly to the dresser and pulled open the drawer. He seemed hesitant, looking down at the mound of pale pink cotton, a sad reminder of lost innocence if there ever was one, she mused.

"It is there on top," she called out.

"Ah." He grabbed it up and returned to her.

She did not look at him, but kept her eyes averted,

looking at her gown only briefly as it dropped onto her legs. A moment passed before she took it in her fingers. Very gradually she lifted it, bunched in her hand, and covered her breasts. She felt naked in his eyes. The ugly secrets of herself had been laid bare before him, a virtual stranger.

"I . . . am deeply embarrassed," she said.

He did not speak.

"You must think me something dreadful, and perhaps I am. I have taken you away from your guests, caused you humiliation before the doctor, not to mention having cost you money. I suppose I would not blame you for turning me out. It is nothing more than I deserve."

Without warning she looked up and caught him staring. Not at her eyes, but at her hands twisted together at her breasts. A pink satin streamer had fallen over her fingers and was trailing to her lap.

Finally, as if forcing himself, his eyes came back to hers. "Would you like tea?" he asked.

"Yes."

"Do you need some help with that?" He motioned toward the gown.

"I can manage, I think."

"All right." Yet he continued to stand there until she chanced him another glance. Finally he turned back toward the stove and set to preparing the tea. Her gaze followed him as he stoked the fire and continued to crouch before it while the flames took up their snapping and crackling at the green kindling, spewing a small cascade of embers at his feet. With a force of will, she focused on unbuttoning her dress, smiling a little to herself as he poked and prodded the fire, making far too much noise to be considered normal.

By the time he finished the tea, she was dressed and had rested back on her pillow, covering herself with a blanket. He grinned at her, an expression so unexpected and warm that it went straight to her heart.

"You look better already, Miss Dansing. A cup of my world-famous tea and you will be ready to dance the quadrille for Victoria herself."

"That good?"

"Stout enough to curl your hair."

"Heaven knows it needs it."

"I don't know. You have very pretty hair."

Mercy looked up at him in surprise. Having never received a true compliment from a man, she was uncertain of how she should respond. Coyness would be out of place, considering what had passed between them.

"I should thank you," she said.

"For what?"

"For everything. For holding my hand."

"I daresay I may someday need your hand to hold. I trust it will be there if I need it?"

"If you declare it should be, sir."

She smiled up at him as he handed her the tea. He smiled faintly back.

Reaching for his coat, he said, "You are to follow the doctor's orders implicitly. No work for forty-eight hours."

"Then you still want me, sir?"

He looked at her in surprise, then laughed and pulled on his coat. "Want you, Miss Dansing? Did you expect me to toss you back to the East End on your ear?"

"In truth, I don't know what to expect."

"Because I'm a strange man?"

She felt herself blush.

D'Abanville walked to the door, coat in place now, every bit the aristocrat, dashing, virile, handsome enough to turn the head of every woman awaiting him downstairs. Opening the door, he looked back, flashing her his most charming smile.

"I shall give these good people their money's worth, then come back to check on you. If you need anything, the bell-pull is there."

"Sir?"

He stopped.

"I meant what I said. I shall forever be grateful."

Mercy continued to watch the door for a long while after he had gone. She watched until her head grew too heavy to hold up any longer, until the fatigue and the relief dragged her down into her bed and her head to her pillow. And still she struggled, dozing fitfully, occasionally becoming confused. One moment her nightmare was ended. The next she was back on Sultan Street, expecting

Oliver to come stumbling through the door with one of his girls. When the door finally opened and closed quietly, what seemed like hours later, she was too tired to look up.

But she knew he was back.

And she finally rested.

3

She did not remain in bed for the next two days, but neither did she venture any farther from her bed than the chair before the window.

Mercy sat and contemplated her future. She daydreamed about the present. She wept over her past. She stared out over the courtyard and watched the sky turn from gray to blue to gray again as the afternoon showers moved in. She smelled the musty, rich scent of damp loam, listened to a distant woodpecker drum against the trunk of some high tree beyond her perspective, and considered the possibility that she had found paradise.

Greystone Manor seemed a thousand miles and a thousand years away from the East End. Once she had thought, not many days ago, that she would never rid her nostrils of the stench of unwashed bodies, sewage, and, oftentimes, death. She had thought never again to sleep on a bed that was not made up of heaps of dirty rags, shavings, or straw. After the fiasco with Balfour she had briefly considered killing herself. Suicide in the East End wasn't unusual, after all. Just before her coming to Greystone, a husband and father of five had hanged himself from an upstairs balustrade, leaving his family without any sort of income at all.

But there had been that lingering hope to sustain her. The same hope that kept her surviving, from one day to the next, the elements, the hunger, her half-brother's cruelty. Now she was here and the smells that filled her nostrils were perfumed with cleanliness. Her bed was a mattress with white sheets, and the promise of kindness and hope made her weep with a melancholy every time she thought of it. Dominick D'Abanville had saved her. She owed him her life.

Mercy continued to wait eagerly for D'Abanville's return. Having angled her chair just so, she had a perfect view of both the courtyard and her bedroom door; she would see him the moment he entered. She had rehearsed her thanks a hundred times before noon: she would be forever grateful for his kindness and consideration . . . she would be fastidious in her duties as his assistant . . . The day grew later, the shadows longer.

Yet he did not return.

At just after two, the door opened and Mercy felt her heart skip with anticipation. Miriam entered with a tray. After her initial disappointment, Mercy felt relieved and grateful. Her breakfast of tea and toast at eight that morning had done little to appease her appetite; she was voraciously hungry.

Mercy noted immediately that Miriam was without her glasses. Her chestnut hair had been tied up in a coil on the top of her head; soft curls fluffed over her forehead, making her look much younger than she had appeared the day before. She looked striking in her crisp white blouse with standing collar. Frills of lace spilled in tiers across the bodice of the blouse, accentuating the width of her shoulders. As was the norm, she no longer wore a bustle, but neither was her red skirt flounced. It clung to her body, outlining her round hips and reminding Mercy how slim and almost boyish were her own.

"Are you feeling better?" Miriam asked, standing over her.

"Very much, thank you."

"Dominick never explained your illness to us. Roger is quite concerned, as is Dominick, of course."

"It's nothing, really. I feel much improved today." She glanced at the food.

"I wouldn't say it is nothing if you have been ordered off your feet for forty-eight hours." She stared until Mercy felt discomfited by her intense interest and looked away.

Finally Miriam placed the tray on Mercy's lap. It held a bowl of rich pea soup, thick slices of bread, raspberry cake topped with heavy cream, and a glass of chilled milk. Mercy wasted little time in lifting her silver spoon and eating.

Miriam said, "I have brought up the *Times* if you would care to see it. There is an article on Abigail Russell's murder I feel you should be aware of. Dominick's name is mentioned numerous times." She handed Mercy the paper, folded to expose the drawing of a young woman's face. "The *Times* does not feel that her murder has anything to do with the murders in the East End, but the police feel otherwise."

Mercy stared at the slain girl's picture. "She was very pretty."

"She was a nuisance."

Mercy looked up. Miriam's eyes were cold and her mouth was grim as she explained.

"Abby Russell was constantly underfoot, making demands of Dominick's time and money. She would have bled him for every penny he owned had he not broken off the relationship."

Miriam walked to the dresser and studied her reflection for several minutes before meeting Mercy's eyes in the mirror. "Dominick doesn't have room in his life for hangers-on. You will do well to remember that, Miss Dansing, thereby avoiding any complications in your life. Dominick D'Abanville has almost reached the pinnacle of his career. His ultimate goal is to perform for the queen, and he shall do so the evening of the lord mayor's celebration. He is at the Royal Palace Theater now attending to preparations for the event. Nothing should stand in his way now. Nothing . . . unless those imbeciles at Scotland Yard make trouble. They shall come to regret their stupidity if they do, I promise you. Dominick will brook no interference from anyone during this final climb to the top."

"He certainly sounds determined," Mercy said.

Miriam faced her. "Indeed. And so are those of us who have helped him achieve this glory. You understand why we must be very careful of anything that could cause him harm in any way, whether matters of the heart or matters of business. It is imperative that a man like Dominick, who is scrutinized so thoroughly by the public eye, be beyond reproach. That includes those of us around him. I trust, Miss Dansing, that you have nothing in your past that could somehow surface and damage his career?''

Thinking of George Balfour, Mercy forced her eyes from Miriam's and stared down at her soup.

"Well, Miss Dansing?"

"If it is a crime to be hungry and homeless, then I am guilty of both," she snapped.

"I understand that you are a socialist," Miriam returned.

"If that is a crime, then I am guilty. So are growing numbers of West Enders, if not in actual practice, then in ideals, for whatever good their high ideals do us. As I recall, even D'Abanville hinted of socialistic ideas, and as I told him, it is a very popular way to think now among the upper classes. It gives them something to debate hotly while they sip their tea and nibble their crumpets."

"As long as you are not using this position D'Abanville has given you for an opportunity to publicly beat your breast and howl at his audiences about the deprivations of the poor."

"I had no such intentions," she replied angrily. Forcing her attention back to the news, Mercy turned the paper over and read: "Balfour Nuptials Today."

"Is something wrong, Miss Dansing?"

She shook her head and tossed the paper aside. "Do you expect Mr. D'Abanville to return soon? I should like to talk with him at length about my position as his assistant."

"Oh?"

"Certainly." Mercy forced a calmness into her voice that she didn't feel. "I would like to know what the position entails."

"That would depend on you, I suppose."

Mercy broke off a bit of bread and buttered it.

"How old are you, Miss Dansing?"

"Nineteen."

"You are very young. The youngest so far, I think."

"What do you mean? The youngest for what?" Mercy looked hard into Miriam's eyes.

Miriam smiled. "Nothing. I was just thinking aloud." She walked to the door and looked back. "We will be leaving for Liverpool day after tomorrow. We had planned to leave tomorrow, but considering your illness, Dominick chose to postpone our traveling another day. I will attend him this last time before you step into my shoes. I trust you will watch closely and take note. The Great D'Abanville is a master and expects mastery from those around him.''

''I shall do my best to please him in whatever way I can. He is a very kind man.''

The caustic smile fading from her mouth, Miriam regarded her without blinking. Finally she said, ''If you need me for anything, my room is just down the hall. Don't hesitate to call, Miss Dansing.'' She stepped from the room and closed the door behind her.

Mercy shoved the food aside, having lost her appetite.

Mercy napped for the remainder of the day and awoke at just after seven to find her dinner tray placed on a table near the stove. She rose and ate it in semidarkness, had just finished when she heard D'Abanville's voice in the hall. She closed her eyes and listened, vaguely aware that her heartbeat had accelerated, that her breathing had become shallow. She told herself it was nerves. After all, she had not spoken to him since the night before. She wondered how they would approach the subject of what had taken place here.

He did not come to her door, but stopped up the hall, where he rapped softly on another. Mercy left her chair and slightly opened her door. He stood at that threshold with his midnight-dark hair tousled boyishly about his head. He was without his coat. His galluses cut into his shoulders, making his shirt blouse slightly at the sleeves and about his neck.

The door opened and Mercy heard Miriam say rather harshly, ''You're late.''

''I was held up by the theater manager. I'm sorry.''

He walked into the room and the door slammed behind him.

Mercy was about to close her door when Miriam's voice carried shrilly down the hall.

''Have you seen the papers? . . . Then you saw the story about Abby Russell. . . . What do you mean, ignore it? I told you that bitch would be trouble, didn't I? Didn't I? . . . Of course I've been drinking. What in God's name am I supposed to do with my time besides drink? There are only so many letters to write, Dominick. . . . Yes, of course I made arrangements with Madame Cartier. As soon as we return from Liverpool I'll take the little mouse down to have her properly attired. . . . Oh, my, have I hit a nerve? Forgive me, darling, I hadn't realized you two had become so cozy so quickly. Just what *did* go on up here last evening while your guests were waiting downstairs wondering why they had spent ten pounds each— Where are you going?''

Mercy stepped back into her room as Miriam's door opened.

''Don't you dare walk out on me, D'Abanville!''

''I don't intend to stay here and watch you do this to yourself.''

''Me? Me!''

''Be quiet.''

''Don't tell me what to do. Do you know how sick I am of taking orders from you?''

''We can terminate the arrangement anytime you so desire, madam.''

''You would like nothing better. I gave you the best years of my life, and you would turn me out on the street as if I were some tawdry little matchbox girl like—''

''Shut up!'' The door slammed again, and for a moment their voices were muffled.

''You owe me everything,'' Miriam cried. ''You would be nothing without me.''

''Keep your voice down, dammit.''

''I am the one who talked Jacques into taking you on. You would still be in some flea- and drunk-infested cabaret begging for food—''

''I don't intend to listen to this.''

The door opened again and D'Abanville stormed out, Miriam hot on his heels, her hair flying around her shoulders and her gauzy red nightgown swirling around her ankles. Mercy caught her breath as the woman screamed, ''Toss me out and I'll ruin you. I can, you know! I'll sell the *Times* all I know about you and your goddamn magic. You're a fake, Dominick. A phony! A cheap charlatan!''

Miriam stumbled to the wall, where she leaned heavily against it. There were footsteps, and suddenly Roger was before her, taking her shoulders in his hands and turning her toward her bedroom. For a moment she fought him.

"Where's he gone?" she muttered.

"To the tower, no doubt. He was most distraught. He told me to sober you up."

"He used to like me like this. He thought I was exciting."

"He never liked you like this. You are not a likable woman when you are like this. Now, come to your room."

"I was younger then. And prettier."

"Come along."

"He likes them young and pretty. The younger the better these days."

"He likes them sober, which you rarely are."

"He wants to get rid of me."

"If he wanted that, he would have done so already. He cares for you, Miri."

Mercy closed her door.

Mercy did not see D'Abanville the next day. Neither did she see Miriam. Her food was delivered by a somber young servant who came and went so quickly there was little time for conversation. For countless hours Mercy sat by her window and looked out on the peaceful world, or what she could see of it. The day before, she had wondered how such a paradise as this could exist, when outside the gates all bedlam teemed around them. After viewing Miriam's and D'Abanville's performance the night before, however, she had begun to wonder just how heavenlike Greystone really was.

Other, less pleasant thoughts had begun nagging at her mind as well. Abigail Russell's slaying was being highly publicized; certain investigators for the CID suspected that her murder and the East End murders had too many similarities not to be related. The *Times*, however, felt that because the East End murders had been thoroughly explored by newspapers interested in revealing every horrible detail of the killings, anyone on the street could have mimicked the brutalization with little effort. The

Times, however, did not stop short of rehashing D'Abanville's stormy romance with Abigail Russell. An unnamed source was quoted: "I saw her slap his face once and run weeping from the room." Another said, "Miss Russell once told me, 'He has a heart made of ice. Sometimes Dom frightens me so!' " There was even a beautifully sketched picture of Russell and D'Abanville together at a hospital charity ball only two weeks before Russell's brutal murder. It was that picture Mercy saw in her mind as she closed her eyes for sleep that night.

Sunlight flooded upon her, not so harsh and yellow as it had been the past long summer weeks, but with the mellowness of soft candlelight. Mercy sat up and rubbed her eyes, hearing the far-off hammering and sawing of lumber as she stared at the sunlight that poured through the window. A slight breeze stirred the curtains and filled the room with the smell of roses. Mercy yawned, taking the time to stretch and sigh deeply before throwing the counterpane from her legs.

Recalling last night's troubled dreams, Mercy moved to the window and stared toward the tower. She had worried throughout the night about the police and the public's interest in D'Abanville's possible involvement in Abigail Russell's murder. How could the man who had shown her such kindness be the same man who could murder a woman, or women? She refused to believe it.

But there was that damnable ruby ring, after all: enough evidence to put him behind bars, or possibly hang him. She knew by reading the papers that the country's passionate obsession with catching the East End Butcher was growing almost out of hand, that Scotland Yard was desperate for any evidence that might yield some clue to the murderer's identity. However, T. P. O'Connor of the *Star* had mentioned less than a week ago in his column, "Mainly About People," that the CID should take care with their investigation or they were likely to find themselves murderers in their own right. Law-abiding men were growing frightened of walking the streets after dusk for fear they would be taken into custody by the CID and accused of the killings. The populace, too, had grown so fearful they were beginning to suspect anyone who appeared even slightly unorthodox.

A rap at the door startled her. Miriam called out, "Miss Dansing, are you there?"

"Yes," she responded.

"You were to meet D'Abanville by eight. You are fifteen minutes late."

"I'm sorry. I shall endeavor to be more prompt from now on."

"See that you do. We shall be leaving for the train at ten. Make certain your things are ready."

Mercy stared at the door until she was certain Miriam had departed. She then rushed to dress, brushed out her hair, and hurried downstairs.

Miriam showed Mercy to D'Abanville's office, leaving her alone to wait for her employer. The apartment was cluttered, tables piled high with papers and books, many of them tattered and yellowed with age. The windowsills, as well as the massive oak desk to one side of the room, were strewn with empty cups and saucers, brandy snifters, and china plates. Wadded pieces of paper littered the floor in the vicinity of the rubbish bin near the knee hole of his desk.

A movement at the corner of her eye caught her attention. Sitting on a perch, the jackdaw cocked its head and peered at her with glittering black eyes.

"Hello," it said.

Mercy stared.

"Hello," the bird repeated. Then with a flap of its gleaming wings it flew to the desk, landed on a stack of papers, and hopped up and down. "Where's Roger?" it said. "Time for work!" The bird hopped again and screeched, "Abracadabra!"

Mercy turned and walked out into the hall, stood there for several minutes before returning somewhat hesitantly to the room. Stepping through the doorway, she stopped.

"Good morning," D'Abanville said. Sitting back in his chair, his eyebrows raised in anticipation, he asked, "Is something wrong?"

"Where did you come from?" she asked. "You weren't here a moment ago."

"Are you certain?"

She narrowed her eyes. "Oh, I see. I am to believe that you appeared there magically. Well, I shan't believe in such an impossibility." She glanced about the room.

"Looking for something?"

Her eyes came back to his. There was amusement in their blue depths. She saw it too in the quirk of his lips. "Where is the bird?" she asked, aware her voice sounded dry.

"Bird?"

"The blackbird."

"His name is Malphas and he's a jackdaw. He becomes somewhat offended if you refer to him any other way."

"I beg his pardon," she said a little angrily.

D'Abanville left the chair and walked around the desk. Mercy noted he seemed different today. Less austere. Less formidable. Dressed in leather breeches and a loose-sleeved white shirt, he looked more like a stablehand than a world-renowned magician. Sitting upon the edge of his desk, he crossed his arms and looked at her directly. His eyes were the color of deep, still water.

"Are you feeling better?" he asked. "Did you rest well these past two days?"

"Very well, sir. Thank you."

"Are you up to the trip to Liverpool? If not, you are excused and may remain here."

"I'm fine." She glanced again about the room, again at the empty perch.

He said, "We have not discussed this problem with the CID. I trust you won't let Inspector Chesterton's curiosity distress you overmuch."

"Only if you are not overly distressed by my skepticism of your occupation."

"Touché."

"Where is the bird?"

"What bird?"

Mercy leveled him with an indignant stare. "I don't believe in your hocus-pocus, Mr. D'Abanville, so you can save your theatrics for your gullible audience."

"Then why are you so concerned about my bird?"

"I have never seen a bird that could talk."

"Ah. Well, then . . ." He walked to the window and raised it. Within seconds the bird flew in and landed on D'Abanville's shoulder. Dominick fed it a sunflower seed he dug out of his shirt pocket. Looking back at Mercy, he asked, "Are you ready to begin, Miss Dansing?"

"That would depend on what we are about to begin."

"Magic, of course."

She must have looked incredulous.

"Something wrong?" he asked.

Folding her hands before her, she said, "I have told Roger of my feelings. I suppose you should be aware of them as well. I do not approve of your profession, Mr. D'Abanville."

"You would not be the first to disapprove of my profession, Miss Dansing."

"And at the risk of sounding redundant, I do not believe in your hocus-pocus."

"Not even a little?" He fed the bird another seed before slipping one into his own mouth.

"No, sir. Not even a little."

"Well, Malphas," he said to the bird, "I suppose we'll have to turn her around. What do you think?" The jackdaw fluffed its feathers before hopping atop D'Abanville's head and flapping its wings. Turning his eyes on Mercy again, D'Abanville directed her, "Please hand me the kerchief from that chair, Miss Dansing."

She turned her head briefly, just long enough to sweep the delicate article of white lace and linen from the chair. When she looked at him again, she stopped short, her mouth falling open in surprise. The jackdaw was now a snow-white pigeon cooing softly from his shoulder.

There was a smug curl to D'Abanville's lips as he watched her face for surprise. She *was* surprised, and distressed too. For a fraction of a minute she had almost allowed herself to believe . . .

"Impressed?" He looked at her expectantly.

"No," she replied with a huff of impatience.

"You dropped your kerchief," he reminded her.

Drawing her eyes from the pigeon to the floor, she stared down at the scarlet square of silk lying over the toe of her shoe. Dumbstruck, she focused on the object while her mind wrestled with the impossibility of his turning a square of white linen into scarlet silk without having moved away from the desk. Closing her eyes, she whispered, "It isn't possible."

"But everything is possible, Miss Dansing, if only one believes—"

"I deny it." Her eyes blazed back at his. "I don't believe in miracles. Not anymore. I stopped believing when I watched my father lose everything he'd worked for all his life. I stopped believing when both he and my mother died of a broken heart, and I deny any deity who would allow the human race to suffer in poverty for no more reason than they were born in the East End!"

After that she was embarrassed to look at him again. She closed her eyes while she struggled to control her breathing, then glanced down at the white kerchief on her shoe.

So much for miracles.

By the time Mercy had extinguished her anger enough to face D'Abanville, he had turned his back and was in the process of lifting the covers off several cages of birds, a cage of rabbits, one of white mice, and a glass box of what looked like tree limbs and grass. Then the tree limb moved, blinked, and stuck out its forked tongue. Mercy almost swooned.

D'Abanville proceeded to catch one of the mice and deposit it into the case with the serpent. As the rodent shrank into a corner, its sides heaving in and out with fear, Mercy grew weak enough to look around for a chair. Perhaps she had left her bed too soon after all.

"You aren't afraid of fire, are you?" D'Abanville asked, diverting her attention briefly.

Wistfully eyeing a chair filled with books and yellowed newspapers, she responded, "Fire?"

"As in smoke and brimstone."

"As in Satan and hell?"

He rolled his shirt sleeves up to his elbows before whirling around to face her. His lip curled sardonically as he replied, "As in hot, Miss Dansing." Then his arms moved so swiftly and his body shifted so suddenly that her eyes became confused. Before her mind could come to grips with what her eyes had seen, a flash of light exploded before her, engulfing D'Abanville in a blinding bright flame. Mercy stumbled backward, crying out in surprise as she covered her face. When the acrid smoke cleared, he was gone.

Silence.

Hesitantly dropping her arms, Mercy waited, glanced about the room. She called out softly, "Sir? . . . I don't appreciate this. You might give me more warning next time . . ."

"Abracadabra!"

Mercy spun toward the desk. The jackdaw hopped up and down on the back of D'Abanville's chair and said, "Hello!"

Mercy ran from the room.

Mercy was standing in the hall outside Roger's office, doing her best to rationalize what her eyes had just seen, when Forbes popped his head around the door and smiled. "Ah, there you are, my dear! Are you feeling up to your first full day at work?"

That is debatable, she thought.

"Have you seen D'Abanville this morning?"

"Off and on."

Roger chuckled. "Been at it again, has he? He does so enjoy disappearing. It took him years to perfect the feat, you know. Please come in, Miss Dansing, so we might better discuss our business."

Miriam left the office in that moment. Without affording D'Abanville's secretary a second glance, Mercy followed Roger to his desk.

"There are papers to sign," he said. "When the formalities are finished, then you may go back to D'Abanville if you so desire."

"And if I don't?" she asked.

Roger's eyes crinkled merrily as he laughed. He shuffled through the great mire of papers on his desk before spotting the object of his intense search. "Ah!" He perused it a moment before staring directly at her. "It is quite simple. You have asked for an advance of five pounds, a month's wage, have you not?"

She nodded.

"Then you shall have it. However, D'Abanville requires your signature on this contract, stipulating that should you leave this position before the required month is up, you shall be obligated to return the salary in full.''

Mercy accepted the paper, placed it in her lap, and regarded it carefully. ''What if D'Abanville and I don't suit each other?'' she asked, thinking still of his disappearance.

''Not suit?'' Roger removed his glasses, pressed his thumb and forefinger against his eyes before replying, ''Dominick approves of you very much, Miss Dansing. Very much. He told me so this morning. To quote him, 'Miss Dansing is just the sort of woman I've been looking for.' '' Replacing the spectacles, he smiled. ''Have you some reluctance about working with him?''

Staring down at the contract, she thought of the ring in her pocket. She thought of Chesterton three nights before . . . she thought of Abigail Russell. Then she thought of D'Abanville standing at her side, holding her hand, bestowing on her more compassion and kindness than she had experienced since her arrival in London.

She picked up the pen and signed.

''Mercy?''

Forcing her eyes away from her signature, she looked up at Roger, who was leaning slightly across the desk.

Frowning concernedly, he said, ''You've grown quite pale. Please don't let what you've recently heard about D'Abanville's reputation distress you.''

Mercy looked quickly to the paper he extracted from her hand.

''That will be all,'' Roger said.

She noted the flame of the nearby candle reflecting in the cloudy lenses of his spectacles as she raised her eyes to his. He watched her intently, the pupils of his eyes glowing with the flickering firelight.

''That will be all,'' he repeated, smiling this time.

She glanced once more at the paper in his hand before leaving her chair. Not until she left his office and stood in the musty corridor did she finally realize that she had not taken a breath in what seemed like minutes.

Resting against the wall and closing her eyes, Mercy tried to rid herself of the feeling that she had, somehow, just sealed her fate. But perhaps she had known that since the first moment she put eyes on Dominick D'Abanville.

''Ey! There y' are, y' silly bitch, nappin' on the job already, I wager.''

Startled, she turned to find Oliver grinning at her from the shadows. ''What are you doing here?'' she demanded.

''Wot d'you think, imbecile? Me money, of course. Give it over and I'll be on my way.''

Mercy moved away, realizing the impossibility of escaping Oliver, but attempting it nevertheless. He made a sudden move, catching her arm and slamming her back against the wall so forcefully she momentarily lost her breath.

''Bloody bastard,'' she hissed. ''What's wrong, Ollie, your girls kipping on the job? Didn't they earn you your ha'penny for breakfast?''

His eyebrows shot up. ''Wot's this? The wee lamb is speakin' back to her master? Careful, darlin', you know how I hate sass.''

''You're not frightening me any longer, Ollie. You've got no control over me here.''

His smile turned under. ''Don't I?'' he asked softly. ''I'd think that over very carefully, me lovely little pet. Who got you this friggin' job in the first place? Methinks you should be showin' yer appreciation a mite. You could be back in some rat hole workin' yer fingers to the bone twenty-two hours a day while stitchin' some blueblood's frilly drawers, you know. And who knows. Maybe D'Abanville will take a special fancy to you . . . the way yer high-brow junior politician did. I always suspected it would take somethin' just short of a miracle—or money— to get you to spread those long white legs for a man.''

She swung her hand toward his face. He caught it with a force that brought tears to her eyes.

''Don't even think it,'' he said. ''Whatever would our dear deceased father think of yer strikin' his only son? He's no doubt rollin' in his grave this very minute.''

''He cursed the night you were born,'' she said.

Grabbing her jaw in his fingers, he sneered. ''Aye, I'm certain he did. He told me enough times that the hounds of hell turned their noses to the moon the moment I let out my first shriek. Born bad, he said, and it's the truth, I vow, so if I were you, me darlin' sister, I'd turn loose of that money before you come to regret the day you were born.''

Mercy shook her head, her anger making her breathless. "I haven't got it yet," she told him.

"Liar. You've been here three bloody days."

"I've been ill."

"I think maybe you thought you'd go to Liverpool with the lot and disappear before givin' me my cut."

"I wouldn't get very far on five pounds," she told him. "Now, let me go."

"Give me the money and I will."

She did her best to turn her face away, but his fingers only dug more cruelly into her skin until it was all she could do not to cry out. "I . . . don't . . . have it," she finally managed. She then twisted from his grip, did her best to turn away.

The shadow came from nowhere, looming suddenly over Mercy as she turned her face toward the wall, expecting the blow that would undoubtedly follow. It didn't happen, however. Cautiously turning, she discovered why.

D'Abanville stood beside her brother, Oliver's raised fist caught firmly in his hand. Oliver, his mouth slack, stared up into her employer's glittering eyes in surprise.

"If you have some argument with the young lady," Dominick said, "you will take it up with me."

It was a moment before Oliver recovered from his shock enough to answer, "Is that right?"

"Aye," he said. "That's right."

"And just who the bloody hell do you think you are to interfere with family business?"

"Her employer," he said silkily, his mouth grim and his face immobile in the erratic lamplight.

Mercy backed away, well-acquainted with her brother's temper. He was a street fighter, an alley cat. He played dirty and showed no pity or remorse over his brutality.

Looking to D'Abanville again, frightened of the outcome should he be forced to face down Oliver, she said, "Sir, no harm's done. He only—"

"I know what he wants," he said slowly. Lowering his eyes to hers briefly, he finished, "I forbid it."

"You wot?" Oliver laughed in disbelief.

"Should I be forced to repeat myself, you will sorely regret it, Mr. Dansing." D'Abanville's fingers flexed more tightly about Oliver's wrist, his knuckles white in the half-light. "I abhor violence in any form," he continued. "But what I loathe even more is being driven to it . . . especially by the likes of you."

Oliver made a strangled sob of outrage in his throat. As Dominick thrust him away, he stumbled over his own feet and fell flat on his back.

Mercy swallowed back the sick fear that her brother's temper had been pushed beyond its limits. Reaching out and grabbing D'Abanville's arm, she beseeched him, "Please, you don't know his temper."

Lunging to his feet, Dansing sneered. "You son of a bitch, the last man who laid me on me back got his tongue cut out. Let's see if some of that hocus-pocus'll keep me from cuttin' out yers."

"Don't tempt me," came the quiet threat.

The lights flickered and dimmed. D'Abanville stood stolidly in the center of the corridor, his hands relaxed at his sides but his face dark and his eyes like ice burning as he watched her brother. She felt weak suddenly, as if her strength were slowly being drained from her, as if the lack of oxygen in the corridor were suffocating her to unconsciousness.

Vaguely she saw her brother move; an object glittered in his hand as he lunged toward D'Abanville. But as she tried to scream a warning, she found herself incapable even of that. For a moment she became lost in the confusion, in the sudden flurry of dust and debris that rose from the floor in a cloud to blind her. She caught a glimpse of D'Abanville raising his hand; fire flashed at his fingertips, or perhaps it was the glint of lamplight on the steel of Oliver's knife. The air snapped like an ax blade against dry tinder, and suddenly Oliver was hurtling back against the wall, sliding to the floor, and clutching his stomach with both hands.

Slowly D'Abanville approached him, grabbed him by the collar, and hauled him to his feet. Easily lifting Oliver to his tiptoes so he could look him squarely in the eye, he said in a cold voice, "Leave here and don't come back. Should you even consider crossing those gates, I shall turn my dogs loose on you. Do you understand me?''

"Yer gonna regret this," Oliver said.

"I doubt it. Now, get out of my sight before I lose my temper, Mr. Dansing." Then he added, "God only knows, I have a considerable temper when antagonized. And you *do* antagonize me, Mr. Dansing." He lowered Oliver to the floor.

Mercy's brother straightened his clothes, shifted his eyes to hers. "You'll pay for this, gel," he said. "I'll be waitin', Mercy." He swept his knife up off the floor, then walked away.

Only after Oliver's departure was Mercy able to breathe. Only then did she look toward D'Abanville.

His back to her, he leaned against the wall and stared up the dark corridor in which her brother had disappeared. Suddenly he released a long, harsh breath of air. "Dammit!" It was vicious, painful. He lifted his face toward the steady yellow light above him and groaned so quietly she thought she imagined it.

Her voice quavered as she asked, "Are you injured?"

He shifted a little and shook his head.

Moving closer to him, she said, "I must apologize—"

He raised his hand to silence her, then reached into his coat pocket and withdrew an envelope. He handed it to her.

Mercy found inside the envelope two five-pound notes. She stared at them before looking back at D'Abanville.

Without returning her appraisal, he demanded, "Take it."

"Take what, sir?"

"All of it." He stood a little straighter and began brushing off his black suit coat. Before Mercy could recover from her shock, he tilted his head toward her and added, "It will be our little secret, of course. Roger would require a reckoning should he learn of this, and I'd rather not debate it with him. You understand."

"No," she said, "I don't. I cannot accept—"

"Are you not in need of money, Miss Dansing?"

Her mouth opened and closed without response.

Lifting one black brow, he looked down at her again.

"Buy yourself something pretty. God knows you deserve it."

"Not with money I did not earn," she told him. Her fingers lightly brushed the crisp notes before she looked at D'Abanville again. His blue eyes were warm now, his countenance less severe. She almost hesitated before asking, "Exactly what are my responsibilities, to warrant this sort of wage?"

He shrugged. "Don't consider it a wage. Consider it a bonus for a job well done."

"But I've done nothing yet."

"Haven't you?"

She stood rigid, staring into his magnificent face, the memory of his touch tumbling like an avalanche through her mind and body.

"Loyalty commands a high price," he continued, "a price I am more than willing to pay. But know too that disloyalty demands a higher price." Mercy flinched as he gently caught the tip of her chin between his thumb and forefinger and tilted her face up toward his. He added quietly, "Don't ever forsake me, Mercy. *Ever.* If you did . . ."

His touch burned.

Her fear must have shown, for he backed away and regarded her with less emotion. "Your bags have been delivered to the front door. Miriam is waiting for you, I think. You will ride together to the train station. Roger and I will be along shortly."

Without responding, she turned up the hall, concentrated on each step before she took it, crumpling the money in her fist and clutching it to her stomach. Reaching the end of the corridor, she looked back.

D'Abanville was gone.

4

On the Liverpool train, they had the entire stateroom carriage to themselves. Mercy sat alone for a majority of the trip, watching the countryside fly by faster than she had imagined possible. She was not uncomfortable. Her chair was covered in rich plush velvet and swiveled to whatever angle she desired. She was swiveling back and forth once when she looked up to find D'Abanville watching her. He only smiled and went back to reading whatever material had kept him occupied since the start of their journey.

The walls of the coach were black walnut embellished with marquetry. Mirrors adorned each glossy panel. Above the many glass windows were painted colorful landscapes, and the ceiling was hung with red silk. There was matching carpet on the floor so thick and soft Mercy had trouble walking on it. From a burled walnut table she ate her lunch: several small meat pies she had purchased from an urchin who had dashed up to their group just as they were boarding the train.

"Cud y' spar a penny for a pie?" the young man had pleaded, tugging her skirt.

"A pie!" She was startled.

"Aye, miss. They's 'ot pies, guaranteed. There's tarts and puddin' balls too."

"Have you potatoes?" came D'Abanville's voice beside her, and Mercy had looked up, surprised, to find him grinning rakishly down at the eager young man.

" 'Course I do." The boy laughed, thumbing back over his shoulder. "Me mum's got baked taters just there, kept 'ot over charcoal burners, they is."

"I'll have two," D'Abanville told him. "And they'd

better be hot as you say. And they had better have butter and salt provided.''

The boy turned his eyes up to Mercy. "Certainly I'll have a pie,'' she told him. "Two! And a tart and a pudding as well!''

He had pointed toward Miriam, who stood scowling with Roger at a distance. "Will the lady and gent be buyin' nothin' ?''

"Certainly,'' D'Abanville responded. "Give me a pair of those trotters for the lady. I happen to know they were once her favorite before she got so uppity.''

The boy scrambled to do D'Abanville's bidding. Mercy's last sight of the lad was his running alongside the moving car, his hands full of coins, calling, "Y'll be likin' them pies, miss; they's beautiful!''

She was eating one of the boy's pies when D'Abanville sat down beside her.

"Hello,'' he said softly. "Would you like to share my potatoes?''

"Only if you will have one of my pies.''

They exchanged pies and potatoes.

"I think you'll enjoy Liverpool,'' he told her. When she made no response, he glanced at her sideways and whispered, "You don't talk much, do you? Are you timid? Not put off by crowds, I hope.''

"No, sir. I am accustomed to crowds.''

"Will you do me a great favor?''

"Anything, sir.''

"Stop calling me 'sir'.''

She felt her cheeks turn hot.

"I'm sorry we haven't had a chance to talk the last two days. I trust Miriam has seen to your comforts.''

Some irritation must have shown on her face, though she tried to hide it. He looked solemn. "I trust she has at least behaved herself where you are concerned.''

Mercy smiled and took a bite of potato.

He said with all seriousness, "I don't share my potatoes with just anyone, you know.''

"Are you fond of potatoes, Mr. D'Abanville?''

"Dominick. Certainly. What country boy wouldn't be?''

"Do you eat them a lot, Mr. D'Abanville?''

"Dominick. As often as I dare.''

"Would you like your potato back, Mr. Dominick? I should hate for you to be hungry."

"I'll survive, Miss Mercy." His eyes flashed as he smiled. "Mercy, mercy, Miss Mercy, what is this?" He placed his hand against her face. The contact was jolting, unexpected. Mercy drew in her breath as his fingers brushed her ear gently. He held up a gleaming new penny between two fingers. "Good lord, woman, what sort of place is your ear to be lugging about pennies?"

She stared at the penny, her mouth full of potato.

"And here!" He laughed and brushed her other ear. "Another bloomin' penny. You've heard of pennies from heaven? How about pennies from ears? Close your mouth, Miss Mercy, you've potato in it. Aha! What is this?" He held up his elbow.

"An elbow," she said, swallowing her potato.

"And what are elbows good for, young lady?"

"Bending your arm?"

"Louder. Don't be shy. Speak up so the entire audience can hear you."

Mercy repeated herself, but not much louder.

He shook his head, looking very serious. "They make starving magicians a great deal of money. Give me your penny." She did so. Holding the penny in his right palm, he said, "I shall make this penny dissolve into my left elbow by rubbing it into said elbow. Watch closely." He rubbed the penny against his elbow a little clumsily. The coin fell to his lap. He picked it up and tried again, dropping the coin again. He picked it up with his left hand, switched the coin to his right, and tried again, rubbing it gingerly against his elbow. When he turned his hand over, the coin was gone.

"Voilà! Another mystifying feat by the Great D'Abanville. Hold your applause until later." He dug into his breeches pocket, withdrew a pocketknife, opened the blade, and held it up for Mercy's inspection. "You will see that the blade is clean, tainted with nothing."

She nodded.

He laid it on her lap, then withdrew a handkerchief from his shirt pocket, held it up for her to see, flipping it from one side to the other. Holding up his thumb, he added, "You see, the thumb is totally unscathed." He then rolled up the handkerchief and tied it around the first joint of his thumb. Taking up the knife, he proceeded to slice into the pad of his thumb.

Mercy gasped, covered her mouth with her fingertips as he turned up his thumb to reveal a terrible bloody gash.

Looking surprised, he said, "Oh, gosh, are you squeamish? Well, we can't have that." Whipping off the handkerchief, he covered his thumb with it and held it up to Mercy's mouth. "Kiss it and make it better," he said.

She looked at him skeptically.

"Come now, Miss Mercy, you wouldn't want me to bleed to death right here in your lap?" Very gently he raised his thumb to her lips. Her eyes on his, she lightly pressed her lips against his covered thumb. "Very nice," he whispered. "But you'd better do it again just to make certain."

She did, her eyes never leaving his. She could not conceive what he might be thinking behind those eyes, behind the smile that revealed the pleasure he was feeling over this small performance.

Pulling his hand away, he slowly unwrapped the kerchief, revealing a thumb totally undamaged by the knife.

Mercy stared at it in amazement.

"You know what they say," he said, grinning. "Love heals all wounds."

Looking back at his eyes, cerulean pools that were both bright and dark, she thought of saying, "But I don't love you." But the words, strangely enough, wouldn't come.

After a nine-hour journey they reached Liverpool. Less than a half-hour later they were off through the dark streets of the city on their way to their hotel. They passed the Empire Theater on the way. Great banners proclaimed the coming of D'Abanville the Magnificent! The Greatest Magician of All Time! Direct from the Alhambra Theater in Paris! Mercy found it hard to visualize that the man sprawled lazily over his seat across from her, his sleeves rolled up to his elbows and the collar of his shirt unbuttoned, exposing his throat completely, could be the same man. He seemed not in the least affected by the proclamations. Just glanced at them, laid his head back on the seat, and appeared to drift off to sleep. Mercy, however, continued to stare until their coach was long out of sight of the theater.

Their hotel was the finest in the city. Mercy waited with D'Abanville and Miriam as Roger checked them all into their rooms and paid several young men to see to their luggage. Mercy was given a room to herself, directly across from her employer. She did not fail to notice that Miriam's room was adjoined to his.

Mercy had just begun to unpack when there came a quiet rap on her door. She opened it to find D'Abanville smiling down at her.

He said, ''It is customary for us to celebrate our first night in a new city. You are invited to share champagne and dinner in my room.''

''When?''

''Now. The unpacking will wait.'' He took hold of her arm and escorted her across the hall, into his room, closing the door behind them.

Mercy looked about the spacious apartment, noting the table in the center of the room that was laden with silver-covered dishes, burning candles, and flowers. Several bottles of champagne lay chilling in buckets by the table.

''Where are the others?'' she asked.

D'Abanville stepped around her and walked to the table. ''What others? Did I say there were others? Roger and Miriam can have their own party, blast 'em. Do you like champagne, Miss Mercy?''

''I think it is not very proper for me to be here with you alone,'' she said.

''You'd better get used to it. As my assistant, you will be alone with me the majority of the time.''

She remained where she was, watching his hands roll the champagne back and forth in the ice. Finally he lifted the bottle and poured two sparkling glasses of the fizzy drink. He carried one to her, put it into her hands. ''Relax, Mercy, or I might be forced to pull pennies out of your ears again.''

She smiled a little.

''That's better. You are very pretty when you smile. I hope you'll do it often.''

''For your spellbound audiences, sir?''

''Absolutely not. For me. It does wonders for my soul.

Now, drink your champagne and relax. The others will be joining us any minute.''

She followed him into the room. He indicated a chair and she sank into it, sipping the champagne, feeling it tickle her nose and the inside of her mouth as she tried to swallow. Miriam entered the room without knocking and D'Abanville glanced at her with a frown forming between his heavy brows.

''I should be very careful of that from now on,'' he said to her quietly. Miriam appeared to ignore him and poured herself a glass of champagne. ''I should be very careful of *that* too,'' he added, the warning obvious in his voice.

Miriam laughed and leaned against him. Pressed against him, rubbing her full breasts against his arm. Throwing her hair back with a toss of her head, she cut her eyes to Mercy and said, ''Lesson one, Miss Dansing. Don't ever believe a word he says. If he says he wants to be alone, he's lying. I happen to know what he's like the night before a performance. He's about to explode with anticipation. Aren't you, darling? Let me know when it gets too painful for you, won't you?''

Roger entered the room then, beaming them all a smile. ''You will be thrilled to know that the performance to-morrow night is sold out. Some five hundred people will be watching the Great D'Abanville bedazzle them with his wizardry.''

More glasses were passed. Soon they were seated at the table and were enjoying pheasant under glass, asparagus spears with hollandaise, glazed carrots with almonds, and bread still warm to the touch. Mercy listened to the others discuss business while she ate to contentment. When she finally looked up from her food, she found D'Abanville watching her with a delighted smile curving his mouth. He surprised them all by lifting his glass of champagne and saying, ''A toast to my hungry new assistant. May her days with me be nothing but pheasant and champagne, as much as she can eat.''

Having downed several glasses of the pleasant drink, she laughed giddily and raised her glass. ''May I not disappoint you,'' she returned, meeting his twinkling eyes boldly. ''May I be all that you expect me to be.''

"You already are," he replied.

Soon the tables were cleared away. Roger and D'Abanville continued discussing matters pertaining to tomorrow's performance while Miriam sat back in her chair downing glass after glass of champagne. Occasionally Mercy would see D'Abanville's eyes stray briefly to Miriam, and Miriam's countenance would challenge him or tease him openly.

Suddenly Roger stood up. "Impossible. The act has not been perfected. Not only would it endanger your own life, it would pose a danger to the entire theater full of people."

"The fire is contained," D'Abanville argued. "I would jeopardize no one but myself."

"When your present acts are already applauded? Why risk the chance of killing yourself, or, less important, failing before your audience?" Roger looked at Miriam. "For God's sake, talk some sense into him, Miriam. That act is a death trap."

"He doesn't listen to me anymore," she said, swigging her drink and eyeing Mercy with a sleepy look. "Perhaps Miss Dansing could plead your case, Roger. That's part of his assistant's responsibilities, isn't it? Making certain her employer isn't idiot enough to torch himself in front of five hundred people?"

They all looked at Mercy.

"I fear I can hardly argue anything without knowing what I'm arguing against," she stated.

D'Abanville dragged up a chair before her and sat down. Elbows on his knees, he leaned toward her and explained. "Imagine a glass case center stage. I step inside. The case is closed and chain-locked so it appears that I have no way out. The entire floor of the case appears to be black powder, enough to consume me in flames if set afire. I light a match, toss it to the floor, and am instantly engulfed by fire and smoke. My assistant—that being you—hurries to unlock the door and open the case, releasing the smoke, and . . . *voilà*, I am gone."

"And where are you supposed to have gone?"

"You walk to a trunk on the opposite side of the stage and open it. I step out—unscathed, of course."

"How have you done it?" she asked.

"Done what?"

"Disappeared from here to there?"

Miriam spoke up. "Don't ask him that. There are some things assistants are not allowed to know, Miss Dansing. It's ethics, I think. Some mysterious code the great conjurers live and breathe by. Oh, he'll confide to you the trivial matters, like the pranks he showed you this morning. If you are wondering where the coin he supposedly dissolved into his elbow went, I'll tell you."

She left her chair, walked up behind D'Abanville, and ran her hand slowly up his back. With one fingernail she teased his ear as she explained. "As you recall, during the performance he twice appeared to drop the coin clumsily. The second time he dropped it, you only thought he transferred the coin from his left hand to his right. When he raised his left elbow again, he let the coin drop into the back of his shirt. And the cut thumb? It was rather gruesome, wasn't it? When he reached into his pocket for the knife, he barely pricked his finger with a needle he has hidden there. Not enough to bleed right away, mind you. But when he applied the kerchief to his finger, the pressure was enough to bring the blood to the surface. All there was left to do was to draw the knife blade lightly down his thumb, smearing the blood so it looked cut. When he cleaned the blood away his thumb appeared uninjured."

D'Abanville left his chair abruptly and walked across the room. He refilled his glass.

"Oh, dear, I've upset him again," Miriam said. Taking the chair next to Mercy's, she leaned close to Mercy and smiled. "You see, Dominick doesn't like to be reminded that he's a fraud. It makes him feel mortal. That's why he keeps attempting these asinine feats like torching himself to a crisp. He has to try to prove not only to the world that he's a flesh-and-blood wizard, but to himself as well."

"Shut up," he said evenly, staring at the glass in his hand.

"He used to bilk little old ladies out of their purse money by pretending he could communicate with their dead loved ones. He was quite good at it. As I recall, one suffered a light heart attack when she thought her deceased husband had rapped three times on the table. Of course, he makes up for it now by condemning the practice and doing his best to uncover such schemes. It's easy to be judgmental when you no longer have to fight and claw for your dinner money.''

Roger set down his glass. "I think it is time to say good night. May I see you back to your room, Miriam?''

"No, thank you. Dom and I have matters to discuss. You might see Miss Dansing to her room, however.''

"*I* will see Miss Dansing to her room,'' Dominick responded, his tone brooking no further discourse on the matter. With movements more stilted than his usual grace, he took one last swallow of his drink, then put the glass down on a little table next to the window overlooking Warwick Street. Walking by Miriam, he said, "I will deal with you later.'' Then he caught Mercy's arm and helped her from the chair.

Neither of them spoke as they left the room with Roger. They each said their good-nights to D'Abanville's manager, waiting as he disappeared into his room, closing his door soundly behind him. D'Abanville then led Mercy to her door, opened it for her, and showed her in. She turned to find him leaning against the doorframe, his hands tucked a little way into his trouser pockets.

He looked at her, returning stare for stare. "May I come in?'' he asked quietly.

When she did not respond, he stepped into the room, pushing the door shut with his hand. Mercy stepped away, her mind reeling with the effects of too much champagne, and something else. The intensity of his look disturbed her, but she did not know why. She could not think; her heart was racing too fast. She felt very queer, light-headed and foolish.

"Champagne becomes you,'' he said. "You should drink it more often. It puts roses in your cheeks.''

She blinked and tried to think straight.

"Nice room.'' He looked around, toward the bed, then back at her. "I suppose I should apologize for Miriam.''

"Is it true?''

"True?'' He nodded. "I dropped the coin down my shirt, I confess. Guilty as charged.''

"No. I mean the other. Did you really bilk those old ladies out of their money?"

He looked away, ran one hand through his black hair. "That was a long time ago, Mercy. A *very* long time ago. I try not to think about it. Neither should you. Miriam should never have brought it up."

The room seemed unbearably warm and suffocating. D'Abanville's presence was, in itself, suffocating. She thought to step away, to escape his disconcerting closeness, but he caught her arm, stopping her and turning her back around. The heat of his hand seemed to burn through the thin cotton of her blouse. She stared at his fingers before forcing her eyes back up to his.

"I'd like to kiss you good night," he said.

"Kiss me good night?"

He smiled and brushed her lips with the tip of one finger. "There. Please. I would like to do so very much."

"Why?"

"Because I like you."

"Do you go about kissing every woman you simply *like?*" she asked him.

"Contrary to what you might have been led to believe, I don't."

Mercy stared at his mouth. She would be lying to herself if she thought, even for a moment, that she would not like to be kissed by this man. His dark hair shone with midnight flickers of fire in the lamplight. His eyes looked a little sleepy, and his face was shadowed by beard stubble. But she had already made one mistake where a man was concerned, a very costly mistake. It wouldn't be wise to—

He pulled her toward him, the gentleness gone from his touch, catching her wrist as she lifted her hand to deny him. His mouth closed hard on hers, punishing, then tender, forcing her head back while his hands released her and his arms wrapped around her, pinning her against his hard body. A confusion of sensations enfolded her, sharp, blinding, a hot urgency blooming in the very pit of her stomach.

Someone moaned. Herself, she realized as his mouth, hot and demanding, forced hers open roughly. Then he was driving deep with his tongue, making her world spin crazily, filling her senses and mind with forbidden images that had once brought her shame and disgust. Odd, how they made her ache now with need, how they made her tremble. She felt her resistance shatter like tiny fragments of bright crystal, and without realizing it, she began to kiss him back.

Suddenly his hands fell free and he backed away, leaned against the door, watching her strangely with his deep blue eyes. Then he reached for her again and dragged her against him, held her tightly, almost too tightly. So tightly she could hear the drumming of his heart against her ear, could feel the tremor of his hands as he slowly rubbed them up and down her arms. Finally he slid his fingers into her loose hair and said:

"I wasn't expecting that."

He did not smile as he pushed her to arm's length. His eyes were intense, his countenance stern as he appeared to consider her for a long moment. Finally he dropped his hands and reached for the door. Without another word he left the room. Mercy waited a long while at the door, watching for Miriam's departure. When the minutes ticked by and Miriam did not show, Mercy closed the door of her room and turned in for the night.

Roger showed Mercy to a front-row seat in the Empire Theater. Anticipation vibrated the air around her as men and women chatted and waited for the performance to begin. She had seen nothing of D'Abanville or Miriam all day. According to Roger, they had left very early in the morning for the theater, to rehearse and become acquainted with the stage. Roger had returned to the hotel only to transport Mercy to the theater, handing her a ticket and showing her to her seat. At the foot of the raised stage an orchestra was tuning up. The cacophony of sounds added to the expectation building around her. Occasionally Mercy was able to overhear several conversations:

"Saw him at the Alhambra on the Rue de Malte. Paid thirty francs to sit in the *avant-scène,* certain I would be able to decipher how he does it all. By gosh, but I couldn't, not a time."

"I've heard he walks through walls."

"They say he is breathtakingly handsome!"

"He hypnotizes women with his eyes."

"Then, by golly, don't look at him, Ethel!" a man exclaimed.

"I've heard he dismembers his assistant, then puts her back together."

The woman next to Mercy slumped in her chair and fluttered her fan before her face. "Oh, dear . . . oh, dear," she whimpered. "I may faint. I'm certain I shall."

The lights lowered. The stage went completely dark. The orchestra's discordance suddenly struck into a harmonization of violins and drumrolls that shook the floor beneath Mercy's feet. A small man walked to center stage and announced loudly that the program would begin with an overture by the John Jacobs Theater Orchestra, followed by the Three Gibson Brothers as the Jovial Jugglers, then the ventriloquist Herbert Edwards, and finally the Magnificent D'Abanville. He walked offstage as the audience hooted and applauded.

The show began.

The orchestra's playing heightened the suspense as the jugglers bumbled their way through their performance. Their departure brought a smattering of applause. The ventriloquist was very funny but he too was rewarded with a less-than-appreciative farewell when he vacated the stage. The stage went black again, the orchestra silent. Not a sound could be heard throughout the entire auditorium as everyone waited and watched in anticipation.

Slowly the curtain began to open.

A single hazy light shone down on Miriam, and Mercy felt her heart give a squeeze of disconcertion as she realized, for the first time, that she would soon be in Miriam's place. Miriam looked beautiful in a sleek form-fitting red dress, her hair like a rich brown mantle around her shoulders. Her facial features were made more striking by the color she had added to her cheeks and eyes and mouth. She bestowed on the audience a brilliant smile that brought about an appreciative whistle from someone in the crowd.

She stood alone on the stage in a circle of light, her arms down by her sides and her eyes straight ahead. Then slowly, very slowly, she began to tilt sideward. Her feet left the floor and she appeared to float in space. A murmur rose from the crowd. The women on either side of Mercy sat forward in their chairs, their fans fluttering rapidly. Drums began to roll as a smoky form began to materialize beyond Miriam. Then, with a flash of fire, D'Abanville stepped from the smoke, bringing a deafening explosion of applause from the audience. Dressed in a flowing black cape, black suit, and white shirt and gloves, he proceeded to cover Miriam's suspended form with a vivid blue satin cloth, passing his hands around her completely, as if to prove that she was held aloft by nothing but air. Then, with a drumroll, he lifted the corner of the blue cloth and grabbed it away.

To Mercy's amazement, and everyone else's, Miriam was gone. A moment later she walked onto the stage wearing a glimmering gold dress, her hair expertly coiffed atop her head.

For the next hour D'Abanville was larger than life. Mercy found herself spellbound no less than the others, caught up in the magic of his performance and the memory of the magic he had spun about her the night before. For the first time she was hit by the reality of who and what he was: a dream-weaver, a sorcerer, a magic man who was idolized by hundreds, no, thousands of people. She gasped and screamed and covered her eyes as he appeared to slice Miriam in two with a sword: then, at a few words and a snap of his fingers, the woman jumped to her feet, displaying no injury at all. Mercy watched in amazement as he materialized cards and flowers and bright-colored scarves from thin air and threw them to the audience. He flirted with the women to the point of maddening their escorts, then made light of the matter by performing feats to make the agitated gentlemen look foolish, so they could not help but laugh along with the others. For a while Mercy forgot that he was the man who had bought her potatoes and pies the day before, who had wrapped her in his steely embrace only the night before, and kissed her. He was not the friend who had shared with her the most intimate secret of her life, nor was he the employer who had saved her from the starvation and humiliation of London's East End; he belonged to every woman in the audience, and Mercy realized in one blinding moment that his sleight of hand was not the only reason for their admiration.

They wanted him.

The realization sent a stab of something disconcertingly like jealousy through her heart, and for a frantic moment she stared at the woman next to her, who, despite the fact that she was with a male escort, was peeling off her glove and tossing it onto the stage at Dominick's feet.

By the time D'Abanville had returned to the stage for a third encore, the crowd was on its feet. Women nearest him were pitching their gloves on the stage. Many he picked up and turned into flowers, throwing them back to the awestruck young women. One young woman fainted into her escort's arms. Another swooned delicately back into her seat, displaying a good deal of her ankle as she did so. Mercy was frowning openly at the woman when Roger appeared through the crowd, caught Mercy's arm, and escorted her backstage. She watched from behind the curtains as her employer and Miriam each took turns at bowing, smiling brightly, and waving to the audience. Dominick then gently took Miriam's hand in his, kissed it adoringly; then they hurried off the stage.

As D'Abanville swept by Mercy, barely glancing her way, he tore off his gloves and threw them to the floor. Roger was there immediately to help him off with his coat, which was immediately replaced with another. His face was wiped dry and he was given a glass of what looked like straight whiskey, which he tossed back with only a swallow.

Miriam walked up to Mercy, her face looking not nearly so attractive up close. The powder appeared thick and had settled into the fine lines around her eyes and mouth. Her lipstick had smeared around her mouth and had slightly stained her teeth. Pulling the coiffured wig from her head, releasing her own damp hair down her back, she grinned and said, "He'll knock a few of those back until his knees stop trembling. The only time he drinks is when he's afraid of something. Come with me,

Miss Dansing, while the Great D'Abanville performs his greatest feat yet.''

"And what is that?" Mercy asked.

"Stomaching his adoring public. He doesn't need us for that.''

Miriam caught Mercy's arm and they walked down a dark and musty hallway, squeezing between crates and stacks of ropes and pulleys, bumping into backdrops that looked like cities or landscapes. Finally reaching a door, Miriam shoved it open and showed Mercy inside. The room was hardly bigger than a small larder. On one wall was a mirror desperately in need of resilvering. A dim yellow light shone above it, casting Miriam's face in harsh gold as she sat down in a chair beneath it.

Among the bottles and boxes of powders and rouges strewn over the table beneath the mirror was a bottle of liquor and a glass. Miriam poured a small amount of the whiskey into the glass and offered it to Mercy. Mercy declined and Miriam smiled, shrugged, and began drinking it herself. Mercy watched then as Miriam picked up a small pearl-encrusted case, flipped it open, and withdrew a thin black cigarillo. She lit it, closed her eyes, and blew a stream of smoke into the air.

Arching one heavily kohled eyebrow at Mercy, Miriam asked, "Shocked?"

"No."

"Not even a little?"

"Women smoke a great deal in the East End. It is nothing I haven't seen before," Mercy replied.

"Dominick doesn't like it. He won't allow my doing it in public. Might somehow taint his reputation, you see. What did you think of the show?"

"I was very impressed."

"He is very good, isn't he? The Society of European Magicians has recently proclaimed him the best in the world, even greater than Robert-Houdin, which is quite an accomplishment, considering the French magician probably achieved the highest artistic magical performances of anyone during his lifetime." She looked around thoughtfully, alternately smoking and sipping her drink. "This is all yours now, Miss Dansing. Every dust-clotted and rat-infested corner of stardom. It's enough to make you want to . . . drink." She tipped up her glass, swallowed, then added, "It's not all bad, mind you. The good times make it worth it, I suppose. Those moments on the stage, hearing the roar of applause and approval: those are the moments you live for. They are like a fever in the blood that won't go away. Once you get a taste of it, you have to have it again and again. To some of us, of course, it means different things. For you it may mean money to buy your next meal. For Dominick it is that and more, I think. It's acceptance and recognition. It somehow proves not only to his adoring audience that he exists, but to himself as well." Looking at Mercy through the curling smoke of her cigarillo, she said softly, "He must have been a very neglected little boy."

Placing her drink aside, she left her chair and began undressing. When Miriam had pulled her new dress up onto her shoulders, she called, "Would you mind, dear?"

Mercy approached and began buttoning the back of Miriam's dress, aware Miriam was watching her in the mirror. Miriam said, "I think Dominick has had plenty of opportunity to get to his dressing room. Therefore it is time for your next lesson, Miss Dansing: sharing him with his public. It is a burden that can and will break your back eventually, if not your heart. Look at me. I'm a prime example." Bending closer to her mirror, she smeared away the creases in her powder, rubbed the color off her teeth, then turned for the door.

The crowd trailed out the door and into the hallway. Women stood on tiptoe, doing their best to see over the heads and shoulders of others between them and D'Abanville. Miriam took hold of Mercy's arm, wedged them through the smiling people until they stood inside the door against the wall. In the distance stood D'Abanville with Roger at his side. Clinging to D'Abanvilles right arm was a stunning woman whose blond hair was stylishly piled atop her head, exposing ears that were dripping with diamonds. Her plunging décolletage all but exposed her white breasts entirely, and she seemed to take every opportunity to offer him any unobstructed view she could manage.

As a waiter walked by with an uplifted silver tray of champagne in glasses, Miriam reached for two and forced one into Mercy's hands. "If I'm any judge of character at all, you're going to need this before the night is over."

Mercy took the drink, but responded loudly enough to be heard over the din of laughter and conversation, "I don't know what you mean, Miriam. Why should anything about this disturb me?"

"Ask me that in another two hours," she responded, lifting her glass to her mouth. Then, smiling broadly, she said more quietly, "Smile, darling, we've been discovered. This is your only chance to make our darling boy think you don't give a damn when he disappears for twenty minutes with that little blond she-cat. Smile, darling, smile, and you won't hurt so badly tomorrow."

Mercy did smile—forever, it seemed—as Miriam introduced her as D'Abanville's new assistant. Within the space of the next half-hour she was asked no less than fifty times about what D'Abanville was *really* like. She heard "Do you think you could introduce me?" enough times to make her head ache.

Several times she found herself cornered by men who charmed her with flattery one moment and the next offered her money to "walk" with them down by the Mersy River. By the third proposition she had gone from blinking in dumb stupefaction to "accidentally" spilling champagne down the front of the man's trousers. "That should cool you off," she told the portly bald leech who had openly touched her breast. Miriam, standing not far behind her, threw her head back and roared with laughter.

Mercy caught D'Abanville glancing her way occasionally. She avoided his eyes at first, pretending not to notice. She had found soon enough that Miriam was right. She felt a stirring of disapproval in her chest over the woman on his arm, and with each glass of champagne she drank, the feeling intensified. By the time she had downed her fourth, she was meeting his eyes directly, enjoying the subtle glint of anger she detected there each time she was approached by another man. No doubt it was all right for him to flirt with and fondle his admirers, but his assistant was not allowed such privileges.

By two in the morning the crowd had thinned out. D'Abanville sat on the settee between two women, the same blond and a brassy redhead who Mercy learned was a dancer with a troupe performing at the theater the next night. Each of the women was more than obvious in vying for his undivided attention. Mercy could not hide her shock as the red-haired woman took his face in her hands and kissed him fully on the mouth. Huffing in displeasure, Mercy dropped into a chair and closed her eyes; life back on the farm in Huntingdon had certainly been nothing like this.

"Miss Dansing."

She opened her eyes briefly and closed them again.

"Mercy."

Mercy peeked from behind her lashes to find D'Abanville crouched before her, looking at her concernedly.

"I think it is time to say good night, sweetheart."

"Good night," she mumbled.

He caught her arm. "Shall I carry you to the coach or do you think you can walk?"

"Of course I can walk." She tried to stand, then made a grab for D'Abanville as the world swayed beneath her feet. "Oh, my," she said. "Are you going to exterminate me?"

"Don't you mean 'terminate'?"

"Whatever."

"I hardly think so. How much champagne have you had?"

She held up two fingers.

"Two glasses is all?"

"Bottles."

"Ah. Will you take my arm while I assist you back to the hotel?"

She shook her head and started toward the door. "I shan't take you away from your. . . . what do you call them?"

"Friends?"

"Bloody close friends, I'd say. Miriam tol' me what you do with your 'friends.' "

"Did she?"

Stopping abruptly, Mercy looked around, up into his amused eyes, and said, "You should be ashamed, sir."

"Should I?"

"You should find yourself some respectable young woman and settle down."

"I've given it some thought of late."

"You are too old to be gadding about like some lad just out of knickers."

"Too old, you say? Watch you step here, love. When I open this door, I want you to take great deep breaths of this fresh air—I am hardly old, Mercy—now breathe."

She tried.

"Again. Once more. Very good. How old do you think I am, anyway?"

"Twenty-eight or twenty-nine, I should think."

"And you think that is old."

She nodded, then stumbled as he tried to lift her into the coach. Settling in across from her, he rapped on the ceiling and the vehicle lurched away.

"I fear I am in grave trouble, then, Miss Dansing. You should be packing me off to some institution for the enfeebled if I divulge my true age."

Looking at him as squarely as she could in the dark coach, she leaned toward him and said, "You mean you are older than that?"

"Much older. I fear I've just turned three-and-thirty. Virtually decrepit in your eyes, I would imagine."

She sank back into her seat, gripped it with her hands, feeling as if she were being tossed about on some stormy sea.

"How are we doing?" came his soft voice from the dark.

"Very well, thank you."

She saw him brush at the knee of his trousers. Then he said, "From now on I'd like you to stay close at my side during these functions. I can better keep my eye on you that way."

She hiccuped and he laughed.

"Mercy, Miss Mercy, you are going to keep me on my toes, I fear. I may have gotten more than I anticipated by taking you on. . . . Are you shivering, love? Are you cold? Come here and let me warm you."

She shook her head.

"Why not? I thought we were friends."

"You've no doubt got a blond and a redhead tucked inside the folds of your cape."

He flashed her a smile. "Nope. Just me." He crooked his finger at her. "Come here, Miss Dansing, or I may be forced to exterminate you."

Staring hard through the dark, she asked, "Are you going to be fresh?"

"I am not above a grope in the dark with a pretty girl on occasion. Alas, Mercy, I'm not a saint."

"That is an understatement, sir, if you don't mind my saying so."

"Come here, Miss Dansing, before you freeze of cold."

"Nope."

"Please."

"Umm."

"Pretty please."

She began to giggle. Suddenly his arms were around her, lifting her, settling her on his lap, and drawing his fur-lined cape around her so she nestled warmly against his chest. For a moment she listened to his strangely racing heart, allowed her senses to soak up the smell of his skin, the rough texture of his cheek against her forehead. As her head slid back and she looked up into his face, she heard herself say, "The women think you hypnotize them with your eyes."

"Do they?"

"Aye. Do you?"

"Would you care to see for yourself?"

"I don't know."

"Think about it and let me know."

"I shall," she replied sleepily, thoughtfully. "Perhaps I shall."

5

___

D'Abanville awakened Mercy at noon. Banging on her door, he called out that she was to be dressed and ready for a ride out in ten minutes. Holding her head and wondering if she would survive the next ten minutes, Mercy rolled out of bed.

She heard him bang on Miriam's door. He pounded and pounded until doors could be heard opening and closing up and down the corridor. Several voices rose in protest, but D'Abanville kept pounding and calling Miriam's name. Slipping on her dressing gown, Mercy walked to the door of her room and looked out. Roger had joined D'Abanville and both were staring at Miriam's door in concern.

The door opened in that minute and a man stumbled out, stuffing his shirttail into his trousers and snapping his galluses into place over his shoulders. He smiled at D'Abanville, placed his bowler hat on his head at an angle, and stepped by him, stopped, then, digging into his pocket, dragged out a handful of coins and tossed them back into the room, onto the floor. As he strode by Mercy, the overpowering stench of liquor about him made her stomach turn.

As D'Abanville and Roger entered Miriam's room, Mercy followed, concerned over the woman's welfare. She stopped short upon seeing Miriam, totally nude and staggering toward D'Abanville, her hands clenched into fists as she screamed, "You damned bloody bastard, how dare you come waltzing in here as if you own me!"

Mercy slammed the door behind her, briefly closed her eyes in surprise as Roger tried to throw Miriam's robe around her. Miriam kicked it to the floor. Then, drawing back her fist, she slammed it so hard into D'Abanville's shoulder that Mercy flinched.

"Friggin' frog, get out of my room. I'll kill you if you don't!" She hit him again before he could grab both her wrists in his hands.

"Shut up," he said. "The entire hotel can hear you."

She threw back her head so her wild hair streamed to her white buttocks. "That's all you care about, isn't it? Afraid something is going to hurt your precious reputation."

"You're stinking drunk," he told her. "Shut up."

"And you just stink. I'd like to know who you slept with last night. The blond or the tramp with red hair? Maybe both!" She laughed in his face and tried twisting from his grip. "Think you're such a stud, magic man. Well, there's plenty more where you came from. The Paris gutter spits 'em up every day. Take your hands off me, you fake. You fraud. I allow only men to touch me, and you're no man, you're a bloody machine."

"And you are a whore," he said through his teeth, shoving her backward.

Miriam stumbled before righting herself. Only then did she notice Mercy's presence. Her eyes, smeared with kohl and red from whiskey, widened as she said, "Well, if it's not the Angel of Mercy herself, direct from Sultan Street. My darling innocent child, run as fast as you can from that one." She pointed at D'Abanville, whose face looked dark with suppressed rage. "He cares for nothing but his damned magic and his upstanding reputation. Take either of those away and you may as well cut off his manhood. God help anyone who thinks she can take the place of either. Get in his way and you end up like Abby Russell, crawling on your knees and begging for one more—"

"Shut up!" he roared. He took two steps toward her, his hands clenched into fists, one drawn back with threat.

"Go on and hit me, big man. Prove to Miss Dansing that you aren't the saint you profess to be. What's wrong, would slamming me go against your religion? Afraid you won't make it to the Temple of Divine Wisdom if you hit a woman?"

"Don't tempt me, Miriam."

D'Abanville pointed to Miriam's robe. Roger picked it up and handed it to him. Dominick tossed it forcibly into Miriam's face and said, ''You disgust me.''

Her face suddenly pale, Miriam stared at him with tears in her eyes. ''You haven't always thought me so disgusting, Dominick.''

''You haven't always been a wretch.''

''And a whore. Don't forget you called me a whore.''

His lips curling, he said in a voice of sudden icy calm, ''You have always been a whore, Miriam, from the day I met you.''

D'Abanville turned and swept out of the room. Roger followed. Mercy remained, still too much in shock over what had transpired to move. Finally coming to her senses, she took several steps toward Miriam, thinking to do what she could to help or comfort her. But Miriam only turned her eyes, full of anger, on Mercy and said emotionlessly, stopping Mercy in her tracks, ''I don't want or need your pity, Miss Dansing.''

''I only meant to help,'' Mercy said. ''Can I do anything? Get you anything?''

Turning her back to Mercy, Miriam responded, ''Why the hell would you want to?''

''Why not?''

The response brought Miriam's head around; she stared a long silent moment at Mercy.

''God,'' she finally said. ''Another do-gooder. Just what I need in my miserable life is another do-gooder. You and D'Abanville will make a pair. Yes, ma'am, a real duo. I'm beginning to understand now why he chose you over all the others he's interviewed over the months. You're just like him. Do unto others, and all that crap. Well, you can have him with my blessings, Miss Dansing. I was tired of him anyway, as you can see.'' She nodded toward the mussed bed and laughed. ''There's plenty more where he came from. You'll do well to remember that, sweetheart, and save yourself for someone who deserves it.''

''I don't think you mean that,'' Mercy responded.

Miriam's red-rimmed eyes widened; she staggered slightly as she turned fully around. ''Is that so?''

"I think it is only the drinking that makes you this way. Why do you do it?"

"Why not?" Miriam mocked her. "What is there left for me?"

"Your pride, for one."

A smile curling her mouth, Miriam said, "Pride? Come talk to me of pride, Miss Dansing, when the Great D'Abanville turns you out."

"It is not a crime not to be in love with someone. You are only hurting yourself with these spiteful displays."

Miriam pulled on her robe before facing Mercy again. Her voice had begun to quaver slightly as she said, "You asked if you could help me. All right, you can. You can get out. But first you can get me a drink."

Mercy shook her head. "I won't get you a drink, but I will tell you something I think you should know. D'Abanville did not leave the theater last night with the blond or the tramp with red hair. He left with me. He saw me to my room, then turned in for the night himself."

Miriam's face, already pale, blanched even more.

"I wonder how many times you left the theater on someone's arm assuming something that never took place, Miriam."

Miriam buried her face in her hands as Mercy turned, stepped over the coins strewn over the floor, and left the room, closing the door behind her. Up and down the corridor people were returning to their rooms and had, no doubt, been privy to the entire ugly shouting match between Miriam and their employer. Mercy returned a white-haired woman's perusal forcibly until the eavesdropper turned and slammed her door hard enough to vibrate the floor. D'Abanville's door remained slightly ajar, and as Mercy stepped by it toward her own, she heard him say with no emotion:

"Get rid of her. Sober her up, pack her things, give her three months' salary, and tell her to get the hell out of my life before she ruins me."

Mercy, Roger, and D'Abanville boarded the coach some twenty minutes later. They rode in silence through the busy Liverpool streets, D'Abanville's interests seemingly in the busy cavalcade of life teeming around them and not on her. He appeared tired. His mouth was pressed in a disapproving line she was not accustomed to seeing on a man who had been so quick to smile on previous days.

Mercy was loath to bring up the subject of his secretary, but she could hardly forget the weeping she had heard coming from Miriam's room as she was leaving her own. Well aware of the straits in which an unemployed woman could so easily find herself, Mercy felt compelled to plead Miriam's case.

Glancing first toward Roger, she cleared her throat, then stared a long moment at D'Abanville. His face, turned toward the window, was mostly in shadow, but Mercy could clearly make out the tense line of his jaw. She took a deep breath and said, "Sir, about Miriam?" Her mouth went dry as he turned his cold blue eyes to hers, waiting.

"What about her?"

"You don't really mean to release her?"

"I don't? Why, pray tell, not, Miss Dansing?"

"The unemployment—"

"She is not without resources. She made enough on her back last evening to tide herself over nicely for several days."

"That is very unkind," she responded hotly.

"Pardon me, m'lady," he told her. "I had forgotten how sensitive you were to the subject of whores."

He might as well have slapped her. Unable to summon any form of response, she could only stare into his hard countenance and wonder miserably if he had actually meant the double entendre she had heard in his biting comeback. Was he actually insinuating that she was no better than Miriam? Or was it her own sensitivity to the subject that made her grow suddenly physically ill?

Looking away from D'Abanville, she did her best to focus on the traffic outside her window, cursing the mortifying sting of tears that made the world a watery blur.

"Mercy."

He touched her hand. She drew it back, buried it in the folds of her skirt, and stared harder out the window.

"Mercy."

"Don't," she said, curling her fingers into her palms as he closed his hand over her small fist. "Don't," she repeated. By now hot color had risen to her cheeks and her voice quavered dangerously close to breaking. "I don't like you very much right now, sir."

Her honesty set him back. Even Roger looked at her in surprise.

"I didn't mean anything by what I said. I only meant—"

She leveled Dominick with a look that made him appear to forget exactly what he did mean. He closed his mouth momentarily and sat back in his seat, shoulders squared, hands gripping his thighs.

"I think you know that I am sympathetic to the women's plight in the East End," he said stonily. "I understand—"

"No, you don't," she snapped. "Don't tell me you understand when you don't. How could you? To understand, you must know what it is like, and no one can know what it is like without having experienced it."

He drew a breath and released it loudly, his aggravation and weariness audible even with the clattering of traffic around them. "I need a holiday," he said to Roger.

"I wholeheartedly agree."

"I wonder if there is anyplace on this earth where there are no emotional women?"

Roger chuckled until Mercy darted a speaking look his way. He said, "I doubt it."

"Perhaps after the royal performance I'll go home to Paris for a while."

"Good idea."

As the coach stopped, held up in traffic, D'Abanville turned his attention away from Mercy and whistled to a paper boy on the nearby corner. The lad hustled between several hansoms, shoved the paper through the window, and waited as D'Abanville flipped him a penny. The pungent smell of the lampblacked ink filled the cab as D'Abanville fingered through the three-page paper. Mercy was the first to see the headline adorning the lower corner of the back sheet. D'Abanville saw her frowning and turned it over.

He stared at it a long moment, long enough so she was certain he had read it several times.

Forgetting her earlier anger, she said, "I'm sure it is nothing."

His eyes looked very blue and his face very white as he looked back at her.

She could think of nothing to say except, "I'm certain there's some mistake." When he made no response, she said, "To think Miss Russell's death is linked to the East End killings is one thing, but to suspect that you are in some way involved with either is another."

"What is it?" Roger asked, coming out of his musing. As D'Abanville dropped the paper in Roger's lap, exposing the caption "D'ABANVILLE QUESTIONED IN DEATH OF FORMER MISTRESS," Roger cleared his throat.

"That Inspector . . ." D'Abanville searched his memory but could not come up with the name.

"Chesterton," Roger reminded him.

"He is no doubt behind this. I want you to talk to his superior—"

"That would be the commissioner, Sir Charles Warren, I should think."

"I want this stopped."

"Certainly."

"You'll talk to the *Times* as well when we get back to London," Dominick ordered.

"Of course."

"Tell them I'll sue them for libel."

"Certainly."

Anger having replaced his momentary shock, D'Abanville's face turned a slow-burning red as he looked back out the window. "Dammit," he said quietly, viciously. "Dammit."

They arrived at the Liverpool Hospital just after one o'clock. Although Mercy had no notion of why they had come here, she did not ask. D'Abanville's dark mood had become so tangible the last quarter-hour of their drive that she could hardly breathe, much less speak. So she chose to remain silent.

No different from London Hospital on Whitechapel Road, Liverpool Hospital was a backended-stone fixture with sprawling wings that reminded Mercy of something from the medieval age. While other, more welcoming institutions were scattered about the cities, offering better care to private citizens, these wretched institutions were supported mostly by government funds and were therefore where the indigents of the cities were forced to apply for help when ill or injured. She knew them well enough, for it had been London Hospital where she had volunteered those hours that were not spent trying to find paying employment. The dark corridors of this hospital were the same, the stench of illness and death and disease no different.

As they walked down the bleak corridors, footsteps ringing in the quiet, Mercy glanced at the poorly painted green walls, noted the dusting of black soot and grease from the furnaces that had settled near the ceiling and along the floors. In the distance a young woman moved about on her hands and knees, scrubbing the floor with a brush. Its soft *swoosh swoosh* made Mercy think of the many hours she had spent doing the same job, only to look back and discover someone had soiled it with muddy shoes. Lifting her skirt several inches, she took a precautionary glance at her feet.

"Mr. D'Abanville, what a pleasure to see you again!"

Surprised, Mercy looked up to see several men smiling and holding out their hands in greeting.

"We've told the children you were coming. I daresay they thought we were joking. Come in, come in. Caught your performance last evening. Splendid, my good man! Just splendid!"

The smile was back on D'Abanville's face. Mercy caught herself staring at it, smiling herself at the warmth she could see there and in his eyes. She bit her lip and tried to force this warm image from her mind, but was unable to do so. She could only stare, realizing the dangers of acknowledging her growing fascination for D'Abanville. After all, there had been hundreds of women in the theater last night who had felt the same. Perhaps it was that very aspect of the man that made him so appealing to her now.

The dark-suited man who Mercy determined must be the hospital administrator caught D'Abanville's arm and

led him down the hall. Caught up in her musing, Mercy
lagged behind, watching the graceful way her employer
moved. Listened to the way his deep voice echoed about
the nearly empty corridors.

The administrator continued, "I think you'll be pleased
with the changes that have been made since you were last
here, Mr. D'Abanville. We opened a new ward with the
money provided, painted the existing ward, and purchased a half-dozen new beds."

D'Abanville stopped and looked around. In the dim
light of the hall his eyes were unreadable. "Are you coming?" he asked. He raised his outstretched hand to her.

Mercy forced herself to move. She did not, however,
take his hand. Just took her place at D'Abanville's side
and tried to concentrate only on the constant swooshing
of the distant mop girl, and not on the fact that she had
purposely ignored his proffered tenderness.

There was a moment's pause as D'Abanville dropped
his hand, long fingers curled in rejection as he contemplated the top of her head. Finally they continued their
walk.

They turned a corner. Mercy caught glimpses of nurses
moving about in drab brown dresses, crisp white aprons,
and white caps. She must have looked wistful, for suddenly she heard D'Abanville say, "My new assistant,
Miss Dansing, fancies herself another Nightingale, I
think."

Mercy felt color rise to her face as the administrator
turned his beaming eyes on her and smiled.

"We are always in need of more nurses, my dear. Have
you any training?"

"Only volunteer duty at London Hospital," she told
him. "Although I hope someday to attend the Nightingale School of Nursing at St. Thomas."

"A laudable sacrifice, my dear. When you have done
so, contact me immediately."

"No, you don't, Jefferson," D'Abanville cut in, laughing and catching Mercy's hand in a grip that was more
spiteful, she thought, than affectionate. Until she looked
up into his face and found him watching her intently. He
added in a softer tone, "I looked a very long time for a

woman like Miss Dansing, so I'm afraid she's mine. You can't have her."

Mercy was still considering her breathlessness over the touch of his hand and his teasing, almost flirtatious admission as they turned yet another corner and stopped. Before them were double doors. On the wall to the right was a bronze plaque, which Jefferson pointed out.

In Loving Memory
The Charlotte Reed Ward
for
Orphan Children

"I was in hopes you could have been here for the dedication," Jefferson said.

D'Abanville regarded the plaque for some time before replying softly, "I would have liked nothing better. Unfortunately, I was performing in Paris at the time and could make no other arrangements."

"Well, I am certain you will find everything satisfactory, sir. Come right this way."

D'Abanville hesitated, his eyes still on the plaque, his hand tightening almost imperceptibly about Mercy's. Almost. She noted the minute flexing of his fingers and the slight trembling against her palm. It was enough to cause Mercy to look up and watch his features for some emotion she could not quite place. The ensuing silence seemed to stretch forever before Jefferson called out:

"Just through here, sir."

They followed Jefferson through the double doors into a white-walled ward of immense proportions. Each long wall was lined with beds. The windows near the high ceiling offered soft light that spilled over the children's pale faces as they looked up.

Stepping forward, Jefferson clapped his hands. "Hear up, lads and lasses, your guest has arrived. D'Abanville the Magnificent!"

A moment passed.

" 'E don't look like no bloody magician t' me," came a skeptical voice.

His eyes twinkling, Jefferson looked at D'Abanville and

said, "That would be Bobby Brown. He'll give you trouble."

"They always do at first," he responded, smiling. "I'll turn 'em around."

"I'm certain you will. Therefore they are all yours, sir, and good luck." Jefferson stepped from the room, where he joined Roger, leaving Mercy and D'Abanville alone with the children.

Sliding off his suit coat, D'Abanville glanced at Mercy and said loudly enough for everyone to hear him, "None of these boys and girls believes in magic, I wager."

"Naw!" a couple of voices cried out.

"It ain't nothin' but a boonch of bloody slei'-a-hands," one said.

"Who said that?" D'Abanville asked.

"I did." Bobby, the dark-haired youth of some nine or ten years, raised his bandaged hand and waved it in the air. "Want t' make somethin' of it?"

Fixing the boy with a stare, D'Abanville walked toward him. He lifted his hand and a card appeared in his fingers. He threw it on the boy's bed.

"I ain't impressed," the boy said.

D'Abanville did it again, and again.

The boy rolled his eyes. "Y've got the damn things up yer sleeve. I seen it once. 'E's got this gadget attached to his arm under 'is sleeve. It feeds 'im the bloody card evertime he cocks 'is elbow."

There were numerous groans throughout the room and a single "Hang the scoundrel."

Stopping at Bobby's bedside, D'Abanville asked, "What's your name again?"

"None of yer bloody business."

"Well, None of Your Bloody Business, I think you should clean your ears out." As he had done with Mercy the day before, he produced a penny from the boy's ear.

"I still ain't impressed."

He did his coin and elbow trick.

"Y' dropped it down the back of yer bloody shirt. Me da use to' do it all the time when he weren't popped up at the pub."

Mercy glanced around as the children began to sit up in their beds. One young boy was too weak, and she hurried over to him, lifting his shoulders and cradling his head against her breast so he could better see D'Abanville's performance.

"Take yer shirt off!" someone called.

" 'E won't take 'is shirt off, stupid," Bobby retorted. "If 'e took 'is shirt off 'e'd give up the game."

"Is that so?" D'Abanville said.

"That's so."

"Take yer bloody shirt off!" several voices called out.

"I'll catch cold," he said.

"Y' see?" cried Bobby angrily. "Take 'is bloody shirt and 'e won't be able to' do nothin'."

The children started hooting. A pillow sailed across the room, barely missing D'Abanville's head. He only laughed. "All right, all right. I'll take off my shirt, but there are ladies present. At least give me a screen."

Several children pointed to the privacy screen at the end of the ward. D'Abanville walked behind it. Mercy had barely glanced back toward the children when he left the screen, shirt in hand. The entire process had taken no more than five seconds. As he tossed Mercy the shirt, she noted it was still buttoned. Surprised, she glanced back at D'Abanville, only to find him grinning at her rather smugly.

"Impressed?" he asked softly.

She averted her eyes from his, but in doing so found herself staring fixedly at the light curling fleece of black hair on his chest. Before she could respond, he turned on his heel, raised his arms to shoulder height and said a little sarcastically to the dark-haired boy called Bobby, "As you can see, I've nothing up my sleeves. No gadgets feeding me cards when I cock my elbow."

"Ah, hell," the boy said, "y' left yer gadgets behind the screen."

Two boys tumbled out of their beds and ran toward the screen, their legs thin and their feet bare beneath their long white hospital gowns. Looking behind the screen, they called back, "Ain't no gadgets here, Bobby!"

"Oh, yeah?" Bobby smirked at D'Abanville and said, "Well, then, let's see you produce a bloody card now!" He was joined by a chorus of similar prompts.

"In a minute. First I think it's a little too dark in here.

Does anyone have a candle? Wait, what is this?''
D'Abanville reached into his right breeches pocket and
withdrew a burning candle. A gasp of appreciation riffled
the room. He reached into his left pocket and withdrew
another.

A sprinkling of applause sounded from the far end of
the room as Mercy hurried to take the candles from his
hands. His eyes flashing with candlelight, he smiled down
at Mercy, and suddenly she was all too aware of the skin
of his broad shoulders, bare of everything but the dark
galluses that exaggerated the width of his chest and the
tautness of his stomach. The musky scent of his smooth
flesh filled her nostrils and his skin shimmered a little
with the sunlight from the windows overhead, making
her feel confused with feelings that both dizzied and disturbed her.

She turned away quickly, barely hearing from that moment on the excited cajoling of D'Abanville's audience.
She did her best to focus her thoughts on the children,
making certain they could all see the performance, making certain those who were too ill to sit up were each
given turns in her arms. Gradually the children's shouts
of disbelief and disapproval were replaced with cheers
and squeals of laughter. Even the most ill, whose faces
upon their arrival had been solemn with sadness or pain,
were, for that moment, bright and smiling with joy.

D'Abanville astounded them by turning clear water into
red by merely pouring it from a pitcher into a glass. He
turned bright-colored scarves into flowers, and scraps of
paper into pound notes, rewarding each of the children
with one of his or her own, which left them gaping with
wonder at the crisp bills in their hands. By the time he
had completed his performance, the children were out of
their beds, running about his legs, hugging him in something just short of worship. Even Bobby was laughing,
and offered his unbandaged hand in friendship as
D'Abanville said good-bye.

"I don't believe a bloody bit of it," the boy said. "But
yer all right, I guess. You'll do, sir."

As Mercy, laughing herself and baffled by his wizardry, joined D'Abanville at the door, he stopped her,

turned her back to the bright-eyed, laughing faces of the children, and whispered in her ear:

"Tell me now you don't believe in miracles, Miss Dansing."

She was still staring in wonder at the transformation when Roger and Jefferson came up behind them. Having redonned his shirt and in the process of slipping on his jacket, D'Abanville laughingly admitted, "They are always my toughest audience."

"But most gratifying," Jefferson added.

"Absolutely. Who is Bobby?"

"A street urchin. He was run down by a bus and left for dead."

"No parents?"

"Both dead."

Another silence as D'Abanville considered Jefferson's words. His eyes were now on the boy in the distance; when the lad looked up, a shadow of a smile touched D'Abanville's mouth. He said to Jefferson, "Keep me abreast of the boy's condition. You'll send me all pertinent information . . . ?"

"Of course."

D'Abanville finished slipping his coat into place before looking around at Roger. "Have you taken care of business?"

Before Roger could respond, Jefferson said, "The donation was beyond our expectations, Mr. D'Abanville. On behalf of the Liverpool Hospital we extend our most heartfelt gratitude and I want to personally assure you that every penny will go toward the improvement of the children's circumstances while they are interned here. As you stipulated, the best in nursing assistance, food, medication, and environment will be provided, thanks to your sizable donation."

"As well as new clothes for each child to wear when released from the hospital," Roger added.

"By all means."

Buttoning his coat, D'Abanville said, "As is customary, I don't wish this to be publicized."

"Certainly."

"You'll write to me if those funds run short before I am back to Liverpool."

"As you wish, although I suspect the funds provided will last us some time."

They turned and walked up the hall, Mercy at D'Abanville's side, his hand holding hers as they left the hospital. She stared down at their clasped hands while they hurried through the drizzle that had begun falling through the fog overhead, denying to herself that his simple caress was the reason for her pounding heart. Her reaction was owing only to her surprise over D'Abanville's philanthropy and nothing more. Perhaps she was a bit in awe of the man himself.

Roger boarded the coach last, slamming the door hard as he sank back into his seat. D'Abanville directed his eyes onto his manager, and for a moment his smile turned hard.

"Is something wrong?" he asked.

Roger stared out the window as the coach lurched away. A moment passed before he said with a lift of one gray eyebrow, "Do you realize you have just given away three-quarters of what you took in last evening?"

D'Abanville responded with a simple nod of his dark head.

"Do you understand that by the time we pay salaries and expenses, there will be nothing left of the take?"

"I assumed as much."

"Then for God's sake, tell me why you did it!"

"Because I chose to," he said.

"You cannot better the plight of every filthy-faced urchin in Britain," Roger snapped, surprising Mercy with his vehemence.

"Have you ever been left without your wage, Roger?" D'Abanville asked his manager in a patient voice. As Roger hesitated, he prompted, "Well? Have you? Can you name a time when you were unable to pocket your own salary, or give Miriam hers? Or any other servant who is on my payroll?"

Roger's quick, discomfited glance toward Mercy told her D'Abanville had made his point. Turning his face toward the window, Roger sank back into the seat.

They made the ride to the train depot in silence. Mercy spent that time thinking about D'Abanville the renowned magician and D'Abanville the man.

The more she knew of him, the less comfortable she became in his presence. She tried to tell herself that it was because of his notoriety and not because she found herself attracted to him physically. Though she was. How could she deny it to herself, when her eyes kept straying his way when he wasn't looking? How, when her private moments were filled with the memory of his kissing her that first night in Liverpool . . . of his holding her hand that first night at Greystone, offering her the first kindness and compassion she had experienced since coming to London? Yet, as much as she hated to admit it to herself, there was more to those feelings in her breast than just physical attraction. That was what bothered her most. She could cope with the desire. Deny it if she must.

But, dear God, how easy it would be to fall in love with Dominick D'Abanville. His wit, his charm and kindness, not only to her, but to those ill, orphaned children, had moved her to tears. But therein was the danger. Miriam was quite obviously enamored of him. Abigail Russell had been, and how many before them? Yet, despite that glowing, almost-too-good-to-be-true caricature he had painted of himself to others, there was a dark side. A strange sort of desperation that lurked just beneath the surface of that witty smile. A cold-blooded determination driving him like the machine Miriam had professed him to be.

Closing her eyes, she tried to force his image, his presence from her mind. Impossible. How could she, when he was so close, when his scent filled her nostrils, when the close confines of the coach were filled with his every movement? Mercy smiled bitterly to herself. One moment she thought she could deny the physical urges he stirred within her; the next, her body was tautening like a damnable bowstring. She had no one but herself to blame for those feelings. By doing what she had done with George Balfour, she had opened herself to urges a woman of innocence would know nothing about. She wasn't a whore. Not yet. But if these feelings grew stronger, could she fight them? More important—more disconcerting—would she want to?

She was given little time to consider her answer, for sooner than she had anticipated, they had arrived at the train depot. The train stretched down the tracks like a long, snoozing gray cat, white steam creeping from its smokestack and hissing occasionally at the passersby.

Their belongings having already been transferred from their hotel, they went immediately to their stateroom carriage. Mercy was the first to see Miriam. With her small tattered valise at her feet and her eyes large and sunken in her pale face, Miriam looked like an orphaned child herself.

Instinctively Mercy put her hand on D'Abanville's arm, stopping him. She almost regretted the move, for she realized from Miriam's pained look how intimate the gesture must have seemed. D'Abanville followed Mercy's gaze. He regarded Miriam for some time before looking back at Mercy.

"Please," she said.

The simple request was enough to defeat any doubt he harbored on the matter. The stubborn clench of his fine jaw relaxed and he smiled faintly as he said, "I think you don't really realize what you are asking of me. But I acquiesce for you because I know you are probably right. I only hope that neither of us comes to regret it, that you remember that you encouraged it."

He almost touched her face, but didn't. Then he turned on his heel and strode gracefully to Miriam. Watching, Mercy thought Miriam hardly seemed like the same woman who had, only that morning, fought like a wildcat in D'Abanville's arms, kicking, screaming, and crying that she hated him. With her hair pulled into a matronly knot on top of her head, she might have passed as Mercy's mother.

His hands in his coat pockets, D'Abanville spoke to Miriam quietly. Suddenly Miriam covered her face with her hands and openly wept. Even from her distance Mercy could hear her desperate pleas of: "I'm sorry. I won't ever do it again. You and Roger are the most important people in my life. I'm sorry. I'm sorry. If you'll only forgive me again . . . I'll be good. I swear I'll be good."

Hesitantly D'Abanville raised his arms and took her against him, cradled her there at his chest, rocking her back and forth until the train let out a mournful whistle that sounded to Mercy's ears like a sob. Somewhere far

down the tracks the bell of departure began to ring and
the passengers who had delayed too long about the plat-
form began to hurry to their cars. Roger, who had
boarded already, waved his hand to Mercy to come
aboard.

Yet she couldn't. All she could do was stare at D'Abanville and Miriam, feeling sharp pangs of regret shiver up
her spine.

They had just turned back for the train, Dominick having grabbed Miriam's valise from the ground, when they
were fast approached by several men. One grabbed
D'Abanville's arm brazenly, stopping him in his tracks.

"Kyle Barker from the Liverpool *Times*, Mr. D'Abanville. Is there any truth to the rumors that you are about
to be brought up on charges in London for the murder of
your former mistress?"

Another man stepped forward. "Ain't it true that the
Criminal Investigation Department has questioned you
already on the matter?"

"Is it true that you and the young woman were seen
arguing heatedly only three hours before her death?"

"Ain't the CID also investigating the fact that Miss
Russell's murder could also be tied in with the gruesome
East End killings?"

"Don't you use knives in your performances, Mr.
D'Abanville? In fact, don't you, in one of your acts, sim-
ulate the mutilation of a woman?"

Mercy looked toward Roger as he jumped from the
train and ran toward the encounter. D'Abanville was
shaking his head, his face white with shock and then
anger as the questions came faster and faster, giving him
no time to respond.

Roger shoved his way through the crowd, grabbed
Dominick's and Miriam's arms, and began propelling
them through the reporters. "No comment!" he barked
to the frantic newshounds, but as one made some comment Mercy could not hear, Miriam stopped short,
rounded on the man before Roger could stop her, and
shoved him hard enough to topple him to the ground.
Roger grabbed Miriam before she could do more damage
to the irate reporter. With some effort he then walked
D'Abanville and a cursing Miriam onto the train, by-

passing Mercy so she was forced to jump for the train alone or be locked out with the reporters.

Standing at the back of the car as the train steamed away, Mercy watched as D'Abanville fell into a seat, Miriam beside him, cooing over him like a concerned mother hen. Hardly the defeated, pitiful wretch she had appeared moments before. Even her hair had begun tumbling from its coil, spilling like a chestnut rope over her shoulder as she bent over D'Abanville, her white hands cradling his face and comforting.

"I need a drink," D'Abanville said.

"Certainly, darling, that's what I'm here for," Miriam hurried to the liquor cabinet at the front of the car and returned with a glass half-full of whiskey.

"All this will be straightened out as soon as we reach London," Roger assured him.

They rode in silence for some time. Having dropped into the nearest chair, Mercy stared out the window, watching Liverpool's slums and businesses flash by faster and faster as the train gathered speed.

The clickety-clack of the wheels was almost enough to soothe Mercy's state of distress . . . until she looked at D'Abanville again. And Miriam. Miriam sat at D'Abanville's side, her head on his shoulder as he drank the potent liquor and brooded over what had transpired moments before their departure. But eventually the liquor relaxed him and his head dropped back against the chair as he spoke softly with Miriam.

Mercy was still watching him as the train rumbled southeast over the countryside, away from a sun that was round and blazing . . . and the color of blood.

6

The train pulled into King's Cross Station just before midnight. Roused from her dreamy state by D'Abanville, Mercy allowed him to see her out of the car and to the coach. Shivering from the damp chill, she watched as he then walked Miriam and Roger to the coach behind them, expecting him to join them and leave her to return to Greystone alone. Why shouldn't he? He had said hardly two words to her throughout the entire journey back to London.

She had turned to board the coach alone when he joined her, catching her arm, helping her into the comfortable confines of the luxurious vehicle. With some relief she sank back into the leather seat and closed her eyes, more to dismiss D'Abanville's presence than to rest, she realized.

D'Abanville stepped up into the coach, making it rock, filling the narrow space with his body and the pleasant aroma of the whiskey he had been drinking. Before closing the door, he leaned out and spoke quietly to the driver. Mercy felt the cloth of his coat brush her arm as he sat back into the seat, but they did not touch.

The coach moved on. There was silence for perhaps the first quarter-mile or so. She knew he was watching her but she did not say anything.

"Is something wrong?" D'Abanville asked.

"No."

"Are you certain?"

"Yes."

She rolled her head and peered out the window, pretending she found some interest in the gaslit street choked with fog.

She heard him release his breath before saying, "Perhaps you're tired."

It had not been a question, so she did not respond.

They rode in silence down one narrow street after another. After a while Mercy lifted her head and frowned at the unfamiliar landmarks they were passing. "Where are we going?" she asked.

"I thought you might be hungry."

"But it is after midnight."

"I know a place that keeps irregular hours for special clientele. Are you opposed to Italian food?"

She stared at him and repeated, "But it is after midnight."

"Are you afraid to be alone with me after midnight? Concerned I might turn into a bat and—"

"Don't be absurd," Mercy interrupted. She sank back into her seat, wishing she could better see Dominick's face in the shadows. Occasionally a dim light would flash through the window and briefly brighten his features, but they were too swiftly gone to make any sense of his mood.

They rode for another fifteen minutes before the coach stopped. D'Abanville stepped out onto the walk, offered his hand to Mercy, helping her alight to the ground before catching her arm and propelling her to the dimly lit door of the restaurant. A plate-glass window, steamy with condensation, read in scrawling yellow letters: "Romano's."

A bell rang out as they entered the establishment. They were greeted immediately by a swarthy man with dark flashing eyes and white smile.

"What a pleasure, Mr. D'Abanville. Will you have your regular table?"

He nodded. They were shown to a back corner, where a table with a white cloth glowed with candlelight.

The waiter seated Mercy and asked D'Abanville, "Will you have your usual, sir?"

"Yes. Thank you."

When the waiter had gone, Dominick looked at Mercy and sat back in his chair. "You have been very quiet," he said.

"Have I?"

"The entire journey to London."

"As you said earlier, I am only tired."

"Is that all?"

She looked at him, her fingers toying with the scalloped edge of her napkin. "Should there be any other reason?"

"I think only you can answer that. If you will."

She had no response.

The waiter returned with glasses and wine. Mercy watched curiously as the bottle was uncorked, the cork handed to D'Abanville. He sniffed it, then nodded for the wine to be poured. The waiter poured a small amount, which D'Abanville swirled about the glass, then sampled. He nodded and the waiter poured them each a full glass.

When they were alone again, Mercy stared into D'Abanville's face, full of candlelight and shadow. "Why did you bring me here?" she asked.

"Because I'm hungry." He watched her over the top of his wineglass. "And because I wanted to be alone with you," he added quietly.

The answer was startling. His look held a hidden danger and a passion that might have been only a product of her vivid imagination. "Miriam won't like it," she said.

"I do not give a damn what Miriam thinks. Do *you* like it?"

The vague unease that had plagued her since leaving the train seemed to take hold of her senses, turning into something solid. She could not find her breath and gulped more deeply of the claret than she intended.

"I think I shall enjoy you, Miss Dansing." He placed his wine on the table, rested his forearms on the table too, hands clasped as he leaned slightly toward her. "You are a babe and I shall have great fun in spoiling you."

"Hardly a babe," she countered.

"I did not say 'innocent.' There is a difference."

She gave him a fierce look and he laughed.

"I like it when you look at me. Often you—there you go, looking away, lowering your lashes like some demimondaine. Look at me." He reached across the table and laid his hand against her face. "I enjoy talking to your eyes, young lady. I love your eyes. I like you very much,

Mercy Dansing. Very much. Does my saying that bother you?''

''I wish you wouldn't. It makes me feel like one of those others.''

''Who do you mean?''

''The Abigail Russells and Miriams and all those who came before them. I do not wish to be your mistress, sir, and if my position as your assistant hinges on that sort of arrangement, I regret to say that I will leave Greystone promptly.''

D'Abanville sat back in his chair and eyed her speculatively. ''You don't care for me, then,'' he stated in a tight voice.

The sudden strong ache in her heart squeezed off her breath as she stared back into his dark eyes. A heartbeat passed while she carefully considered her words. ''I . . .'' She swallowed and started again. ''I am very grateful, sir—''

''Grateful!''

The word seemed to boom in the quiet restaurant. Several patrons turned quizzical gazes their way.

''Grateful for what?'' he demanded in a lower voice.

''For this position. For standing with me that first night and not thinking of me too unkindly for my error in judgment. You were very kind, sir, and I *shall* be grateful to you for as long as I live. But I do not wish to be anyone's mistress. Please don't ask it of me because then I shall be forced to think that all your kindness was only because you wanted something in return. That is not the case, is it?''

''No.'' He shook his head.

''Please understand that if I became involved in such a relationship I would be no better than any woman who barters her body from any street corner along Whitechapel. I have my pride, and though I injured it terribly once, I shall not do so again.'' Her hands twisted together in her lap; she was glad they were hidden from his eyes, for they would give her feelings away more than her surprisingly steady words ever would.

In a low voice she said, ''As one friend to another . . .'' She flashed him a look to see the impact of the term ''friend'' on his bearing. His hands clenched on the table. That, however, might have been coincidence. Her voice quieter still, she asked, "You do not think me a whore, do you? I would rather die than have anyone think that of me."

He turned his face away and stared for some time at a table where a man and woman were smiling warmly into each other's eyes. Finally he looked back down at his own glass of wine and said in a heavy voice, "Of course I do not think you are a whore. Although"—he smiled almost regretfully—"I must admit to feeling that at this moment I almost wish you were."

It was a relief when the waiter returned to their table and Dominick was forced to concentrate on something other than Mercy. It gave her time to collect her shambled thoughts and smash any nagging doubts she might have harbored over her decision not to become involved more deeply than she was with D'Abanville.

Nothing else was said during the wait for their food. He stared into his wine like a prophet into his crystal ball, then turned it up to his mouth and quaffed deeply.

Their food arrived and they ate in silence. Occasionally the lovers next to them would laugh that seductive laugh that flowed around them like warm honey. The sound was like the crash of cymbals in Mercy's ear; each time she heard it, she felt the food catch in her throat so she could hardly swallow.

She picked at the luscious portion of rich pasta and red sauce so thick she could stand her fork in it. She poked at the melted white cheese that stringed from the tines of her fork, and found she could think of nothing but the kiss they had shared two nights before. She, too, drank her wine, thinking she was beginning to understand a little more why Miriam found such consolation in drink. Mercy decided she would try to be a little more compassionate toward the woman's addiction from now on.

"It seems neither of us is really hungry," D'Abanville said. "Are you ready to go?"

Mercy nodded and stared regretfully at the food once more. Then he helped her from her chair, slipped the waiter money for the meal, then gently took hold of her arm and walked her out of the restaurant.

A light rain had begun to fall. They hurried through

the fog to the coach and boarded, taking seats across
from each other, each looking out opposite windows at
the dark street. They rode that way for some time before
Mercy worked up her courage to look at D'Abanville
again.

"You're angry," she said.

His response was a long moment in coming. Finally,
when his eyes came back to hers they were warm and
gentle. The smile he returned left her breathless.

"No, I'm not angry. Disappointed, perhaps."

"There are other women."

His eyebrows shot up, and he laughed, a mellow sound
that exaggerated the lightheadedness Mercy always experienced in his presence. Even in the shadowy interior
of the coach his eyes seemed to twinkle, his body became
lazy as he rested back into the seat. His legs were outstretched, one knee flexed, the posture casually attractive. "You are the first woman with whom I have been
involved who actually invited me to fool around with
other women."

"But we aren't . . . involved," she responded.

"No?"

"No."

"But we will be."

". . . no."

"Ah. A hesitation. I must be making progress."

Mercy ducked her head and smiled.

He shifted to the seat beside her, surprising her. "What
are you doing?" she asked.

His smile grew. "Attempting seduction, I think."

"Do you do this often? I mean in a coach."

"Seven, eight times a month I would calculate."

"With different women?"

"All different." He began to laugh, and Mercy smiled.
A companionable silence filled the coach then. They sat,
shoulder to shoulder, arms brushing, as the coach swayed
on its journey down King William Street.

In the darkness, Dominick's hand covered hers and
gently tightened.

"When I am alone with you," he said, "I feel very,
very good."

Mercy closed her eyes, floating on the cadence of his

words. When his arms came around her she looked up. His face, near her own, carried an inscrutable emotion that was too fragile to name. It took her breath away, stole all resistance to the rush of feelings expanding inside her. He did not kiss her, but pulled her closer, cradled the back of her head with his spread fingers, gently pressing her face into his shoulder.

"This is crazy," he said. "And I'm not certain I even know how to do it."

"What?"

"Seduce you. It's been a very, very long time since I've had to worry about it."

She swallowed, her denial melting away beneath the warmth of his hand like snow under a hot sun.

His breath came, warming her skin, gently blowing the fine hair at her temples as he whispered, "Mercy . . ."

She squeezed close her eyes and shook her head.

"Look at me."

"No."

His finger tipped up her face; his mouth met hers in a motionless kiss before he repeated, "Look at me."

"I'm afraid to."

"I wouldn't hurt you. Ever."

Slowly, slowly, she opened her eyes. She could hardly see him. His head appeared to be wreathed in star shine. She parted her lips as he kissed her. The kiss was soft. A wave of longing washed over her as his tongue touched hers, but she fought it, or tried to. She wanted him to do this, but she did not want him to. She yearned to acknowledge the bittersweet pain he aroused inside her, but dare she? No, no, she mustn't, her mind cried, but her body screamed something else.

She lost her breath as his hand closed over her breast. Then his weight and the hard male shape of him pushed her down into the seat, pressing her into soft-cushioned leather while his fingers made quick work of the buttons on her blouse, then plunged beneath to tug aside her chemise and expose her breasts to his hand.

He moved his head down to the breast that he was teasing with his fingers. Struggling to breathe, Mercy lifted her head to watch. His tongue flicked out to lick her erect nipple once, then twice, before taking it completely in his mouth.

She groaned as the surge of desire raced through her veins. Feeling her denial of him crumbling, she managed desperately, "Don't. Please! I thought you were my friend!"

His dark head came up slowly, and between unsteady breaths, he smiled and said, "My lovely child, I don't want to be your *friend.*"

"But I don't want you like this!"

"No?" His body pressed harder against hers, and to Mercy's horror she felt her own respond, until her skin grew moist and feverish against his caressing fingers. It was so easy now to understand how those others slipped so easily under his spell. One look into those smoldering, desirous eyes and she was ready to forget every promise she had made herself when leaving Sultan Street.

The coach rocked unsteadily as they rounded a corner. The clopping of the grays' hooves on the deserted street sounded eerily loud, loud enough to drown out the ridiculous pounding of her heart as she awaited his next move.

He said her name in a whisper before kissing her again, his tongue raking like a flame to set her afire inside with a desire she was reluctant to admit even to herself. He left her mouth wet and swollen as he backed away and helped her to sit up on the seat. His hands were not so gentle now as he righted her blouse and rebuttoned it. His mouth took on its old line of sarcasm, and Mercy was given the impression that her plea for friendship had actually hurt him. She felt ill with regret.

Wetting her lips, Mercy opened her mouth to speak. He stopped her with a lift of his hand. "You want to be my friend and nothing more," he said. "Well. It seems I am beginning to understand a little more how Miriam—"

He stopped in midsentence as the coach skidded to a halt. The driver's whoa! was a confusion of jangling harnesses and whinnying horses together with a roar of angry male voices. Mercy glanced out one window and noted Greystone's walls rising out of the fog to her right. D'Abanville shifted in his seat and reached for the door.

It was snatched out of his hand in that moment and flung back against the coach.

The next awful seconds passed through Mercy's mind in slow motion. D'Abanville seemed suspended in space for an infinitesimal amount of time, his hand still stretched toward the door that was no longer there, his face motionless with concern and some confusion. Suddenly a man, his head covered with a hood, filled up the doorway and reached for D'Abanville, gripping his coat with his hands and dragging him toward the door opening.

Mercy tried to cry out but nothing came.

Dominick grabbed for the wall of the coach, his fingers clawing impotently at the upholstery as he attempted to thwart his attacker's efforts. Mercy sprang for the door but it was slammed in her face and held in place by the body of a man whose eyes glittered at her through the slits in his hood. They were laughing at her, those eyes. Taunting her. They seemed so familiar, and yet . . .

As if he had read her thoughts the man abruptly turned away, blocking her view from the window. To Mercy's horror the awful dull thud of body blows reached her ears. There was scuffling, and more blows, so sickeningly violent that they seemed to make her heart stop beating.

"Bloody murderin' bastard!" came the vicious words. "Devil. Son of Lucifer. We'll send you back to hell for what you done to them women. We'll send you back to hell if the CID won't."

Mercy beat on the door with her fists.

The sudden shrill sound of a policeman's whistle pierced the night air. There was a sound of running feet. Mercy threw back the door, blinking the cold mist from her eyes as she searched the dark street. Finally she found Dominick lying on his back some distance away, the gaslamp overhead washing his still face in yellow light.

She ran to him and fell to her knees beside him. There were footsteps approaching and suddenly two policemen were stooping over him, firing questions into her face that she could not yet understand. Finally she raised her head and looked up at the coach's driver. His eyes were stony in his face as he watched her.

"Why didn't you help him?" she asked. "You sat there and did nothing. Why didn't you help him?"

"Who did this?" one of the policemen asked.

Forcing her eyes from the driver, she shook her head.

"Robbers more'n likely," the other said.

"No," she said. "Not robbers. They only wanted to hurt him."

"Did you recognize them, miss?"

"They had on hoods. Please, let's get him to the house. I fear he's terribly injured."

They put him in the coach, and she cradled his head in her lap. Roger answered the front door and directed the police to take D'Abanville to the nearest drawing room where they placed him on the settee, the very one on which she had been placed her first night at Greystone. They were no more than settled when Miriam swept into the room, pushed them all aside, and took up D'Abanville's hand.

"Who did this?" she demanded.

"I don't know," Mercy responded. "They must have been laying in wait. They wore hoods and called him devil and son of Lucifer. They said they would see him in hell for what he had done to those women."

D'Abanville groaned and opened his eyes. He seemed confused at first and frowned when seeing Miriam.

"Don't try to move," she told him. "Should I call a doctor?"

"No," he said.

"Did you know any of the men who attacked you, sir?" one of the police asked him.

He shook his head and tried to sit up. Miriam attempted to stop him, but he shoved her away. "Leave me alone. I—" His head came up suddenly and he looked around frantically. Finding Mercy, he appeared to relax. "You're all right?" he said in a relieved voice. "They didn't—"

"I'm fine."

There was a great deal of commotion then as Miriam and Roger tended to D'Abanville's wounds and discussed the atrocity with the police. Mercy stood by the window and looked out, collecting her nerves, fighting back the surge of irrational distress she experienced each time

Miriam touched D'Abanville or spoke to him in that possessive, clinging tone.

They removed his shirt. Already there were bruises staining the flesh of his chest and stomach and ribs. He would be sore tomorrow, he informed them, but he was fine.

Miriam asked him outright: "Did you even bother to fight back? Silly question, of course you didn't. Someday, D'Abanville, we will bury you with a copy of *The Theosophist*. You'll contact us from the beyond, I hope, and tell us whether your passivity on earth was worth it or not."

Mercy saw the police to the door and thanked them again for their timely intervention. She did not, however, return to the parlor. Miriam had everything firmly in hand, it seemed. Mercy felt she really wasn't needed. She doubted that D'Abanville would even miss her.

Still, she paused before passing from the foyer and looked back toward the door. She was still shaking slightly, as much from the encounter with D'Abanville as from her reaction to the ruffians' attack. She had denied his desires—and hers—this once. What about next time?

She closed her eyes briefly, no longer unaccustomed to the shudder of regret that seemed to shake her each time she turned him away.

She retired to her room, glad to be back amid its threadbare simplicity. There was a comfort here in the familiar surroundings. Her kettle was where she had left it, the cup and saucer of blue china alongside it, ready to use when she so desired. Once these small idiosyncrasies might have seemed strange even to her, but after being forced to share even those most private moments of her day-to-day life with strangers on Sultan Street, this aloneness was like a holiday to her battered senses.

Mercy started a fire in the stove and put her kettle of water on to heat. She stared into the fire for some time, warming her hands over it, watching the small gold flames dully reflect from the smutted belly of the old kettle. Then she walked to her window and looked out.

The mist had thickened, not so much as to obscure all within the courtyard and beyond, but enough to give what she saw a dreamlike quality. Through the mist small yellow lights glowed from the distant towerhouse windows. The towerhouse itself seemed taller and blacker than it had before, stark behind the moving clouds of gray mist. The distant rumble of thunder and vague flash of light in the night sky told her another storm was brewing.

A sense of unease crept over her. Then the lid on the kettle began to rattle. She turned back to the stove and made her tea, purposely keeping her mind empty of all thought, ignoring the odd chill that kept crawling up her back each time she ventured too far from the glowing stove.

She drank her tea and fire-gazed until her eyelids grew so heavy she could barely raise them. After a while she roused herself enough to walk to her baggage and dig out her gown. It fell to the floor in a heap, however, as she dropped onto the bed with an exhausted sigh.

Footsteps sounded in the hallway, but they seemed a long way off. She threw a brief but intense look toward the door and waited. Nothing. She fell back on the bed, closed her eyes, shuddering a little from the damp cold that the stove could not seem to drive away. Odd how her skin seemed cold while inside her body she felt hot and unsettled.

With her hands she pulled at her blouse until it lay open. She tugged at the ties on her chemise until it too was thrown back. In the mirror she caught a glimpse of her breasts, pale and rounded and high. The small nipples took on a rosy glow from the distant dying fire. She touched one briefly, felt it tauten. She thought of D'Abanville and how he had taken it into his mouth, his head so dark against her white flesh and his hand so large as he raised her breast to his tongue and lips.

As the nipple jutted like a hard pebble against her fingers she moved her hand away, down to the waistband of her skirt, peeled away the layer of calico material until it slid down over her knees to the floor. She pushed down her drawers, thinking she really should retrieve her gown, but somehow she could not make herself rise from the bed.

The mirror reflected her outstretched form, a pale statue in the dimness. Her head lay in the soft white halo

that was her hair. Her belly curved inward, accentuating
the line of her hip bones and the mound of curling light
brown hair between her legs. There was a stirring of feeling inside her there, but although she tried, she could not
stop the images that flashed one after another through her
mind's eye. Images of men and women together. She had
seen it all while living on Sultan Street with Oliver and
his girls. Nothing a man could do with a woman would
ever surprise her.

What did surprise her was that the images she had once
thought deplorable were arousing a discomfiting longing
in her senses. Images taking the shape of Dominick
D'Abanville and herself. Images of his hands on her,
touching her in those private places that had brought gasps
of delight from Oliver's girls. George Balfour hadn't
touched her there, or anywhere, with his hands. Had just
raised himself up over her on his hands and knees and
thrust himself inside her so abruptly she had had barely
enough time to cry out before he was done and rolling
to his side with a groan. From what she had witnessed it
was that way a lot with men, but not always.

She closed her eyes and listened to the quiet. Embers
shifted in the stove and sparks crackled and died,
drowned by the intense silence. Then something . . .

She opened her eyes and looked at the ceiling. Nothing. It was nothing. She glanced about the room, dimly
made out the vague shape of the dresser, the mirror, the
reflection of her body stretched out sensually over the
white sheets of her bed. She should try to relax, Mercy
told herself. She closed her eyes and finally slept, or
thought she did.

A sudden spasm awoke her, as if she had just fallen
into a black abyss, had grabbed for a hand hold and found
nothing. Mercy opened her eyes. Perspiration dampened
her hair. She ran her fingers over her brow and down her
face, trying to force herself awake. The wet chill of outside seemed to permeate the walls of her room and settle
like a blanket around her so that she shivered. The air
had turned into a sort of vacuum, a freezing vacuum like
starless space: she couldn't breathe.

She slipped into a sort of purgatory, caught between
wakefulness and sleep, vaguely aware of the crash of

thunder and an occasional flash of lightning that briefly lit the room. Her arms and legs seemed strangely leaden, unable to move, she tossed her head from side to side, struggling against the consuming darkness, afraid of falling completely into it, afraid she would never return.

Turning her head, she tried to focus on the tumbling sleaves of fog drifting through her open window. She did not remember leaving her window open . . .

A figure stood there, on the verge of the dreamlike darkness. Pushing herself up on both elbows, she watched and waited as he moved forward through the shadows and stopped at the end of her bed. He was naked, all curving, flexing muscle and tendon and bone, with flesh like shimmering wet gold where the firelight touched him. The desire at the apex of his legs left no doubt in her mind that he was more man than most, and that he wanted her badly.

She could not speak, but her mind told her over and over that this was a dream. A fantasy she had been too cowardly up until now to acknowledge. The very acknowledgment made her smile.

Silently he moved over her, his presence surrounding her, his warmth fanning her like a summer breeze, filling her to such wondrous degrees she could not catch her breath. His weight pressed down on her, but though she yearned to wrap her arms around his shoulders she could but lie there beneath him, her arms outstretched and pinned as they had been in the carriage by some force she could not even see.

His hands moved over her, gently, brushing her hips, her waist, her breasts. She looked up into the odd shining blue depths of his eyes and raised her mouth to his, opening it beneath his, feeling the startling heat of his tongue as it embraced her. Then came the words, whisper-soft, next to her ear:

"I want you. I want you, Mercy, I'm going to have you."

The tears came, rolling down her cheeks.

His head moved down, nuzzling her throat. Down, to the soft hollow between her breasts. Then up to the pulsating peaks that seemed to burn beneath the scalding touch of his lips and tongue. *Love me!* she longed to cry

out, but couldn't. All the words and tears had knotted in
her throat and she could do nothing but lie there silently
and let the magic grow to ever greater heights. The feel
of him inside her, moving, sliding, flooding her being
with such sweet torment that she almost wept aloud, until
she was rising hard to meet his every drive, her body
demanding a release. With closed eyes she groaned as he
rocked her, at first gently, then powerfully, low sounds
rumbling from his throat like thunder. The storm settled
between her thighs, building, building, and she lifted her
arms to embrace him.

A sudden flash of light brought her upright on the bed.
She was alone.

Slick with sweat she huddled there, feeling her body
throb in the most intimate of places. Rising, she stumbled toward the open window, flung her hair back and
turned her face into the wind, praying it would extinguish
the frightening fire inside her. Again the lightning, setting
the world momentarily ablaze. And in the silence that followed—that breathless stillness of anticipation—there came
the music, chimes that seemed to float suspended in the
air around her. Then with a brilliant flash of light it was
gone, and as Mercy looked toward the tower silhouetted
against the black sky, the tiny yellow light in the distant
window flickered . . . and went out.

7

Unable to sleep, Mercy arose before dawn, poured a basin of bracingly cold water, and washed herself. She shivered, as much from her troubling night as from the cold.

Try as she might, she could not forget the dream of D'Abanville, or the thoughts that had plagued her throughout the night. At three o'clock she had left the bed and paced the floor, certain that to remain in his employ would be folly. By four she had fallen back onto her mattress and tried her best to conjure up the same dream that had racked her mind and body before, but the only image to send her sitting upright in bed was the one of a jackdaw dropping Abby Russell's ruby ring at her feet.

Consciously or unconsciously she had managed to put the memory of the ring from her mind the last few days. There could be any number of reasons for that ring to be at Greystone Manor, none of which had anything to do with murder. It just wasn't possible that the man who had donated the entire earnings from his Liverpool performance to help ill and orphaned children, who had shown Miriam untold patience and understanding, could be the same man who was butchering women in the streets.

Mercy dried her face, slipped on the last of her clean and not-too-tattered garments, then pulled her chair to the window and sat brushing her hair. As she stared out the window at the weed-infested courtyard, she plaited the pale skeins into a thick braid and tied it with her only ribbon.

She caught a glance of the newspaper Miriam had

brought her during her convalescence. She picked it up, ignored the story about her employer and Abigail Russell, and flipped over the paper. "DR. JEKYLL AND MR. HYDE A SMASHING SUCCESS AT THE LYCEUM!" the headline read. "RICHARD MANSFIELD, THE AMERICAN ACTOR WHOSE *Dr. Jekyll and Mr. Hyde* OPENED AT THE LYCEUM IN AUGUST, CONTINUES TO SUCCESSFULLY ENTERTAIN HIS AUDIENCES ON THE STRAND, HIS INTERPRETATION OF THE MONSTER HYDE IN PARTICULAR GIVING SATISFACTION . . ." Mercy threw down the paper and looked away. Ridiculous notion: kind men turning into monsters because they drink a potion.

She looked toward her dresser, left her chair, and pulled open the drawer. The ring lay buried beneath a pair of patched stockings. Mercy took the ring and returned to the window.

Long minutes passed in silence except for the occasional trill of a nightingale announcing the coming of morning. Mercy turned the ring over and over in her fingers, looking not at it but out her window at the distant hedges of hawthorn and dog roses. With any luck, the sun would soon burn the mist away and splash the earth with color, however briefly. By noon the sky would be blotted by one of the sulfurous fogs the city so fancifully called "London particulars." Suddenly Mercy had a need to be out of this room. Away from the doubts that had plagued her throughout the night. Sliding the ring into her skirt pocket, she left her room.

She was almost to Greystone's gates when the dog ambled out of the woods by the drive and sat down, its yellow eyes fixed on her. Mercy stopped dead in her tracks, heart racing as she waited for the inevitable attack. Then the bushes parted again and a dark-haired man stepped out onto the drive. He glanced at Mercy and clapped his hands at the dog. Obedient, the animal heeled and took his place at the man's side.

"Thank you," Mercy said. "Do you work here?"

The man smiled and nodded.

"I only thought to go for a short walk. Do you think that will be all right?"

He nodded and smiled again.

Mercy walked by him, discomfited by his intense stare and silence. She did not breathe until she had closed the gate behind her and had walked a comfortable distance from Greystone's boundaries. Then she stopped and stared back at the wall of brick and the line of dark trees that separated the reality of London from the fantasy of Greystone—for that was what it seemed like, standing on the outside looking in.

Dawn had always been her favorite time in London, before the streets became crowded with traffic and the sidewalks with pedestrians. Yellow lights glowed through town house windows. One by one, streetlamps were being doused and shop doors were thrown open as shopkeepers swept out their establishments in preparation for the day's business.

It was only natural that Mercy would return to Spitalfields. She had friends there, after all, many of them already taking their places on street corners, readying for the first onslaught of businessmen who would pass through the area by foot or carriage. She recognized the one-legged street sweeper stumping his way to Chancery Lane. A dustman and his nag clopped down the street, and stopping before a line of tenements, he yelled, "Dust hoi! Dust hoi! Bring it out today, I shan't be here tomorrow!" Seeing Mercy, he threw up his hand and waved her a cheerful hello. She smiled in return and waved back.

The landlord of the Star and Garter threw open his door and tossed a pail of dishwater into the street. His round cockney face broke out in a smile as Mercy walked by. "Get 'omesick, lass?" he called out.

"Ay," she responded, laughing.

"Give over, gal. Yer out now, bless yer soul."

"I still think of you, Danny. How's the business?"

"Not good. It's them murders what put people off. It'll see me to bankruptcy, I wager. Since the killings started, I hardly get a soul in here of a night."

"Perhaps it will get better soon."

He shook his head and retreated into his tavern.

She wandered down by Christ Church and watched those too destitute even for the fourpenny lodging houses as they stirred from their sleeping places along the church's railings. Mercy knew that they hadn't slept much because of the storms throughout the night. She had spent her first night in Spitalfields clinging to the wall of that church, afraid to sit down or even to close her eyes, unaccustomed to the ragged people around her. Not so much afraid of the people themselves as of becoming one of them.

D'Abanville had saved her from that. Still, she could not help but feel guilty as she continued walking, the money in the purse she had stuffed into her pocket feeling like an anchor weighting her down. Coming to White-chapel Road, she picked up her pace and pulled her shawl more closely about her shoulders. She walked the same route she had traversed the last two months that she had lived on Sultan Street. Finally arriving at London Hos-pital, she stood outside the sprawling structure and won-dered what had brought her back here. Something was bothering her. The hospital had flashed through her mind each time she recalled D'Abanville's performance at Liv-erpool Hospital.

The nurses gave her no more than passing interest as she walked the hospital's corridors, for many a morning Mercy had arrived by dawn and worked several hours be-fore hitting the streets to look for paying employment. Few of the women responded with more than a nod to her quiet good-mornings, for their position as nurses de-manded that they be aware of their purpose at all times. "Sober as nuns," Mercy had often thought with a gri-mace, but she knew the real reason behind those stoic demeanors. They were bored and bitter and cared not a whit for the patients within those rooms. Unlike the pri-vate hospitals, which could be particular about whom they hired, these public institutions had little choice, forced to hire women who thought nursing no more than a way to make ends meet, a way to keep themselves off the street, a way to stave off starvation's hand. How often Mercy had found them idly chatting in their offices, eating the choic-est foods—what little there was—and leaving the weak broth and stale hard bread for mouths that were more often than not too sore or weak or toothless to chew it.

A rumor had been running rampant about the halls of the hospital when Mercy first arrived, that a doctor on staff had actually experimented with untried drugs on pa-tients who were too enfeebled or sick to realize the dangers. Many had died, poisoned horribly, or were left to gape at the ceiling in some sort of senseless state. But there were some caring doctors and nurses who had encouraged Mercy with a smile or a cheerful wink—a kind of silent thank-you and God-bless-you-for-your-kindness—that had given Mercy the energy and the will to return to London Hospital day after day.

She headed directly for the children's charity ward, where she had spent most of her volunteer hours. Odd, but never before had she realized how little she had noticed about the ward. Now her eyes took in the fresher paint, the cleaner floors, the fact that there were more nurses on duty than in any ward except, perhaps, the ones used for contagious diseases. Her eyes scanned the walls along the corridor near the door. There was a small plaque on the wall that she had not noticed before. She somehow knew what it would read even before approaching it. That did not lessen the impact of seeing the actual engraving, however.

In Loving Memory of Charlotte Reed
1855–1865

"Has anyone seen Dominick this morning?" Miriam looked first at Roger than at Mercy. "He is not in his room, or should I say his tower." When both Roger and Mercy shook their heads, Miriam left her chair at the table and grabbed up a decanter of peach brandy from the nearby sideboard; she poured a portion into her empty juice glass. Glancing at Roger, she sat back in her chair and dismissed him with a wave of her hand.

"Sorry, but I need it. Something about this house gives me the creeps. I couldn't sleep all night. I kept waking up thinking I heard noises in the walls. Rats, no doubt. God, I hate rats. Reminded me of the nights I spent in Paris."

"But you promised Dominick," Roger argued.

"I promised him I would behave. I never said anything about stopping completely." She looked back at Mercy. "Where did you two disappear to last evening after leaving the train?"

"Romano's."

Miriam smiled her a smile that said: I thought as much.

Mercy concentrated on buttering her scone before looking toward Roger. His head bent over a stack of papers, he appeared intent on reading silently to himself.

"Roger, I think you should know . . ." He looked up and peered at her so steadily through his glasses that Mercy momentarily lost her train of thought. Putting down her scone, she said, "D'Abanville's driver did absolutely nothing to help Dominick last evening. He watched the entire affair and never left his box to offer assistance."

"I suppose I should speak with him, then."

"Only speak to him? I think he deserves far worse than a tongue-lashing. D'Abanville might have been killed."

"I don't think so. This is not the first time something like this has occurred. Unfortunately, with D'Abanville's profession there are always going to be those fanatics who think that he accomplishes his illusions because he's in league with the devil. They only thought to shake him up."

"I fear these were no religious fanatics. Their concern was the women who have been killed of late."

He dropped his papers on the table and reached for his glasses, cleaned them with his napkin. "Well, I'm off this morning to speak to the *Times* on that matter, as well as to Commissioner Warren at the Yard, for what good it will do. As long as Dominick persists in cloaking himself in secrecy, this sort of gossip is going to continue. It always does. It is what has helped to build his success."

Miriam said, "But the rumors of his being some sort of spirit or devil incarnate could hardly be taken seriously. These murders are very real, and Dom's relationship with Miss Russell was under public scrutiny from the moment they first met at the opera."

"I will do what I can," he told her. "For God's sake, you would think D'Abanville is the only man under suspicion for these crimes."

"What about the driver?" Mercy asked.

"I cannot fire him, my dear. He came with the house."

"What difference does that make?"

"Lady Casimire stipulated in the deed that the servants must be retained. The servants you see here today are from the same families who served the Casimires one hundred and fifty years ago." Leaving his chair, he looked at Miriam and the glass in her hand. "If you see Dominick you might remind him where I've gone . . . if you can remember."

Miriam smiled sweetly, then turned up her brandy and drained the glass.

As Roger turned for the door, Mercy said aloud, stopping him, "Who is Charlotte Reed?"

His head came around and he looked at Miriam. They both looked at Mercy.

"Why do you ask?" Miriam said.

"I noticed the plaque at Liverpool Hospital. There is one at London Hospital as well. Both outside the children's charity wards. D'Abanville seemed greatly interested in the one in Liverpool, and since he mentioned he had once seen me at the London ward, I assume he has something to do with that plaque as well. Who is—was— she?"

"Would you believe that we don't know either?" Roger responded.

She shook her head and reached for her tea. "No, I wouldn't."

"Well, we don't," Miriam told her. "There are certain things you do not question the Great D'Abanville about. The most important of those is his past. You couldn't pry that information out of him, Miss Dansing, with a barrel of black powder. As far as we know, the man did not even exist until he walked in off the street and into our company five years ago."

"Of course he existed," she argued.

Miriam and Roger exchanged looks, then Roger quit the room, leaving Miriam to raise one eyebrow at Mercy and say, "Did he? Then why had he never mentioned family or home? I have even tried to trick him into some sort of admission, but all I get for my effort is a look so damned blue and cold I think I'm looking at a corpse." Miriam outwardly shivered and her face became strained. Lowering her voice, she said, "He scares the hell out of me when he looks that way. Only time he ever really frightens me; he's usually a generous man. A kind man, and tolerant beyond belief, you'll learn soon enough. But there's a line you don't cross, Miss Dansing. He won't let you, and if you try to force it . . . well, just don't do so, Miss Dansing. You'll sleep better at night if you don't.''

Sitting back in her chair and forcing a lightness to her tone that did not match the frown on her brow, Miriam said, ''Are you up to a day at the couturière's? Our darling Dominick has suggested that we get you outfitted as soon as possible. I shall be looking forward to an outing, I think. Anything to get out of this musty old mausoleum. God knows why Dom wanted to buy this place. He could have bought himself a palace with what he paid that decrepit Casimire woman for Greystone. The old bat robbed him blind, told him she was giving up a very infamous part of her past by turning over the house.'' Miriam held up her glass and appeared to study the intricate etching of flowers around its base. More softly she said, ''There is something not quite right about this house. About this city, for all that. Do you ever feel that way, Miss Dansing?''

Mercy nodded.

''Good,'' Miriam said. ''Then I am not totally losing my mind. At one point this summer I remember standing on a walk on Oxford Street and thinking the very air smelled like blood. I looked up and—''

''The sky was red as blood,'' Mercy told her.

Miriam put down her glass, her eyes on Mercy's.

Mercy remembered that day clearly, could feel again the cold wedge of fear that had sluiced down her spine at the sight of the fiery sky. She remembered the teeming streets, the jostling of pedestrians on the walk. For perhaps thirty seconds the frantic human race had paused and stared at the sky, silent in fear and contemplation. One woman, certain the end of the world had come, had fainted to the walk, where she lay unheeded by anyone but her distraught companion. A kind of madness had gripped the people then, and Mercy as well, as they looked down at their own hands and into the faces of friends and strangers, only to find that the blood-red sky had cast the same ghastly hue to their flesh. When she could force her limbs to move, Mercy had run all the way back to her apartment on Sultan Street, had passed Cornhill and Leadenhall street, and Aldgate Pump, had taken a shortcut through Spitalfields, down Buck's Row, past Barber's Horse Slaughterhouse, where the alley ran with animals' blood, and the stench and sounds of dying animals had filled her with such desperation she had almost screamed. That same desperation had driven her into George Balfour's arms that night, and had driven her friend Polly Nichols into the arms of a fiend who had murdered her with enough savagery to alarm the entirety of London. Oh, yes, Mercy remembered that day. She suspected all of London would remember it: the thirty-first of August, when the blood-red sky was a portent of things to come for them all.

Mercy did not see D'Abanville again until preparing to board the carriage for town. As he stood at the top of Greystone's steps talking with Miriam, she tried to look away, finding the effort impossible. Her eyes were continually drawn back to the pair, noting his height compared to Miriam's, the ease with which she faced him . . . how closely they stood. Had he dropped his head and Miriam lifted hers . . .

Hot color touched Mercy's face, and this time she did manage to look away. She felt sick inside, more over her own jealousy than over Miriam's and D'Abanville's relationship. Or so she tried to force herself into believing. Her odd dream, her own body's betrayal at his touch inside the coach the night before, was proof beyond any shadow of a doubt that her resolve to keep a safe distance from her employer's appeal was sorely failing.

Out of the corner of her eye Mercy saw them move toward the carriage. Her throat went dry from the thought of facing him again. Forcing herself, she turned her head, centered her gaze on the man in the distance, the same man who had met her by the gates that morning. Tall and broad-shouldered, he stood in a tunnel of trees, a pair of hedge shears in his hands. She noted with a sense of surprise that he was watching her as well. She lifted her hand in recognition and he smiled in return, a smile so boyishly elated that his entire face lit up.

"You know what I expect. Only the best," came D'Abanville's voice.

Mercy forced her eyes away from the stranger and stared down at her hands in her lap.

"Of course. Perhaps I am not so stunning as I used to be, darling, but my mind rarely fails me . . . contrary to what you might believe," was Miriam's slightly sarcastic response.

The carriage swayed slightly as Miriam climbed aboard. D'Abanville closed the door so it clicked gently into place. He said, "Enjoy yourself, Miss Dansing."

"We shall," Miriam responded. "As I recall, the sky's the limit. Madame Cartier is well aware of your tastes, Dom, and, as always, will do an impeccable job outfitting the newest lady in your life."

"Dress her subtly," he said.

"Certainly."

"Pale blues and pinks and greens," he told her, and Mercy looked around.

"I don't care for pinks," she said evenly.

His look told her that he was not bothered in the least about what she wanted, but he responded, "Very well. No pinks for m'lady." As the driver boarded the carriage, Dominick raised his hand to the hat Mercy wore and let his fingers play a moment with the blue streamer trailing from the tiny straw crown. "And buy her a new hat, Miri. We want no reminders around here of her days down on Sultan Street."

"There is nothing wrong with my hat," Mercy told him hotly.

"It is atrocious."

Mercy had to concentrate on keeping her hands in her lap or she might have slapped him, as much over the beguiling glint in his eye as for his rudeness.

"Did you buy that during your outing down Rosemary Lane this morning?" he asked.

"And what if I did?"

"Commendable of you to help your friends' economy,

I suppose. I understand you didn't bother to haggle the price.''

"You had me followed!" Furious, she gripped her purse in her hands. "You have no right—"

"Nonsense. Would I do that?" He looked at Miriam. "Would I?"

"Certainly not." Miriam pulled her glasses from her purse and set them on her nose. "He saw it all in his crystal ball, Miss Dansing. He sees all. He knows all. He is, after all, the Great D'Abanville."

"Did you sleep well last night, Mercy?"

Her head snapped around again. With the recollection of her dream tumbling through her mind, she stared at him fixedly, noting that his eyes lingered longer than necessary on her lips. "What do you mean by that, Mr. D'Abanville?" she forced herself to ask.

"Since when is it a crime to ask whether someone slept well or not? I thought that you might have been bothered by the trouble last evening, is all."

Mercy gave him a small, hard smile. "Why don't you consult your crystal ball for the answer?"

"Perhaps I don't need to. Perhaps I already know—"

The carriage lurched into motion at that moment, leaving D'Abanville staring after them, unsmiling, until they turned the first bend in the drive. Not until Greystone's gates swung closed behind them did Mercy force herself to relax enough to look over into Miriam's eyes. The woman regarded her narrowly, her lips curled in a knowing smile.

Miriam said, "He is an enigma, isn't he?"

Mercy nodded. Then they rode without speaking for some time. Finally growing uncomfortable with the silence, Mercy asked, "Have you worked for D'Abanville long?"

"Five years," came the response. "We met in Paris."

"But you're English."

"I was living and working there at the time." Miriam looked away, studied the traffic for several minutes before adding, "I was in the entertainment field myself."

"And that is how you met D'Abanville?"

Lost in thought, Miriam studied the bustling traffic,

then watched a blind street seller barter with a woman over shoe laces and combs. Finally she responded quietly, "I was working in the cabaret of Mère Catherine in the Montmartre district of Paris. D'Abanville walked into the manager's office one stormy night and coerced my employer into allowing him to perform for the audience. He was dressed in rags, and was very, very thin." Smiling a little at the memory, Miriam shook her head and looked directly at Mercy. "I thought he was crazy, and even told Jacques so. Maybe it was his eyes . . . like staring into flames and seeing at their very center a core of ice. He was desperate. At first Jacques turned him down flat. Told him to get out of his establishment. D'Abanville stood there before Jacques and me and said if we would not give him this opportunity he would kill himself on the front step of the cabaret. He then looked directly at Jacques and said haughtily, 'Could you live with that on your conscience, monsieur?' Jacques relented. After Dom's performance he was given a standing ovation by the spectators. All he asked in return was a plate of hot food and coffee. He asked, too, that he be allowed to perform every night for the next week—asking no wage except food and coffee, guaranteeing the manager that by the end of the week Jacques's business would have doubled."

"And did it?" Mercy asked. Miriam looked away from Mercy again, and her countenance softened. "No," she replied. "It tripled. By the end of the month he was performing four times a day to a full house. He was beautiful and bright and charming and totally unaffected by his success. There wasn't a woman who saw him who didn't fall a little in love with him. I have never seen him fail at anything he set out to do. What he wants, Miss Dansing, he gets—or takes—one way or another."

It was Mercy's turn to look away, the words having distressed her more than she wanted to admit.

"Take Abby Russell for instance. Do you know that Miss Russell was engaged to a count when she first met Dominick? When she made it clear that she was interested in a relationship with Dominick, he told her he would not cuckold another man and that if she wanted a 'relationship' with him she would have to break off her engagement. That alone caused quite a scandal.''

"She gave up the opportunity of marriage to a count for marriage to—''

"Dominick said nothing about marriage to Miss Russell. Ever.''

"But what could possibly persuade a woman to sacrifice such as that which was being offered to Miss Russell by her fiancé for the role of mistress?''

"Among other things, I think Abby, and all those before her''—Miriam adjusted her glasses—''thought they could eventually convince him to marry them.''

"He must have made promises.''

Miriam shook her head, looked back toward the traffic. "Never,'' she said so softly Mercy had to lean forward slightly to hear her. "As much as they yearned to hear those important words, he never said them; he never makes false promises, Miss Dansing, and he *never* cheats. With Dominick it is all or nothing. If he finds himself becoming interested in a woman who is not his current paramour, he exits the current relationship. And he never leaves one woman unless his interest in another is far greater.'' She looked back at Mercy. "That's why we were so surprised when he suddenly dropped Abigail. He'd shown not the least bit of interest in another woman for months, that we knew of.''

Mercy sat back in her seat, discomfited by Miriam's intense stare.

Her voice suddenly colder, Miriam said, "For a while we thought that finally the Great D'Abanville might have found himself interested in a married woman. Note that I said 'interested.' Let me stress that he is never in love with these women. I think inwardly he laughs at them, if the truth be known. I recall overhearing an argument between Abby and Dominick just three days before her death. Abby demanded to know whom he had become enamored of. He responded, 'You wouldn't know her.' Both Roger and I knew at that point that Abby didn't have a chance of rekindling that spark in Dominick if what he said was true.''

"Then you believe he is involved with someone?'' Mercy sat upright in her seat, hands clasped, hearing the noise around her multiplied a thousand times by her own heightened anticipation.

"Yes, Miss Dansing, I fear he is."

"Do you know who it is?"

"I have an idea."

"Who is it?"

"Are you so interested?"

"Yes."

"Why?"

Mercy closed her mouth and swallowed. She looked toward the traffic, aware that her cheeks were deep red. She felt revolted by her own admission and because there was no graceful way to sidestep the issue.

"Never mind," came Miriam's voice, barely discernible over the increasing racket outside their carriage. "You will learn who she is soon enough."

They began their buying spree in a tiny shop on Oxford Street. Mercy was fitted for numerous dresses of Italian and French silks while Miriam stood in the shadows and watched. Only once did she step forward and make a suggestion, pointing out to the proprietress that the décolletage of Mercy's gowns was not to be overly revealing. Relieved, Mercy smiled her thanks, but Miriam only turned away, refusing to look at her again.

There were several ready-made dresses that caught Mercy's eye. She tried each of them on, noting how fashionably they suited her slimness and flattered her bust. Since the bustle was a thing of the past, the skirt of the last dress she tried was much more trim and slightly shorter than those she was accustomed to seeing. Her ankles showed. Standing before a full-length mirror and staring at her feet, Mercy nibbled on her lip and thought the length was scandalous, really. The neckline seemed daringly low compared with the styles Miriam had chosen for her to work in, and the skirt wasn't pale at all, but a vivid blue with stripes of intense green running down the entire length. The close-fitting bodice with a pointed front was a subtle fawn, but the tight sleeves were of the same material as the skirt.

Miriam walked up behind Mercy and their eyes met in the mirror.

"He won't like it," Miriam said.

Mercy smiled.

"You'll need shoes to match," Miriam told her.

Mercy's smiled widened.

"And a hat. He likes simplicity."

Mercy glanced about the shop and her eyes fixed on a bonnet with bright green ribbons and a stiff green bird feather that stuck straight up toward the ceiling.

Turning back toward the beaming couturière, Miriam announced, "She'll wear the dress home, Madame Cartier."

By the time Mercy stepped out of Harrods late that afternoon, her head was pounding. The boned seams of her bodice felt like knives cutting into her skin and the bead-embroidered pointed toes of her new shoes were killing her feet. Miriam had assured her that she would eventually grow accustomed to the discomfort, but Mercy wasn't so certain.

As a young girl she had often tried to imagine how exciting such a shopping spree would be, but she had fast learned that the reality of being pricked by pins and forced to stand on one's feet all day was not nearly so appealing as she once might have believed. The constant roar of business traffic did nothing to help her head. The penetrating noise from iron-shod horses' hooves and the running of iron-rimmed wheels on the granite road top made her close her eyes and pray that Miriam would quickly settle D'Abanville's account so they could return to Greystone without delay.

Rubbing her temples, she watched a barrel organist pipe a tune that sent a tiny monkey dressed in a top hat and tails spinning round and round, shaking a tin cup for contributions. From the street the stench of straw gone bad in the sun and rain, along with the equally revolting smell of horse droppings, drew enough flies to form a buzzing black cloud above Mercy's head. All this dulled in importance, however, as she noted the stack of newspapers tucked beneath a young man's arm.

"Paper! Read it here!" the vendor cried. "Paper! Special! Whitechapel! Scotland Yard investigating magic man for latest murder! Murder! Special! Read it here for a halfpenny!"

Even as she watched, several gentlemen hurried up, flipped the lad a coin, then continued their journey up the walk, their heads bent attentively over the sensational headlines. Mercy walked toward the crier slowly as she attempted to make out the words across the page.

"Allow me," came a familiar voice behind her. Before she could turn, Inspector Chesterton had tossed the boy a coin and snatched the paper from him. He smiled down at Mercy as he slipped the paper into her hands. It took only a brief glance at the bold black headline to confirm what she already suspected.

"Interesting, don't you think?" he asked her.

"This is appalling," she replied. "Libelous."

"But it is the *Star*'s duty to report the news, Miss Dansing. Dominick D'Abanville is the news in London right now. Whether it be the article in 'Mainly About People,' enlightening the population about his extraordinary trickery, or the fact that he is now my number-one suspect in the Russell murder, as well as the East End murders. . . . Are you feeling better, Miss Dansing? I must compliment you on your appearance—"

Mercy threw the paper to the sidewalk and turned away.

Feigning surprise, Chesterton said, "But there is so much there of interest, my dear. Why, the editor of the *Star*, T.P. O'Connor, was himself among the gathering at Greystone seven evenings ago. He witnessed the sudden magical appearance of D'Abanville among his guests. I find the idea of such a feat fascinating. Imagine how easy it would be to elude the police if one could somehow devise a trick to disappear at the snap of a finger."

A hansom cab rolled by, harnesses jingling and wheels throwing the morass along the street up onto the walk. Moving farther from the curb and running her gloved hand protectively down her skirt, Mercy said, "Men simply do not disappear at the snap of a finger, Inspector Chesterton."

"Oh, my good lady, I did not mean to imply that they did. Certainly no mortal man could accomplish such a feat. No, I meant only that should a man—or woman— be able to effect the illusion of such a feat, how incredibly easy it would be to commit the ultimate crime . . . that being murder, of course.''

Facing Chesterton fully, Mercy said forcefully enough to surprise even herself, ''D'Abanville is not your killer.''

''No?'' Raising one brow, he smiled. ''Do you know him so well, Miss Dansing? Tell me, how long have you been employed by Mr. D'Abanville?'' When she refused to respond, he centered his eyes on the bustling traffic before them. ''There is something odd about D'Abanville. In my many years of working for the CID, rarely have I come up against a man so—how shall I put this?— indifferent to his friend's brutal slaying.''

''People handle grief differently, Inspector,'' she countered.

''He certainly handled his well, Miss Dansing, very well.'' Looking down his thin nose at her, he added, ''Much better than you did, I would say.''

''I was overly tired—''

''Ah, yes, of course. D'Abanville did mention that you were excited that evening. Forgive me if I say frankly that I don't believe you. The look of shock, then fear, that crossed your face before you collapsed was most apparent.''

She could not think of what to say to refute the charge. All that came to mind was how stiflingly hot the air suddenly seemed. Looking to the sky, she watched the tumbling clouds pile high atop one another. She prayed that Miriam would soon finish her business so they could be off to Greystone and away from the prying inspector.

Realizing she had not responded to Chesterton, she said, ''Perhaps the shock of hearing the victim had been found so near to Greystone—''

''But you did not swoon from that disclosure,'' he interrupted. ''You swooned when hearing that Miss Russell was wearing a gift from D'Abanville. The rubies, if I recall rightly.''

Her hand went immediately to her purse, where she had tucked the ring.

''Are you all right, Miss Dansing? You've grown quite pale again. I wonder what it is about the mention of those rubies that causes you such distress. Here, let me offer you my hand. Should I hail a hansom for you? No? Miss

Dansing, if you know something about D'Abanville, I urge you to tell me. If you are frightened . . ."

She turned back to the inspector, her mind a jumble of confusion as the traffic noise and Chesterton's insistent questions whirled frenzily around in her head. It was wrong withholding such evidence. If D'Abanville was the killer . . . Dear God, what was she thinking? Of course he was not Abigail's killer. Neither was he the East End slayer.

She closed her eyes for a brief moment as Chesterton continued. "We must all do what we can to stop this monster, Miss Dansing. He is a heartless devil and is frightening these people to panic. Just recently a Mrs. Burridge, a floor-cloth dealer, was so overcome in reading the *Star*'s lurid account of the last murder that she fell dead, a copy of the late final still clutched in her hand."

"No doubt you will blame D'Abanville for that death as well," she snapped.

"There is something to be said for the article, I must confess, for it summarizes the CID's feelings about this beast. If you will allow me to paraphrase, it went something like this: 'A nameless reprobate—half-beast, half-man—is at large . . . Hideous malice, deadly cunning, insatiable thirst for blood—all these are the marks of these mad homicides. The ghoullike creature, stalking down his victim like a Pawnee Indian, is simply drunk with blood . . . and he will have more' Whoever this 'beast' is, he has a lurid hate for women, Miss Dansing. Especially whores."

He walked more closely up behind her. "But he is a master of illusion. For he is pleasant enough to convince these lost souls that he is eager for their company. Do you realize that none of the women appeared to struggle against their aggressor? What is it about him that makes them simply lie down on their backs while he slashes their throats?"

She covered her ears with her hands.

"Did you understand what I said, Miss Dansing? They did not fight him. They made not one sound of protest."

"Were you there?" she answered furiously. "How do you know?"

"The last victim was murdered on Hanbury Street, directly beneath a family's bedroom window. Would you like me to recount what he did to her?"

"I would not! I have read it a hundred times in the papers!"

"Can you imagine what it must have been like for Annie—"

She whirled on the inspector and shouted, "Stop it. I know what you are trying to do and I will tell you once again: Dominick D'Abanville is not your murderer!"

"You would stake your life on that assumption, Miss Dansing? Because that is what you are doing if you are withholding any evidence that might prove in some way that D'Abanville is responsible for Miss Russell's death."

She closed her eyes again. When she opened them, Miriam stood just behind the inspector, her face a mask of rage as she regarded them both.

"How dare you," she said to Mercy. Stepping between her and Chesterton, Miriam faced the inspector and demanded, "What has she told you?"

"Quite frankly, nothing. Never fear that she has disparaged the Great D'Abanville, madam. Miss Dansing's loyalty to her employer is most impressive."

"You will leave him alone," she continued. "He had nothing whatsoever to do with Miss Russell's death. He was finished with her, Inspector; why would he want to kill her?"

"They were intimate. It is not beyond the realm of possibility that he inadvertently said or did something in her presence that would have incriminated him in the eyes of the law, had it been brought to our attention."

"If she knew of some evidence against him, why come to Dominick with it instead of going directly to Scotland Yard?"

"We are dealing with a man so fiendishly twisted and brilliant that he manages to lure women into his trap with seemingly little effort." Chesterton's eyes came back to Mercy's. "He is either very handsome or very wealthy or both. For despite the apparent danger, these women went with him willingly, ladies. It is not beyond the realm of possibility that Miss Russell was so infatuated with D'Abanville that she thought to blackmail him back into her arms. Greater crimes have been perpetrated in the name of love." He continued to look directly at Mercy.

"London is hardly without its wealthy and handsome gentlemen, sir," Miriam retorted. "Neither is it without its Don Juans."

"Ah, but how many are capable of disappearing into thin air, madam? Illusion or not, D'Abanville pulls off the feat more than competently or he would not be considered the world's foremost magician."

"You are grasping at straws!"

"Perhaps. Only time will tell."

"And in the meantime, you destroy D'Abanville's career, a career he has struggled and sacrificed his entire life to achieve." Grabbing Mercy's arm, Miriam propelled her toward their coach. To Chesterton she stated, "You have no right to accost us like this."

"*Au contraire, madame.* When a police officer is trying to discover whether, or by whom, an offense has been committed, he is entitled to question any person, whether suspected or not, from whom he thinks that useful information may be obtained. In this case, I feel Miss Dansing knows more than she is willing to admit about Miss Russell's murder."

"Impossible. The young woman did not even come to Greystone until after Abby's death. She did not know D'Abanville or Abigail at the time of the killing."

"I never insinuated that she did. But she learned something after arriving at Greystone. Of that I am certain."

Miriam shoved Mercy toward the carriage. Rounding on Chesterton one last time, she hissed, "You are a disgrace to your position, hounding frightened young women—"

"She is frightened, all right. I will agree with you there, madam, and I intend to find out why." He caught Miriam's arm. "Madam, the police are not the representatives of an arbitrary and despotic power, directed against the rights or obtrusively interfering with the pleasures of law-abiding citizens. We are simply a disciplined body of men engaged in protecting the masses as well as the upper classes from any infringement of their rights on the part of those who are *not* law-abiding."

"You're a frigging bloodhound, Inspector, and you're

barking up the wrong bloody tree.'' She turned for the
door. Chesterton reached it before them, opened it, and
offered Mercy his hand. She turned her face away and
did not look at him again.

8

"What in God's name did you think you were doing, Miss Dansing?"

Mercy sank back in her seat, rubbing her throbbing temples, praying a bolt of lightning would rip through the threatening clouds overhead and strike her. Put an end to this excruciating headache and Miriam's overzealous recriminations.

"Well? Have you no sense of loyalty for the man who took you off the streets, virtually saved you from starving?"

A single raindrop spotted her silk skirt as Mercy looked toward the sky. A finger of sunlight moved across her face, but it failed to warm her.

Forcing herself to meet Miriam's accusatory stare, Mercy said, "I defended him. I said absolutely nothing that would incriminate him in Chesterton's eyes."

"I don't believe you. Dominick will be furious when I tell him—"

"But I didn't say anything. It was Chesterton who did the accusing. I denied it all!"

Without taking her eyes from Mercy, Miriam dug into her purse and extracted her case of cigarillos, one of which she lit, then inhaled deeply. "I should not be surprised if D'Abanville dismisses you for this breech of loyalty. I shall certainly suggest that he do so as soon as we reach Greystone."

Mercy struggled for control over her rising anger and the sudden leap of fear that closed off her throat. Flashes of Oliver and Sultan Street brought the pain in her head to an excruciating peak.

"Fine!" she countered. "I know you would like nothing better than to rid D'Abanville of any interest outside yourself. Go ahead and have him turn me back to Spital-fields, but I highly suspect that there will soon be another young woman to take my place. And another and another, because he does not love you, and no matter how you continue to cling to him with your tragic dependency, he will not love you that way again—if he ever loved you at all!''

Mercy's head rocked to one side as Miriam slapped her face. Covering her cheek with her hand, Mercy stared out one side of the carriage and fought back the flood of tears that made the world waver unsteadily.

She did not look at Miriam again the entire journey. Miriam did not speak. Whatever truce they had shared throughout the morning had vanished with the appearance of Chesterton.

By the time they arrived back at Greystone's wrought-iron gates, Mercy had had enough of Miriam's company. No defense on her own behalf would vindicate her in Miriam's eyes, so why bother? Mercy almost hoped that Miriam was right about D'Abanville's releasing her. She was tempted to quit herself, but the idea of returning to Sultan Street agitated that lingering hollow of hunger in her stomach.

Upon arriving at Greystone and leaving the carriage, Mercy chose not to return to the house immediately, allowing Miriam the freedom to do her worst without the fear of Mercy's intrusion. Whatever D'Abanville decided, she would accept it with as much pride as she could muster, Mercy told herself. Still, she could not help but clutch her purse in dread and frustration as she hurried down the walk, leaving Miriam outside Greystone's steps, staring at her.

Mercy continued down the pathway until she had finally lost sight of Miriam. Slowing, she touched her face again, recalling the times Oliver had struck her, sometimes out of anger, most times out of malicious spite. Somehow Miriam's striking her bruised more deeply. Her pride was wounded. For a short time that morning she had hoped that whatever animosity and jealousy Miriam held for her could be overcome. In light of what had just taken place between them, however . . .

She took a deep breath and looked up. The rain clouds had diminished somewhat and the sky looked very blue. Deciding to try to enjoy the last of the afternoon sun, she strolled more slowly down the pathway that wove around and through the many rosebushes and flowerbeds surrounding the house. She imagined that at one time the gardens had been grand, fashioned after the Prince of Wales's Carlton House. In contrast to the more formal garden, it had—or once had had—the appearance of beautiful nature. Trees were planted around the periphery to shut out the neighboring houses and enclose and arcadian world of grassy glades and winding paths and water. Once, the encircling belts of trees and the secret landscapes within must have struck an exotic note to the surrounding activity of the busy London streets. But now . . .

Mercy stopped and turned her full attention on the imposing house. She decided that Greystone suited D'Abanville, dark and mysterious and overwhelming. The house was certainly grander than anything she was accustomed to, even before leaving Huntingdon and coming to London.

Continuing her exploration, Mercy moved leisurely down the gravel walk that reflected the day's last rays of sunlight. There was no point in dwelling on the past, or the future either for that matter. If D'Abanville turned her out, as she suspected he might, she would survive. She had done so before.

She looked about the gardens and imagined that the parterres had once been managed meticulously, but now the eye reposed on nothing but beds of earth half-covered with vegetation. Having a great love of gardening, she could easily imagine the beds blooming in masses of colors: pinks, purples, scarlets, whites. She thought of stooping and pulling a few of the spiny-looking weeds, but she refrained and continued walking.

She came upon the carriage house unexpectedly. From a distance it had looked no more than a dense growth of wild rosebushes and tangled ivy all twisted amidst stunted fir trees, furze thorn, ferns, and rhododendron. But as she looked toward the sky, the very tip of the ventilator caught her eye. Unable to contain her curiosity, she tugged away the vegetation until the casement window came fully into view.

It took some doing to work her way through the overgrowth, but finally she stood in a clearing staring at the crumbling facade of the carriage house. There was something oddly appealing about the structure, despite the fact that most of its walls had been eaten away by the elements.

Mercy stood on the threshold and peered into its dim, musty quarters. Within the shadows she made out the bulky shape of a carriage, its black-lacquered coating a dull gray beneath many layers of dust. Entering the carriage room, she walked to the stables, noted there were enough stalls to accommodate ten horses. Walking back across, she found the tool room, and next to that a workshop. An uneasy feeling passed over her as she studied each small chamber, for each looked precisely as it must have looked a hundred years before. All the tools were laid out neatly on tables. There was even a pair of boots resting beneath a stool to one side of the door. Like the carriage, everything was covered in a thick blanket of dust.

She noticed then the furthermost door at the end of the carriage room. A feeling of disquietude overcame her with the discovery, a shortness of breath. She told herself it was simply the excitement and mystery of exploration, and though her better judgment told her to leave her gloomy surroundings, something else compelled her forward, to ignore the spark of fear that ignited in her breast with each step she took toward the room.

The door was half-closed. She cautiously nudged it open.

The smell of old leather permeated the dank air. A shaft of sun wedged through the tree limbs outside and spilled through the window, refracting off the steel of bridle bits, then pouring across an overturned stool, and beyond that . . . a bed. As she stared at the bed, a bridle slid from its tenuous perch on a nail and fell crumbling to the floor, as if her very presence in the room had somehow disturbed the stagnant air enough to dislodge it. Startled, she backed toward the door.

With an effort, Mercy forced herself to turn her back

on the room and quickly leave the house. She had not realized until that moment how oppressive the air had been inside the building. Eager to put the disturbing place behind her, she struggled through the thick vegetation, dodging limbs that smote her face and arms and threatened to tear her dress. She paused in a slight clearing, took a breath while looking back through the trees. But as she moved forward again, her toe caught on something and she went down, hard, on both knees.

She stared at the pale gray stone for some time before realizing what it was. A gravestone. Half-submerged in the earth and mostly covered over by fallen leaves, it might have passed as a boulder to anyone happening by. But from her place Mercy could make out the distinct grooves of letters etched deeply into the stone.

She struggled to sit up as she tried to rationalize the fact that here, lost within this wild wood, was a grave. Not merely one grave, she noticed then, but . . . four. She could just make out the eroded hillocks lined up across the plot. Dear God. She had stumbled onto some forgotten cemetery!

Stunned by her discovery, she failed to hear the rustle of leaves nearby. When she looked up, it was into unblinking yellow eyes.

The dogs. They stood not ten feet away, their massive heads lowered so the coarse hair on the backs of their necks and shoulders stood up.

"Mercy," came a quiet, familiar voice behind her. "Don't move. Micah, take the dogs."

Someone moved up beside her. She glanced up to find the man she had earlier seen tending garden, and though he did not speak, he smiled and nodded in an attempt to convey that she was safe. At a clap of his hands, the dogs backed away, and within a moment both he and the animals had disappeared through the trees. Only then did Mercy release her breath and turn back to D'Abanville.

He towered above her. For a moment she read nothing in his face, in the eyes that regarded her with ice-hot intensity.

"Are you injured?" he asked.

She shook her head as he moved toward her. He went to one knee beside her.

"I told you about the dogs—"

"I forgot," she said, feeling foolish.

"Have you hurt your leg?"

She shook her head. Their eyes met briefly before Mercy forced herself to look away, to concentrate on standing. Then he caught her arm and helped her through the trees, into the sunlight.

Caught in her hair were bits of grass and leaves. Her shoes were slightly muddy, as was the hem of her new dress. She slapped away the debris, her dread of facing D'Abanville as strong as her anger over so stupidly mussing her new clothes. Feeling conspicuously unkempt and uncomfortable under his scrutiny, Mercy thanked Dominick and turned back for the house, inwardly hoping to avoid the inevitable confrontation. His voice stopped her.

"What did you say to the inspector?"

She stood rigid, refusing to answer.

"I have asked you a question," he said.

"Nothing. I told him nothing."

He caught her arm, not so gently this time, and stepped before her. "Miriam said—"

"I am well aware of what Miriam probably told you." Lifting her chin, Mercy forced herself to meet D'Abanville's fierce scrutiny. She could see it clearly now: the ice behind the fire in those blue eyes.

As she tried to step away, his fingers closed more tightly about her arm. She said, "Miriam wasn't there, at least not until Chesterton was about to leave. Miriam knows nothing about our conversation. Nothing."

"What did he say about me?"

"He thinks you are strange."

His laughed humorlessly. "Most times I would welcome such news. In this case, however . . ." His eyebrows drew downward as he asked, "Is that all?"

"He is fairly certain that you are guilty of murdering Abigail Russell, and he suspects you of the East End killings as well."

D'Abanville had released her arm and turned away. Now he looked back at her savagely.

"Bastard," she heard him hiss. Then he walked toward her again. Sunlight reflected off a trace of perspiration that trailed down his right temple to his jaw.

Mercy looked away, centered her eyes on the distant tower as he openly regarded her. He asked softly, "Do you believe I killed Abigail Russell? . . . Mercy?"

She took a deep breath before responding. "For my sake I hope you didn't." Finding some courage in his silence, she started to move up the path.

His voice gave her pause as he said, "I trust you will remember that anything that happens at Greystone is not to be talked about to anyone outside of Greystone."

"I can hardly stop anyone from approaching me on the street," she replied.

"Then walk away."

"I tried."

"Miriam said—"

She spun around. "I don't give a fig what Miriam said. I told Chesterton nothing about you because I know nothing about you. How could I? But let me say this, Mr. D'Abanville: if I thought you were guilty of murder, I would not keep it to myself. I would have told Chesterton immediately, had I any proof at all that you were Miss Russell's killer."

"Indeed," was his reply.

"Indeed," she repeated after him.

"Then why are you hiding the ring?"

Mercy caught her breath. She backed away as he approached. The sun was behind him now and looked like fire over his shoulders. "R-ring?" she stammered.

He stared down at her, his face hard and without emotion. "The ring in your purse—Abby's ring. Where did you find it?"

Mercy set her lips with her tongue before replying. "A bird flew to my window and dropped it at my feet." As he shifted to one side, the sun spilled into her eyes, blinding her. Closing her eyes, she threw up her hand to shield her face. "How do you know about the ring?"

"I know," came the answer, chilling in its softness. Mercy blinked rapidly, her heart turning over when she discovered D'Abanville no longer stood before her. Panicked, she searched for some sign of him. It just wasn't possible for a man to . . .

She spotted him some distance away, studying a rose bramble, his back to her. Seeing him postured there before that backdrop of vibrant pink, she felt a stirring in her blood that warmed her skin.

He snapped the rose from its thorny branch, then turned around to face her. She watched his fingers as they idly twirled the rose forward and back.

"I didn't kill her, Mercy. She left the ring the last time she came to Greystone to see me."

"And not the necklace and bracelet." It wasn't a question.

"She removed them, along with her clothes. Afterward, when I told her to leave, she seized the jewels from the table and dropped them into her purse."

The intimate confession jarred her. Taking a deep breath, she tried to make her heartbeat settle to a more rational pace.

He continued, "Forgive me if I sound vulgar, but I'm certain you are woman enough to realize that Abby and I were beyond hand-holding." His fingers suddenly closed about the rose and ripped it from the stem. The petals floated like feathers on a breeze to the ground and looked like tiny pink paint splotches against the yellowing grass. "Do you believe Chesterton, Mercy?"

An oblique shaft of sunlight had found its way through a rift in the clouds and poured over D'Abanville's shoulders, into his hair and eyes, likening his eyes to the color of gunmetal, hard and cold as he watched her. There was anger in that gaze, in the hands that could crush a tender rosebud and turn it to waste. But there was fear there too, and desperation. It came and went as quickly as it took him to look down at the mangled petals about his feet, then back to her.

What could she answer? She half-believed and half did not. The logical part of her said she should leave Greystone that moment, but some other part of her demanded she stay, give this man who had shown her immeasurable kindness the benefit of the doubt. But there was more to it than that, and she knew it the moment she raised her eyes back to his.

Mercy thrust her hand into her purse, withdrew the ring, and threw it at him. As it struck the center of his chest, she said, "Take it. Why I kept the abhorrent thing, I cannot guess. Now, if you will excuse me, I intend to

gather my few belongings and leave Greystone. I should never have allowed my brother to coerce me into accepting this position, but I did, and what's done is done. I'm certain you will have little trouble in finding a replacement, and I'm sorry for inconveniencing you, but . . .''
She backed away as he approached, a sudden wind slapping the coattails against his thighs and ruffling his hair. Her skin grew hot with the flush of panic, and as he reached for her arm, she could only freeze and wonder if he meant to harm her.

"I cannot let you go," he said. "You understand that, don't you? You signed the contract."

She looked down at the hand on her wrist, feeling its heat burn into her flesh. Her heart began to pound in anticipation.

"You must understand how much this royal performance means. For most of my life I have worked for this . . . fought for this. When little else existed in my life beyond hunger and loneliness, my devotion to success sustained me. I have come this far, Miss Dansing; nothing should keep me back now. How many men can honestly say they have achieved their life's goal?''

Mercy shook her head, unable to speak as the warmth of his hand on her arm seeped ever more intensely inside her. He moved nearer, a faint smile on his lips. Smoothing her pale hair away from her cheek, he reminded her, "You signed the contract. And even if you hadn't, I think you would find escape impossible. I have no intention of letting you go. In case you aren't aware, a great deal of consideration went into my decision to bring you here. The woman I would ultimately choose to stand at my side during this momentous occasion in my life had to meet certain criteria."

The enormity of what he was saying flooded through her. "You are insinuating that my coming here with the hope of being hired was a farce. Is that what you are implying—that the matter had already been settled?''

"I am saying that my seeing you those weeks ago at London Hospital was no accident. I was taken there by Roger to watch you. Gaining my approval, he investigated you thoroughly. I wanted nothing in your past that could in any way harm my own reputation. Ironic, is it not, that it is *my* reputation that now seems to be in question.''

She regarded him with a grave calm before saying, ''And did you find many skeletons rattling around in my closet, Mr. D'Abanville?''

''Obviously none of any importance, or you wouldn't be here, Miss Dansing. You are a compassionate, beautiful young woman of superior intelligence and some education. Other than one mistake—George Balfour, with whom you slept once, on the night of August 31—your reputation appears spotless. And since Mr. Balfour is now married to a young lady of good birth, I rather doubt that he will stand and shout out the conquest—it was difficult enough to make him confess in the privacy of my coach.''

Mercy turned her face away, shame and anger burning her cheeks. He released her arm, and without looking at him again, she returned to the houses.

Mercy felt defiled in some way, as used and foolish as she had the moment she discovered that George Balfour had been less than sincere about his feelings toward her. She had no one else to blame for that mistake. She accepted that now. George Balfour had never mentioned love even once. Nor had she. But there had been mutual caring, and in a fragment of her mind, perhaps a tiny hope that the sacrifice of her innocence would buy her a ticket out of poverty. She had gambled and lost. But she had learned a valuable lesson: self-respect is not easily regained once lost. God knows she was trying, but it was hard. She had her mind and body to contend with now. No longer a child, she saw the world through a woman's eyes, all the bare truths and ugly realities. She could no longer view the world through the eyes of naiveté, for she was no longer naive. She must accept that. Live with that. Learn from the mistake and never repeat it, and she would, in the end, be a stronger person.

But life is full of hurdles.

No sooner had she cleared what she thought to be the highest and widest, that being London and Oliver Dansing, believing she was on the very threshold of escaping them both, than she ran smack into the next.

Dominick D'Abanville.

A knock on the door interrupted her thoughts. Upon answering the door, she found Micah with a pail of steaming water in each of his hands.

"Thank you very much," she told him.

He ducked his head and smiled, hurried into her room and poured the water into her tub. When finished, he reached into his pocket and pulled out a note.

"What's this?" she said. When he didn't respond, she opened the paper and read the message: "Miss Dansing, Please join us for drinks at four. Respectfully, D."

Looking up, she noted Micah watching her intently. He seemed entranced.

"Is something wrong?" she asked.

Lowering his eyes, he shook his head.

Sensing his discomfiture, Mercy smiled and held out her hand. "I am Mercy Dansing. And you are Micah . . . ?"

He stared at her hand, wiped his own on his breeches before tenderly taking her fingers in his and giving them a shake.

When he still made no response, she decided he was overly shy. Hesitant to press him further, she thanked him again and added, "Please tell Mr. D'Abanville that I shall see him at four." His blue eyes came back to hers once more before he moved out the door, closing it quietly behind him.

She spent the next hour preparing for dinner, choosing another of the ready-made dresses she had purchased that morning from Madame Cartier. Trim-fitting in the bodice, with a low square neck, the long-sleeved dress spilled to the floor in a skirt of soft silk with a gauze overskirt that was edged in scalloped lace. The snow-white color of the dress enhanced the pale, almost translucent quality of Mercy's skin and the darkness of her brown eyes.

She brushed and plaited her hair before recalling that D'Abanville preferred it down. On impulse she released it, shook her head so the hair spilled like a soft white mantle around her shoulders. Looking again into her mirror, she thought: Will he think me pretty? Prettier than Miriam? Or Abigail Russell?

That slight acknowledgment took her aback and

brought bright color to her face. She pressed her fingers
to her cheeks, as if the act could somehow swipe away
the telltale sign of her weakness. If she could blame
George Balfour for anything, she blamed him for that.
For turning her into the kind of woman who would admit
to herself that she desired a man, especially a man like
Dominick D'Abanville. A rake. A rogue. A womanizer
of the worst degree.

Besides, D'Abanville would not think her pretty. Her
neck was a little too long, her eyes too big, and her
cheeks too gaunt. Men liked women who were rounder
and softer, full of color and fire, whereas she was like a
snowflake, so pale and delicate she would vanish in a
moment in a room full of women.

She glanced again into the mirror, noted the high spots
of color on her cheeks, the rich red of her mouth. A faint
smile touched her lips. Her mother had once said that
snowflakes were unique. No two were ever alike, and
when they first touched your skin the feeling was more
like a burning than a coldness.

Mercy took a deep breath to clear her head, chiding
herself for even considering the idea of partnering with
D'Abanville for any other reason than business. She had
not survived the fiasco with Balfour only to turn around
and compromise her pride and self-respect over a man
with so notorious a reputation. She was trying very hard
to trust him, to believe in what he said, but how could
she totally accept his reasons when obviously his entire
existence was built on the premise of illusions, on outright lies? On convincing the public that what their eyes
were seeing was the truth, despite what their common
sense told them was false.

Oh, but he was handsome, though not in an ordinary
or sophisticated sort of way. Beneath that stoic exterior
he was a contained storm, driving and powerful, threatening to shatter those confining walls of civilization with
the slighest provocation.

Taking a deep breath, she turned and left the room.

Everyone was congregated in the renovated drawing
room east of the vestibule. Mercy paused outside the

door, took another deep breath to calm her nerves, then entered.

She noted the visitor immediately. A robust man in a Norfolk jacket stood with D'Abanville near a window. His voice carried pleasantly across the room.

"So pleased you are happy with the restoration, D'Abanville. Certainly we are doing our best to capture the house's original character in every way. We were most fortunate to come across those old plans; you must realize what a find they are, at least from my standpoint. Why, they must be one hundred and fifty years old if they're a day."

Roger noticed Mercy first. His face lighting with a smile, he said, "Ah, Mercy! So glad you could join us. You look lovely, doesn't she, Miriam?"

Noticing Miriam for the first time, Mercy felt her face drain of color. Reposed on a settee, she wore an evening dress of scarlet satin and gauze, the daring décolletage revealing the upper half of her white breasts quite brazenly. Like Mercy's, Miriam's hair flowed freely over her shoulders, its chestnut color capturing the light from the nearby lamps. Her rouged lips were turned up in a smile.

"Charming," Miriam said.

Mercy glanced again toward the dark figure dominating the far side of the room. The stranger continued to talk, but D'Abanville's eyes were on her now rather than on his companion. He held a glass in his hand, lifted it slightly to her before turning it up to his mouth. He set the glass on the table then and raised his hand to her.

"Come here," he said.

His hand closed gently about her arm as he said, "Mr. McMillian, meet my assistant, Miss Mercy Dansing. Mercy, Stan McMillian is an architect. With his help I plan to restore Greystone to its original worth."

"How do you do?" McMillian said.

"Very well, thank you," she replied.

"Miss Dansing has become quite captivated by Greystone," D'Abanville continued, and Mercy wondered if his voice hinted of humor or sarcasm as she looked up to find him smiling at her.

Looking back at Stan McMillian, she replied, "I have always held a fascination for old houses. I often told my mother that I think I should have been born in a previous century. It was such a romantic age.''

''Indeed it was,'' McMillian responded. ''Certainly no one builds homes like this anymore. It is a shame it has been allowed to deteriorate to such a degree, but with my expertise she shall be magnificent once again!'' Cocking a conspiratorial glance at D'Abanville, he added, ''Perhaps the mademoiselle would care to see the plans after dinner?''

''Plans?''

''D'Abanville and I have made the most exciting discovery. Shall I tell her, D'Abanville?''

D'Abanville nodded, his eyes still on Mercy.

''As my men were tearing out a wall in the ballroom, we come upon a safe. Within the safe were the original plans of Greystone. The descriptions were very detailed, down to the style of moldings on the ceilings. It is our most fervent desire to restore each room at Greystone precisely as it might have been found one hundred and fifty years ago.''

''That sounds like quite an undertaking,'' she said, but she was thinking about the hand still gently gripping her arm.

''Oh, indeed, it will be. After the house was built, there were numerous alterations in the original structure. The tower was an afterthought, I believe, and looks as if it were built some fifty years after the house. At least, there is no reference to such an addition on the original plans. I find the tower most interesting. While it has the usual rounded facade, the room inside is very irregular.''

''How odd.''

''Indeed! In my many years of design and restoration I have never seen one quite like it.''

Joining in the conversation, Roger said, ''Perhaps it is somehow related to astrology.''

''You might be right,'' McMillian responded. ''I had not thought of that.''

A servant appeared at the door then and announced that Lady Casimire had arrived.

''Smashing!'' McMillian exclaimed. Then to D'Abanville he said, ''She has been most anxious to finally meet you in person, D'Abanville. I'm certain she will approve wholeheartedly of the improvements you've done on the old place.''

Dominick reached for his glass on the table and replied evenly, ''Then by all means see her in, sir.''

McMillian left the room with a flourish, and D'Abanville poured himself another drink.

''She's a bloody battleax,'' Miriam said from the settee.

Roger chuckled in agreement as he too poured himself another sherry. More quietly than Miriam, he said, ''Don't let her age deceive you. The old lady's mind is yet sharp.''

''I wonder how sharp it is,'' Dominick said mildly. He looked down at Mercy then. He seemed inordinately tall. The black fitted coat and breeches set off the deep color of his thick hair and the darkness of his complexion.

They all turned toward the door as McMillian escorted the dowager Casimire into the room. All, that is, except D'Abanville. His back to the door, he continued to regard Mercy until her face grew warm and she was forced to raise her eyes back to his.

''Sir,'' she whispered, ''you have a guest.''

''Indeed,'' he replied dryly. His eyes twinkled with amusement. ''The only woman I see in this room tonight is you, Miss Dansing.''

Mercy ducked her head, wishing he would not jest with her so.

He caught her chin with the tip of his finger and lifted her face back up to his. Then, sliding his left hand into his coat pocket, he withdrew a small black velvet parcel and pressed it into her trembling fingers. ''A truce,'' he said. ''Among friends.''

''D'Abanville!'' McMillian cried. ''Come meet Lady Casimire!''

He placed his drink on the table and turned back toward his guests. The dowager Casimire stood in the doorway, frail and small compared with McMillian's robustness. But her eyes, pinned on D'Abanville, were as gray and sharp as flint as she regarded him.

''So,'' she announced, ''you are the young man who gouged me out of my family fortune. You are much younger than I might have suspected. And you're good-looking, but then, I knew that. I knew Abby Russell, you see.''

Miriam turned away, her face abnormally placid.

D'Abanville accepted Lady Casimire's offered hand and bowed slightly over it. ''She mentioned you fondly,'' he responded. ''Numerous times.''

''No she didn't, but you are kind to have said so. I told her mother once that Abby would end up on the wrong side of a smoking gun if she wasn't careful. She didn't disappoint me. Tell me, young man, did you kill her?''

They all looked at D'Abanville.

He flashed her a smile. ''Lady Casimire, do I look like a killer?''

''No, but neither did Burke and Hare, my good man.''

McMillian cleared his throat, then made introductions all around. When Mercy's turn came, the dowager stared at her for a long minute before saying, ''What an unusual child. And such pale hair.'' To D'Abanville she added, ''She is rather beautiful, don't you think? Of course you do or you would not have greeted me so rudely on my arrival.''

A hard smile curved Dominick's mouth as the dowager took hold of McMillian's arm and the both of them began to walk about the room. Mercy followed them with her eyes, but her senses were too tangled to make out the continuing conversation between D'Abanville and his guests. She had never been called beautiful before, and to think that D'Abanville might possibly think of her that way . . . The idea was preposterous, of course.

She glanced down at the box in her hand, ran her thumb slowly over the plush velvet, and told herself over and over that she could not accept it, whatever it was. She would not look, not even a peek, and at the first opportune moment she would thank him very much, but . . .

She turned her back on the crowd, as they were busy discussing the reparation of the ceiling moldings, and very slowly raised the lid on the box. She stared down at a chrysanthemum brooch whose petals were pearls and whose long curving stem and leaves were encrusted with diamonds.

"Do you like it?" came the masculine words over her shoulder.

Mercy closed her eyes, her shock over the extravagant gift enough to make her feel faint. Then he took her shoulders gently and drew her back against him.

"I bought that last year from George Kunz when he traveled to Paris on a search for fine gems for Tiffany's in America. The petals of the flower are made of freshwater pearls from a tributary of the Mississippi River. I've saved the piece all this time. Do you like it?"

She snapped the box closed and walked away from him. McMillian's enthusiastic ramblings about neoclassic plasterwork, denticulated cornices, and elaborate friezes buzzed around in her head like a swarm of bees, making no sense to her.

"As you can see, we have duplicated the center medallion exactly," McMillian said. "Come closer, Miss Dansing, so you can see the effect it gives the entire panel."

She blinked and looked at the ceiling. From the corner of her eye she could see that D'Abanville was still watching her, one hand now in his breeches pocket, the other raising his sherry glass to his mouth. She tried to focus on the leafy molding surrounded by winged angels' heads that were enclosed by a foliated square, but found the effort useless.

The dowager Casimire took her place on the red velveteen rolled-arm sofa before the black marble fireplace. She looked about the room, then back at D'Abanville. "I thought to meet you before this," she told him. "Why have you not responded favorably to my invitations to tea?"

"I don't like tea."

"You are quite impertinent. Has no one ever told you to respect your elders?"

"I fear my mother was working too hard to feed me to teach me etiquette."

"Who is your mother, and where does she come from?"

He drank his sherry and watched her over the top of his glass before saying, "She's dead."

McMillian took a chair beside the sofa. Roger showed

Mercy to a chair, then Miriam. He hurried to pour them all a drink. D'Abanville remained standing alone in the center of the room, the pressed-brass chandelier over his head shining like an odd halo above his black hair.

"I take it you are much interested in antiquities, Mr. McMillian," Mercy said.

"Oh, yes. Very much. I am a historian in my spare time. I take special interest in the houses I restore. I like to know their history. It is like getting to know a beautiful woman. Until you know what lies at the heart of that beauty, you cannot say you know her at all. You must search out the personality, the secrets. You become friends first, then lovers. Right?"

His eyes twinkled at Mercy, and she smiled. "And what do you know of Greystone?"

He looked to D'Abanville, then at Lady Casimire before responding. "Only as much as Lady Casimire can supply me, which is not nearly as much as I would like, my dear. Greystone's history is somewhat murkier than most, due to her rather unfortunate reputation. But I will not delve too deeply into that. I wouldn't like to distress you."

It was Miriam who spoke then. "Perhaps you should, Mr. McMillian. Mercy is new to Greystone and she will no doubt become somewhat curious over why many of the servants won't stay in the house after midnight or return until dawn."

Mercy met Miriam's eyes directly and responded, "Are you implying that the house is haunted?"

"Would it bother you?"

"Frankly, no. I don't believe in such nonsense."

Slanting a look toward Roger, Miriam, said, "My goodness, Roger, what have you done? It seems we have a disbeliever in our midst."

As Roger laughed good-naturedly, Miriam looked to D'Abanville. "However will you perform successfully, darling? Conviction means so much to you."

Mercy smiled her thanks to Roger as he brought her a glass of sherry. She spoke to McMillian again. "I would be interested in hearing anything you know about Greystone."

Lady Casimire responded. "There's not much, really.

Considering the house is one hundred and fifty years old, she has actually been lived in a fraction of those years. Until D'Abanville bought the property, my family had not inhabited it for twenty-five years.''

''But you lived here once?''

''For five years. We then moved back to our home in Essex. A certain number of servants, those who chose to, remained in residence to make certain the house was kept in some sort of repair.''

Miriam spoke again. ''The house is cursed, you see. The families who have resided here have all met with misfortune or have been frightened away by the ghosts.'' She sat back in her chair and smiled at Mercy. ''Oh, yes. You don't believe in ghosts.''

''Have you seen the ghosts?'' Mercy asked her.

''One does not always have to see them, Miss Dansing, to know they are there,'' Lady Casimire said. ''I, however, did see and hear something one night that I could not explain.''

''Rattling chains and stomping feet, no doubt,'' Mercy said.

''A woman weeping.''

''And who is this weeping woman supposed to be?''

''One hundred years ago the house was occupied by Francois Casimire, my husband's uncle and the original builder of the house. Although he was advanced in years, he had taken a much younger wife, and they had a son and daughter. It was the son who went mad and brutally murdered the family and several servants as they slept in their beds. He then climbed to the roof of the tower and threw himself to the ground.''

''Then you believe it is the wife who is haunting Greystone?''

''On the contrary. All evidence points to the daughter, my husband's cousin.''

''Evidence?''

''I saw her walking the corridor near the tower. She was a young woman with long blond hair. Rather like yours, I suppose.''

''Why should the daughter walk the corridor?'' Mercy asked.

''You must understand, my memory is no longer sharp,

and little has actually been recorded; truth becomes distorted by hearsay, and my husband, while living, was very reluctant to speak on the matter. But according to legend, his cousin had a lover. He was in the house when her brother went on his rampage, and was murdered as well. Some believe his soul passed on to the hereafter. She is waiting for him to return for her.''

Mercy smiled. ''I feel someone has a very vivid imagination,'' she said.

Lady Casimire sipped her sherry and looked at D'Abanville as he moved toward the fire. He stared down into the flames, his back to his guests.

Cutting her eyes back to Mercy's, Lady Casimire said in a more feeble voice, ''It is said that to see her ghost is a portent of death for whomever she appears to.''

''Then you are proof of the foolishness of such fairy tales. For you are certainly alive.''

''I am. But I was not alone that night, my dear. I was attended by my lady's maid.'' Lady Casimire again drank from her sherry, and the lines in her soft skin became harsh. ''She was killed the morning after in a fall down the stairs. I left Greystone soon after. This is the first time I have returned since then.''

''And why did you return now?'' came D'Abanville's voice. He turned from the fire, his face shimmering from the heat as he regarded the dowager.

''Curiosity, my good man, over why you were so obsessed about owning Greystone. And to warn you one last time about this house.''

''I am not afraid of this house.''

''Perhaps you should be. You are in trouble, thanks to Abigail Russell. If you remain here, you could be destroyed.'' With McMillian's help she left the settee and stood up before D'Abanville. Dwarfed by his size, the top of her iron-gray head barely reaching his shoulder, she stared up into his dark face and pursed her lips thoughtfully. ''You aren't French,'' she finally said. ''I would wager you're Irish if you ain't English.''

Dinner was announced.

Roger left his chair and took the dowager's arm. ''Will you stay and have dinner, Lady Casimire? You can see the rest of the house later.''

"I don't care to see it," she told him. "And I've already taken my dinner." She turned to Mercy and took her hand. Her flesh was cold and her fingers shook against Mercy's. "Good luck, my dear. I have a house on Park Lane if you should ever need anything—"

"She won't," D'Abanville said in a sharp voice. "And if she does, she will get it from me . . . m'lady."

Without looking at D'Abanville again, the dowager walked to the door of the drawing room, escorted by McMillian. Pausing, but not looking back, she said, "Good-bye, Mr. D'Abanville."

"*Adieu,* Lady Casimire."

Soon McMillian returned, and in the strained silence glanced about the room. Mercy set her sherry aside, thankful she could finally breathe. "She has a rather fanciful imagination, I think."

"No doubt you are right," McMillian responded. "But the idea of a young woman pining for her lover after all these generations is a romantic notion, is it not? Imagine a love so strong that it never dies, but follows each lover to the grave and the hereafter. I'm certain if they were meant to be together, as must be the case if the young woman pines for him still, God would see that they find one another again."

It was D'Abanville who spoke next. "Miss Dansing came across a graveyard this afternoon. It was hidden beyond the old carriage house. You might find it of some interest, since you're researching the house's past."

"Indeed!" he exclaimed. "By gosh, I would like to see it. Do you think we could?"

"Of course." D'Abanville's eyes came back to Mercy's. "Perhaps Miss Dansing would do us the honor of joining us, since it was her discovery."

As steadily as possible, she returned his look.

Raising his sherry glass between them, he said, "To lovers, then and now and . . . forever. To *you,* Miss Dansing." Slowly tipping the glass to his mouth, he smiled and said, "Welcome to Greystone."

9

Dinner was a pleasant affair, full of continuous light-hearted banter from Stan McMillian. He babbled good-naturedly about Greystone's renovations, decorations, and furnishings, while D'Abanville drank his wine and responded with an occasional "Ah!" and nod of his head. Mercy knew D'Abanville well enough to know his interest at the moment lay not in petit-point fire screens or Persian rugs or Chinese-pilgrim vases, circa 1800. Nor was it in the Les Terrines d'Alouettes Truffées, followed by Les Faisans de Sologne Rotis aux Perles Noires et Legumes Primeurs the cooks had taken such deliberate care in preparing. He was watching her, perhaps looking for some hint of her feelings about the brooch. "A truce," he had called it, "between friends." A very expensive show of friendship, she thought.

Once she looked up from her pheasant and found him watching Miriam. Unlike Mercy, who shied like a timid colt under his perusal, Miriam returned his look with a smile, the diamonds in her ears sparkling like bright stars. Mercy found herself growing tense the longer he watched Miriam. And desperate. Very desperate. So desperate that her hand trembled as she reached for her wine.

Her hand went to her lap and grasped the box. She decided she would return the brooch as soon as possible. As soon as they were alone.

"I say let the dead rest in peace. What good could possibly come out of snooping around that old cemetary?" Roger, who had removed his spectacles to clean them, squinted up at D'Abanville before adding, "Isn't

170

there something in your religion about disturbing the dead?''

D'Abanville laughed. It was such a warm, clear sound that it gave Mercy pause. She watched from beneath her lashes as he stepped past her, his hands in his pockets, his stride light and quick. She thought again of the brooch, thought of returning it to him now before she weakened and changed her mind. But as he looked around at her, she turned away.

They moved as a silent group down the bricked pathway. When finally arriving at the carriage house, they stared momentarily at the copse of bramble and ivy before McMillian spoke.

"You say the cemetery is here, Miss Dansing?"

"Just beyond the carriage house, actually," she replied.

It was Miriam who spoke next. "What were you doing there?"

"Curiosity. Nothing more."

Miriam looked from Mercy to D'Abanville. "And you?"

Hands in his pockets, he stared toward the bramble, silent, while a sudden breeze blew his black hair around his face. He was half a head taller than the men around him, demonic, beautiful, his white shirt billowing in the rising wind. His dark breeches were cut close to his strong legs, accentuating the length of his thighs and the slimness of his hips.

Finally he slanted a look down into Miriam's troubled face and replied, "Looking for Miss Dansing, of course."

"Then you were alone here together?" A panic rose to the edges of her voice. She looked pale in the shallow light.

D'Abanville did not respond. Another gust of wind flapped open his shirt, revealing a glint of dark hair at the top of his chest. Mercy found herself staring, unable to tear her eyes away before Miriam looked her way. Caught, Mercy felt her face warm under Miriam's scrutiny.

"The carriage house was most interesting," Mercy said to McMillian, aware her voice sounded less than steady, a little like Miriam's. Too much like Miriam's, she realized too late.

"Carriage house?" Roger left his place by McMillian and walked over to Mercy. "You investigated the carriage house?"

"Briefly."

Roger removed his glasses again and cleaned the lenses.

Micah joined them then, and D'Abanville told him to bring a shovel. Micah's face paled. Backing away, he shook his head.

"Is something wrong?" D'Abanville asked him.

Again Micah shook his head, looked at Roger, then at Mercy. D'Abanville approached him, placed a comforting hand on his arm, and said, "We don't intend to dig up the dead, my friend, just the markers. Perhaps we might even clean up the area and consider renovating the stables as well."

"Smashing idea!" McMillian exclaimed. He then plunged into the overgrowth with all the exuberance of a hunter on safari.

The group watched him disappear before looking expectantly back at Micah. "Hurry," D'Abanville told him. "The light is short, and from the feel of this wind, we're in for another wet night."

"Can't this wait until morning?" Roger called out to McMillian.

The only response was a sharp snapping of twigs and a rustle of leaves. Then, "By gosh, I've found them, D'Abanville!"

Dropping his hand from Micah's shoulder, D'Abanville turned for the lair and was soon swallowed by its shadows. Miriam hesitated before following, carefully avoiding the long sharp thorns that shone like ivory teeth in the fading sun. Mercy remained by Roger's side, aware he was watching her intently.

"Did you find anything unusual in your investigation of the carriage house?" he asked.

She responded, "No." Then Micah returned with shovels and they joined the others at the graveyard.

By the time all four stones were cleared, the clouds had blown in, blotting out what little of the day was left them. Micah was sent to bring lanterns, then they all huddled over the marker that had tripped Mercy that afternoon. Brushing away the damp compost, McMillian studied the engraving closely before looking at the others.

"This appears to be the resting place of the murdered Casimire family. Here lies François. There is his wife, and there his daughter. This one, however . . ." He walked to the farthest headstone, holding his lantern low to the ground. The spectators waited, hearing the quiet hiss of the flame as it flickered within its flumed glass chimney. Going to his knees, McMillian swept the refuse away with his fingers, held the lantern closer to the ground while he squinted to make out the faint traces of engraving, following each etched letter with his finger. "Definitely not 'Casimire'."

"You mentioned the daughter's lover," Miriam said.

McMillian's eyes widened. "Of course! No doubt you are right, my dear." He worked harder to decipher the name. "D-e . . . Deveraux!"

"His first name?" Mercy asked, caught up in the anticipation as well.

"It looks as if . . . P-i-e-r—"

D'Abanville, who had knelt close to McMillian's side, suddenly stood up. He towered over them all like a dark sphinx while McMillian read aloud, "Pierre."

"Peter," D'Abanville whispered.

They looked at D'Abanville. The lamplight barely reached his face, painting it in vague shadows of light and dark. His face held an expression Mercy had never seen before: empty yet fearful at once, as if he had looked upon the tombstone and seen his own name etched into the time-worn granite.

"Is something wrong?" Miriam asked.

He did not respond, just continued to stare down at the engraving while the silence grew heavy.

"Perhaps we should get back to the house before it rains," Roger said. He helped Miriam and Mercy to stand, took one of the two lanterns from the ground, and helped Micah with the shovels. They were halfway back to the house before the first fat raindrops began to fall

. . . before they realized that D'Abanville had remained at the grave.

Drenched and breathless, they met in the saloon, waited eagerly as Micah prodded the coals in the hearth into a crackling warmth. The sudden rush of autumn briskness had left the women pink-cheeked and shivering slightly. Standing before the fire, Mercy glanced occasionally toward the door, wondering when—if—D'Abanville would join them.

Roger left the room and returned soon with tea and biscuits placed decoratively around a pink-and-white flowered platter. He had just placed a matching cup and saucer in Mercy's hands when Miriam left her chair and paced toward the door.

She said, "Someone should check on him. He was obviously upset."

"He's a big boy," Roger responded.

"This Russell thing has disconcerted him. You know how sensitive he is. My God, he's so sensitive. Too sensitive. You know how he is, Roger. People don't understand him. He holds himself back from them, so they think him odd."

"Would you like sugar, Mercy?"

Mercy smiled her thanks at Roger, sipped her tea as she watched Miriam continue to pace. As Roger turned back to Stan McMillian, Miriam regarded Mercy for a long moment. Mercy felt that, had a gauntlet of challenge been present, Miriam would have flung it at her feet.

Finally Miriam looked away. "If anything happened now to damage his career, he would be destroyed, Roger. How can you ignore this matter with the police? You'll go down to Scotland Yard again and speak with them, won't you? Tell this Chesterton person to leave him alone."

"I have spoken with them," he replied, "and was told quite frankly that Chesterton is only doing his duty as any investigator of the Yard would do. My advice to you, Miri, is to have patience. Eventually the true murderer will be found and Dominick's name will be cleared."

Hugging herself and rubbing her arms, Miriam walked to the hearth and gazed into the fire. "I cannot understand how you are taking this so calmly. This could de-stroy Dominick. But then, no one understands him the way I do. I remember what he was like in the beginning, how hard he worked so each performance was perfection. He used to lie in bed at night and imagine what it would be like performing for the queen.'' A silence pervaded. As she realized what she had admitted, Miriam's face, already flushed with the heat of the fire, turned a darker shade of red. Her look at Mercy said—think what you will—I don't care.

She continued, ''I knew he would be great, and he is. He could have the world at his feet, yet he cloisters him-self in that dreadful tower, in this awful, foul-smelling old house, as if he were a pauper. Doesn't he realize that people would respect him more if he lived up to his im-age? He should be living in Mayfair, attending opera, making himself accessible to his admirers. Instead, he continues to withdraw, to shut us out, to shun everything he once dreamed of achieving . . . the adulation and rec-ognition. He throws his money away on—''

''Miriam.'' Roger peered over the top of his spectacles and smiled. ''You are no longer on the stage so may save your theatrics for a more appropriate time. I'm certain Miss Dansing and Mr. McMillian are hardly interested in how our employer spends his idle time.''

Miriam closed her mouth and continued staring down into the fire.

For a while Mercy feigned interest in McMillian's and Roger's rather uninteresting conversation, but finally gave in to her boredom and excused herself, thinking to return to her room. Passing the corridor that led to D'Aban-ville's office, she slowed. A shaft of light streamed across the floor from the nearest room. She ventured closer, wondering if D'Abanville were there. Pushing open the door, she found a grand library, whose walls of shelves were empty but whose floors were stacked with enough crates of books to furnish the shelves many times over.

She entered hesitantly, thinking the room occupied. It had been, recently. A lamp still burned on the marble-topped table beneath the window. A snifter of what must have been brandy was placed alongside it. And beside that, a book. Having a great love of the written word,

Mercy wasted little time in approaching the nearest crate and lifting the first book she came to.

Carefully she opened the leather cover, her senses detecting the deteriorated condition of the pages. Walking nearer to the light, she tilted the flyleaf toward the lamp and read: *The History of Magic and the Foremost Magicians.* She turned the page, found a bold scrawl slanting neatly to one side, and read it.

She closed her eyes and rubbed them. She bent nearer the light and reread the passage, experiencing the same skip in her heartbeat she had felt the first time she had read it.

"I don't understand," she said aloud.

Again she read it, saying the words aloud, as if hearing them would somehow assuage her confusion: "To Dominick D'Abanville. Happy fortieth birthday! Paris, France, 1848. H. Lavoisier."

Eighteen-forty-eight. That would mean . . . D'Abanville was eighty years old!

Mercy laughed aloud before catching herself. Obviously there was some mistake. Perhaps the inscriber had meant 1888. But . . . no. The ink, like the page, appeared faded with age.

Dropping into the chair by the table, Mercy carefully thumbed through the book, stopping long enough to read a passage or two. Near the end of the book were biographies of the best-known magicians, beginning with the sixteenth century, the first entry being someone called Faust:

Of German decent, Faust (1480–1538) amazed his audiences in the early 1500's with weird exhibitions and farfetched boasts. He claimed to be in league with Satan, boasting of having sold his soul to the devil in return for magic powers. (See Philippe Goethe.)

Philippe Goethe (1600–1640) boasted of being a descendant of the infamous Faust. Was acclaimed in the early 1600's by both German and French audiences as a wizard. Performed numerous times for royalty, but was burned at the stake when he purportedly cast a spell on the cousin of Louis XIII. The cousin, after viewing Goethe's performance, denounced him as a hoaxer then fell dead to the floor. (See Henry Richelieu.)

Henry Richelieu (1740–1807) was said to have attained his expertise from the writings of his greatgreat-grandfather, Faust of Germany. Richelieu was never to attain his ancestor's greatness, however. He died a pauper in Paris. (See Dominick D'Abanville.)

Dominick D'Abanville (1808–) is the most promising young magician to influence the craft of wizardry in over a century. Undisputed descendant of Faust. Said to hold the complete works of Faust and is a devout student of both Buddhism and Hinduism. He has traveled and studied extensively throughout India.

Closing the book, Mercy looked about the room, searching for . . . what? She wondered. Some evidence that would prove Dominick D'Abanville was not some doddering old man with parchment-thin skin and a feeble mind?

Her eyes scanned the crates again. *Isis Unveiled* and *The Theosophist* caught her attention. She looked then to the book on the table. It was much newer than the one she held in her lap. Lifting it in her hands, she carefully turned it over, brushed her fingers over the gleaming leather and gold-embossed lettering: *The Secret Doctrine*, by Blavatsky.

She opened the cover: "Published by the Theosophical Society. Copyright 1888, in accordance with the teachings of the Theosophical Society, est. 1875 by Madame Elena Petrovna Blavatsky."

She turned the page:

Theosophy is the belief in a certain system of philosophical and religious thought. Theosophy is based on claims of a mystic insight into the nature of God and the laws of the universe. It is the belief that the truest knowledge comes not through reason or the senses, but through a direct communion of the soul with divine reality.

Hindu and Buddhist thought and doctrines are prominent in theosophical teaching. Theosophy is the belief in reincarnation, in accordance with the Hindu doctrine of karma. This doctrine states that the spirit advances to its goal through a succession of earthly lives, and that the consequences of a man's actions in his present life are reaped by his successor on earth in a fresh incarnation.

Mercy closed her eyes briefly, the words having made her head swim dizzily. She didn't quite understand them. Words like "reincarnation" and "theosophical teachings" were confusing. What did "a succession of earthly lives" mean exactly?

She turned the page and read:

Behold the truth before you: a clean life, an open mind, a pure heart, an eager intellect, an unveiled spiritual perception, a brotherliness for all, a readiness to give and receive advice and instruction, a loyal sense of duty to the Teacher, a willing obedience to the behests of Truth once we have placed our confidence in and believe that Teacher to be in possession of it; a courageous endurance of personal injustice, a brave declaration of principles, a valiant defense of those who are unjustly attacked, and a constant eye on the ideal of human progression and perfection which the sacred science depicts—these are the Golden Stairs up the steps of which the learner may climb to the Temple of Divine Wisdom.

Frowning, she snapped the book shut.

She looked toward the crates, the window, the lamp. The wick was nearly gone and the flame was licking in a tiny sputtering tongue at the encroaching dark. Walking to the crates, she perused the many volumes of history and science books. There were books on philosophy, poems, plays, and stories, many of which were written in French and Latin, and a few in Greek. Opening the cover of one of the few English books she had discovered, she read the slightly wavering inscription:

My Son: Each of these books represents a world of contrasts. By opening your mind and heart, you will learn from them and understand, your spiritual perception and brotherliness for all mankind will flourish and make you one with God, the Divine Wisdom. If the world should turn a blind eye to your endeavors and rob you of your most cherished possessions, know that here the word is forged upon the page, your mind and heart. Reap from them their message, be it science or history or poetry. Cleave to them and be rewarded forever.

Closing the book, she sat back into the chair, allowing the faint hiss of the nearby lamp to fill the quiet. She sensed in this writing a great sensitivity, a generosity, and—yes—even pain. There was an aloneness in the words that spoke of reaping life's fulfillments from the written text, that if all else forsook the beneficiary of this gift, the written word would always be there to comfort.

She herself had found comfort in books on a few occasions, had often imagined writing them herself. Nonsense, her father had called her aspirations. What good were all the fanciful words when there was wheat to cut or butter to churn?

Forcing her attention back on the books, she decided to borrow a few and spend the evening reading. She thought too that the books might offer her some insight on her employer: what he did, who he *really* was.

She had gathered several in her arms when that chilling sensation of being watched came over her. Upon entering the room, she had briefly noticed a mirror on the wall; she stared in it now, noting that behind her dark image the room was reflected in shadow. She focused her eyes, doing her best to pierce the corners of the library that were reflected in the glass, certain she would discover someone staring at her. Her face in the mirror was the only brightness, a glowing white-faced statue with frightened wide eyes. She bit her lip for courage and turned.

She looked toward the partially closed door, sensing

that someone stood there. There was no one that she could see. No shadow intruded upon the beam of light spilling over the floor from the hallway. Yet . . . someone was near. She could sense it. Perhaps it was the person who had earlier sat in this chair drinking brandy and studying theosophy. D'Abanville?

The blood started its slow, arousing strum through her veins, quickening the beat of her heart, flushing her skin with warmth. She tried to force the feelings aside, to ignore them. Impossible. As impossible as it was to ignore D'Abanville himself.

Focusing again on the door, she strained for a sound, but there was nothing. It was almost too quiet, she thought. A house this old should creak or pop or rattle.

She peeked into the hallway, still expecting to come face-to-face with someone. Nothing. She looked one way, then the other. The light at the far end of the corridor gave the narrow space a hazy appearance. She could just make out a closed door at the end of it. Odd that she should think of the door as unusual. But it was. All the others along the corridor were massive walnut fixtures carved out of solid wood that had endured many lifetimes and would endure many more. But that one . . . It looked so unstable, as if it should have crumbled from its hinges long ago.

She left the library and moved down the corridor. Reaching the door, she tugged it open.

Somewhere around the highest curve of the narrow, spiraling staircase a lamp shone. The steps were barely discernible at her feet, but higher they glowed with luminescence. She took one step, then another.

Realization came as she rounded the first bend: the towerhouse.

A shadow on the steps above her moved just a little, and she realized that someone stood there, waiting for her to round the bend.

She backed away, and the shadow advanced. Stalking.

The growl sounded low and throaty. Then the click-click-click of the animal's claws filled the suffocating silence. Then a massive dog was before her, the muscles of its haunches rippling, its eyes abnormally bright.

Odd that she should think of the Greystone ghost in

that moment. Perhaps it was because this corridor was
the one the girl was said to haunt. Of course, she did not
believe in such silly superstition . . . so why did she seem
to feel warm breaths down the back of her neck?

Stepping back into the hallway, she closed the door
soundly between her and the animal. Feeling more certain of her safety, she leaned her head against the door
in relief.

Her relief was short-lived, however, as she turned back
down the corridor.

The image stood in the distance, pale hair streaming
over her shoulders to her hips in a wild array of curls.
The girl's face was white, her eyes wide with fear. She
lifted one hand toward Mercy and . . .

Mercy closed her eyes, stumbled backward, shaking
her head in refusal. No, no, it wasn't possible!

She forced open her eyes.

The image was there yet, staring back at her, her face
even whiter. Dear God, she was looking in a mirror. She
had been frightened by her own reflection!

Had she not felt so ridiculous, she might have laughed.
Instead, she covered her mouth with her hand, waited for
the frantic racing of her heart to ease. It did so, gradually. That was when she heard the footsteps descending
the stairs behind her.

Clutching her books, she ran to the nearest door, found
it unlocked and slipped inside the room. She did not
close the door completely, but left it ajar just enough so
she had a perfect view of the tower door. She felt like
laughing at her childish desire to see D'Abanville without
his knowledge.

The door opened and D'Abanville stepped out, the dog
following at his heels. Mercy held her breath. Should the
dog sense her behind the door, he would give away her
presence. A hundred lame excuses flew through her mind
for being found in a pitch-black room with her arms full
of D'Abanville's books.

Dressed in a black cape, D'Abanville swept up the corridor, forcing Mercy to open the door further to better
see him. The dog stopped. Mercy closed the door again
as the mastiff, his black-and-yellow head held high
walked slowly back down the hall. Mercy thought she

heard that low, throaty growl as he neared the door, and she held her breath.

"Kan, come," D'Abanville called.

The dog hesitated.

D'Abanville called out again.

The dog turned and padded after his master, leaving Mercy limp with relief. Then the realization hit her: D'Abanville was going out.

Even as she listened, her heart still pounding like a drum in her ears, she heard the tall case clock chime the hour: nine. Swinging open the door, she moved down the corridor, out through the foyer, into the ballroom and to the mammoth windows that looked out over Greystone's front gardens. Although the rain had ceased some time ago, puddles of water shimmered on the pavement. She thought she saw D'Abanville walking down the drive toward the gates, but she couldn't be certain. One moment he was there . . .

The next he was gone.

She lay on her back gazing wide-eyed at the ceiling high above her head. The rain had once again begun its gentle patter upon the roof. Any other time, its calming effect would have lulled her to sleep. Tonight, however, her thoughts continually strayed back to D'Abanville. And the brooch. After watching him leave the house, she had returned to his office and placed the box on his desk, where he was certain to find it first thing in the morning.

She tossed and turned for hours before finally succumbing to an exhausted half-sleep. In some drowsy corner of her mind she realized she was doing her best to coax back the dream of his coming to her room. What harm could come from it, after all? She could live out her fantasies in the privacy of her mind and no one would be the wiser. Especially not D'Abanville. God forbid that he find out what sort of effect his presence had on her.

Yet, the dream, no matter how she willed it, did not come. Instead, an uneasy restlessness continued to plague her. Once or twice she awoke with a start, believing she heard music. Not the chimes that she had heard upon arriving at Greystone, but something deeper, throbbing like her heartbeat. She thought she heard voices as well, distant, rising and falling like the sighing of the wind in the trees. When finally rousing herself from her sleep-drugged state, Mercy sat up in bed, rubbed her eyes, then looked toward the window.

She recalled having closed it—or had she? It was open, allowing the rain to pour in a fine mist over the foot of her bed. Leaving the warm comfort of her counterpane, she walked to the window; the slick feel of the floor against her bare feet made her shiver.

Mercy moved into the spray of rain, feeling it soak her nightgown so it clung to her hips and thighs. Leaning her head and shoulders out over the windowsill, she searched the towering peaks and the gray-tiled roof slanting to the narrow ledge some three or four feet below her window. She was withdrawing again into the room when she raised her sights to the distant line of dark trees. A pale white light glimmered there briefly, like a firefly zigzagging through the trees. Shielding her eyes against the rain, she focused harder, thinking that she had imagined the ghostly glow, for no sooner had she acknowledged the light than it was gone, leaving darkness in its wake. Though she waited several minutes, it did not return. Had she imagined it? Perhaps dreamed it like the odd music just before she awakened?

She didn't think so. She wasn't asleep now. The cold rain covering her body was real enough.

Changing out of her gown, she redonned her dress and started a fire in the old black stove. For the remaining hours before dawn she sat in her chair by the inviting warmth and read her employer's books on theosophy and magic. At the first sign of daylight she was up and out of the house before the servants started their duties.

Perhaps summer was behind them for good now. The woods surrounding Greystone were thinning. She could look out over the birch and elm trees and see the distant grounds fall away toward the outlying walls that cloistered the estate from the city. A pretty patchwork of colors shimmered from the tallest birch as a chilly breeze swept over the grounds, smelling of frost and wet earth, reminding Mercy of autumn days back in Huntingdon.

She walked with purpose down the pathway, looking back time and again until she could clearly see her bedroom window. This would be the place where she had seen the light. She stared at the copse of ivy and bramble . . . and the ventilator she could see just above the trees. The light she had seen from her window last night had come from the carriage house.

Staring into the thorny lair, Mercy considered exploring further. Instead, she glanced about the dripping leaves and the boggy black earth and told herself that to venture there now would be foolish. Best to wait and watch another night. If she spotted the light again and was absolutely certain it wasn't her imagination, then she would say something to D'Abanville or Roger.

Returning to the house, Mercy was stunned to find a coach outside Greystone's door. Wondering who might be calling so early in the day, she entered the house, only to find Miriam and Roger talking quietly. As Miriam looked round, her face pale and her eyes wide with worry, Mercy stopped. Just beyond Miriam and Roger stood a familiar figure. It was a moment before she realized the visitor was Lawton, Inspector Chesterton's partner.

As if she were in the bottom of some deep well, Mercy heard Roger's voice come to her, echoing slightly in the immense foyer. "Miss Dansing, what are you about so early in the morning?"

"I went for a walk," she replied.

"Chesterton has come back to see Dominick," Miriam said.

"Oh?"

They all fell silent as D'Abanville's angry voice carried up the corridor. "I told you I did not know the young lady, Inspector. Have you some evidence that I did?"

"She attended your last public performance, sir. I have spoken to several people who said they saw you with your heads together once or twice during the evening."

D'Abanville entered the foyer then, his eyes snapping with anger and frustration. Upon seeing Mercy standing in the open door, he stopped, watched her face for some display of emotion, and, when finding none, turned back to the inspector.

"It is no secret that the women find my occupation rather fascinating, but if I dallied with each one who threw herself at my feet, I would be too exhausted to roll myself out the door for my next performance. They come and go, Inspector Chesterton. I give them a moment's notice and nothing more.''

"An enviable position, it would seem." The inspector smiled. Raising his eyes to Mercy, he brightened. "Ah, Miss Dansing, you are looking as lovely as ever, even on so dreary a morn. How do you do?"

"Well," she replied softly.

"I suppose you are unable to vouch for your employer's whereabouts last evening?"

"Why, Inspector?" She looked at D'Abanville. "Has something happened?"

"Indeed it has, my good lady. Indeed it has." Hands behind his back, his mackintosh slapping about his shins, Chesterton approached her. "While we all slept safely in our beds last evening, another young woman was killed."

"At Whitechapel?"

"Alas, no. She was killed a mere quarter-mile from here. It was a ghastly ordeal, worse even than the Whitechapel killings. Her throat was torn out, as if brutalized by some rabid animal."

"The dog."

"I beg your pardon?"

Too stunned to realize she had spoken aloud, Mercy blinked slowly, focused on the gleaming white tiles of the marble floor, and prayed she did not lose consciousness. Slowly, very slowly, she brought her eyes back to Chesterton, refusing to look beyond him to D'Abanville.

"I beg your pardon?" the inspector repeated.

"I said . . ." She took a breath. "You think it was a dog?"

He did not blink. "Did I say that?"

She opened and closed her mouth.

"I said only that it appeared that she had been attacked by an animal."

"Oh."

"Were you home last evening, Miss Dansing?"

She nodded.

"What were your activities during the evening?"

She glanced at Miriam and Roger, aware that they had been asked the same question. Miriam watched her intently, her mouth pinched with worry. Roger had removed his glasses, was wiping the lenses furiously with the tail of his coat.

"Miss Dansing?"

"I . . . took tea with Miriam and Roger and Stan McMillian."

"At what time?"

"Seven, I think."

"Was D'Abanville with you at that time?"

She shook her head.

"What did you do then?"

"I retired to the library, where I read for some time."

"Did D'Abanville join you?"

"No."

"What time did you adjourn to your quarters?"

She stared at the floor.

"Miss Dansing?" Chesterton repeated. "What time did you adjourn to your quarters?"

"Nine o'clock."

She looked at D'Abanville. His eyes narrowed.

"And you neither saw nor heard anything from D'Abanville before or after that time?"

"Not before. No."

"You are certain of the time?"

"Absolutely. I had left the library and had stepped into a room further down the corridor when I heard the clock chime nine." Forcing herself to face the inspector, she asked, "When was the young woman killed?"

"Sometime after ten." Chesterton then turned to D'Abanville. "It seems you have no alibi, sir."

"And you have no evidence against me," he responded calmly. "I tell you, other than the fifteen to twenty minutes that I walked about the estate grounds, I was alone in my room all night."

"But no one saw you return from your walk. Do you often walk after nightfall, Mr. D'Abanville?"

D'Abanville's hands clenched at his sides. "I am growing weary of your snide insinuations that mean nothing. If you intend to arrest me, Chesterton, then do so. If not, then leave me alone. I have a performance to prepare for and I cannot do it with your constant snapping at my heels."

"Very well."

Miriam gasped.

Chesterton turned and allowed her a smile. "I will leave you alone for the time being, Mr. D'Abanville. However . . ." Stepping up beside Mercy, and joined by Lawton, he turned back toward D'Abanville and asked, "Would you mind if I take a look at your dogs before I leave Greystone?"

Roger stepped forward then. "Impossible. The dogs are much too dangerous to be approached by strangers."

"Indeed. Then perhaps you or Mr. D'Abanville will do me the honor of introducing us—from a respectable distance, of course."

When Roger hesitated, D'Abanville spun on his heel and tugged on the bell-pull, which brought a round-faced young maid into the foyer. "Have Micah bring up the dogs," he ordered. With a curtsy she hurried from the room, white apron and dress hems swishing in the quiet.

Chesterton looked fleetingly into Mercy's eyes, then turned and left the house.

10

D'Abanville stood away from the gathering, his face white with worry and temper. Only once did he take his eyes off Chesterton, and that was to look at Mercy. There was a touch of madness in the cerulean eyes that stared back at her. A madness that she found frightening and dangerous and totally alluring. Those eyes, unblinking and all-knowing, stole her breath away. In that moment Mercy thought herself to be just a little mad. She would have to be. For even as she watched him pace back and forth, his hands clenched in fury, her mind would not accept that he was guilty of the heinous crime that Chesterton was ready to accuse him of.

Micah rounded the house then with the dogs. Four of them lurched against their leashes, shoulders bulging against their harnesses as they struggled for escape. Micah, grim to the task, set his heels into the soft earth as he held them back.

Chesterton stood before them, hands clasped around his back as he regarded each snarling, snapping monster. Mercy herself could only shudder, tremble, and back away as a pair turned on each other and growled ferociously, only to be thwarted by Micah's well-aimed boot in their ribs.

"Not exactly pets," Chesterton said to his partner. "Would you say they were killers, Lawton?"

"Definitely, sir."

"Capable of tearing out a young woman's throat?"

"Undoubtedly."

Chesterton turned back to D'Abanville. "Why do you keep them?" he asked.

"Because it pleases me."

"They are obviously killers."

"They are well-trained."

"Indeed. Would you mind showing me how well-trained they are?"

For a long moment D'Abanville stood, his dark figure motionless, his face carved in ice. Mercy felt his tension mount until the cords in his broad neck stood out under the strain of keeping his anger in check.

With a vicious curse, D'Abanville strode past Chesterton and motioned for Micah to release the dogs. Mercy noticed that as Micah released the slavering animals, D'Abanville turned a smug, almost taunting smile on the inspector. The unspoken threat hung in the air, tangible enough to cause Chesterton to back slightly away. She saw his hand move suspiciously beneath his coat. She was not a little nervous about the animals, but recalling how easily D'Abanville had controlled them on her first arrival at Greystone, she felt confident he could control them now . . . if he so desired.

Released from their leashes, the dogs bounded forth. As the group standing in the center of the drive watched the animals streak toward them, there was not one among them who did not cower slightly. Except for D'Abanville. He stood silently, his eyes pinning Chesterton's, his mouth slowly curling in a smile as the dogs approached.

Just as it appeared he would allow the dogs the freedom to do as they wished with these obvious trespassers, D'Abanville raised his hand and spoke quietly.

"Heel."

They stopped in their tracks, yellow hackles raised and their massive heads down, close to the ground. Their sides heaved in and out in anticipation of the attack.

Chesterton, grown quite pale, his voice trembling slightly with nerves, glared at D'Abanville with obvious anger and said, "Good show, sir. You are obviously in complete control of these . . . monsters. Would they also attack if you gave them the order?" Dropping his hands to his sides, he released his breath. "Yes, I think they would." Looking sideways at Lawton, he said, "Let us be off, my friend. I have seen what I came here to see."

Turning back to Mercy, he tipped his hat. Boarding his coach, he slammed the door and the pair of grays pulling the coach were off, spitting up gravel and mud with their hooves as they lumbered toward the distant iron gates.

Miriam, Roger, and Mercy all waited for D'Abanville to move or speak. Minutes passed as he watched the coach disappear from sight, and still he stared, until the rain began to fall again, until Micah moved and with a gesture of his hand instructed the dogs to follow him back around the house. Miriam and Roger retreated first, dodging the icy raindrops that suddenly, with no warning, deluged the already saturated earth. Mercy huddled beneath the porte-cochere, watching the rain wash the mud from D'Abanville's boots and plaster his fine white shirt against his skin.

When he at last turned, his fierce gaze met her own and he said, "That bloody bastard is going to destroy me." Then he swept into the house, leaving Mercy to stare down the drive through the rain.

When she finally reentered the house, the vestibule was empty. Vague voices, Miriam's and Roger's, drifted to her from Roger's office.

"You cannot think he is guilty," Miriam cried. "Dear God, Roger, you mustn't. Without our trust, he has nothing. Nothing!"

"There were those women in France—"

"Stop it. I won't hear it. Do you understand? I won't hear it!"

"The Paris police never found the killer."

"It wasn't Dominick. It couldn't be. Why would he kill them?"

"Because he hates them. Will you deny it? He has every right, I suppose, if we are right in our assumption that his mother deserted him."

"My God, do you know what you are saying? How could you speak of him this way? The next thing I know, you'll be turning him over to Chesterton."

"Don't be an idiot. I love him like a son, but that doesn't blind me to reality. The fact is, while he lived in Paris, several women were brutally murdered. The killer was never found. Now we have come to London and the killings have begun again."

The words faded with a soft click, and Mercy realized they had closed the door of Roger's office. She stood without moving, her mind a blur of incoherent thoughts, until she was forced to press her fingers to her skull and close her eyes. The peaceful tick of the distant clock was as steady as a heartbeat, soothing the first rush of fear that had momentarily closed off her breathing.

Where was he? she wondered. Cloistered again in that forbidding tower, shunning the world and its madness? She crept from the foyer, ventured down the corridor, some instinct prodding her on. Coming to his closed office door, she listened, hearing nothing but feeling his presence. She waited, motionless. Finally she turned the knob and pushed open the door.

He sat in his armchair, staring sightlessly over the stacks and stacks of books and papers, his damp shirt still clinging to his flesh and his filthy boots propped on a footstool of needlepointed roses. In his hand he clutched the black velvet box he had given her the night before.

He turned to stare at her as she entered the room; she forced herself to walk fearlessly to his desk and meet his eyes.

"I won't be needing you this morning," he said. Then he threw the box onto the desk. When she made no move to leave, he snapped, "You are dismissed!"

She closed her eyes briefly, then turned and left the room.

It was ten before Mercy ventured from her room again. She barely heard the familiar hammering and sawing of renovation as she stood in the foyer, trying to decide what she should do until D'Abanville called for her.

"Miss Dansing!"

She looked around, blinking away her lethargy at the sound of McMillian's cheerful greeting.

"Miss Dansing, good morning!"

"Hello." She returned his smile.

His pace slowed as he noted how drawn her face appeared. "Oh, dear, word must have already reached you."

"Word?"

"Of the newest murder. Ghastly ordeal, it was. The streets are humming with it."

"Inspector Chesterton was by just after dawn."

McMillian pursed his lips before nodding. "I was afraid of that. As soon as I heard the murder had occurred not far from here, I suspected there would be trouble for D'Abanville. I am almost afraid to ask. They haven't . . . ?"

"Arrested him?" Shaking her head, Mercy replied, "Not yet."

"Not yet. Well, it doesn't sound promising, does it?"

"I'm afraid it doesn't."

"Perhaps he should try to conjure up some magic to exonerate himself," he said with a chuckle. "He is so good at his craft, he can almost make me believe in his wizardry."

Mercy laughed. "He is not *that* good. Nothing could make me believe that he really performs miracles. In truth, I find his abracadabras rather objectionable."

"Indeed?" McMillian appeared genuinely surprised.

"I cannot accept that which cannot be readily explained."

"But that's all part of the mystique, isn't it? *How* does he do it? *Does* he really do it?"

"Of course he doesn't really do it. It's all a trick, an illusion. He's a hoaxer."

McMillian chuckled before turning his attentions to the roll of papers in his hand. Raising them for Mercy to see, he announced, "Here it is: the Greystone print. We are about to discover exactly what sort of alterations have been made along this corridor since these plans were drawn up. Would you care to join me in my inspection?"

"I suppose I've nothing else to do until D'Abanville calls for me," she replied.

As they moved slowly down the corridor toward the towerhouse door, McMillian carefully unrolled the brittle yellow paper. "It appears that very little has been changed here," he said. "Other than the addition of the tower door at the end of the hallway."

Recalling her exploration here the night before, Mercy glanced over her shoulder toward the mirror at the end of the corridor. Her reflection stared back, pale and troubled.

"You do realize that this is the corridor the Casimire girl is supposed to haunt? . . . Miss Dansing?"

Forcing her mind away from the mirror, Mercy looked at him and smiled. "I walked this corridor just last evening and neither saw nor heard any ghost, Mr. Mc-Millian. Surely you don't believe in such nonsense, sir?"

Mercy waited for his response, realizing that in his zest to study the print he apparently had not heard her reply. His eyes suddenly wide, he pointed to the drawing. "By gosh! Something has changed, Miss Dansing. There should be a room precisely there!"

Mercy peered down the long corridor wall, then back at the print.

Stepping up against the wall, McMillian gave it a hard rap with his fist. His face brightened even more. "By gosh!" he repeated. "It's hollow here. Do you hear it, Miss Dansing? There appears to a room behind this wall!"

Mercy waited in D'Abanville's office for an hour, sitting in a chair as far from the snake as she could get. Then Miriam entered the room and said, "What are you doing sitting here alone?"

"Waiting for D'Abanville," she replied.

"He is in the front parlor with Mr. Gladstone of St. Bartholomew's Hospital. There is also a representative from St. Thomas waiting." With added sarcasm she said, "Seems the old buzzards smell blood. D'Abanville will be lucky to get through this with the shirt on his back."

Mercy waited until she was certain Miriam was gone before leaving the room. Curious over Miriam's meaning, she walked to the vestibule and found a gentleman in a cutaway coat and pin-striped pants lounging in a chair near the door. He checked his watch repeatedly and tapped his foot on the floor in impatience.

Mercy walked to the parlor door and looked in. D'Abanville stood before the window, arms crossed over his chest as he listened to Gladstone.

"As you know, with the opening of the hospital's new wing, we are short of beds. After some checking, I located a supply of used cots from a smallpox hospital that is being torn down. The beds would be adequate—"

Dominick interrupted. "I wouldn't think of allowing you to furnish your new wing with beds infested with smallpox disease. How much do you imagine it would take to purchase new beds?"

Gladstone fumbled in his coat, withdrew a paper that he thrust eagerly toward Dominick. "I took the liberty of calculating that figure, just out of curiosity's sake, you understand."

"Certainly."

"As you can see, the amount is quite sizable." He cleared his throat. "Just short of one hundred pounds."

"I will have my manager deliver you that amount first thing in the morning."

"Smashing!" Gladstone exclaimed.

Mercy left the vestibule and returned to D'Abanville's office. She continued to wait, her mind only half-acknowledging the rapping of hammers and the splintering of wood as the workers went about their task of renovating the house. Occasionally McMillian's pleasant voice boomed over the racket, instilling patience and care into his men, and Mercy would rouse from her daydreaming state long enough to listen with interest.

She didn't notice the quiet immediately. Then, curious, she left the room and stared at the unmoving men at the end of the corridor.

She would think later that she moved down the hallway like an automaton. Stopping beside McMillian, she stared, along with the others, at the gaping hole in the wall. A hazy yellow light spilled through the window and cut through the room's dim interior, illuminating a place on the floor. The red, blue, and gold of the carpet merged in the light like the tiny fragments of glass in a kaleidoscope.

Someone mumbled, "S'like openin' a bloody tomb."

Mercy stepped forward, the only one to move.

"Hey, lady, stay away from there," came a man's voice. "No tellin' wot's been holed up there all them years."

She ignored him and walked up to the opening. Cold wrapped around her like a glove. She looked toward the window, saw it was open, and told herself that was the source of the cold. A voice in the back of her mind said,

"But it isn't that cold outside, Mercy." The rational part of her mind responded, "But it's an explanation. There's nothing to be frightened of. It's only a room."

"Miss Dansing," came McMillian's voice. "Perhaps you should wait until D'Abanville returns. We have no way of knowing why this room was walled up. Perhaps it's not safe . . ."

She stepped over the fragments of lumber barring her way. Her heart beat hard in her chest as she studied the interior, the wardrobe, the dresser, and the vanity decorated with its once white doily of French lace. A chair stood before the window, as if someone had sat in it looking out over the gardens in the distance. Yes, she could see the gardens through the thickly draped ivy crisscrossed over the glass panes. There grew the rose brambles, a splash of vibrant pink against the sky.

She turned then toward the bed.

The dress draped from the bed to the floor. It had been white once. It looked the color of candlelight now. There was a touch of lace around the neck, along the cuffs of the sleeves, and along the hem.

"I'm leavin'," came a voice from the hallway.

"Somethin' ain't right about this," came another.

"Gentlemen, gentlemen," came McMillian's voice. "I suggest that you reconsider. Please! You simply cannot put down your tools and leave!"

"If ye don't mind me sayin', sir, the whole place gives me the creeps. After wot I heard this mornin' 'bout that D'Abanville feller . . ."

The voices faded and Mercy stood in the room alone. She looked toward the wardrobe, walked to it.

She barely touched the wardrobe door and it opened. Inside were dresses with high waistlines, plain and spotted prints with delicately printed borders. Leather shoes with sharp-pointed toes and tiny heels lined the floor of the wardrobe, along with stacks of neatly folded neckerchiefs, frilly muslin tuckers, and plaid and checked scarves and sashes.

"Welcome to the eighteenth century, Mercy Dansing," a little voice within her whispered.

Noting the drawer at the bottom of the wardrobe, Mercy went to her knees and tugged it. It didn't open.

She wasn't surprised. After a hundred years the wood would be warped. The dust would have settled thickly into the grooves. It came open on the second try, and Mercy found herself staring down at a book with a tattered needlepoint cover.

Carefully lifting the book, she held it in her hands. It was so fragile she could feel it disintegrate in her fingers. She opened the cover, noting with some disappointment that many of the first pages rested in dozens of tiny jigsawlike pieces that fluttered to the floor when she breathed too heavily on them. But across the top of the first page was the heading: "This diary belongs to Mary Casimire, 1788."

Mercy gently closed the book, tucked it beneath her arm, and returned to her own room.

Mercy sat in a chair by the window, gazed at the courtyard, visualizing how it must have appeared one hundred years ago. Micah was working nearby, hoe in hand as he chopped away the knee-high grass and brambles that cluttered the parterres. The wind whipped his black hair over his brow, and occasionally he would stop and sweep the lightly curling locks out of his eyes before resuming his chore. Mercy watched him a long while before he seemed to sense her. He stopped his labor and turned his face up to the window. Their eyes met and held and Mercy was swept by a sensation of familiarity that took her breath away. It was his eyes—blue as heaven. They reminded her of D'Abanville.

He smiled and waved. Mercy waved back. She then carefully opened the book in her lap and began to read:

1 April, 1788.

Will the rain ever cease? Perhaps if it ceased father's health would improve. He grows weaker by the day and I suspect it is only a matter of time before he dies. Why? I ask the good Lord a hundred times a day. How could a man in such apparent good health grow so deathly ill overnight? My mother is frantic. Despite the differences in their ages, I believe she loves him devotedly. What will happen to us when father dies?

I met a man today. His name is Peter, and he has the most beautiful—

Mercy ran her fingers over the ragged edge of the page, disappointed that the remainder of that particular entry would be forever lost to the ravages of time. Then the wind barreled through the window and Mercy quickly but gently closed the cover of the book and looked again to the courtyard. Micah was gone.

It had begun to rain.

Mercy did not see D'Abanville again until three that afternoon. He was standing in the vestibule speaking with Micah when she entered from the drawing room, a letter she had received that morning from her brother gripped in one hand and her reticule in the other. Each man looked around, stopping her in her place. Micah smiled and tipped his head. D'Abanville only smiled. But although Mercy returned Micah's smile, she only stared at D'Abanville. He appeared to be in a better frame of mind, for his mouth continued to carry the faintest smile. His eyes were warm and inviting and twinkling slightly with amusement.

"Hello," he said.

Mercy smiled, feeling herself flush as his gaze took in her appearance. She wore the same dress she had worn the day she had first arrived at Greystone, tattered but mended. The shoes she wore had been patched and bought from Rosemary Lane, and her bonnet was the one he had called atrocious the day before.

"I did not expect to see you," she told him.

"Obviously." He looked down at some mail in his hand, then back at her. "I still live here, do I not?"

"I only meant . . ." She lowered her eyes.

"Relax, Miss Dansing, I know what you meant."

Roger entered the vestibule then, his face slightly flushed as he regarded the newspapers in his hand. "D'Abanville," he said, "have you seen the papers?"

"I haven't." He was still regarding Mercy. She noted a shadow of disapproval now in the narrowing of his eyes.

Seeing Mercy then, Roger said, "By the way, a letter

arrived for you earlier. If you will step down to my office, Miriam will see that you get it.''

She tucked the letter into the folds of her skirt as she thanked him. Miriam had delivered the letter earlier, and Mercy had hoped to leave Greystone before D'Abanville returned. She preferred that he not know of Oliver's demands, considering the confrontation that had passed between the men before.

Regarding Micah, Roger said sternly, ''Haven't you something to do? We don't pay you a wage to—'' His eyes widened as he noted the muddy footprints Micah had tracked over the polished white floor. ''Get that cleaned up immediately. Do you understand me?''

His face red, Micah nodded and looked away. He was going to his knees when D'Abanville clapped a hand on his shoulder and forced him to stand. ''That will be all,'' he told the gardener. Then, as Micah hurried out the door, he turned his eyes on Roger. Mercy thought she had never seen such restrained anger in a man's face before.

''Don't *ever* speak to him in that manner again,'' D'Abanville said.

''The man is a moron,'' Roger continued. ''I cannot fathom why you continue to employ him.'' Without a second glance at his employer, Roger left the room.

D'Abanville closed his eyes, apparently willing his anger under control. When he opened them again, it was to look directly at Mercy. ''I've brought the coach around,'' he told her sharply. ''Come along.''

''Where?'' she asked.

''To see your brother.''

She felt her heart turn over. ''Wh-why?''

''To deliver his money.''

''But how did you know—?''

''Who else would have written to you, Miss Dansing? You have no other family, as I recall.''

Her face turned darker. Reminded that he had pried rather furtively into her personal life, Mercy responded hotly, ''I can see to Oliver myself as I have the past nineteen years. I hardly need another 'big brother' to hold my hand in times of crises.''

When a moment of silence had passed, Mercy looked

at him directly. She was surprised when he began to smile pleasantly.

"Big brother?" He laughed softly. "Good God, what a disappointment. I hardly had brotherly intentions when hiring you as my assistant, young lady."

A wave of disconcertion left Mercy momentarily speechless. She could hardly deny she had suspected his intentions, but to hear him finally admit them aloud left her somewhat dazed.

His smile thinned a little as he looked her over once again. "You mustn't look so terrified, Miss Dansing. Inspector Chesterton has sufficiently gelded me. I fear one sniff at a woman's skirt hems and I will be hanging from a beam at old Newgate." He raised his hand to her. "Come along. You're safe enough."

She hesitated.

"I promise: no more moonlight seductions in coaches. You have dismissed my gift of friendship, therefore you have made yourself perfectly clear: it is to be business only between us . . . or perhaps you are afraid to ride alone with me?"

She watched him a moment longer, an odd disappointment settling into the silent space between them.

His hair was very black against the white light of the window behind him, waving slightly over his ear and curling ever so gently at the nape of his neck. He waited for her response without speaking, perhaps anticipating the resignation she had rehearsed giving him all night. The frightening thought occurred to her that he might accept it now. She remained quiet.

"Well?" he prompted. Humor touched the corners of his mouth. "Are you frightened of me?"

"No."

He didn't believe her, she could tell.

Throwing his mail onto the table by the wall, he said, "I see I have my work cut out for me. You're not an even passably deft performer, my love, but that will come with time and practice. But for now let's pretend that it is your brother you're afraid of. I assure you, he won't hurt you again, Mercy. I'll see to it."

It was more than her dread of facing Oliver, she realized. More than D'Abanville's presence too. She had faced down Oliver too many times to allow that threat to frighten her now. No, it was much more. Her pride—what little pride she had managed to maintain since her arrival in London—was at stake. She didn't want D'Abanville to see the hovel on Sultan Street she had shared with her brother.

"You can't hide from him forever," he said, apparently misconstruing her hesitation as fear of her brother. He walked to the front door and opened it. Forcing herself, she moved to his side, and offered little resistance as he took hold of her arm and escorted her out the door to the coach. The driver had already boarded and sat high above them on his chair. He turned his head slowly and peered down at her over his shoulder, his eyes barely visible beneath the brim of his high-topped black hat. Then Dominick opened the coach door and helped her in.

She sank back into burgundy seats that were soft as glove leather. They made her forget about the inclement weather, the driver, and, for a moment, her brother.

D'Abanville said nothing as the coach got under way. Mercy wished he would stop staring at her as if she were one of the little white mice he was about to drop into his serpent's mouth.

"Is something wrong?" she asked.

He looked at her clothes.

She squared her shoulders. "Surely you did not expect me to flaunt what you have given me in their faces? I really should not have accepted them at all, considering. But—"

"You did." He smiled. "Didn't you?"

As they rolled through Greystone's gates, Mercy forced her eyes from his and looked out the window in time to catch a glimpse of a white banner proclaiming "The End Is Here!" and another stating "Repent, for the Son of Satan Is Among Us!" When she chanced a brief look back at D'Abanville's face, she found his features sober, his mouth pressed in irritation. He caught the velvet casement in his hand and let it drop down over the window.

"Idiots," he muttered.

As the sounds of the London streets surrounded the coach, Mercy managed to relax. There was something comforting about the clattering of hooves and the hum of iron wheels. She hadn't realized how much the quiet of Greystone Manor had begun to affect her.

Glancing out the window, she said, "You might tell your driver to make the next right."

"He knows his way to the East End," he replied.

She looked around, surprised. "Oh? I wasn't aware the privileged took turns through the impoverished side of town. Do you do so for entertainment or just curiosity?"

He removed the gloves from his hands, slapped them absently against his thigh. "I think we get to the gist of the problem," he said. "You don't dislike me because of my occupation, or because the world thinks I'm a murderer, or even because I am a man. You dislike me because I reside at Greystone and not some tenement house on Sultan Street or a doss house east of Aldgate Pump. Does that make me a fiend, Mercy?"

"It makes you ignorant and I despise ignorance in men who should know better."

"I wager you were as ignorant before your father lost his farm."

She looked away.

"Mercy, there are men—good men—who are trying to change these people's circumstances. But changes take time. You cannot change the course of life overnight, you know."

"Oh, yes, we are well aware of the infamous aristocratic socialist awareness. The socialist rich are encouraged to buy up East End property. With proper management the Whitechapel slums can be made to pay better than preference shares in the best railways or Prussian stock or any foreign rents. A net and safe four percent is something to be desired, I suppose. There is a landlord who owns six lodging houses on Thrawl Street. He does so well with the property he has purchased himself a country house in Hampstead. One of those very lodging houses turned Polly Nichols onto the streets because she could not afford the fourpence for a doss. She was murdered merely for being homeless and poor."

"I grant you there is a need for reform among certain Social Democrats," D'Abanville said.

"According to Frank Fitz, secretary of the Socialist

League, 'The gutters of London and their terrible human wreckage shall be made to yield a four-percent profit and even more.' So you see, there are no true socialists among you. There are only opportunists who would take advantage of the idea to make their customary profit.''

They rode in silence for some time. Finally, attempting to change the subject, Dominick asked more softly, ''Are you enjoying your stay at Greystone?''

''Very much.'' She looked at her hands.

''What do you think of Roger?''

''He is very . . . intense.'' Mercy looked up into D'Abanville's eyes. ''But so are you.''

He responded with a smile.

''What do you think about the room McMillian discovered?'' He shifted slightly against the back of his seat.

''It is very sad. It is as if someone walked out of the room and never returned.''

''A sobering thought.'' He flicked with his fingers at a spot of lint on his knee. ''Further evidence of the uncertainties of life, I suppose. Here today and gone tomorrow, as they say.'' Lifting the shade off the window with his fingertip, he watched the busy street before looking at her again. ''Did you enjoy the book on theosophy?''

Her mind momentarily diverted from Mary Casimire's room, Mercy shook her head. ''It was difficult to understand. Perhaps I'm wrong, but does it not ascribe to the belief that when a person dies, his soul continually comes back to life as someone else, and in that new life he pays for the sins perpetrated by the soul in a former life, and will continue to do so at least until he lives a life that is worthy of heaven?''

''That's about the essence of it.''

''Then our present existence would be a sort of . . . purgatory.''

''We prefer the term 'Avici.' In Avici an individual remains after death in exactly the same physical entity he had before physical death. He is subject to the cravings, desires, and appetites felt in the physical world, but in Avici he is totally unable to experience the satisfaction of these desires. He may, however, work himself out of Avici after an indeterminate stay.''

There was silence as Mercy considered the explanation.

She knew the very moment their coach entered her old neighborhood. The screams of children playing, and their crying, could be heard even over the clattering of the coach. It was a rare occurrence that a vehicle such as this was seen along these streets, so Mercy knew without looking that their passing would cause great curiosity among the dwellers here.

As the coach veered onto Sultan Street, Mercy, with some hesitation, lifted the shade and peered out into the twilight. How ugly it all seemed. Even uglier than she remembered. The squalid tenements rose from the black streets, paved with ironstone slag, to a gray sky that endlessly poured rain onto the houses' red-tiled roofs. Even as she watched, lightning flashed blue-white, brightening the dreary bleakness so she could see every filthy, crumbling form down the street. Despite the rain, the foul air, reeking of human and animal waste, took her breath away so she was forced to close the window quickly and sit back in her seat.

D'Abanville was looking at her again, much to her discomfort. How could he sit there so nonchalantly, unmoved by the bedlam going on around them? Could he not hear the crying of hunger, of pain, of anger? Did he care nothing that the men, women, and children were screaming out their anger at whoever dared trespass into this world with his fine coach to remind them of how poor they were?

"Perhaps you should let me out here," she told him.

"Nonsense."

"You won't be welcome here. There might be trouble."

"I am fully capable of dealing with trouble, should trouble arise."

"They are tired of listening to big talk and shallow reasoning. You could say nothing more than they've heard before many times. From men just like you. You think that by donating occasional money to charity you are doing your share to stamp out poverty in the world. When will you understand that it is not your money that will help, but your time and influence to change the ways of governments and how they deal with the people.''

Mercy shook her head. ''No, you are no different at all. You could be just another of the many young and beautiful socialists sent from Toynbee Hall or Oxford House to live among the unfortunate, to rouse the local bodies, to establish town councils, Poor Law guardians, and school managers so they might bring reform and awareness of their own social responsibilities. When in the end they will use the experience as a tool to better their own position in the Houses, and that is all.''

Watching her intently, D'Abanville argued, ''I would like to think I am of better character than George Balfour. Your anger should be directed at him and what he did to you personally and not toward the gentry populace at large. I highly suspect Balliol College had higher aspiration than seduction for such a charismatic gentleman as Balfour. Although, in my opinion, Balfour is not an unlikable chap, nor is he heartless. I would be forced to alter my opinion of you if I suspected you thought of him as a fraud when you allowed him—shall we say—liberties with your reputation.''

Mercy sat back in her seat, her face burning as if he had slapped her. ''He used me.''

''And you used him, or tried to. That makes you even. Keep in mind why he came to Sultan Street in the first place. He gave up the comforts to which he was accustomed, in hopes he would learn about the dark realities of life and labor of the urban poor—yes, perhaps he did it so that he could carry that impression with him into his later career. Indeed, he called himself a junior politician and in his naiveté knew beyond any shadow of a doubt that his existence on Sultan Street would raise these inhabitants' level of culture, both social and intellectual. You cannot fault him for his ideals.''

Her hands twisted into her skirts as she countered, ''Oh, yes. He should be knighted for his superior dedication to the cause. That dedication lasted until Samuel Barnett's *Practicable Socialism* had been printed—''

''Proclaiming 'a poor man might seem deprived compared with the owner of some stately mansion,' '' D'Abanville interrupted, '' 'and yet that man may be the head of a happy home and family. Such a man's poverty is not an evil to be cured. It is a sign that life does not depend on possessions. The existence of poor men alongside rich allows for a pleasing variety of earthly experience.' As I recall, Mercy, several of your friends here—"

"Who had lost wives and mothers and sisters and children to starvation and disease!"

"—heaved the junior politician into a pile of horse dung, then tried to set him afire. Were you there to help light the match, Miss Dansing? Did you expect him to rise from the flames, take your hand, and as your under-privileged friends pelted him with excrement, ignore your own radicalism and propose?"

"Radicalism!"

"Aye. They are screaming so loudly they cannot hear themselves talk, and you know it. They wait in their gutters to be spoon-fed by Parliament, to be handed improvement on a silver platter. They should work for it with their minds and hands and less with their wagging tongues."

"They try! There is only so much employment to go around in London."

"Then they should leave London. There is an entire world out there in which to look. There are entire resources to build upon, yet they linger in their squalor and whine."

She might have slapped his face, but he caught her wrist in his fist and gripped it tightly. Mercy turned her face away, feeling the tears rear up behind her lids so they scraped like sandpaper over her eyes when she blinked. In a calmer voice she said, "Even when they find employment, they are underpaid."

He released her. "I have no argument with that. But isn't something better than nothing at all? At least with a pittance you can begin to build. Teach a child the basic fundamentals of reading, and if he has any aspirations at all, he will educate himself. But the drive must be there, Mercy, as well as the desire and the belief that they can change their own destiny, or all the books and universities in the world will not help them."

It was the truth. She had thought it herself. Perhaps it

was only her conscience that constantly reminded her of
these people's plight. She had made it out, after all. Almost. Perhaps it was her fear of being forced back into
it that made her frantic. The same fear that kept her at
Greystone despite the controversy surrounding D'Abanville.

She had to be honest with herself; she could deny his
philanthropy all she wanted, but there was something different about Dominick D'Abanville. She felt it as his
eyes held hers. They had a way of probing her in a way
she had never experienced before, and all the pain and
resentment and, yes, hate she had felt toward her brother
for bringing her into this 'pleasing variety of earthly experience' felt as if it were whirling around in her head
for escape. Perhaps he did understand what she was feeling. It was there in his eyes. No ice now. No fire. Just
. . . compassion.

Sixteen-thirty-two Sultan Street was a dove-gray limestone tenement that cost Mercy and her brother two shillings, sixpence per week, roughly one-fifth of Oliver's
wage when he was gainfully employed and not dependent
totally on his girls. She had learned from George Balfour
that when the seventy six-room houses were first built in
1870 they had been occupied at once, and by 1871 were
filled by six hundred and sixty-one persons. By 1881 the
population had risen to over a thousand. Two-thirds of
the inhabitants were now living more than two per room,
as many as twelve to thirteen per house. Mercy shared
one such room with Oliver and whomever he decided to
entertain throughout the evening. Regardless, she had
done her best to make the accommodation a home. Her
cracked pottery vase boasting a wilted geranium sitting
in the window was evidence of that.

She stared through the rain at the long-dead flower,
knowing without looking that there were faces staring
back at her from the windows around her and overhead.
As the footman appeared at the coach door with umbrella
in hand, she shook her head in refusal, then stepped
lightly into the rushing stream of water along the curb,
then onto the sidewalk. Several barefoot children dashed
by her, splashing water onto her skirt. Then several more
moved cautiously from their doorways or from the alley-

ways to examine the coach more closely. They scattered like rabbits as D'Abanville stepped from the coach as well.

An odd hush sounded throughout the street as Mercy turned to face him. Did they sense it too, the women with suspicious eyes and the children whose little noses were flattened against the window glass? Did they sense the presence of this unusual man the way she did? Somewhere at the far end of Sultan Street a horse and cart clopped by, but those were the only sounds to drift though the tension-charged air as Mercy regarded him with rain running down her cheeks.

"I'll do this alone," she told him. It was her pride again. What she really wanted was to climb back into the comfortable, safe confines of those burled walnut walls and forget all about Oliver Dansing and Sultan Street. She wanted to apologize to D'Abanville for doubting him.

He didn't respond, just dipped his head and lowered his eyes to the walk. The rain had already soaked his hair and was running off his cheeks in rivulets. Mercy stared at him hard before forcing her eyes away. She started to turn, when the words came.

"I'm here if you need me, Miss Dansing."

As she looked back over her shoulder, the reality of her surroundings seemed to fade in and out of the bruised light. It was as if she were looking at him through smoky glass.

She turned and entered 1632 Sultan Street.

11

There was a fine sweat on Mercy's forehead as she leaned back against the door and surveyed her surroundings. Strange how she had managed to forget the stench that rose up through the floor from the miasma of liquid sewage that flooded the cellar below. The accumulated piles of rags and rubbish strewn over the floor stank of rot, and even as she watched, a rat scurried from beneath the filthy heap and disappeared beneath the stairs.

There were new faces staring down at her from the second floor, young faces, barely older than three and four years. About their mouths was the residue of their dinner: skilly, a mixture of Indian corn and hot water. Mercy knew it well enough. For the first week after coming to London, until she landed her first sewing job, she had existed each day on one pannikin three-quarters full of skilly. As she smiled up at the children, they scattered back to their rooms without responding.

Three doors led off the entryway. Two were open, emitting conversation and the constant whimpering of a sick child. Chancy Blake, a robust hag who worked for Oliver three nights a week, and who had a penchant for gin, leaned back against the doorframe of her apartment, arms crossed over her chest as she regarded Mercy. Chancy had never liked her, always thought she was out to get her husband, as if Mercy would want him. The man sold his own wife for a penny and used the money to buy gin.

"Well, now, look 'oo's come 'ome, Shirley," the woman said to the stringy-haired child clinging to her skirt.

"Ah'm 'ungry," Shirley responded.

"Ain't we all?" said her mother. "Or most of us. I suppose some what got jobs ain't doin' too poorly."

Mercy ignored the remark and started for the door.

"Get 'omesick, Mercy?" Chancy asked. "Maybe if yer real nice, Ollie'll take y' in."

"I wouldn't dream of usurping your place on his pallet, Chance. I'd hate to see the poor lass starve." She glanced down at the child, then turned back to the door, her mind too occupied with other thoughts to remember to knock. Seconds later she was staring red-faced at the wall while Oliver pulled up his pants and his companion wrapped the dingy white sheet around her torso.

"Stupid twit," came her brother's voice. "Ain't you got no brains, Mercy? How's a man to take care of business if he's always bein' walked in on?"

"You might try locking the door," she countered. "Or waiting till after dark to do your business."

"I'll bloody well do me business when I've got the urge, gal, and don't you forget it." He kicked one of the two chairs at the table, sending it tottering on its back legs. Before it could spill to the floor, he dropped onto it with an animal grunt.

Pig, Mercy thought.

"I'm reckonin' you got my letter," he said.

Mercy nodded, doing her best to avoid looking at the other woman. Then, as her eyes strayed to the pallet where she had found them, Mercy felt swept with revulsion. They had been in her bed, and the horrifying thought occurred to her that Oliver and his girls had no doubt entertained in her bed before, and she hadn't realized it. She suddenly felt filthy and longed for a bath.

When she looked at her half-brother again, he was regarding her in that way that made her flesh crawl. It wasn't natural, that look. It was the same look he gave to the women he brought home for the night, the same way he looked at some of his girls, the ones who were still young and who had not yet been turned into wretches by their poverty. But then, Oliver had often insinuated that he might be interested in her in *that* way, regardless of the fact that they shared the same father. He thought that she might be swayed by his good looks, the way the other girls were, but she had told him that she would rather rot in debtors' prison than let him touch her that way. Despite his fair looks and curling golden hair, he smelled foul, and the few times he had laid a gentle hand on her, his palms had been overly warm and very damp. Her mother had secretly warned her, just after her sixteenth birthday, to stay clear of Oliver.

"So where's me bloody money?" came his voice. As the harlot bent over his right shoulder for a kiss, he shoved her away, keeping his eyes on Mercy instead. In a moment the door slammed and she realized with sinking desperation that she was alone with him. He sensed her fear like a cat might sense fear when cornering a rat in an alley, and he grinned.

She plunged her hand into her reticule, withdrew the note, and flung it onto the table beside him. He didn't look at it. His eyes remained on her.

"I'll be leaving now," she finally said. But she had no more than turned toward the door when he was out of his chair and against her, his fingers digging like five separate vises into her arm.

"Wot's yer hurry?" he asked. "Ain't you got a few spare minutes to spend with yer brother?"

It would do no good to fight him. It never did. Besides, it was the fight he enjoyed the most.

"Things've been right lonely round here since you've gone, Mercy."

"I'll bet," she said. "You've had to fetch your own food, I suppose, and wash your own clothes." She cast a disgusted glance about the filthy quarters.

He shrugged and one golden curl spilled over his forehead. "Chancy's been obligin' now and again."

"I'll bet. Why don't you get some of your other girls—"

"I don't pay me bloody whores to clean, Mercy. I pay 'em to—"

"I am well aware of what you pay them for," she said.

Mercy looked down at her aching arm. There would be bruises tomorrow, and she thought how they would look with the French silk dress she had been fitted for the day before. "I'm leaving now," she said. As his fingers bit more cruelly into her arm, the ache coursed like fire to her shoulder. "You have your money, Ollie, what more do you want?"

"As if you didn't know."

The blatant insinuation startled her. For a moment she allowed her surprise and fear to show in her eyes. A mistake.

"Let me go," she told him. "Or I'll scream."

"Never did you any good before, Mercy. Besides, you ain't got yer princely protector here for you now, you know."

"Wrong."

His eyes narrowed.

"D'Abanville is outside in the coach." She took a much-needed breath, certain the information would help rectify the perilous situation in which she had gotten herself. Still, the grip on her arm did not relent, but grew harder, until she was biting back tears, hurting too badly to scream even if she needed to.

Without warning, Oliver moved to the window, dragging her along with him. He yanked back the yellowed muslin cloth that passed as a curtain, stared over the top of the vase at the coach for a long moment before releasing a quiet, relieved laugh.

"Nice try," he said. "But you know how I feel about liars, darlin'."

"He's there, I tell you!" She pulled back the curtain with her free hand. The coach was there, where she had left it, parked in the gaslight's gold halo. Rain fell more steadily now, but the light from the streetlamp was bright enough to illuminate the inside of the coach. It was empty.

Feeling panic rise inside her, Mercy looked up and down the walk. There were several children playing in the rain, one jumping in the mud puddles and another doing handstands in the center of the street. A pack of drenched mongrel dogs rummaged through a pile of refuse littering the alley between two buildings.

But D'Abanville was gone.

She glanced at the vase; then, as if Oliver had read her thoughts, she was jerked away from the window so quickly she almost stumbled.

"I wouldn't advise it, darlin', not if you plan on col-

lectin' another wage from D'Abanville next month.''
Twirling her hair round and round his fingers, he smiled.
'' 'Course, judgin' by the stories the papers have been runnin', D'Abanville may be arrested, tried, and hanged before you ever see another quid from him.''

"Let me go.''

"What do you think, Mercy? Think the magic man is capable of murder? The papers say the coroner can't tell whether he molests his women before he kills them, but I imagine he does . . . or maybe it's after he kills them. Imagine them peering up into his eyes as he slides the knife into their—''

"Stop it.'' She struggled again.

"The papers say the man has a real hate for women, though he hides it well enough at first. The women never suspect until it's too late. Tell me, do you like him a lot?''

"That is none of your affair!''

"An interesting choice of words. Affair. I like the sound of it. Reminds me of mistresses and the like. Perhaps if you are very nice to the man, you might earn an extra few shillings on the side.''

She could not hold back her gasp of outrage. "Bloody whoremaster!'' she cried. "Release me or I'll scream!''

"Come, now, Mercy, it ain't like yer a virgin.'' As her eyes flew to his again, he laughed. "I don't for a minute think you didn't put it to old Balfour. A woman's got a certain smell about her after she's been with a man, and I remember how you smelled that last time you seen Georgie Porgie. Then there was yer sickness. Wot 'appened to the kid, me darlin'? Did D'Abanville call in an abortionist . . . or did he take the knife to you himself?''

She screamed and drove her fist into his chest.

He laughed and caught her wrist. "Say, if you were nice to me, it wouldn't be as if I'd ruined you for anyone else. It ain't like I was really your brother. You know our pa always questioned whether I was truly his or not. Seems me mum got around a bit on the side before she died.''

Turning her face up to his, she hissed, "I don't care if you were sired by the Prince of Wales, I would still loathe

you for what you are: a wretch! Now, release me before
I call for D'Abanville.''

"He won't come, 'cause he ain't there." His dark eyes
narrowed. "Or maybe he is. Maybe he's floatin' over our
heads this very minute and is about to pierce me wicked
heart with a bolt of lightnin'.''

"He's there, I tell you. He's stepped out of the rain is
all. He's just outside this door and—''

A knock at the door interrupted. Mercy closed her eyes
in relief.

Oliver froze, stared at the door for some time before
responding, "Who's there?''

Nothing.

"I said, who the bloody hell is there?'' Oliver yelled.

They both stared at the door, waiting, Mercy counting
the seconds that ticked by, praying silently that D'Abanville would open the door, sweep into the room, and save
her as he had before. Then she realized he was there
already. As always, she could feel the presence—the
power—of his nearness. It was in the silence, the deafening absence of sound that wrapped around her, making
her ears hum.

She looked up into Oliver's face. He sensed it too. She
could tell. A small line of sweat had beaded over his
upper lip, and his usual ruddy complexion had turned a
sallow yellow that made him look jaundiced. He felt the
presence, all right, and that pleased her. For the first time
since her father had died, leaving Oliver in charge of her
welfare, she had power over him. By fearing D'Abanville, he feared her.

She pulled her arm away and ran to the door. Behind
her, Oliver threatened, "I'll see you soon, Mercy."

Mercy threw open the door, ran into the hall. She stood
there a full ten seconds before realizing she was alone.

Leaving the building, Mercy stood outside the door,
putting the last few minutes of her life into perspective.
She might have imagined the knock at the door. No, her
brother had heard it too. Perhaps someone had knocked
at one of the other doors and they just thought it was
theirs. Certainly that would explain there being no one
there when she opened the door.

Squeals of laughter brought her head around. Shielding

her eyes against the rain, Mercy looked toward the end of the street.

Six children clustered under an umbrella, their usually haunted and hungry faces beaming now with wonder as they watched the performance before them. Heedless of the rain, D'Abanville stood in an island of light, his hands moving rhythmically up and down as he juggled a set of yellow balls in the air. As Mercy watched, spellbound, one by one the balls disappeared and were replaced by bright gold coins. There came a gasp of awe from the children as each one's eyes grew as round as the coins. Their hands raised and opened in silent behest. The coins landed with wet plops in their palms, and without another word the children whirled and disappeared into the alleys that were, more likely than not, their homes.

Then D'Abanville turned toward Mercy, his face smiling and boyish. Looking from his eyes to his hand, she found a bouquet of vibrant pink roses.

Forgetting about the ache in her arm, forgetting even her brother, she turned her tear-streaked face into the rain and began to laugh.

Postscript:
    Since Father has been ill, Richard has taken over as head of the family. I worry about Richard. He's changed over the months, become remote and oft-times surly. He spends a great deal of time away from Greystone. Mother says he's taken up with a bad crowd, but I don't know. Richard was always so quiet and withdrawn. I cannot image his going bad, as Mama terms it. But he is impressionable and very easily manipulated.
    He announced after dinner that he's decided to build an extension to Greystone. When Mama asked him why, he explained only by saying: "It is what I want. As head of this house I can do what I please." He made Mama cry. Oh, how I wish Papa would get well soon. I don't like what Richard has become.

Mercy, propped up in her bed, stared down at the book without really seeing it. After returning from Sultan Street she had come directly to her room, had picked up the diary without a thought, and opened it to the page after the entry she had read that morning, surprised to find the postscript. But realizing that her mind was not on the diary, she carefully closed it and laid her head back on the pillow. Her arm hurt abominably, and just as she had suspected, a row of four violet-blue bruises shone against her white arm like ink spots.

She didn't dwell long on the bruises. She never did. In this case she simply filed the incident away in her mind in order of importance—slightly more painful than the time he had pinched the skin of her underarm, much less painful than the day he pushed her out of a tree, breaking her arm.

By the time she had turned six she understood that if she simply avoided him he would leave her alone. Which he did, right up until the time she began to mature. Then he seemed to always be around—''sniffin','' as her mother called it, though at the time she had not understood what the term meant. She understood now. Understood much too clearly. The last six months had been interminable hell. Living night and day under the fear that he would come ''sniffin' '' at her sometime during the night had nearly driven her insane. Thank God for Roger Forbes and . . .

Thank God for Dominick D'Abanville.

Mercy closed her eyes, listening to the constant patter of rain against the window. She saw D'Abanville again, standing in the rain, the light from the lamp behind him reflecting like pools of gold off the shoulders of his jacket. She saw again the children's faces, the wonder, the *belief* that what their eyes were seeing was the truth. Tonight they were no doubt lying in their beds—if they had beds—their young, innocent, gullible minds wondering on the magic that could turn a half-dozen yellow balls into gold coins.

It wasn't magic.

It wasn't even right, now that she thought about it.

Mercy left the bed, absently rubbed her arm. The image of pink rosebuds beaded with raindrops kept looming up before her mind's eye, along with the question: How? She saw again the flame, so intense that she had closed her eyes, then found him gone. Oh, yes, she knew how those children felt. For an instant she had almost believed in the miracle.

They were still believing, but she wasn't. Belief brought disappointment, and besides, she was an adult now, and even if she thought she might like to believe—which she didn't—it was the adult's role in life to see the way clearly, to maintain reality in this unsettling world.

Mercy stood at the window staring at nothing, and tried to think of when she had actually lost total faith in God, the faith that led people to believe that the misery they were suffering was going to be righted by a simple whispered prayer or reverent glance toward heaven. It wasn't as if she was the only one. Since her arrival in London she had watched the people of the middle and upper classes march into their towering chapels on Sunday mornings, their faces slack and their eyes already glazed with boredom even before entering the holy shrine. Anthony Trollope had written several years before that it was "very hard to come at the actual belief of any man." Mercy believed it. Observance did not necessarily mean faith. Watching those well-dressed patrons filing into that stone and stained-glass cathedral, Mercy had realized, as did they, that regular church attendance was necessary for *social* reasons, whether they actually believed in God or not.

Queen Victoria herself had admitted to having "flashes of doubtfulness," and if her majesty could get away with such thoughts, why not the whole of Britain? The world, for that matter? But Victoria had quickly, and eloquently, added that it was impossible also to believe that lives cut short such as her beloved Prince Albert's, could really have come "to an utter end." The queen regretted that fear of eternal damnation had disappeared as a spur to faith. With the gradual abandonment of acceptance of the literal truth of the Bible, theologians were emphasizing the subjectivity of the concepts of heaven and hell, describing them as states of mind, not as physical entities. But Victoria was unhappy about the unsettling effects of the new biblical scholarship, and also about the impact of new scientific ideas—including Darwin's theory of evolution—upon religious belief. *The Pall Mall Gazette* had quoted Victoria not long ago: "Science is greatly to be admired and encouraged, but if it is to take the place of our Creator, and if philosophers and students try to explain everything and to disbelieve whatever they cannot prove, I call it a great evil instead of a great blessing.''

Well, there was evil aplenty in London town, Mercy thought. Its face was starvation, unemployment, and ignorance. It was also manifesting itself in people like the East End killer. It was Oliver Dansing who got his fun from abusing anything and anyone who was smaller than him. How dare Dominick D'Abanville saunter into this den of iniquity and cause her, even for a fraction of a second, to believe in his idiotic magic? How dare he make those children believe? If they continued to believe that such generosity tumbled into her palms from heaven, they would never strive to work their way out of their squalor.

Work was the salvation. Both Dominick D'Abanville and George Balfour had agreed on that matter.

Work was going to get her away from Oliver and away from London. No more hunger. No more pestilence. No more bruises that looked like ink spots.

She left her room, feeling but not hearing the continuing thunder shake the house. She was too busy formulating her recriminations of D'Abanville's behavior to even care about the storm.

D'Abanville wasn't in the library.

She walked further, not so fast now. Slower. She thought she heard voices . . . no *a* voice. It was D'Abanville's. She walked to his office door and stared in at him and Micah. They sat on the sofa directly across from the snake and below the jackdaw, so closely the outside of their legs brushed. D'Abanville was reading aloud from what sounded like a children's book. Something about a girl falling down a rabbit's hole. D'Abanville pointed to each word as he read it.

Without taking a breath or even looking up, D'Abanville said, ''Won't you join us, Miss Dansing?''

Micah looked up, surprised. Their eyes met, as they had earlier in the day when she had watched him in the courtyard.

D'Abanville continued reading and eventually Micah looked down, again centering his attention on the words, while Mercy as quietly as possible sat down across from them. Rarely had she heard a more melodious reading. Not long after her arrival in London, during her first visit to Hyde Park, she had happened upon a group of young Shakespeareans reciting from *Romeo and Juliet*. She had been drawn into the very heart of those voices, but this . . . this tide of sound slid around her as smoothly and effortlessly as the moon rising against the black sky. Ethereal yet powerful enough to unsettle the sea. But more discomposing than that effect was the realization that was very slowly coming upon her as she watched Micah's face as he listened to the words.

"The end," D'Abanville said. He closed the book and placed it in Micah's hands. "We'll read another tomorrow night if you'd like."

Micah turned the book over and over in his man's hands while his child's smile responded yes. He then slid from the sofa, dipped his head toward Mercy, then quit the room.

Mercy said nothing. Her throat hurt too badly to speak at the moment.

Dominick's eyes met hers briefly before he looked away. He plucked at a loose thread, a frayed silk cord that jutted up from the sofa arm, and rolled it between his fingers.

"He has the mind of an eight-year-old," he said matter-of-factly, but Mercy noted the tightness and slight hesitation in his voice, as if he had run out of breath and needed to swallow.

She had heard the pain for what it was.

Wetting her lips, she said, "And he can't speak."

"No."

"Has that something to do with his . . . his—"

"No." He left the sofa and stood by the glass case, staring down at the serpent, gripping the edge of the case so tightly his knuckles turned white. For a moment it seemed as if the world had speeded up around her, as if she were sitting in the eye of a hurricane, calm, while the walls of reality roiled all around her.

She closed her eyes. When she opened them again D'Abanville had gone to his desk.

"You were wanting to see me?" he asked.

She glanced toward the door, still thinking of Micah.

Finally she nodded. "I came here to say I think you were wrong to make those children believe."

"Why?"

"For the very reasons we discussed this afternoon. They must face reality, which is that there is nothing free in this world. They must work for what they wish to achieve."

"I've no argument with that," he said. "But take away a child's dreams and you rob him of hope. Without hope he will never bother to strive for the dream. Without the dream I would never have worked as hard as I have to achieve my goal. I have worked very hard to get where I am."

"Indeed." She looked about the office a little skeptically.

"I was not always wealthy."

His tone startled her. She went cold to the tips of her fingers as she looked into his eyes.

"Did you think I was born with a silver spoon in my mouth?" He raised one black brow. "Did you?"

D'Abanville left his chair. "Well," he said, "I wasn't. I fought and scratched for everything I own. It took me thirty-three years to get where I am, and by God, I will let no man destroy it."

She realized he was no longer talking to her. In truth, he looked a little mad. His clothes were slightly wrinkled, his hair lay disheveled all over his head. He had the look of some pagan god, and in the core of her being Mercy felt a fluttering pain.

"Do you know that everywhere I went today I was followed by Chesterton's lapdog?"

"Can you not ignore him?" she asked.

He laughed aloud.

"Ignore him!" he said. "Good God, lass, haven't you seen what he's done? You saw the men outside my gates. Chesterton has them believing I am some devil incarnate."

"You exaggerate."

He stopped his pacing, swept up a paper from his desk, and flung it into her lap. "Read it and tell me I exaggerate, Mercy."

She stared down at the illustrated broadsheet, at the

ink etching of a cloven-hoofed demon with D'Abanville's face. Beneath it was written "Who is D'Abanville? What is D'Abanville? London demands to know."

Mercy looked away.

Running his hand through his hair, he stared at the ceiling and released his breath. "They will be burning me at the stake soon, all because they are afraid of what they cannot understand. They are afraid of change, afraid of anything or anyone that rattles their comfortable existence. Imbeciles." He growled it.

Stopping again at the serpent's cage, D'Abanville stroked the snake on the back until it raised its broad, flat head and slithered partly up his arm. "Somehow I've got to stop him," he said softly, giving Mercy the impression that he had totally forgotten her presence.

Mercy left her chair, backed toward the door. She didn't want him to say any more. Didn't want him to reveal more of himself than he already had.

"May I go?" she asked.

He did not respond, just wrapped his long fingers around the snake and stroked it. When finally he looked in Mercy's direction, his eyes meeting hers, she knew she could not bear to stand there a moment longer, looking at the expression on his face, part despair and part suffering . . . there was nothing she could do to help him.

With no further word, she left D'Abanville's office and returned to her room. She did not realize until after closing her door just how tense she had been while in his presence. But her nervousness could not compare with D'Abanville's. He was close to breaking. His anger at Chesterton was as great as his desperation and fear of losing everything he had attained over the years.

Was he capable of murder?

Closing her eyes, she did her best to rid her mind of the thought, but the conversation she had overheard between Miriam and Roger that morning kept rearing up to remind her that she knew next to nothing about Dominick D'Abanville. Therefore the feelings she was experiencing toward him were ludicrous. They were nothing more than physical longing, and such desires could be denied.

Dear God, but she would have to be made of stone not to desire him. Aside from his appearance, she had never met a kinder, more compassionate man—at least toward those orphaned children. Of course, it could all be an act, a ruse to paint himself as a philanthropist to the rest of the world while in reality . . . He *was* a performer, after all. A very good performer. The best in the world.

She hurried to build a fire in the stove, stood beside it while the kettle began to rumble, then hiss steam into the air. Closing her eyes, she felt the humidity settle on her eyelids, making them heavy, making them hot. She made tea, heaping the leaves in great spoonfuls into the china pot, then adding the boiling water and letting it steep. Straining it into her teacup, she added a teaspoon of sugar, then a second spoonful when finding the brew was too strong and bitter.

Mercy settled into her chair by the fire and thumbed through D'Abanville's book on theosophy, determined to know him better. Ah, yes, the theosophists. Another of the nonconformist groups to be put up there with the Hallelujah Band, the Free Grace Gospel Christians, the Christians Who Object to Being Otherwise Designated, not to mention the Methodists.

She flung the book away, rested her head against the back of her chair, and closed her eyes. And as always, she saw D'Abanville again, his piercing eyes moving over her features. They seemed to be boring into her soul, and the brilliant glitter in them dizzied her.

She dozed.

When she roused herself enough to realize that she had fallen asleep, she tried to rise, managed to do so clumsily. The heat seemed unbearable. She really should raise the window or put out the fire, but her dreamy state was too enticing. How long had it been since she had last slept deeply, without worries about her brother, or starvation, or, more recently, Dominick D'Abanville? That made her smile. Perhaps the dream would come again, allowing her to free her spirit of her bothersome worries and love him. She could love him. So very easily. *If* he was for real . . . if only . . .

Not bothering to pull back the covers, she sank down on the bed. So hot. Mercy licked her lips, tasting the almost syrupy sweetness of the sugar that lingered there. Her hands came up, fumbled with the buttons of her blouse, and pulled it open. She felt the perspiration wetting her chemise. She really should get up and open that window. . . .

She drifted.

A soft knock awakened her. She tried to open her eyes, but it was easier just to keep them closed. She tried to call out, but her throat was too parched. Her legs were on fire. She reached for her skirts and pulled them up over her knees, over her thighs to her waist.

The rap again. *Rap rap*. It wasn't coming from the door, she realized. The window. It was coming from the window.

That wasn't possible.

Rap rap. The windowpanes rattled.

Mercy raised her head, stared at the dark glass, waiting for the sound again. She saw a shadow move behind the window, then slowly the window began to rise. A leg appeared over the windowsill, then another, until the entire frame was filled with the figure of a man. She could not see his features, but his hair seemed silvered by some light beyond the window. His shoulders were wide and he moved with an easy grace that was familiar.

"Hello," came the soft voice.

She had the sense of being in a vague nightmare, able to see but struck deaf and dumb, unable to move. This was not like the dream before. This was frightening, too real and . . . He was different. Threatening. She tried to raise her head and open her eyes, but her eyes were already open. She closed them and opened them again. Her throat grew sore from the scream that would not surface.

Looking beyond him to the window, she saw that the panes had become red, glowing like the coals inside the stove.

He sat down on the bed beside her, as he had before, the night she first came to Greystone. His arms was across her, his nearness pinning her to the bed. She touched his arm, expecting him to vanish. He didn't. The flesh and bone and muscle beneath her hands was solid and warm, bringing a rush of desire that made her roll her head and groan.

"Don't do this." They were her words, hoarse and rasping, scoring her throat as she tried to convince herself that he wasn't real. "Don't do this to me."

His breath brushed her throat. Warm. Arousing. He buried his face against the damp soft skin below her jaw, and her breath became a panting whimper. Real. This was real. He had finally come, and meant to take her, and she was glad. She wanted it. Just like Abby. Just like Miriam. Just like all the women who rushed to his dressing room after his performances for the opportunity of touching him and being touched by him. To share in the magic that made him what he was. Still, she tried to remember her pride. Oh, how she tried. She should not allow him to touch her like this. It was wrong, so wrong. No decent woman would let him touch her like this—

"But you're not decent," he whispered. "Are you, Mercy? You may as well enjoy it."

His hand slid up her thigh, touched the soft, aching place between her legs. She heard his breath quicken, a warm flame in her ear. Then his weight was pressing her down, pressing the air from her lungs. There was the quiet ripping of cloth, and suddenly her breasts were free of the chemise, filling his hands, the nipples straining high and hard as he circled each one with his fingers. Raising her hands, she slid them over his smooth bare shoulders, threaded them through his black hair, feeling it coil around her fingers. Then down, over the hard, broad muscles of his back, until her fingers touched . . .

"Mercy," he whispered. "Look at me."

Her heart began to pound. Again she tried to force open her eyes—yes, her eyes were open, they were open—focused on the dark hand cupping her white breast.

"Mercy, I have something for you," came his voice in her ear, whisper soft. "Look at what I have for you."

Slowly, slowly, she turned her head and met his eyes. She did not believe what she was seeing. It was part of the nightmare, the long, continuing nightmare that had plagued her since arriving at Greystone. Surely it would end at any minute. She would rouse herself and find that she had been asleep. This was too horrible to be real, yet she could not drag her gaze away from the dreadful thing above her. For those eyes held her, mesmerized her. They were D'Abanville's eyes, but this was not D'Abanville. Its thin, narrow nose was more of a snout. Its mouth was drawn back in a grin to show prominent pointed teeth, and its eyes, no longer despairing or suffering, gleamed with an unholy light. Atop its head was hair resembling a ram's fleece, and sprouting from the sides of its head were—

"I have something for you."

Dumbly she raised her eyes to the upraised hand. It sparkled with pearls and diamonds—the brooch—then something else: dark drops that oozed from the chrysanthemum petals like teardrops. Only now they were red and the brooch was no flower at all. She stared in horror at the knife, saw the light from the stove reflect like a blue star on the steel blade high above his head.

Throwing her head back she began to scream. She screamed and screamed until, suddenly, there were hands on her arms and shoulders, shaking her, a voice calling her name over and over.

"Mercy! Mercy, for God's sake, snap out of it!"

Someone slapped her face.

"Mercy, open your eyes and look at me."

Covering her face with her arms, she whimpered, "No, no. Don't make me."

"Mercy, it's Miriam. Miriam! Look at me."

Gradually she opened her eyes.

Miriam took Mercy's face in her hands. Her fingers were cool and gentle as she swept a strand of hair from Mercy's cheek. "You were dreaming. Do you understand me? You were only dreaming."

Mercy released her breath.

"What's going on here?" Roger stood in the door, his ankle-length nightshirt looking dingy yellow in the light from the candle he was holding. His quick eyes took in Mercy's disheveled state, and he asked, "Is she all right?"

"Fine," Miriam responded. "It seems Miss Dansing had a bad dream, is all. It's over now."

"Shall I get Dominick, do you think?" Roger asked. He padded closer, his spectacles reflecting the light from his candle.

"No!" Mercy responded. "Please, I don't want to see him. He . . . he . . ."

"He what, Mercy?" Miriam took Mercy's face in her hands. "Are you frightened of Dominick?"

She shook her head, feeling foolish and still confused. Something still was not right . . .

"Why don't you get out of these clothes? Let me help . . ."

Mercy looked into Miriam's eyes. She looked at her smiling mouth.

Miriam's hands came up and clamped about her wrists.

"Let's get you out of those clothes now."

Mercy shook her head.

"Get you ready. He's coming. Listen. He's already here."

She raised her eyes to the door. "No," she said. "No."

The beast moved toward her, cloven hooves striking the floor like flint.

Her head fell back and this time the scream of terror tore at her throat until it was raw with fire and she was crying. She fought the hands that reached out for her.

"Mercy, for God's sake open your eyes. Mercy, you're dreaming. Love, you are dreaming!"

Suddenly she was looking into *his* blue eyes and—

She tore herself from his hands, fell to the floor, and crawled toward the window. She heard him call out her name and she screamed again, stumbled to her feet, and backed away.

D'Abanville rose off the bed, the dim glow from the stove casting shadows over his features. He looked so real, so normal now, and concerned. She closed her eyes and opened them again. He was there yet. She waited for him to change, for the horrible calcifications to erupt from his head and back and feet.

"Mercy," he said gently. "Mercy, love, be careful. You're too close—"

"Don't!" she screamed. "It's a trick. Only a trick. You'll change again into that horrible monster!"

He looked as if she had struck him. But that was a trick too, to make her let down her guard, so he could get close enough to . . .

"Mercy, the stove. Watch out for the stove!"

She felt it then, the heat, burning into her back. She looked down at her smoldering skirt, then dumbly back at D'Abanville. He moved forward so quickly she could only cringe and await the thrust of the knife in her throat. But his hands only grabbed her away from the open stove and slapped at her skirt, sending tiny slivers of singed calico to the floor, where he stamped out the sparks.

Realizing in that moment that this was no dream, Mercy threw herself against him, pressed her face against his bare chest, and wrapped her arms around his shoulders. She clung to him until the sensation of his cradling her in his arms began to replace the terror with something far less disturbing.

"Is everything all right?" came Miriam's voice from the door.

Mercy opened her eyes and found Miriam standing just inside the doorway, her face pinched, as if seeing them together, holding one another, was like a lance to her senses.

"Fine. She's fine now," Dominick said. "Aren't you, love?"

Mercy nodded, her eyes still on Miriam. *I have him now,* a voice in her head whispered, much to her own consternation. As if Miriam understood, she bowed her head a fraction and smiled a little thinly.

"I'll leave you, then," she said. Stepping out into the hall, she closed the door behind her.

They were alone, and Mercy didn't care.

Closing her eyes, she breathed deeply of his scent, listened to the steady thump of his heart against her ear. He rocked her slowly back and forth, and gradually she began to relax.

"Better?" he asked.

She nodded.

Very slowly he pushed her back and looked down into her face. He swept away the lingering trace of tears from her cheeks with the pad of his thumb. He did not speak, nor did she. When he held up his hand before her, she raised her own and pressed it firmly to his.

Their fingers interlaced.

She heard him swallow. She raised her eyes to his and found him staring at their hands.

"I think," he said, "that I have only now realized what a child you are. *Prends garde, mon enfant,* that you do not trust me so unguardedly in this moment." He backed toward the bed, his hands still holding hers. "I'd like to stay with you tonight."

She shook her head in refusal, yet her feet moved of their own accord and she followed him.

He sank back on the bed, his hands still holding hers, his eyes holding hers with their strange blue light. He pulled her gently down onto him so her breasts were pressed against the damp skin of his chest and his heartbeat was an echo of her own.

He slid his fingers into her tangled hair and dragged her face down to his. He brushed his lips across her mouth, then kissed her cheek.

"Bonsoir, ma bonne amie; bonsoir."

Mercy laid her head on his shoulder and closed her eyes.

12

Mercy awakened late in the morning. Dominick was gone. The effect of his presence throughout the night remained, however. She could smell the scent of his maleness on her hands. Holding them to her face, she inhaled deeply.

The effect of her dreams remained also. Her throat felt raw and swollen and her head pounded when she tried to move it.

She forced herself to roll from the bed, holding her head as she did so, uncertain if the pain in her temples would kill her if she moved too abruptly. She moved carefully to the window and raised it. Rain streamed down her face, wet, bracing, making her shiver with relief and cold. Resting her head against the window frame, she stared out over the distant trees and wondered if she had actually spent an entire night in D'Abanville's arms. He hadn't kissed her, no more than the chaste brush of his lips on hers before she fell asleep. And though his arms had held her tightly throughout the night, he had done nothing more to her with his hands than to stroke her hair and occasionally her face.

Turning her face into the rain again, Mercy lifted her hand and held it beneath a continuous stream of icy water that ran off the eave, cupped it in her hand, then tipped it to her mouth. It tasted a little brackish, but cooled her throat. She drank again, more awake now, more aware. She recalled having awakened just before dawn, when the room was all in grey shadow and the wind drove the rain in a constant drone against the window. She had awakened wanting him. Not just his arms about her or his lips pressed into the soft hair on top of her head.

She had wanted him inside her. Deeper than George Balfour had ever been.

Pretending to be shifting in her sleep, she had moved her hand from his chest to his stomach, thinking him to be asleep, but he wasn't. Suddenly his dark hand had caught hers, shifting hers to the waistband of his breeches and slightly lower. Not much. But enough so she felt the stirring of him beneath her palm, the hardening and growing, until she was certain he would feel the trembling of her palm against him. He had pressed her hand to the shape of him and she had stopped breathing, waiting, wondering if he realized after all that she was awake. His hips had moved slightly. Restlessly. His body warmed and tensed against her and his heart began a forceful throbbing against her cheek.

Then he had groaned deep in his throat. He pressed her hand again, slid it slowly down the rigid length of him as his hips raised again, then fell. Raised and fell slowly enough not to awaken her. The arm on which she was cradled came up around her, squeezing her ever so slightly to him.

"God," he had whispered. "God."

He cupped her hand to him again, harder this time, so it was almost painful, so hard she felt him move and throb and swell, so hard she felt her own breathing quicken, until she was breathing deeply of his aroused male scent and perhaps a little of her own. Then suddenly he shoved her hand away, took his straining shape against his own palm, the best he could, and drew his hand sharply up and down until the bed jumped in quick rhythmic strokes, vibrating the ache inside Mercy until the need for him was so strong she almost lifted her head, almost reached out. Then suddenly his back arched a little, the free hand buried in her hair fisted against her head; he went still, his hand gripping hard against the straining ridge.

He shuddered, then began to relax. In a moment he had taken her hand again and placed it against him, as if he liked it there. The passion was spent, she could tell. A part of his breeches was warm and moist against her palm. He then kissed the top of her head and drifted back to sleep. Still aching, she had continued to stare down at her hand where it rested on his breeches.

Mercy was to meet Miriam at the couturière's at two, and she was late.

She stuck her head out of the carriage and glanced up and down King William Street. There were two streets to go yet and the traffic was at a standstill. The continuing rain was the culprit. The streets were flooding, some completely underwater, and by the looks of the sky, there was no hope of relief anytime soon.

Will the rain ever cease?

With umbrella in hand, she swung open the door and stepped down from the carriage. As the coachman looked around, she called up, "I'll walk from here."

If he heard her over the shouts of other coachmen and the whinnying of horses, he made no sign, just hunched his shoulders against the rain and looked away.

Mercy made her way carefully around the nearby bus, whose five pairs of horses were stamping their feet and tossing their heads in frustration. Equally frustrated, the passengers within the bus glared down from the windows at her as if she were the cause of the confusion. Mercy ducked beneath her umbrella and used the London General Omnibus Company sign attached to the bus as a handhold so she didn't slip in the morass and ruin her clothes, though she suspected the rain and mud would do that for her anyway by the time she reached the couturière's. No sooner had she stepped beyond the bus than she was nearly trampled by one from the London Road Car Company, then once more by a tram and again by a hansom.

The sidewalks were little better. Mercy took a moment to step out of the rain under the overhang of a building in order to catch her breath. Turning toward the plate-glass window, she stared at the advertisement for travel. Beside the message was a copy of Jules Verne's *Around the World in Eighty Days*.

"See the World with Briggs Travel!" she read. "The route will be over the Great Union and Central Pacific Railway to San Francisco, passing through some of the grandest and most interesting scenery in the world. From

San Francisco the tourist will be taken to Japan and China"—Mercy wondered briefly where San Francisco was—"by the Pacific Mail Steamship Company, and thence by the Peninsular and Oriental Company, via Galle, Madras, Calcutta, and Bombay (over the Great Indian Railway), to Southampton, or London, via Brindisi—all in ninety days!"

"Quite remarkable, don't you think, Miss Dansing?"

Mercy looked up into the face reflected in the glass, her heart leaping momentarily to her throat.

Inspector Chesterton smiled. "Imagine traveling around the world in ninety days. Seems too good to be real. But then, this is the age of thaumaturgy, it would seem."

She spun around, furious. "You've been following me, Inspector. I demand to know why."

"So I might speak with you privately, of course."

"I have nothing more to say to you, sir." She made a slight movement to one side, but he as quickly blocked her way.

"Are you aware that two more women have been killed, Miss Dansing? Of course you wouldn't be. Even the papers have not released the news yet."

Mercy forced herself to look away from the inspector's bland face, turned back toward the window, and focused her eyes on the travel advertisement, her eyes jumping up and down the words "Galle," "Calcutta," and "Brindisi," the only words to leap out at her and snare her mind from the inspector's insinuations.

"Were you with D'Abanville last evening, Miss Dansing?"

"Yes!" she responded.

"At what time?"

Her mind raced back to the first conversation she and D'Abanville had shared in his office. The tall case clock in the library up the hall had been striking the hour when she left the room. She recalled counting the notes—six, seven, eight—she tried to remember what time she had awakened from her nightmares. Think! The clock on her dresser . . . Think! Two. It had been two in the morning. "Eight," she said, "and—"

"The young women were killed sometime around midnight."

She shifted her eyes up to his in the glass. Behind him images moved like ghosts across the window. Then a vague reflection of a man standing in the rain appeared through the crowd, his features too indistinct to make out clearly. But he was tall. Very tall. Half a head taller than the others . . .

"Miss Dansing, do you know beyond a shadow of a doubt that D'Abanville was at Greystone for the entirety of last evening?"

She closed her eyes briefly. When she opened them again, the image in the glass seemed sharper. She thought she caught a glimpse of black hair and—

She spun around, frantically searching the crowd, finally focusing on the man who had now turned his back to her and was tugging his overcoat more closely around his shoulders.

"Is something wrong, Miss Dansing?"

"Yes," she said, her breathing coming fast and sharply. Looking back at Chesterton, she finished, "You are what's wrong, Inspector Chesterton. You are harassing me, and if you don't stop, I shall be forced to take the matter up with your superiors."

"Are you frightened of D'Abanville, Miss Dansing?"

"Certainly not."

"We are contacting the Paris police and—"

"I care little if you contact President Sadi Carnot himself. I have an appointment to which I will be late if you detain me any longer, so if you will excuse me . . ."

The inspector smiled. "Of course. But first . . ." He reached into the pocket of his mackintosh, then withdrew his hand. In his palm were two blue buttons. "One of these was found in Abigail Russell's hand."

"Are you saying you believe that Miss Russell's death is definitely linked to these other killings?"

"That is still under debate. Regardless, she was linked to D'Abanville." He pointed to the buttons and continued, "The other button was located beside her body. They looked as if they might very well belong on a man's jacket, probably the man who killed her. Perhaps torn from his coat during an attempt to escape him. Do they look familiar, Miss Dansing?''

She shook her head, refusing to look again at the buttons, focusing instead on the man by the curb. His back was still to her.

''There is no absolute way of determining if they belong to D'Abanville, unless, of course, we were able to search his quarters. But without stronger evidence . . . You will keep an eye out, won't you, Miss Dansing?''

Mercy turned her face up toward his. ''Are you asking me to search his apartment, Inspector?''

''That might be a trifle too dangerous. And if you are as frightened as—''

''There is absolutely nothing to be frightened of, Inspector.''

''Of course.'' Reaching for her hand, he pressed one of the buttons into her palm. ''Just in case you have the opportunity . . .'' He touched his hat brim. ''I am always at your assistance, madam. Good day to you.'' Turning on his heel, he merged with the crowd and walked briskly down the street.

The rain fell less steadily against Mercy's umbrella as she stepped away from the building, her eyes still focused on the man whom she had noticed regarding her earlier. His shoulders were wide, his hair very black and curling slightly over the collar of his coat. Closing her hand upon his arm, she turned him around.

''I'm very sorry,'' she said to the stranger. ''For a moment I thought you were someone else.''

''That's quite all right,'' he responded.

With embarrassment coloring her cheeks, Mercy stepped away from the gentleman, noting that he did not seem so tall now, and his hair was not black after all, but dark brown. In truth, he didn't in the least resemble the man whose reflection she had seen in the window.

She tried to put the incident out of her mind as she hurried to her appointment. It was not to be, however, for as she rounded the corner, criers from both the *Star* and the *Times* were shocking the horrified public with the announcements:

''Paper! Two More Whitechapel Horrors!'' ''Paper!

CID Investigation Intensifies! . . . Madman Taunts Public with Letters! Calls Himself Jack the Ripper!''

Fifteen minutes late for her appointment, Mercy arrived to discover that Miriam, having another appointment, had been forced to leave. She spent the next two hours being fitted for her wardrobe by the couturière, who, Mercy was certain, believed her reasons for buying clothes were more personal than Mercy was letting on. Once, when Mercy pointed out that the evening dress with the dark green bodice and cream brocade skirt striped with pink sprays was her favorite, the woman had cocked one eyebrow, smiled, and said slyly, "It is a very romantic and dramatic dress, *oui?* Certain to catch and hold D'Abanville's eye, don't you agree?''

She thought of arguing the matter, but decided against it. In truth, it *was* a very romantic dress. Certainly not the sort of thing typically worn to work in. But then, she was not in a typical position. It was becoming more and more obvious to her that her position as Dominick's assistant included being his companion on social occasions. The idea of having to stand at his side while women, both single and married, flaunted themselves before him made her headache return.

It was dusk by the time she left the couturière's. She had just stepped onto the walk when a familiar, friendly voice called out, "Miss Dansing!''

"Mr. McMillian, what a pleasure to see you." Mercy held out her hand. "We missed you at Greystone this morning.''

He appeared thoughtful before asking, "I have a little while before my next appointment—will you join me for tea?''

"Tea would be nice," she responded.

He took her arm as they moved down the walk. The rain had stopped and the gas lamps up and down the streets were being lit.

Breathing deeply of the cleared air, Stan McMillian said, "Ah, it is the London eve that restrains me from quitting the city, that thrilling mood when the eyes of the great city, like the eyes of a cat, begin to flame in the dark. Have you viewed Whistler's *Nocturnes,* Miss Dansing?''

Smiling, she shook her head.

"No? Whistler expressed his love of London after dark by likening the tall chimneys to campanili and the warehouses to palaces."

"You are quite the romantic," she told him.

"What would the lovers' tryst be without the twinkle of candlelight to reflect in the young woman's eye?" Shrugging, he added with humor, "Besides, the lights will make the London streets safer after dark for all concerned."

Reaching the confectioner's shop, they were seated at a table for two beside a window displaying scones and cakes. Mercy ordered tea with lemon and honey, hoping it would soothe her throat. McMillian placed his newspaper aside and ordered coffee.

"I regret having to postpone my renovation of Greystone," he told her.

"Why must you do so?"

"My workers were greatly distressed by our discovery of the sealed room, and refuse to reenter the house. I must admit to a certain reluctance myself. While I am not frightened by the idea of spirits residing in these houses—what great old house in Britain is without its ghosts, after all?—there was something most disconcerting about the room itself. And although the discovery of a walled-up room is not unusual in itself, never have I found one such as this."

"It was Mary Casimere's room."

McMillian sipped his hot beverage before responding, "I thought so."

"It seems no one ever took the time to pack her things away. There are clothes still hanging in the wardrobe. Her brush and combs were laid out on the dressing table. I also found a diary."

His eyebrows shot up with that disclosure.

"I've read very little of it. The writings are badly faded, and in some cases the pages are missing completely."

"I would dearly love to see it," he told her. "I'm certain Lady Casimire would enjoy it as well. Would you mind if I dropped by the house and picked it up? Or perhaps we could meet for tea and look it over."

"Certainly. It belongs to Lady Casimire, after all."

"Imagine, after one hundred years. Tell me, what does Mary write?"

"She writes that her brother instigated the building of the tower." Smiling a little, she said, "I find nothing threatening about Mary's room. I can't imagine why your workers are so frightened. Could there be some other reason for their reluctance, do you think?"

McMillian looked somewhat chagrined. She did not miss his glance toward the paper.

"Is it because there is some question about D'Abanville's involvement in the murders?" she asked.

"It does appear as if the CID is showing a great deal of interest in him. And while I do not believe for a moment that D'Abanville is involved in any way, I must respect my workers' feelings on the matter. I'm certain this madman will be apprehended soon and D'Abanville will be exonerated. But until then I have my own business to consider. I hope you understand."

"Have you heard that two more women have been killed?"

He nodded. "He is taunting the police now. Calls himself Jack the Ripper. Apropos, I suppose, but ghastly. Have you see the *Times?*" He handed her the paper, opened to the facsimile of a letter and a postcard. Holding it nearer to the light, Mercy read:

Dear Boss,
    I keep on hearing the police have caught me but they won't fix me just yet. I have laughed when they look so clever and talk about being on the right track. That joke about Leather Apron gave me real fits. I am down on whores and I shan't quit ripping them till I do get buckled. Grand work the last job was. I gave the lady no time to squeal. How can they catch me now. I love my work and want to start again. You will soon hear of me with my funny little games. I saved some of the proper red stuff in a ginger beer bottle over the last job to write with but it went thick like glue and I can't use it. Red ink is fit enough I hope ha ha. The next job I do I shall clip the lady's ears off and send to the police officers just

for jolly wouldn't you? Keep this letter back till I do a bit more work, then give it out straight. My knife is nice and sharp I want to get to work right away if I get a chance. Good luck.

Yours truly,
JACK THE RIPPER

Don't mind me giving the trade name wasn't good enough to post this before I got all the red ink off my hands curse it. No luck yet they say I am a doctor now ha ha.

The next letter read:

I was not codding dear old Boss when I gave you the tip. You'll hear about Saucy Jack's work tomorrow. Double event this time. Number one squealed a bit. Couldn't finish straight off. Had not time to get ears for police. Thanks for keeping last letter back till I got to work again.

JACK THE RIPPER

McMillian said, "Dreadful business. I understand the CID is investigating several doctors. It seems the killer has a fair knowledge of the human anatomy."

Her eyes studied the beautifully flowing script of the murderer. "Oh?"

"Well, yes. His mutilations have involved the removal of certain organs. It's said that he has done so with such efficiency—oh, I do beg your pardon, Miss Dansing. This is hardly the sort of topic we should be discussing over our tea." He flipped out his gold repeater to check the time. "I really must be going. May I drop you somewhere?" he asked. When she declined, he dug into his pocket and pulled out his card. "My address. Feel free to drop by anytime. And if you need me for any reason, any reason at all—"

"I will not hesitate to call on you," she responded, smiling.

With a flourish, he swept out of the shop, leaving Mercy to watch him dissolve into the shadows down the street.

By the time she finished her tea, the shopkeeper had begun readying the store for closing. She hadn't realized how late the hour had become; she had been too caught up in her musing about D'Abanville and the horrible murders going on in Whitechapel.

The air had cooled considerably by the time she left the shop. Darkness had fallen completely. The traffic had dwindled to nearly nothing, and, walking to the street, Mercy shivered with the realization that finding a cab might be harder than she had anticipated. She tried twice to hail hansoms by raising her hand and waving to the drivers. They didn't stop and she was forced to jump aside or be trampled into the street.

She began walking back to Buckingham Street.

She had been walking a good twenty minutes when she stopped at the corner of Bartholomew Lane and Threadneedle Street. Standing beneath the harsh yellow light of the gas lamp, she noted that in the last few minutes the usual fog had drifted in around her as silently as a cat. She could barely make out the vague images of the surrounding buildings. The distant streetlight was only a hazy, shimmering glow that succeeded, not in illuminating the darkness, but exaggerating the density of the fog.

She shivered.

Beside her feet lay a discarded edition of the *Star*. Mercy stared down at it for several minutes, refusing, briefly, the curiosity that compelled her to retrieve it. Acknowledging the bold headlines seemed treasonous in itself. Reading the story beneath it made her feel like Judas at the Last Supper. Still . . .

She read.

Two more murders of women, even more diabolical than those perpetrated on Buck's Row and Hanbury Street on 31 August and 8 September, were discovered on Berner Street and Mitre Square. At one A.M. a woman, one Elizabeth Stride, was found lying in a narrow court not far from the International Working Men's Educational Club by a steward of the club, Louis Diemschutz. There were no signs of struggle; the clothes were neither torn nor disturbed. The position of the body suggested that she lay down or allowed herself to be laid down where she was found. Only the soles of her shoes were visible. She was still holding in her hand a packet of cachous, and there was a bunch of flowers still pinned to her dress front. Her throat was cut, but no further mutilation had been attempted. At 1:45 A.M. the body of Catherine Eddowes was found in the City of London by a police constable on patrol. She was lying on her back, left leg extended and right leg bent. There was a large gash across her face from her nose to the right of the cheek. Her throat had been cut and she had been brutally mutilated. Her dress, with its pattern of Michaelmas daisies and golden lilies, had been pushed up to her waist and bunched on her chest, together with her drab linsey-woolsey skirt, her dark green alpaca petticoat and grubby white chemise. She wore brown ribbed knee-stockings, darned with white cotton, and a pair of men's laced boots. In her pockets she carried everything she owned: a white handkerchief with a red border, a match box containing cotton, a blunt table knife with a white bone handle, two short clay pipes, a red cigarette case with a white metal fitting, a printed handbill, five pieces of soap, a small tin box containing tea and sugar, a portion of a pair of spectacles, a small comb and ball of worsted. Both of these women were seen earlier talking to a man of average height, broad-shouldered, and well-dressed. It is said: "He had the look of a foreigner, possibly French."

This maniac sexual killer must be stopped. The public's fear and earlier fascination over the killings has been roused to something just short of panic. How long will the Criminal Investigation Department allow this to continue? When queried on the matter, Commissioner Sir Charles Warren responded only by saying, "We have narrowed our investigation to a few possibilities."

There has been much hearsay as to the identity of this killer, speculation ranging from a failed barrister, a doctor, a back-street abortionist, a sailor, and,

most recently, the celebrated hoaxer from Paris,
D. D'Abanville.

The CID issues this warning: Avoid going out
alone after dark. If approached by any stranger, call
for help immediately and report the occurrence to
the police.

Mercy dropped the paper. It fell to her feet and fluttered slightly in the breeze.

A fine mist had begun to fall, adding to the dreariness
of the cold and fog. It felt heavy on her shoulders, clung
to her cheeks like the sweat of fear. Pressing the backs
of her fingers to her face, she saw the words over and
over in her mind: *and, most recently, the celebrated
hoaxer from Paris, D. D'Abanville.*

She looked around, tried to see through the fog, noting
that the vague light from the distant streetlamp could no
longer be seen. She got the chilling impression that
should she step out of the sphere of light she now occupied, she would go tumbling into black space.

Gripping her umbrella tighter, she stepped out of the
light and into the dark, cautiously feeling her way along,
step by step, using the tip of her umbrella as a blind man
would use a cane.

A sound behind her . . .

She spun, looked back at the dim light, saw only the
paper she had read fluttering and snapping like a flag in
the wind. It seemed to wave to her, that paper, reminding
her in bold black that any woman who would roam these
streets alone after dark was asking for trouble.

She heard the clip-clop of a horse somewhere in the
distance. A woman's light laughter drifted to her, then a
man's response. Mercy walked on a little farther before
she was able to make out the hazy image of the laughing
woman. She stood up against the wall, wearing a black
straw bonnet with a trim of veil. The man before her, his
hand at her waist, was tall, his hair dark. Mercy's heart
began to race. She gripped her umbrella more tightly.

They both looked around as Mercy stepped through the
fog.

"I beg your pardon," she said.

Neither of them replied, and Mercy continued on her

journey, pausing as she heard the man ask quietly, "Will you?" and the woman respond, "Yes." Their footsteps diminished in the distance and all that remained were the silence, the dark, and the cold wet drizzle falling from the sky.

Not so, Mercy realized the minute she thought it. There was something other than the silence and dark and cold wet drizzle out there.

Someone was out there.

She could feel him watching her.

Slowly, cautiously, she walked to the next streetlamp, hesitated before stepping into the light. Decided not to. Instead, she stepped out into the street, crossed it, and continued her journey back to Buckingham Street, walking as quietly as possible on the balls of her feet, eyes aching from the effort to see through the pea-soup fog, ears straining to detect any sound of approach.

Where is everyone? she wondered. London was not exactly known for shuttering its windows and doors after dark, not with the increasing popularity and availability of the electric light. True, the climate was not exactly conducive to strolls in the park, but . . .

It's because of the Ripper, her mind said.

She picked up her pace.

He's out there, she thought, behind me or ahead of me, waiting.

She heard it then: the footsteps. She continued to walk, gripping the closed umbrella so tightly her fingers ached. Don't panic, she continued to tell herself. You're almost home. Just another block or so and then . . .

The man moved up behind her so quickly and silently she had no time to react. She froze as his hand came down on her shoulder.

"Here, now," he said quietly. "What's yer hurry?"

She slowly turned to face him. His face looked round and pale in the fog.

"What do you want?" It was all she could think of to say.

"What do you think?"

"Leave me alone. I am not a prostitute."

"No?" He began to laugh. His grip bore down on her

collarbone, hurting. "I'll give you twopence for an hour."

"No."

"A haggler, eh? Four, then. No? Name your price, but I'll not go more than eight. Not one of you bitches is worth that much, but you look clean enough, and I'll pay it if I must."

She tried to back away. His hand gripped harder, freezing her.

"Come now, gel, don't be difficult. All right, all right, I'll give you ten, but not a farthing more. I'll expect extra for it." He dropped the coins down the front of her dress. He began to smile. "It'll be down on your knees for tenpence, and to your doss for the rest. What do you say?"

She shook her head, her mind racing back to when she had lived on Sultan Street, and the many times she had been forced to turn men away who thought her easy or one of Oliver's girls.

Drawing her shoulders back, she said, "All right, but I'm warnin' ya—I've got the clap. Y'll be takin' yer chances, I vow."

He jerked his hand away, tore a kerchief from his pocket to clean himself. Then, without another word, and forgetting his money, he spun on his heel and disappeared through the fog.

Mercy nearly cried in relief upon reaching the corner of Buckingham and Lombard streets. Greystone's towering brick walls rose like a fortress to her left, the black shapes of the trees beyond the walls clustered into one continuing mass of whispering, shifting shadows.

She had rounded the corner, had the gates in sight, when she saw D'Abanville step through the gates and onto the street. Unable to move, she watched, waited for him to notice her. He didn't. With black cloak billowing behind him, he headed in the opposite direction.

Mercy stared after him through the dark, listening as his footsteps were drowned by the swirling fog. She blinked, trying to bring her mind into focus. Then, forcing her feet to move, she followed, plunging again into the darkness, moving swiftly to keep up with D'Abanville's much longer stride. She followed him forever, it seemed, until her legs hurt and her breathing became short, knowing the way too well even through the fog. Down Fenchurch, past Aldgate, beyond the City's businesses and into the dark of the East End, down Whitechapel Road. Her mind cried out: It's him, it's him, oh, dear God, it's him, why else would he be here, why is he here, it couldn't be him, but it's him!

Realizing he was gone, she stopped abruptly. How long had she been running, following nothing, no one? She stared out into the long tunnel of fog and darkness and felt like screaming out her anger at his betrayal.

Through the fog she saw a figure approach. Even though she could not make out his face, she recognized, by the shape of his cap, that he was a policeman. In his hand he carried a stick. His gold buttons reflected briefly the light of the gas lamp under which he was passing.

" 'Evening," he said softly to her. "Mucky night to be strollin', miss."

"I'm not strolling," she snapped before catching herself.

He stared at her a moment before saying, "I'd watch m'self, if I were you. Streets ain't safe, y' know."

"I shall, thank you."

He stopped beside her, looked up and down the dismal streets before saying, "It's a fine night for mischief. We'll be lucky not to see more trouble in Whitechapel after this one."

"Do you think so?" she said, still staring down the street. Finally turning her burning eyes on the policeman, she asked coldly, "Have you no clue who the murderer might be?"

"Could be. We'll know more tomorrow."

She stared into his bearded features. "Oh? Is something happening tomorrow?"

"We're bringing in suspects tomorrow for questioning. Y' know he's calling himself Jack the Ripper now. Making bloody fools of us all, he is. Did y' see the papers?"

"Aye, I saw them."

"Just received a new letter. Sent it from outside London, he did. Bloke gets around. We'll be watching the train carriages more now, that's for certain."

"Outside of London?" She raised her eyes to his, her

heart racing with new hope. There was the proof, the blessed proof that D'Abanville could not be the Ripper. He had not left London since . . .

"Where outside London?" she asked softly.

"Sorry, miss?"

"Where was the letter postmarked, did you say?"

The policeman looked up and down the street before replying, "Liverpool, miss." Tipping his hat to her then, he moved off into the fog, swinging his club at his side and whistling softly.

The quiet closed in on her, and the dark. Guilty, her mind whispered frantically. Dear God, he was guilty. Suddenly her legs felt too weak to carry her. Her body trembled all over. Not so much from fright as denial. While one part of her mind screamed out at him in anger, the other fought back with refusal.

Tugging her cloak more closely about her shoulders, she looked one last time down Whitechapel Road, then turned and walked back the way she had come, determined now to learn the truth by whatever means she could. If he was guilty, he must be stopped, no matter what her heart told her to do. And if he was innocent, then they must find a way to clear him.

She had gone no more than a hundred yards when she realized she was being followed. Slowing, she listened to the footsteps as they neared. Without stopping, she glanced back over her shoulder. There was someone there. She could just make out his shape on the very brink of the fog.

She picked up her pace, as did he. By the time she reached Greystone, she was running outright. Reaching the gates, she frantically closed her hands around the slick, cold iron and pulled.

Nothing.

She pulled again, this time harder, her breath now coming in sharp gasps of terror. The footsteps were nearing. Gritting her teeth, fighting back the hysteria that was closing around her throat, she searched the gate for whatever was holding her back. She spied the latch.

Mercy tried to seize the latch, but her fingers, still frozen in place from having gripped the umbrella so tightly, clawed ineffectually at the rusting piece of ornate iron. She tried again and the latch moved hardly at all.

The footsteps were closer now.

Forcing her fingers around the pronged device, she concentrated on flipping it open and up, guiding it carefully from around the bar until the gate gave a lurch of release. She slipped through the opening, as carefully shifted the latch back into place, then backed up the drive, waiting for whoever had followed her for the last few blocks to come stumbling up to the gate, to show himself . . .

When he did not, she spun and continued running, not realizing until she had nearly reached Greystone's steps that she had dropped her umbrella back at the gate. She took the steps two at a time, flung open the door, and slammed it so hard behind her the sound reverberated throughout the house.

Mercy blinked, still unable to focus clearly, unable to catch her breath. She thought she might faint now that the threat was behind her.

Roger materialized from the shadows, his face curious and concerned. "Miss Dansing, is something wrong? Have you just returned?"

She nodded.

"Are you alone? Is D'Abanville with you?"

"No." Mercy managed. She leaned back against the door for support.

Roger's face looked troubled. "I wish he would quit his gadding about without telling me first. In light of the trouble, I think it's a not a good idea for him to be out."

"Has he been out long?" she asked innocently.

"He went out earlier, just after you, as a matter of fact. He returned soon after, however, and was in his room until recently. I went to discuss a matter with him and found him gone."

A cold chill centered around the base of her spine and slowly crawled upward. She recalled the face reflected in the window, watching her—she had been so certain that it had been D'Abanville's. She looked back at Roger, realizing he had continued speaking. "I beg your pardon?"

"He was most upset earlier. Haven't you heard? Two more women were murdered in Whitechapel."

Closing her eyes, she nodded.

"A police notice was hand-delivered to our door just before dark." He pointed to the mahogany demilune table against the wall. "There it is, if you would like to see for yourself."

Roger peered at her for several more seconds; then, shaking his head, he turned away and retreated into the shadows. Alone, Mercy closed her eyes, doing her best to rid her mind of the idea that somewhere out in that fog was Dominick D'Abanville. The image of those newspaper headlines, as well as Inspector Chesterton's insistent questions, came hurling at her like her brother's fist, stunning, hurting, then frightening her so badly she began to tremble all over again.

Walking to the table, she stared down at the broadsheet where it lay next to a Meissen hunting scene of a boy with dogs. She forced herself to pick it up.

"POLICE NOTICE," it screamed in bold black print.

> To the occupant. On the mornings of Friday, 31st August, Saturday, 8th September, and Sunday, 30th September, 1888, women were murdered in or near Whitechapel. The murderer in external appearance is quite likely to be a quiet, inoffensive-looking man in his mid-thirties and respectably dressed. He must be in the habit of wearing a cloak or overcoat so that he is able to escape down the streets after the murders, hiding all traces of blood from passersby. He is thought to be solitary and eccentric in his habits, also he is most likely to be a man without regular/normal occupation. He is possibly living among respectable persons who have some knowledge or suspicion that he isn't quite right in his mind at times. Such persons who may harbor such suspicions are earnestly requested to communicate at once with the nearest police station.
>
> Metropolitan Police Office

Almost involuntarily her hand slid into the pocket of her dress. There her fingertips contacted the smooth, cold surface of the navy-blue button Chesterton had given her. Proof positive. That's all he needed to stop the killings. Think of Abigail Russell. Once D'Abanville's mistress, she had looked into his blue eyes and had become mesmerized by his magic. Had she been looking into those eyes when he slid the knife into her stomach and . . . ?

Here's your chance, her mind told her. D'Abanville's out. You've been curious about that tower, wondered what he hides up there. Tricks of the trade perhaps? Maybe those infamous writings of Faust bound in a great black book emblazoned with the devil's face?

She heard herself groan. She didn't want to believe it, not a word of it. If he was evil she would know it. As she had known even before he began his cruelties toward her, that Oliver was wicked. Wicked to the bone. But there was something about D'Abanville that, though terribly frightening and disconcerting at times, didn't conjure up images of a butchering maniac on a rampage. She had felt his kindness, had witnessed his compassion. Dear God, he was a practicing theosophist. He would not even lift a hand to thwart the damnable thugs who had attacked them the night they had returned from Liverpool, for fear he would suffer for the act in his next bloody lifetime!

He simply could not be guilty of these heinous crimes!

But she wouldn't know for certain until she proved it to herself and Chesterton. Proved it to all the people of London. And if she was wrong, if she learned beyond any shadow of a doubt that D'Abanville was a killer of women, she would turn him in with no regrets.

She had to know, for London's sake . . . for her own sanity's sake.

Closing her fingers around the button, she started for the tower.

13

She checked Roger's office, found both him and Miriam talking over plans for D'Abanville's upcoming performance for the lord mayor's celebration. She then went directly to D'Abanville's office, hoping to find some clue there of his guilt or innocence.

There was a copy of the *Times* on his desk. So he had seen it already. Of course he had. Every citizen within the borders of jolly old London town would have heard the news of the latest Whitechapel murders. She picked up the paper and studied the Ripper letters carefully. Then, almost without realizing she was doing it, she began to search about the desk for some scrap of paper or correspondence that contained D'Abanville's handwriting. It was not a difficult task. She flipped open what appeared to be a ledger and stared at the entries. Her hand trembling, she placed the Ripper's letter beside it. Mercy squeezed her eyes closed briefly, then looked again. There were similarities and differences. But if anything, the Ripper's script was more fluid, more . . . skilled. D'Abanville's seemed more intentionally neat, as if he had struggled to write each letter as legibly as possible. She was almost certain the handwriting was different. Almost.

She paid no attention to the names listed in the ledger until she was about to close it. The entry at the bottom of the page caught her eye: "No. 30. (Orphanage-Liverpool) Bobby Brown."

Mercy thought a moment. The boy at Liverpool Hospital?

She ran her finger to the other side of the page, where she found a sum of money listed in the column marked

"October." Then she noted the other twenty-nine entries, all similar, all listing names and orphanages throughout England and Paris, and beside them sums of money, many dating as far back as two years.

Mercy closed the book. She could not allow herself to be swayed now by his generosity. She must keep her mind bent on the reality of the situation. Just because D'Abanville had some sort of obsession toward bettering the plight of the homeless waifs in the world did not necessarily mean he would not, in turn, strike out at the women who had orphaned the children in the first place. Recalling the conversation she had heard between Miriam and Roger just after Chesterton's visit, Mercy was suddenly struck with the terrifying possibility of it. If D'Abanville had been deserted by his mother, he would certainly empathize with these children . . . and he would certainly want to strike out at the woman—or the women like her—who had, or might have, hurt him.

She left the room and again headed for the tower, slowed as she noticed that the door to the room where she had hidden the night before was slightly ajar. A light burned within. Cautiously she approached, nudged open the door, making certain the room was unoccupied before entering and closing the door behind her.

Once inside the room, she glanced curiously around her. Empty of furniture, it was stacked with many of the ornate trunks and crates that D'Abanville used in his performances. Some looked ancient, and she wondered if they had been used by his predecessor. There was also a tall glass case positioned in the center of the floor, and Mercy recalled D'Abanville's mentioning the illusion of fire in glass when they were in Liverpool. Curious, she walked around it, examining it closely, finding nothing unusual about it.

On each wall were posters printed in English, French, German, and Italian, proclaiming D'Abanville as wizard, mystic, incredible and celebrated. There were many from England, including the Empire Theater in Liverpool, the Palace Theater in Hull, as well as the Oxford Music Hall. There were also tattered yellowed maps of the universe. There were maps too with geometric designs, many of them being triangular in shape. As in his office, there were papers and books and cups and glasses that had been placed aside and forgotten. Mercy kicked aside several discarded balls of paper before reminding herself of her purpose for being there.

She was turning back toward the door when she spotted the bloody white cloth tossed to one side of a gray metal box. For long moments she stood and stared at the cloth. She could not move. She hardly breathed. Finally, with her heart pounding double time in her breast, she forced herself to think logically. If she did not move soon, D'Abanville would return and all her plans would be dashed.

She moved to the box, went to her knees, her eyes still regarding the repulsive cloth. It lay half on the box, and she was forced to move it to one side so that she could better maneuver the clamps that held the lid in place.

Her trembling fingers released the clamps, first the left, then the right. She opened the box and stared down at five gleaming knives.

With a calm she would not have believed possible, she closed the box and got to her feet. She did not look at the cloth again as she turned for the door and escaped the room. She refused to allow her mind to consider the knives. There were knives in every house in England. He used them in his performance. That did not mean he was murdering unsuspecting prostitutes and disgruntled mistresses with them.

She made her way cautiously up the tower's winding stairs, relieved to find that the dog that had greeted her before was no longer there to terrify her with his strange eyes and throaty growl. At the top of the stairwell she found a door, massive in size and heavy enough to withstand a battering ram if necessary.

She knocked; then, just to make certain there was no one there, she called out, "Hello!" There was no response, so Mercy opened the door and stepped hesitantly over the threshold into the dimly lit tower room.

"Hello!"

The sudden shriek froze her until she realized the greeting had come from D'Abanville's bird. Malphas strutted across his perch, fluttering his black wings so strongly they sounded like muffled gunshot in the quiet.

Then he left his perch and swooped over her head, taking a turn around the room before alighting on the windowsill. He appeared to consider the open window briefly before returning to his perch, where he cocked his head and eyed her suspiciously.

Releasing her breath, she looked again about the room. The smell of decay prevailed. The room was very old—one hundred years old—and had been closed up for most of those years. Still, aside from the old smell, the room was nothing like she might have suspected. It had a low ceiling, hardly taller than D'Abanville. He no doubt was forced to duck his head slightly upon entering the door. She noted there was neither fireplace nor stove. The window having been left open, the room was extremely cold; Mercy found herself shivering as she glanced about the chamber.

It was an odd-shaped room. The walls to the left and right jutted outward, forming triangular peaks. The walls were bare, but for the curtainless windows. The floor was without carpets. A single bed had been shoved up against the wall. The linens were twisted in an untidy heap, as if D'Abanville had spent a very restless night the last time he slept there. She could just make out the slight indentation on the pillow where his head had rested. Mercy got a queer little twinge in her stomach as she looked at it and remembered that she had slept soundly as a baby in his arms the night before.

She looked toward the washstand beside the window. A linen lay half in and half out of the porcelain bowl. Even from where Mercy stood she could see that it was spotted with blood. She forced herself to cross the room. Within the bowl was a great amount of bloody water, the blood having settled on the bottom of the bowl, staining the white porcelain dark.

With another flap of its wings the bird flew to the windowsill. Opening its beak, it walked back and forth, giving Mercy the macabre sensation that it was laughing at her.

"Naughty girl!" the bird said. "Mer-cy. Mer-cy. Mercy, mercy, Miss Mercy. Pretty girl. Gotta biscuit?"

"No," Mercy snapped.

"Bugger ya, then," he responded. "Bye-bye!" Leaping from the windowsill, the jackdaw flew out the window, disappearing into the night.

Good riddance, Mercy thought, and with a sense of spiteful pleasure she lowered the window so he could not return.

Turning, she looked toward the only other piece of furniture in the room: a towering wardrobe-dresser combination. Her own reflection stared back at her from the silvered mirror over the dresser, which sported a single hairbrush and nothing else.

Mercy then stared at the wardrobe door, the button burning a hole in the palm of her hand.

Somehow she managed to cross the room, to take hold of the wardrobe door and pull it open. A rush of cedar-scented air washed over her. Cedar and something else. She thought of perfume, but it didn't stir up an image of flowers. Instead, that twinge came again, but not in her stomach this time. It was lower, suspiciously around her womb, flooding her lower body with a warmth that brought shame to her face.

There were numerous coats hanging within the wardrobe. She scanned the lineup, noting there were three dark blue coats that might or might not be missing two buttons. Opening her palm, she stared down at the button for several minutes, as if memorizing each nondescript detail; then she reached for the coat shoved to the very back of the wardrobe. That, of course, would be the one. Mercy pulled the heavy jacket out into the light.

The ornate gold buttons on the jacket twinkled in the lamplight. Relieved, she shoved it back into the wardrobe.

She tried the second coat. Buttons all in place.

The third.

Her heart stopped.

A button was missing.

Mercy closed her eyes. The room had suddenly turned unbearably warm, and the tea she had earlier shared with McMillian rose halfway up her throat before she could swallow it back. Don't panic, she told herself. There was nothing unusual about a coat missing a button. She had numerous blouses with missing buttons. Look at the button in your hand and see if it matches.

Very slowly she raised her hand and opened her fingers. She looked fixedly at the button, then shifted her gaze to the buttons on the coat. The place where the button was missing gaped like a mouth with a lost tooth.

Then she recalled: there were two buttons. The inspector had had two buttons, and this coat was missing only one! She checked the cuffs of his sleeves. No buttons missing there. With shaking hand she lifted the button in her fingers alongside the remaining buttons of his jacket. "They don't match!" she cried aloud.

Tap, tap, tap.

Mercy froze, the coat gripped to her chest as her eyes were drawn back to the window. The memory of her horrifying dream came back with a rush. As she watched the dark shadow move back and forth against the glass, she did her best to convince herself that this was reality, no nightmare. There was nothing diabolical beyond those glass panes. It was only . . .

The bird.

She saw it now, pecking on the window.

Tap, tap, tap.

"Go away," she whispered.

Tap, tap, tap.

Only the candle flame moved. For a moment it reflected off the bird's staring eye like a tiny smoldering ember; then the bird took flight again, suddenly, as if in alarm. That was when she heard the dogs barking.

Hurrying to the window, she opened it a tiny bit. Yes, she could hear them, yapping and howling frantically, the way she had heard them do each time they saw D'Abanville.

A rush of fear made her clammy with sweat. Glancing toward the door, she hurried back to the wardrobe, thrust the jacket inside, and was about to close the wardrobe door when she noticed the drawer in the floor of the closet. It wasn't a drawer exactly, more like a trapdoor or the hinged door of a small cupboard. Without thinking, she grabbed the pull and yanked it open. Folded neatly in the bottom of the drawer was a soiled navy-blue jacket.

Mercy knew, even before she dragged the clothing from its hiding place, that it would be missing two buttons. In fact, it was missing all its buttons. All, including the ones on the sleeves and the tucked pleats on the back of the jacket looked as if they had been sheared neatly off. Removed intentionally? To cover up a crime?

She looked toward the bedroom door.

Holding her breath, she listened to the heavy throbbing of blood in her ears. Her body, not just her hands, began to tremble uncontrollably. Her eyes watered with the strain of watching the door and waiting for it to move. Yet it did not. As long minutes passed and still no one had entered she began to relax.

Looking again into the cubbyhole she noted numerous articles wrapped in cloth and yellowed newspaper. Curiosity compelled her to pick up the one wrapped in muslin. She carefully unbound it and found a child's bracelet. Nothing elaborate. Just a very crude band of tin, with the equally simple stamp of P. R. No. 276. She rewrapped the bracelet and returned it to the drawer. She then picked up the paper and found it hid a locket. Inside the silver oval was the aged picture of a young woman, hardly older than herself. Mercy stared for sometime into her dark eyes, noting her dark hair and pale skin. Then reminding herself that her time was limited, she was about to rewrap the locket when she noticed the paper's headlines:

SERVANT FOUND MURDERED AT GREYSTONE

Casimire Curse Continues

Holding the paper closer to the light, Mercy squinted to make out the date. The month and day were too badly faded. The year, however, was 1861.

After rewrapping the locket, she placed it back in the drawer. There was no time to lose. D'Abanville would be returning any moment. Somehow she had to get this coat to her room so she could better inspect it for evidence.

She closed the wardrobe door, hurried to the window and raised it. Everything had to be just as D'Abanville had left it. With any luck, he would not notice the coat being gone before she could return it. She would take it to her room, where she could examine it thoroughly, convince herself of Dominick's innocence or guilt. She would do nothing about contacting Chesterton before that.

She left the room, carefully descended the stairs, her ears straining for any hint of approach. Outside the tower door, she stood at the end of the hallway, stared toward the far end at her reflection in the mirror. She looked slightly mad. She must be, she thought. No one in her right mind would attempt what she had just done. For that matter, no one in her right mind would have continued to stay in this house, in the company of a man who could be Jack the Ripper.

She started down the corridor, clutching the dark blue bundle to her chest fiercely. In that moment Miriam rounded the corner.

"What on earth are you doing, Mercy?"

Mercy stopped abruptly. She felt the blood drain from her cheeks as Miriam's gaze settled on the coat.

"What do you have there?" Miriam asked.

"Laundry."

Miriam frowned. With some hint of a darker thought on her expression she stared at Mercy's bundle. Finally she looked back at Mercy and asked, "Have you seen Dominick?"

"No."

"Do you know where he has gone?"

She shook her head.

"What are you doing down here with laundry?"

"It is only a jacket. I had worn it earlier and had left it in D'Abanville's office."

"Did you meet with Madame Cartier at two?"

Mercy nodded.

"When will the dresses be ready?"

Roger rounded the corner then. Mercy's anxiety intensified as he stared at Miriam, then at her. "Has either of you seen D'Abanville?" he asked.

Mercy checked her own nervousness before asking, "Has he returned?"

"I haven't seen him, but those blasted dogs are in a frenzy and I can't locate Micah." To Miriam he said, "We must sit Dominick down and discuss this matter of his going out at night. Do you know where he goes?"

"I told you I don't. Perhaps he has another mistress already."

"God forbid," he muttered. Taking off his glasses, he vigorously wiped the lenses. "I will be in my office. If either of you sees him—"

"Yes, yes. Good night, Roger."

Before Mercy could bid him a good night, Roger whirled on his heel and was gone around the corner. Looking at Miriam, she said, "Is there anything more?"

"No."

Mercy stepped around her and started down the hall.

Miriam called out, "Miss Dansing!"

She stopped but did not turn.

"Have you spoken to Chesterton again?"

Closing her eyes, she lied, "No."

Silence.

"Is there anything else?" Mercy asked.

The answer was a moment in coming. Finally, "That will be all."

She walked slowly down the corridor, rounded the corner, and picked up her pace. She took the stairs two at a time, hurried down the long corridor to her bedroom door. Her hand paused on the knob while she steadied her breathing, then she slipped into the room, shut the door behind her, and, leaning against it, closed her eyes. She stood that way for a full minute, allowing the strength to return to her legs, allowing her heart to quiet its frantic racing. Then she opened her eyes and looked directly at D'Abanville.

He did not say anything at first. Mercy stared straight into his face and could see nothing but his eyes fixed on hers and the cold, slow curl of his mouth as the minutes dragged by. When he finally spoke the quiet sound was shattering in its gentle fury.

"What were you doing there?"

She tried to swallow.

"I said, what the hell were you doing there, in my room?" He moved out of the shadow and into the light. His hair was wet and clinging to his brow; the lamplight glistened off the rain-wet wool of his overcoat in a thousand pinpoints of light.

She tried to speak, but nothing came out.

"Well?" he said softly. "Is that, or is it not, my jacket?"

Mercy wet her lips with her tongue, though it did little good. Her mouth was too dry to speak. When she tried, the words came out sounding small and hoarse and more frightened than she was willing to admit even to herself.

"I found this button . . . I thought it might be yours . . . I was looking for you—"

"Tell me the truth, Mercy."

Mercy groaned. The coat slipped from her fingers to the floor.

He raised his dark brows. "You saw Chesterton today, didn't you?"

"No."

"Mercy."

"No."

He stared and his face looked savage as he waited for her to continue.

He said in a tone full of bitter anger, "You spoke with him some ten minutes outside Briggs Travel."

She gasped.

"Then you went on to Madame Cartier's, then later had tea with McMillian. You then followed me to White-chapel Road, where you spoke to a policeman. What did you tell him, Mercy—that you were following Jack?"

She began to cry silently. Tears streaming down her face, she waited for him to sweep onto her with a blood-ied knife and slice her into ribbons. She would prefer that to the painful silence that stretched out between them. Prefer it to the bare look of pain she could see in his eyes. She had betrayed him, and he knew it. He had never treated her with anything but kindness and consid-eration, and she had gone behind his back with every intention of proving him to be a murderer. She owed him the truth. All of it. If he was the Ripper, she wasn't about to leave this room alive, regardless.

"Yes!" she finally admitted. "I met Chesterton today, but it was not planned. He followed me from Greystone, waited until he found me alone, then informed me that another two women were murdered last night."

He didn't say anything. He only stood rigid for an ex-cruciatingly long moment, waiting for her to continue.

"Then he gave me this button, said it was found in Miss Russell's hand and must have been torn off her killer's jacket. He asked that I look through your wardrobe for a jacket with missing buttons. I found it." She pointed one shaking finger toward the jacket at her feet.

His eyes shifted to the floor, then back to her face.

"Will you deny it's your jacket?" she prompted.

"Certainly not."

"Then will you deny that you killed that young woman? Will you deny that you are the Whitechapel murderer?"

"Would it do me any good?"

She tried, oh, how she tried, to center her attention on the open collar of his dress shirt. There was a pulse fluttering there, strong and heavy, in the column of his throat, but she couldn't. Against her will her gaze was drawn back to his, and was caught, powerless to look away again.

"Did you kill Abigail Russell?" she heard herself asking. Only it didn't sound like her voice. This voice was deeper, huskier, and slow, drugged by some emotion she had never experienced before. There was fear, yes. There was desperation, but it was a greater desperation than she had felt even at starvation's hand. Her body was a stranger to her, alive and full of heat for a man who could be the devil himself. She was shamed by it. Tortured by it. They weren't right, these feelings. What sort of person was she, that she could not look at him and disbelieve the evidence laid out before her? Dear God, what had happened to her own sense of decency?

Suddenly covering her wet face with her hands, she turned back toward the door, pressed her body against it as if she could somehow absorb herself into the cold hard mahogany. She could not hide. She could not vanish from his sight as he could from hers, no matter how she willed it.

Angrily she wept. "Did you kill her? Did you kill them? Are you the monster Chesterton believes you are?" Silence. "Answer me!" She clenched her fist and hit the door.

"No," he finally responded.

"Liar!"

Spinning back toward him, she swiped the tears from

her eyes and regarded him madly. The confident, almost arrogant manner with which he had acted earlier had vanished. His expression was strained, serious, his eyes dark with emotion, and he looked strangely vulnerable. He did not speak, just stared at her with a longing and pain and bitterness that wrenched at her heart.

"Liar," she repeated, her voice a ragged tear of emotion. "I saw the bloody cloths. I saw the knives—"

"What the hell are you saying?"

"The knives! The knives in that room off the tower! The knives in the gray metal box!"

He shook his head, unwilling to believe that Mercy would even for a moment consider that he could truly be the murderer. Several long moments passed as he stared at her with that terrible anguish. His eyes dark as stones, he tore off one kid glove, then slowly lifted his hand, palm out, for her to see.

"The blood is mine. See for yourself. The knives are a part of my act. You know that. *You know that!* This afternoon I was practicing and caught the blade wrong. Mercy, the blood is mine!"

She closed her eyes and wept.

He moved up against her, smelling of cold night air and a trace of brandy. He was all power and strength. All sunlight and shadow, heat and bitter cold, warming her with his body and chilling her with his eyes. Run! her mind implored her. Yet her body could do nothing more than sway against him as he curled his gloved fingers along the curve of her jaw. She could smell the leather of his glove, could feel the cool bite of the kidskin into her flesh as he molded her lips with his thumb. Then those black-clad fingers were sliding around her head, tunneling through her hair, gripping, dragging her head back so she was forced to turn her face up to his.

"God help me, but I am a lost man," he said, his words soft against her mouth, his eyes bright with a madness born of despair. "Lost! Who is left for me if you don't believe me?"

"You have Roger and Miriam," she heard herself utter.

"I've heard them talking. They don't believe me, but

they need me. Without me they would be back in the gutters of Paris."

Turning her face from his, she said, "Miriam loves you. How can you think otherwise?"

"She loves what I am, what I can give her. Just like all the others before and after her who would not have thrown me a pence if I were an orphan and lay starving at their feet. It is the fame they love, not the man."

He released her suddenly and spun away. The silence was terrible then, as taut as a thread stretched to its endurance, unendurable in its magnitude. He paced the room, his black cloak swirling around his legs each time he turned. Finally he tore it from his shoulders and flung it aside before facing her again.

"Behold the Great D'Abanville!" he said savagely. "The Eighth Wonder of the World! Be he devil or angel? You will be mystified by his magic!" He laughed harshly. "Isn't it rather ironic that once I would have sacrificed anything to become the celebrity that I am now? And now that I am a celebrity I would sacrifice almost anything to be the man I was then."

His face looked tired suddenly, and the violence that had maddened his eyes appeared to dull. "In you I saw the perfect solution," he said more softly. "I saw a woman who would not, for a change, be blinded by my celebrity." He closed his eyes, shook his head, and when he spoke again, the anger was back, biting, caustic, making Mercy shrink against the door as he walked toward her. "Now, by God, I wish that you were blinded by my celebrity. I wish you were impressed by the fame. I wish you *did* believe in the magic I can show you. Because, Mercy, I am very, *very* good at it."

Unable to speak, she sank back against the door, doing her best to escape his nearness, the soft, alluring tone of his voice that could so enchant and mystify, mesmerize.

His hand came up and he brushed her cheek with his fingers. Staring down at her, his face bleak and still, he said sardonically, "Am I so vile? So terrifying that you cannot even pretend to tolerate my touch, Mercy? Many women have before, for a price. For Abby it was rubies. For others it was diamonds or a château on the Riviera. What would you like, Mercy? Obviously its not pearl-

and-diamond brooches. Certainly there is something you want. Perhaps the tuition to nursing school?''

At her soft gasp, he smiled. ''Ah. I thought so. Everyone has a price, it seems. For you it shall be the opportunity to become the next Florence Nightingale.''

Before she could deny his accusation, his mouth closed hard on hers, punishing, overwhelming her, so that whatever insanity had gripped her momentarily was shattered with the abruptness of a blow. She was all too aware of his body against her, hard against hers where hers was achingly soft and disturbed. His hips pressed, rubbed. His tongue darted against her own like a flicking flame, then again, slower this time, mimicking the slide and thrust of his hips upon hers as he pressed her back against the door.

She shook her head, making noises of denial in her throat, yet keenly aware of how hot his mouth was upon hers, forcing hers open with a pressure and possessiveness that were breathtaking. This was no George Balfour, whose ineptitude at lovemaking had matched her own. He was virile and powerful and overwhelming. As she had known he would be. It would be so easy to forget what he might be, and think only of what he was. A magic man. A man whose beauty and masculinity could stop women on the street. A man who had known dozens, perhaps hundreds of lovers and who would, no doubt, love her, use her, and then forget her as easily as he had Abigail Russell and Miriam.

Still, she was powerless to resist him. Her head fell back as he moved his mouth slowly down the pale column of her throat, kissing, licking, nuzzling the fluttering pulse in her throat, tongue darting along the throbbing vein in her neck until she thought she might scream. His black-gloved hand ran up her waist and closed over her breast, causing a flurry of fire to ignite again between her legs, the heat and pressure mounting until her body, already a stranger to her, began to writhe against his in a seductive rhythm that made him groan in response.

She closed her eyes, for the world was tilting and swaying again, spinning round, making her dizzy. Flashes of fog and blackness skirted through her mind, images of those headlines screaming caution to a world grown wild with fear. Rolling her head, she saw his coats on the floor, the one with missing buttons, the other so damp with rain she could smell the heavy odor of wet wool from where she stood.

She groaned as the desire she had felt mere seconds before changed to a sort of blind panic. His hand slipped within her blouse, cupped her breast while his mouth went on kissing her throat, her ear, yet when he tried to kiss her mouth she turned her face away and said, "Don't. Please don't."

"Mercy—"

"No!"

"Look at me, dammit."

She shook her head, closed her fingers around the hand on her breast, and shoved it away. "Let me go or I'll scream," she told him flatly.

"Why should I care?" He sneered. "Murderers usually get their pleasure from screaming women, or haven't you read that far in the papers?"

She pushed on his shoulders.

He caught her wrists in a punishing grip and shoved them back against the door over her head. His face threatening and his drying hair tumbling like a soft black cloud to his eyes, he said, "You *do* believe it all, don't you? Just like the rest of London, you think I killed those women." Releasing his grip on her wrists, he pressed his cool, slightly trembling fingers against her face. "Mercy. You must know that I couldn't possibly have killed those women."

"I don't know you at all," she said breathlessly. "All I know is when I'm near you I change. I'm not myself, and that frightens me. You frighten me. I don't know what to think or feel—"

"You might try a little trust, a little faith; God knows I've done all I can to show you I care, that I'm not the sort of man who could commit murder."

"Like you cared for Abby Russell or the latest—what was her name?—Kinsdale?"

"I did not know that woman!" he shouted, angrier now than Mercy had seen him. "What in God's name must I do to prove to you that I am innocent of these crimes?"

"Tell me why you were going to Whitechapel!" she shouted back.

His face dark, he said more quietly, with a small shake of his head, "Mercy, I can't do that. Just trust me. I need you to trust me. Why must you question my integrity after what I have tried to do for you?"

"Integrity?" She almost laughed. "Dear God, I wish it were that simple—only question your integrity? D'Abanville, I often question whether you exist at all. I fear occasionally that you aren't even human."

He backed away. There was fury now. She could feel it, see it in the stance of his wide shoulders, the way his fists opened and closed like steel traps. She had the horrible premonition that he was about to transform into some grotesque fire-belching monster, and she began to shake.

"Human," he snarled inhumanly. "Show me anything remotely human about this entire rat-infested city." He began to pace the room.

"Human," he repeated. "God help me, how can I do that? It is easier, I think, to convince you that I am not human. I can materialize money, flowers, and birds with a snap of my fingers. I can turn water to wine and wine to water before your eyes, and I can levitate beautiful women in midair. I'll convince you that I can walk through walls, for God's sake, or disappear into thin air, but how do I convince you that I'm human?"

He looked almost frantically about the room. Spying the tea service where she had earlier drunk tea and snacked on cheese and biscuits, he strode to it quickly, picked up the tiny bone-handled knife, and faced Mercy again.

"You want proof that I'm human," he snarled. "So be it." He laid the blade of the knife against the palm of his hand, and before Mercy could cry out for him to stop, had opened the flesh of his palm from his fingers up to his wrist. She wept in alarm as blood rushed in glistening crimson ribbons through his fingers to the floor.

His face pale, he asked in a hoarse, desperate whisper, "Is this proof enough?"

She stumbled away, shielding her eyes from the sight

with her hands. "Oh, God," she cried, "don't. Don't! You don't understand. Chesterton is so positive—"

"I didn't kill them."

"Please!"

"Why would I want to kill them?"

"Those poor women . . . that horrible knife." She shuddered, shrank against the door, certain she could smell the blood from his wound as he neared her. "Stay away!" she told him.

"Chesterton is wrong."

"But the buttons, the coat—"

"Mercy, the coat is several years old. The buttons were used to replace others."

"I saw you! I followed you to Whitechapel! Why were you there? Why won't you tell me?"

"You have to know that I couldn't kill them."

"How do I know? How can I know?"

He tried to touch her face.

"Don't touch me!"

"Please. I would never hurt you. I . . . never would. All I want—"

"I don't care what you want!" With all the force she could muster, she drove her hands against his chest, shoving him backward. She spun toward the door, tripping over the coat, clutching at the doorknob as if it were some lifeline to save her from hell. His hand, hot and slick with blood, closed onto her wrist and she screamed. "Don't. Please don't!"

"Look at me. Mercy, I need you to believe in me. If you don't, I don't think I can—"

She jerked her hand away, opened the door, and without looking at him again, cried, "Get out. Just get out! I have to have time to think."

There was silence then as she waited. He stood in the door, blood running down his fingers in red streams as he watched her eyes. Finally he left the room, and she closed the door, pressed her face against it, feeling, rather than hearing, his footsteps diminish down the hall. Only when she was certain that he was gone did she open the door. Miriam stood in the shadows of the corridor, her face pale, skirts gripped in her hands as she stared down at the blood on the floor.

"Why did you make him leave?" Miriam asked. "I think he cares for you very deeply, Mercy. Very much."

She covered her ears with her hands. "Because he frightens me."

"Does he? Or are you simply frightened by your feelings for him? Afraid of becoming another Abby Russell or another poor alcoholic Miriam whose bitterness drives her into everyone else's bed because D'Abanville won't have her any longer? Afraid of becoming a whore, Miss Dansing? Or afraid of becoming human?"

Mercy shook her head in denial.

The elegant flounced skirt of Miriam's gauze-and-satin evening dress rustled in the stillness as she approached Mercy. Stopping before her, Miriam raised her hands and began tugging away the combs and pins that kept her mass of dark hair anchored to the top of her head. The chestnut coils slid like fine silk over her shoulders, and with a toss of her head Miriam said, "His one dream was to perform for the queen. That suspicious little man from Scotland Yard is ruining that for him. He is suffering, and shouldn't be alone tonight. I've seen him when he's hurting and . . . he shouldn't be alone. If you don't go to his room and comfort him, I will."

Mercy shook her head, too stunned to think.

"Then you're a fool."

Miriam turned and walked down the hall, paused and looked around. "I warn you. I'll do everything in my power to make him take me back."

"I . . . I don't care." It was a lie and she knew it.

Then Miriam was gone, leaving Mercy to stare in mute disbelief before she forced herself to return to her room. She tried to convince herself that the last half-hour had never happened. The fear of being followed, the horror of following him to Whitechapel, then finding that coat, the terror of being discovered—it was too much to cope with. She felt as if she would crumble apart into tiny pieces the way Mary Casimire's diary had disintegrated when exposed to air.

What was even more paralyzing was her behavior with D'Abanville. He had looked at her and she had melted. He had touched her and she had trembled, not with fear, but with longing. Dear God, whom was she fooling? She

was already a whore. *His* whore: D'Abanville's. It made
no difference that she had not actually offered him her
body, she had fantasized it enough times to make it real.

She slammed the door behind her, stood in the middle
of the room, her breasts rising and falling rapidly while
she stared in the mirror at her reflection. Her hands were
clenched. Her disarrayed silver hair spilled like wild spun
cotton to her hips; there were spots of high color on her
otherwise white cheeks, and her mouth was dark and
swollen from the fierceness of D'Abanville's passion. She
didn't look much like Mercy Dansing.

She didn't feel much like Mercy Dansing either.

Dear God, what had she become?

Miriam was right. She was more frightened of her own
sexuality than she was of D'Abanville. She wasn't terrified by his touch, or because the CID thought him a
killer—she knew in her heart he wasn't a killer—she was
angry and terrified of her response to his touch. He made
her feel the way no decent woman should want to feel.
He made her yearn to do those things she had seen Ollie's
girls do with men, wild things, shameful things, dirty
things that made them scream and laugh and cry all at
once, that made men half-crazed with passion so they
pleaded for it on their knees . . . whatever *it* was. She
wanted to know what *it* was. Whatever, it had been
churning around in her body since the moment she first
saw Dominick D'Abanville, expanding to every nerve,
turning her into some restless, aching entity that she could
not recognize any longer.

Mercy walked to the window, found it still open and a
puddle of standing rainwater on the floor at the base of
the wall. Already the water had slightly swollen the old
wood, had bleached it gray. Angrily Mercy mopped up
the water. Then she moved to the blood and scrubbed it
furiously, as if making it disappear would somehow make
the boiling need inside her vanish as well. She followed
the trail of blood to the door, to the place where he had
stood and watched her, with blood running down his
hand. She stared at the puddle of glistening dark crimson,
and thought of him. She touched it, and thought of him.
And laying her hand down flat into it, thought of him as

she then ran her bloodied palm up the inside of her leg and pressed it against the hot, moist apex at her thighs.

1 May, 1788.

Mama and I took advantage of the break in the rain to journey to Brighton. What a wonderful day we spent! What made it even more special was Peter's companionship. Imagine my joy when learning Mama had asked Peter to drive us to Brighton. I fancy I giggled the entire journey there and back. At times Mama seems to suspect the romance blooming between Peter and me. But though she's never spoken of it, I somehow sense she approves. I see her smiling at us a little sadly occasionally. Several times she has commented: "What a nice young man. And so handsome." What good would her approval do us? None, I fear. Papa and Richard would never approve of our relationship, would never accept it. Our backgrounds, after all, are worlds apart.

As always, Brighton was teeming with activity. The three of us walked along the delectable row of shellfish stalls down by the harbor, Peter and I occasionally falling behind Mama so he could secretly catch my hand and hold it. How daring it all seemed. Several times I fancied he yearned to kiss me, there in front of Mama, in front of those boisterous, laughing fishermen. I flirted outrageously, hoping he would. We strolled, the three of us, arm in arm along the walk, selecting little bowls of cockles, mussels, whelks, and oysters; shaking on pepper and vinegar and swallowing the gorgeous things whole.

We met a peddler with a cart full of trinkets. There were bells and ribbons and bolts of brightly dyed cloths. I saw a music box that I fancied. Peter asked the peddler to wind it. When he did, Peter swept my mother into his arms and they danced, laughing, across the Palace Pier. I felt slightly jealous watching them, I must admit. I did not know until much later, during the ride home, that Peter had bought me the box and had hidden it within the folds of my cloak. Even as I write this, it is spinning before me, two lovers dancing round and round. Closing my eyes, I can almost imagine our laughing together on Palace Pier, heady with the smell of fish and the warm sun shining on our faces. I shall cherish those moments, and this music box, forever.

14

3 July, 1788.

Something terrible is happening in London. Several young women have been found brutally murdered, the latest being not far from Greystone. Her name seemed very familiar to me and I believe that she may have been a friend of Richard's. Peter warned Mama and me not to venture away from the estate without proper escort. Perhaps it is my imagination but I felt during my walk about the grounds this afternoon that I was being observed from a distance. The feeling was so strong and frightening that I returned indoors as quickly as possible.

The tower is nearly completed. What is it about the addition to Greystone that frightens me so? Richard has invited Mama and me into it, but we have both declined. It is an evil thing, I told him, and he became angry. But then, Richard is always angry these days. His violent temper frightens me. Just last evening he goaded Peter into an argument. If Mama had not intervened I fear blows might have been exchanged. I fear Richard suspects that Peter and I are meeting, and that is the reason for his antagonism toward Peter.

Today we were forced to call the surgeon for Papa. His declining health weighs heavily on our minds. All except Richard's. Occasionally I actually believe he is eager for Papa's death. How I wish I could leave Greystone and take Mama and Papa and Peter with me. I should gladly leave this miserably cold place entirely to my brother. The longer I remain here, the more depressed I become. Call it intuition, but I feel if I don't escape Greystone soon, something terrible will happen to me. If it weren't for Peter I should feel nothing but unhappiness, I think. If he leaves London, as he's hinted he might, I shall ask him, beg him if I must, to take me to Paris with him . . . as his wife. Peter loves me. I know he does. Somehow I must convince him that regardless of our backgrounds, we were meant to be together as husband and wife.

My brother was visited again by several men, all of whom I considered disreputable-looking characters. They all adjourned to that dreadful tower. What do they do there? They stayed with Richard in the tower until after midnight. I knew the exact moment that they left because I had been awakened earlier by a horrible dream. It seems my nights are plagued with them, dreams of demons and voices and strange—

Mercy looked up from the book, into Stan McMillian's eyes. "Something must have distracted her. She did not finish the entry, I'm sorry to say."

"Have you read any further?"

"The ink is so badly faded it is almost impossible to read."

"I know someone to whom I can take it, if you'd like. It will be a very delicate and tedious chore, but I think he can decipher it."

Mercy stared down at the tattered book on the table.

As if reading her thoughts, McMillian said, "It is most distressing, is it not?"

She nodded. "She sensed that something was wrong with her brother all along. And those men she spoke of. I wonder who they were."

"Perhaps she will tell us later on." He sipped his tea, then frowned in concern. "I think I shall drop it by my friend's business this afternoon, if you don't mind."

She shoved it toward him.

"You seem disturbed, Miss Dansing. Is everything all right at Greystone?"

"I fear the CID will be taking Dominick in for questioning today."

"I'm certain it will turn out all right. I read in the paper that Commissioner Warren does not believe that the Russell and Kinsdale killings were related in any way to the Ripper killings."

"Chesterton does not feel that way."

"There are many investigators in the CID who would like to go down in history as the man who caught Jack the Ripper. I understand that they are bringing in at least a dozen men a day for questioning."

"They are desperate," she said. "That frightens me."

"Commissioner Warren is certainly under fire. There are many who are demanding his resignation. How was D'Abanville this morning?"

"I didn't see him. He lives up in that awful tower like a monk in a cave."

McMillian smiled kindly. "You are beginning to sound a little like Mary Casimire, my dear."

"Perhaps I know how she feels." Mercy closed her eyes. They felt raw and swollen, and gritted like sand against her lids. "There is something about that tower that makes my skin crawl."

"You could always leave Greystone. I doubt D'Abanville would keep you there against your will. I'm certain he would understand, considering the controversy surrounding him."

"Yes," she said, "he probably would." Checking the time, Mercy picked up her purse. "I told Roger I would be back by noon. I'll be late if I'm not off now."

He helped her from her chair. "I'll let you know as soon as I can about the diary. I'm certain you are as anxious as I am to learn the secret of the Casimire murders."

She bade him good-bye and caught a cab back to Greystone. Arriving, she found the gates closed and locked. Along the street people milled about, occasionally stopping and staring up the drive in curiosity. The banner carriers were back proclaiming D'Abanville as "Devil," "Son of Lucifer," "Warlock," and finally, *"Butcher!"* Squaring her chin, she walked through the crowd to the gates. Micah stepped out of the trees, a dog at his side, and released the lock, opening, then shutting the gate solidly behind her. As she turned up the drive, he caught her arm, and as she looked around, he offered her a flower and a smile.

"Thank you," she told him, and he blushed.

The house was quiet, as always. Mercy stopped by the library on her way to D'Abanville's office. Miriam was there, reclining on the sofa, her arm thrown over her eyes as if she were sleeping. As Mercy turned to leave, Miriam's voice stopped her.

"In case you're interested, he didn't want me."

"I'm not," Mercy responded, although there was no denying to herself that her heart had skipped a beat at the woman's admission.

"I suppose I was only misleading myself to think he would. You would have to know him as well as I to have noticed the differences in him since you came to Greystone. With the other women it didn't matter, you see. He used them for the moment, but when they were out of sight they were also out of mind. I should have had more pride, I suppose, but when you've been together as long as we have, been through hell together the way we have . . ."

Miriam stared at the ceiling, wet silver tear streaks running from the corners of her eye to her temples. "He never loved me. I knew that. He never once lied and said that he did, though I imagined that I saw it in those damned blue eyes. He has this way of making you believe it simply because you want it so badly you'll grasp at anything to give you some foundation for the feelings you have for him. I imagine that's what Abby was doing near Greystone the night she was killed. He had broken off with her earlier in the week and she hadn't taken it well. She had already been by twice to see him, thinking she could convince him back into her bed. He was kind the first time she called. He spoke to her for perhaps a quarter of an hour, then sent her on her way. The second time, he refused to see her at all. Do you know what it was like for me, having to tell that woman that the man she loved—or thought she loved—would not see her? Dear God, I hated the ground she walked on, but I sympathized with her. I knew the pain, but I also was brimming over with smug satisfaction because I thought: here is my opportunity to win him back. Can you believe the arrogance of that, Miss Dansing?''

Miriam looked at Mercy, waiting for her response. Mercy shook her head no.

Miriam rose on one elbow and stared directly at Mercy. Her face was pale, her eyes dull and sunken. ''Once I thought it was just that damnable magic,'' she said through her teeth. ''He lived and breathed it. It was an obsession with him, Miss Dansing. Nothing came before it. Nothing. And I shudder to imagine what might have happened to the person who somehow threatened it. It was a living, breathing entity inside him, consuming him, so that eventually it became harder and harder to find the man I first knew in Paris . . . the man I first loved. Dear God, it was so easy to love him then, and painless.'' She left the settee.

Mercy backed away as Miriam neared her. She could smell the heavy odor of gin and tobacco on her breath. Her eyes looked a little mad.

''Now I see it for what it was. It was a game with him, making those women fall in love with him. He always went after the most beautiful or the wealthiest. They were always bitches. Cold-blooded bitches. I could never understand why he wanted them. Then, as I was lying here, wallowing in self-pity, it suddenly struck me. He made them fall in love with him so irrevocably that when he turned his back on them he robbed them of every fiber of pride they owned. I have seen grown women draped in jewels fall on their knees and beg him for one more chance. One more toss in the doss, as they call it on Buck's Row.''

Miriam staggered slightly and gripped her stomach. ''God, what an idiot I am. We all were. I should tell you to get out of this house and never look back, but instead I'm going to stand here and tell you something that you probably don't want to hear.'' She looked at Mercy directly and said, ''The son of a bitch has fallen in love with you, Miss Dansing. Surprised? No more than I, believe me. I should have seen it coming, though. Of course, he would look for someone similar to himself: desperate and hungry but determined to fight her way out. Kind and compassionate, beautiful yet humble. Tell me, Miss Dansing, are you in love with him?''

She shook her head.

''Liar. Were you not in love with Dominick D'Abanville, you would have left Greystone days ago.''

Miriam swayed and Mercy grabbed her shoulders. She helped her to the sofa, where Miriam dropped back on her pillows with a sigh.

''Are you all right?'' Mercy asked.

Closing her eyes, Miriam dismissed her with a shake of her head. ''It's nothing I can't deal with. I didn't reach forty years of age relying on some wet-nosed nursemaid to hold my hand through a crisis.''

Mercy folded her hands in her lap and searched Miriam's features. The silence stretched for one minute, then two. Mercy looked out the window, concentrated on the birdsong that poured like music from a flute into the still room. It was a perfect, breathless afternoon, with the smell of roses hanging in the autumn air and the golden leaves of the beeches surrounding the house rattling like gentle rain on a tin roof. Finally Miriam spoke again.

''He has a good heart, Mercy, no matter what the gin in me says at times. He's been plenty good to me even if he didn't love me.''

Mercy was surprised as Miriam's hand caught her own and squeezed it gently. ''Stop fighting what you feel,'' she said. ''You'll regret it if you do. Believe me, when I look back on the few times I passed up some man's true affections—''

''But the murders,'' Mercy said softly.

''Do you think he did it?''

''Do you?''

''You've seen him as angry as he gets. Did he lift a hand to either of us? He never has, Mercy, and God knows I've given him every reason in the world to knock me to blazes and back. He's a devoutly religious man in his own way. I don't profess to understand his beliefs, but I understand enough to know that to raise a hand against a living being, be it human or animal, is totally against his principles.''

''Then what is he doing walking Whitechapel in the middle of the night?''

Miriam frowned. "That's where he's going?"

"I followed him myself last night."

"Christ." Miriam stared at the ceiling.

Mercy watched Miriam's face as she said, "Perhaps if we both approached him . . . ?"

"It'll never work. He won't talk unless he wants to. Roger and I have tried, since the moment he walked into Jacques's, to get him to reveal his past, if he's got one."

"He exists, so he's got one."

Miriam looked at her lazily. "Sometimes I wonder. There have been times, dearie, when I've questioned that myself."

Chesterton and his forces arrived at Greystone just after noon. Mercy was just sitting down with Roger and Miriam for lunch when a servant entered the dining room and announced that the CID wished to see D'Abanville. Roger was the first out of his chair. Mercy and Miriam followed him to the vestibule.

Despite the fact that the day was clear of clouds and the sun shone brightly, Chesterton still wore his mackintosh. His hands behind his back, he stared solemnly at the floor as he paced.

"What is the meaning of this?" Roger demanded upon entering the room. "Why have you brought these men with you?"

Chesterton stopped and raised his eyes to Roger's. "We have come to take D'Abanville in for questioning, of course."

"Certainly not. He is not to be treated like some beggar from the East End."

"Neither is he the King of England. He will come with us." Chesterton motioned for his men. Immediately they began to walk toward the corridor leading to D'Abanville's office. "We will search the entire premises if you do not call him."

Surprising even herself, Mercy stepped forward. "I'll get him."

Roger and Miriam looked around. Chesterton offered her a thin smile and said, "I trust that you will try nothing stupid. I have men stationed all about Greystone's grounds. He cannot escape."

"I'm certain he wouldn't even consider it," she responded coldly. Then, with a spitefulness she could not dismiss, she added, "Besides, if he chose to try, there is nothing you could do to stop him. His illusion of disappearing is quite remarkable, as you recall."

She smiled a bit smugly before turning her back on the inspector and quitting the foyer.

With a determination she did not feel in her heart, she walked to the towerhouse. No one had seen D'Abanville throughout the morning. Would it not be ironic if she found him missing after all? Closing her eyes briefly, she thought: I hope he is gone. I hope by now he is far, far away, where Chesterton can never find him.

She was not surprised at the thought. She had stared at the ceiling all night coming to her conclusions. Either she believed D'Abanville, or she did not. If she did not, she would leave Greystone and not look back. But she did believe him. Perhaps she did not understand the reasons he had for behaving the way he did, but she knew he could not be a murderer. It was that damnable faith that she had tried so hard to ignore these last months. It kept rearing up at the most inopportune times to rattle her control.

She climbed the towerhouse stairs and knocked on the door. There was no response. Trying the door and finding it unlocked, she shoved it open. D'Abanville lay on his bed, hands behind his head as he stared at the ceiling. He looked around at her as if anticipating her news.

"Chesterton is here," she said.

"Are they going to arrest me?"

"They only want to question you now." She walked to the bed, noting that he had not shaved and was wearing the same clothes he had worn to her room last evening. His hand was bandaged. The sleeve and cuff of his shirt were spotted with blood.

"You'll need to get out of that and into something laundered. Whatever you do, you must not appear defeated. You must appear totally confident of your innocence. I'll get a girl to fetch hot water so you can shave. How long will it take, do you think? Fifteen minutes?"

"Yes."

"I'll be back in ten."

She turned and walked back to the door.

"Mercy."

She looked around.

"I thought you would be gone. Why did you stay?"

"Bobby Brown," she said, starting to smile.

She left him staring after her and returned to the foyer to inform Chesterton that she had awakened D'Abanville and he was dressing. Meanwhile Miriam paced, growing more agitated by the moment. Roger did his best to calm her, but by the time Mercy left the vestibule to return to D'Abanville, Miriam was frantic and ranting at the inspector that he was a fool and she would see him run out of the CID, run out of London for that matter, just as soon as D'Abanville was cleared of all these trumped-up charges. Mercy heard him respond that so far no charges had been made against him, and that there would be no charges if D'Abanville could sufficiently explain himself.

Mercy hurried up the stairs and knocked on his door, waited with growing alarm when no response came. Finally she pushed open the door.

She stared at the steam rising from the basin of hot water before accepting the fact that D'Abanville was not there. His bloodied clothes lay on the floor; his wardrobe was open.

Almost mechanically Mercy turned, her mind blank, and ran down the stairs, throwing open doors along the corridor as she searched frantically for D'Abanville. Then Chesterton was there, at the end of the corridor, his eyes sharp with knowing as she faced him.

"He is gone," he said, "isn't he?"

Before she could respond, the police behind Chesterton began to span out, opening and slamming doors. Mercy heard Miriam's voice cry out, "You have no right to search this house. Get out! I forbid this sort of seizure!"

Spinning on his heel, Chesterton returned to the vestibule. "He cannot have gone far," he told his men. Then he stopped and faced Mercy again. "Of course, we have only Miss Dansing's word that he was ever here. Was he, Miss Dansing, or were you only attempting to protect him again?"

"He was here," she said coldly.

"I hope for your sake we find him."

"And just what the hell does that mean?" Miriam demanded.

"It means, madam, that I shall hold Miss Dansing personally responsible for his escape."

It was in that very moment that the burst of fire and smoke erupted within the open front doorway. One of the policemen cried out in surprise; another threw his hands up over his head, believing the house about to crumble about him. When the smoke began to clear, D'Abanville stepped casually into the room, dusting his black coat and smiling so coldly and smugly at Chesterton that Mercy's blood nearly froze.

"Grab him!" Chesterton bellowed.

The half-dozen policemen converged on D'Abanville, gripping their clubs in their hands in preparation for any hostile move he might make. He raised his hand and a crack of fire and smoke danced between one man's feet. The policeman yelped and jumped and the others all scrambled to a stop, uncertain if they should continue, their faces stricken with fear and doubt as they looked from D'Abanville back to Chesterton.

A long moment of silence passed. Mercy could only stare. The acrid smoke burned her nostrils like sulfur and made her eyes ache so badly she wanted to blink. But she didn't. Suddenly her surroundings seemed far too surreal, as if she were dreaming this entire occurrence.

"Well?" Chesterton raged. "What are you waiting for? Apprehend this fiend before he escapes!"

D'Abanville looked at them casually and said, "The first man who touches me will be turned into a toad."

No one moved and D'Abanville began to laugh. It was a terrible sound; inhuman. Mercy, for the first time since last night, wondered if he were truly insane.

"I am always amazed at how people allow themselves to be manipulated by their imaginations," he stated mildly. Then he moved further into the room, smiling more broadly as the policemen backed away. Walking directly up to Chesterton, his face a smiling mask, he said, "Well? Here I am, Inspector. Go ahead. I'm certain you would not ask your men to do anything you wouldn't do. Or would you?"

Seconds ticked by before Chesterton, visibly trembling in anger, drew himself up and took D'Abanville by the arm.

Immediately the others scrambled toward him, several grabbing D'Abanville roughly by the arms, nearly knocking him to the floor.

"This is an outrage!" Roger cried. "You are treating this man like a common criminal, Inspector!"

Miriam threw herself among them, doing her best to shove the humiliated and angered policemen aside, while Mercy backed up against the wall, her eyes fixed on D'Abanville's face, so black with anger she was afraid in that instant that he might certainly strike out.

Chesterton pulled a pair of shining steel handcuffs from his pocket and slammed them onto D'Abanville's wrists. Mercy looked to Dominick's eyes and saw it coming, the loss of control. It shattered like a mirror breaking; his face turned violent and his hands clenched in savagery as he wrenched his arms apart, attempting to snap the cold metal of the cuffs in two. Then, turning his burning eyes on the smirking inspector, he said through his teeth, "If you think these toys can hold me, Chesterton, you are sadly misled. Now, tell these men to let me go or you will sorely regret the day you were born."

"Is that a threat, D'Abanville? And before so many witnesses too?"

"Aye, and it is not idle."

Sufficiently recovered from her shock to allow some semblance of reason to propel her, Mercy shoved her way through the men to stand at D'Abanville's side. She glared at the inspector. "This is totally unfair. You said you meant only to take him in for questioning. If this is how you treat a mere suspect, I shudder to imagine what you do with a proven villain."

"As far as I am concerned, Miss Dansing, he *is* a proven villain."

"That will be up to the courts to decide, should charges be pressed against him."

Chesterton looked from Mercy to D'Abanville, his sensibilities returning as his anger cleared. That implacable look returning once again to his face, he raised one eyebrow and gave his men a quick nod of his head. "Very well. As long as you pose no threat, sir, you will be treated accordingly." He glanced down at the cuffs on D'Abanville's wrists, and he began to smile. He motioned toward the door. "Shall we go?"

"The cuffs!" Roger exclaimed.

"Remain," Chesterton replied, his eyes not leaving his prisoner. He motioned again toward the door. "After you, sir."

After a moment D'Abanville turned toward the door. Mercy stepped after him, clinging to his arm and placing herself between him and the policemen, who seemed too eager to react to D'Abanville's smallest movement, threatening or not. As they stepped out of the house to the waiting coach, D'Abanville stopped and looked down at her.

"I'm going with you," she told him.

"I don't think that would be a very good idea," Chesterton said. Opening the coach door, he took hold of D'Abanville's arm and smiled. "I fear this may all seem rather grueling to you, my dear, and upsetting to your sensibilities."

"Don't let my looks deceive you, sir. I am much stronger than I might appear to be."

"Indeed." He looked at D'Abanville. "What is it about you, D'Abanville, that enlists such loyalty from the young ladies? It seems they all would walk through fire to remain at your side."

"Why don't you ask them?" he responded in a low voice.

"I would, but two of them—or is it six?—are already dead." Thin lips curling in a smile, he nodded toward the coach door. "After you, sir. And the young lady, if she persists."

They boarded the coach, Mercy and D'Abanville on one side, Chesterton and one of his men on the other. As the vehicle moved away, they could hear Miriam screaming for Greystone's driver to bring their own carriage around.

Micah was at the gates, holding them open for their passage, his face white as he watched the coach drive by. Mercy caught a glimpse of him raising his hand in a childlike wave that made him seem like a suddenly orphaned infant. Seeing him, D'Abanville leaned quickly to the window and called out, "I'll be back, Micah!"

He smiled and repeated, "I'll be back!" Then the policeman across from him took hold of his arm and shoved
him back in his seat. For a moment D'Abanville's face
went dark as he glared at Chesterton's man, and Mercy
held her breath. It was almost reflex that she reach out
and place her hand on his arm. The moment passed.

The crowd outside Greystone had grown to an alarming
number. The coach was forced to slow as the onlookers
surged about them for a closer look.

"They've got him!" a voice called out.

"Hang 'im!" someone else shouted.

Then the coach rocked ominously as several pedestrians attempted to climb aboard. Police whistles shrieked
and the shouting outside swelled to a fever pitch of excitement that brought a hurling of stones against the
coach. Mercy cried out as one well-aimed rock sailed
through the window and glanced off D'Abanville's brow,
just above his eye. Mercy dragged him down into her lap,
even as Chesterton grabbed Mercy and sheltered her
while the policeman attempted to close off the window.

Not until they were finally through the crowds and
speeding off through London's crowded streets did Chesterton allow them up. His brow cut and bleeding,
D'Abanville stared at Chesterton with such bare hate in
his eyes that Mercy feared he might try something foolish. She sat frozen, senses tottering between hysteria and
despair, breathing too fast, her stomach weak and her
ears ringing with fear as she watched a slow, thin stream
of red zigzag through his heavy brow and form a tear at
the corner of his eye. His glance at Chesterton said: *You
did this!* and the contortion of his face hinted at an im-
pending explosion of anger that would destroy him for
certain if he allowed it to happen.

She reached for his hand, pressed it, feeling it shake
even as his long fingers curled into a fist against her palm.
And though he refused to look at her, he sat back in his
seat and used the backs of his hands to wipe at the blood
on his brow. He only succeeded in smearing it over his
face, which made him look all the more demonic, Mercy
thought. But she dared not offer aid. He was treading a
fine line of control. Even the slightest nudge might send
him toppling.

They rode for perhaps twenty minutes before the coach stopped. Mercy glanced out the window, believing they had arrived at the police station on Commercial Street. She was wrong. She recognized the building immediately as Saint George's Mortuary.

She looked directly at Chesterton, unwilling to believe what was about to take place. He motioned for his assistant to see D'Abanville from the coach, while he himself jumped to the street and held up his hand for Mercy. She refused to take it, instead stepping down by herself and waiting for D'Abanville to disembark. He did, slowly and with reluctance, his features becoming tighter as the reality began to sink in.

"Perhaps the young lady would choose to remain in the coach," Chesterton said.

"Out of the question," she responded.

They moved as a group into the building. The wooden floors beneath their feet rang out hollowly as they went past several offices and down a corridor that ended in an open doorway. They stopped at the doorway and Mercy caught a glimpse of a crude wooden coffin in the distance. About it sat several attendants, who left their chairs immediately upon seeing the inspector. They gaped at Dominick in blatant fear.

"After you, Mr. D'Abanville," Chesterton said.

"What is this about?" His voice sounded slightly hoarse. Mercy heard the fear in it, and the dread.

"I only want to reacquaint you with your latest victim. Under cover of darkness, I'm certain you can't be fully aware of the extent of your crime."

D'Abanville's dark head came around and he stared into Chesterton's eyes. "Go to hell. I'm not about to subject myself to this."

"You will go freely or be carried." The policeman put his hand on D'Abanville's back and shoved. Dominick almost tripped before righting himself. Then Chesterton took one arm, the policeman the other. They walked him to the coffin and told the attendants to remove the lid. They did. Mercy, leaning against the wall outside the door, closed her eyes and covered her face with her hands.

"Now, tell me, Mr. D'Abanville, have you ever seen this woman before?"

The answer was a moment in coming.

"Well? Look closely, sir, and try to recollect."

"No."

"You did not approach one Catherine Eddowes on the night of 30 September and offer money for a return of her sexual favors?"

"No."

"You did not lure her to Church Passage leading to Mitre Square and butcher her?"

"No."

"Look more closely and—"

"I told you!" he exploded. "I did not kill this woman. For God's sake, what must I do to convince you of that?"

Turning back to the policeman, Chesterton said, "It is on to Commercial Street."

Once they were boarded and on their way, they passed St. Mary's Church, wound their way down one wide street after another. Whatever anger and fight had bolstered D'Abanville earlier had now gone. Mercy saw it in the slight drooping of his shoulders, in the paleness of his face. Chesterton had set out to put a chink in D'Abanville's armor by forcing him to face the gruesomeness of the ugly, horrible affair, and he had succeeded.

For the first time, Mercy allowed herself to believe, beyond any doubt, in his innocence. Perhaps it was Chesterton's devout belief in his guilt that made her realize the full extent of its absurdity. Then the new realization came upon her, slowly, no thunderous revelation, but an awakening that crept through her, filling her, wrapping around her heart and squeezing until she wanted to weep out loud. She was in love with D'Abanville. Hopelessly in love.

Mercy looked at his hands and found them clasped. Leaning into him slightly, she covered them with one of her own and waited for him to look around at her.

"I believe you," she said.

His eyes questioned her. Doubted her.

She raised her hand and placed it against his face. "I believe you," she repeated. And she meant it.

* * *

They were taken to the back of the Commercial Street police station, then ushered through several long corridors and into a room where they waited ten minutes before they were joined by a very distinguished-looking man. Mercy recognized him from the sketches in the broadsheets and newspapers: Police Commissioner Sir Charles Warren.

He was a very handsome man with kind eyes but with the beleaguered expression of one who is at his wits' end. He smiled absently at Mercy as introductions were made. His eyes became sharper, however, as he regarded D'Abanville.

"Mr. D'Abanville, what a pleasure to finally meet you. I caught your performance at the Alhambra last spring. It was wonderful." He then noted the cuffs on D'Abanville's wrists. "Oh, dear, I'm certain these are not needed." He motioned to the policeman who had applied the cuffs to remove them.

"That's not necessary," D'Abanville said. With a gentle tilt of his hands, the cuffs fell to the floor. His old smugness returning, he shifted his gaze to Chesterton, whose mouth had thinned with irritation. He said, "There isn't a pair of those made that can hold me."

Warren cleared his throat and invited D'Abanville to sit down. Mercy took a chair just behind him and to his right. A man at the far end of the table where they sat took up a pencil and paper and began to draw. Another began to scribble words on a pad of paper.

"I'm sorry to have to put you through this inconvenience," the commissioner said, "but surely you understand our situation. I must tell you, sir, that you are not obliged to say anything unless you wish to do so, but what you say may be put into writing and given in evidence should we bring charges against you. Do you understand this?"

"I understand that your inspector has been harassing me. I did not kill Abigail Russell or Mrs. Kinsdale or the women in the East End. Have you some definite evidence that I did?"

"We will get to that. I want to put some questions to you about the offense with which you may or may not be charged. If you wish to make a statement, a record shall be kept of the time and place during which you made it, and you will be allowed to review your statement and sign it upon completion of this interview."

"Fine," D'Abanville said. "I would like to make a statement. I did not kill anyone. Now, tell me what evidence you have against me."

"For one, your rather stormy relationship with Miss Russell and the fact that she was killed so close to your home."

"There was nothing stormy about the relationship, Commissioner, until I ended it. She wasn't thrilled about it, but when such a relationship such as we had ends, usually there are bad feelings on one or both sides. That does not necessitate murder. And the idea that I am Jack the Ripper is asinine."

"There were some similarities between her killing and the ones attributed to Jack."

"Such as?"

"She was knifed extensively."

"The East End killings were blasted in detail over every London broadsheet. Anyone could have copied those killings. For all you know, each of these killings may have been committed by a different man."

The commissioner sat back in his chair, one arm outstretched over the tabletop at his side, his fingers drumming impatiently as he looked from Chesterton back to D'Abanville. Only occasionally did his intense eyes stray to Mercy, but when they did, she saw the strain of the ordeal on his face, and his desperation. That was what worried her most.

Warren took a deep breath and released it. "Mr. D'Abanville, were you having sexual relations with Amanda Kinsdale?"

"I did not know the woman."

"You met at the charity ball for St. Thomas Hospital in July."

"I meet a great many women."

"Do you often have sex with the women you encounter at these functions?"

"Occasionally. There are always women who find affairs with a celebrity somewhat stimulating."

"Normal sex?" He flashed Mercy a regretful look.

"Define 'normal,' " D'Abanville said.

"Vaginal intercourse, or anal intercourse?"

"I cannot imagine what business it would be of yours."

"Do you practice, or have you ever practiced, homosexuality?"

"I don't intend to answer this line of questioning. It is none of your business."

"I have a witness, a friend of Miss Russell's, who will testify that not long before Miss Russell's death, she confided that you were not 'ordinary.' "

"That could mean a great many things. It does not mean that I'm not normal or that I might be perverted. What has this to do with the murders, anyway?"

"Do you solicit prostitutes?"

"Do you, Commissioner?"

"Remembering that we may or may not already have witnesses to testify to the fact, I will repeat the question: Do you make a practice of soliciting the services of prostitutes, Mr. D'Abanville?"

"Occasionally."

"How often?"

"Only if I am between relationships."

"Between mistresses."

"Yes."

"And you have *never* solicited such a service during your involvement with a young woman? . . . Well?"

"P-perhaps. I cannot remember."

"Why would you do such a thing if you were already 'involved'?"

"I fear I am already on trial here," D'Abanville stated, his voice hard and verging on anger. "What has this to do with anything?"

Chesterton, who had been pacing, stopped suddenly and looked at D'Abanville with obvious disgust. "It has to do with this: These killings were perpetrated by a deviate, and I am quite certain you are that deviate."

As D'Abanville began rising from his chair, the commissioner caught him by the shoulder and forced him back down. "That will be quite enough," Warren said to Chesterton. "Mr. D'Abanville is quite right to be upset. But I hope that he will understand our concerns.

There are certain elements of this case that have been discussed with numerous experts in the field who can and will lead us to the sort of individual who is committing these heinous crimes.''

Warren offered D'Abanville a cigar.

D'Abanville refused it.

"Would you like coffee, then? Or tea, perhaps? Miss Dansing, may we get you something?''

She shook her head.

Warren's smile was kind, but tired. "I regret this line of questioning. It must be very upsetting to you to see your friend go through this. How long have you worked for Mr. D'Abanville?''

"Two weeks.''

"Oh? So short a time? Where did you work before this, my dear?''

"I was unemployed.''

"And lived where?''

"The East . . .'' She bit her lip.

"The East End? I'm certain you are glad to be out of there. Did you personally know any of the women who were killed?''

"Polly Nichols.''

"Ghastly ordeal. Such a crime.''

"I consider what you are doing to Mr. D'Abanville a crime,'' she said. She saw D'Abanville's head turn slightly, as if he were surprised. She looked back at Warren. "He is innocent of these murders. If you only knew him—''

"How well do you know him?''

She knew his meaning; her face began burning.

D'Abanville said sharply, his irritation obvious, "If you have some evidence that I killed these women, then make your charges, sir.''

"We have no evidence as yet. That could change, however. In case you are unaware, Colonel Fraser, the London city police commissioner, has offered a five-hundred-pound reward for information leading to the capture of the Whitechapel murderer. As we speak the reward notice is being distributed throughout the East End. You should know that your picture will be among those included in the *Gazette,* and we will ask that anyone with any information regarding you or your presence in the East End contact us. So if you have anything you would like to tell us, Mr. D'Abanville, I advise you to do so. It will go much easier on you if you are truthful from the outset.''

The only sound in the room was the quiet scratching of a pencil as the artist continued to sketch D'Abanville's likeness on paper.

''I have nothing further to say to you,'' D'Abanville responded. ''May we go now?''

Chesterton stopped his pacing and looked expectantly at Commissioner Warren. Warren appeared to consider the request for some time before he answered with a sharp nod. ''You may go, sir. I advise you, however, not to leave London.''

D'Abanville left his chair, took hold of Mercy's arm, and they left the office.

15

They left the station the same way they had come, with carriage windows closed and with a policeman sitting across from them on guard. None of them spoke. There was very little disturbance from the onlookers as they reentered Greystone's gates. They were driven into the house's front doors, the policeman helped them from the carriage, and without another word reboarded and was driven away.

Mercy and D'Abanville were left alone beneath the porte-cochere.

Unable to tolerate the shadows of the porte-cochere on such a wonderfully bright day, and not willing to seclude herself yet in her room to dwell on thoughts that would only confuse her further, Mercy turned without speaking and walked back down the drive to the rose garden.

Remaining where she had left him, D'Abanville called out, "May I join you, Mercy?"

She did not respond; he took that as an invitation. Her keen ears picked up the sound of his footsteps crunching upon gravel as he approached her. She continued down the walk, occasionally turning her face up to the sun, breathing deeply of the autumn fragrance. Dense clusters of leaf mold nestled at the roots of trees and hedges, smelling musty and rich to her senses. Tender rose petals, their edges having turned brown from the first frost, scattered like soft confetti at her feet as she walked by. She thought of gathering a handful of them and pressing them to her face. She desperately needed something to hide the hot color on her cheeks, color put there by D'Abanville's closeness.

They walked for some time without speaking.

Dominick looked down at her. She saw him from the corner of her eye, or felt him. His look was penetrating, as if he were attempting to read her thoughts. That embarrassed her even more. For the thoughts that were tumbling through her mind like the rose petals scattering wildly over the ground were far afield of the lady she wanted so desperately to appear in that moment. She ached to have him stop her, to force her to face him, then declare his love and devotion and desire . . . if it was true what Miriam had said.

But he said nothing, just walked at her side, his hands in his trouser pockets as he looked alternately at her, then out across the grounds. Finally, when they walked as far as the old carriage house, he stopped walking and spoke.

"I wish we were in Paris."

Mercy walked on before pausing and looking back. Her reaction was to look away, to avoid the intensity of his gaze as she so often had, but she forced herself to look at him as intensely, and wait.

D'Abanville seemed disconcerted by her directness. He looked away, down at a leaf the wind had blown against his shoe. He nudged it aside and watched as it rolled end over end down the pathway.

"They are going to come for me again," he said roughly. "It is only a matter of time if it's true what Warren said about the reward."

"You were seen there, in the East End?"

He nodded and his eyes came back to hers.

"By women?"

"Yes."

"Prostitutes?"

"Yes."

She said nothing, but turned toward the ivy and bramble that cloaked the carriage house.

"It's not what you think," he told her.

She could not resist a look back at him. She waited.

A longer silence commenced before he took a tenuous step toward her. He raised one hand to her briefly, then dropped it.

"I did not solicit them," he explained.

"No? Then why were you there?"

"Not to kill them, if that's what you are thinking."

"Then why were you there?"

"I cannot tell you that."

"It will all come out anyway if any of those women recognize you from the *Gazette.*"

"It will all work out. I have faith that it will."

Mercy laughed harshly. "Faith, sir? I had faith too once. I had faith that the farming economy would somehow be saved from its foreign competition. I had faith that my father would recover from his illness. I had faith that my mother would survive my father's death. I had faith that I would be saved the wretched fate of the eighty thousand whores who live and work in the East End—"

"But you were saved that fate. I brought you here."

"To be propositioned with money and jewels and the tuition to nursing school. To learn that the ladies I always dreamed of being were selling their bodies and souls for money or jewels or houses on the Riviera, I think you said. Nothing is ever what it appears to be, is it?"

"I did not give those things to you in return for sex. I gave them to you because I care for you and I hoped you would care for me in return."

"You cannot buy affection. Not true affection."

"Obviously." Frowning, he looked away. The wind whipped his dark hair, making him look savage.

His head turned again and suddenly her eyes were on his. What madness moved her then to face him completely and confess her feelings, she would never know. Perhaps it was her fear that if she, or he, walked away now there would be no coming together ever again. Suddenly time seemed precious, so very precious. At any moment Chesterton could show up on their doorstep and take him away.

She spoke in a low, rapid voice.

"I care for you. But not because of any gift of jewels or money you might bestow on me. I find those trinkets shallow and false and I would rather have no love at all than to have that which is bought by condition. What good is any love if it is granted by conditions? Should a child feel coveted if he is judged by a parent to be worthy of love *only* if he is perfect? Who among us is perfect? Should love not be unconditional? It is either given unconditionally—freely—or it is not love at all. Rather it is . . ." She searched her mind. "Selfish and self-serving."

Again she faced the carriage house. The wind blew her hair like a silvery spray of water over one shoulder, and for a moment she could not see beyond it to D'Abanville. But she knew he watched and waited for her to continue.

"You are compassionate," she said. "You are kind. Those traits endear you to me far more than all the pearls in the Mississippi River ever could."

Mercy stared a blind moment at the trees. Then she caught the ivy with her hand and pushed it aside, stepped into the shadowed copse, and moved as swiftly and as carefully as possible around the bramble to the door of the carriage house. She looked back once, then ducked through the door, strode with head high and shoulders back to the distant room, where she paused. In the warm gloom of the ancient building she could smell the dusty scent of old straw, could feel its thick softness underfoot. She inhaled deeply, feeling her head reel a little with her emotions, her desire, her fear. Then she began to undress.

She knew the very moment he joined her. It was not in the sound, but in the absence of it. The air stirred. It brushed her legs, billowing her skirt, touched the back of her neck like a lover's gentle caress. And then the chimes, distant, soft, carried on the windtide to tease her ear like sweet birdsong. He was here, standing in the door, watching; she knew it without turning. And knowing it, her fingers began to tremble and her breath caught in her chest, aching for release.

The dress slid from her shoulders and down to the floor. The chemise Madame Cartier had cooed over seemed so frail a barrier in this dim place, so finely spun and hiding nothing from his sight. She tugged on the tiny ribbons holding the fine lawn closed. It parted like a whisper over her breasts, freeing them. Then it too fell to the floor. She pulled the string on her pantalets and they slid like soft white down around her ankles. Slowly she turned around to face him.

He stood in the door, a dark silhouette against the light. He did not move.

Unable to see his eyes, Mercy forced herself to look

away. The stillness was terrible. For an awful moment she believed he did not want her after all. It was all she could do not to cover herself with her hands.

"I suppose I am not as pretty as what you are accustomed to," she stated softly. "Too thin, perhaps?"

He moved into the room with a caution that was maddening. She began to shake with the same violent desire that had obsessed her since the first moment she saw him those many days ago. It seemed an eternity before he stopped before her, when in reality it was mere seconds. She knew his eyes were on her, but she could not force herself to look up. Instead, she stared at her feet, aware her skin had begun burning and her blood was like fire in her veins.

"Look at me," he said with husky urgency. When she hesitated, he caught her chin in his fingers and tipped up her face to his. A spurt of something close to desperation seized her as his eyes gazed hungrily into hers. "You are the most beautiful woman I have ever seen," he told her.

"I would rather you said nothing than to lie," she responded.

"I am not lying, Mercy." He cupped her face in his hands, stroked her cheeks lightly with his thumbs. The rough gauze of the bandage on his palm pressed into her skin. "You're perfect. God, you don't know how badly I've wanted you since the first moment I saw you standing at Tommy's bedside at London Hospital. The way you looked at him, touched him, was so full of caring."

Slowly he bent his dark head over hers and brushed one corner of her mouth with his. His breath caught, and slightly tilting her face to his, she opened her lips in invitation. The breath that had caressed her so softly before became harsher, burning the tender corners of her mouth. "Mercy," he whispered. "The waiting, the wanting you all this time . . ."

His warm fingers trailed downward over the smooth, delicate turn of her jawline to the arch of her throat. Lowering his head further, he opened his mouth slightly and drew his tongue over the pulse that throbbed there. She closed her eyes, suspended, wanting to absorb his touch so badly she could not prevent herself from raising her arms up over his shoulders, but afraid to. Afraid he would vanish again and this would all be a dream, another fantasy that would leave her inconsolably empty.

But he did not vanish.

He buried his hands in her hair roughly and his fingers clenched tightly against her scalp, dragging her head back. "I want you," he whispered again and again. "I want you."

He kissed her with a passion held in check and finally released. Its absolute fierceness invaded Mercy's senses, took her breath, her strength, until she swayed against him, returning the vibrant embrace with as much fire and need, until he groaned and shook beneath her hands like a man who had struggled against a madness but had succumbed to it nevertheless. His hands moved over her slowly, fingers trailing a tingling path along her jawline, down her throat, lightly, down, downward to the rising and falling swell of her breasts. He cupped that taut fullness gently in his palms, brushing his thumb over and over the aching, straining peak until she felt her body abandon all lingering resistance and press against him.

This, *this* was what she wanted. Yes . . . oh, yes . . .

Slowly his body slid down hers until his hot breath touched the valley between her breasts, and she waited, panting in anticipation for him to take them in his mouth, feeling the trembling tension in his shoulders as he balanced there, half-crouching. She could feel the restrained power of his body as he held her gently, his hands played over the narrow, delicate expanse of her back, rubbing. Then hungrily he drew her to him, covered one nipple with his mouth completely, circled it again and again with his tongue, tantalizing her beyond her limits before capturing it once more with the heated passion of his mouth. Awareness of her surroundings receded completely, replaced by such a desire she almost wept aloud for something she could only sense and not know. There was nothing except the two of them and the emptiness of the weathered, crumbling carriage house . . . and the sound of chimes, infinite and distant, blowing to her ear from some dim tunnel of awareness that she could not quite grasp.

More slowly he moved lower, his hands blazing a path his mouth followed, licking, nipping, tongue dipping into her navel like a bee after sweet nectar. He spread his hand over her stomach, lower, fanning widely like slender shadows over the pale velvet skin of her belly. Lower. Kneading, easing lower again, until his fingers brushed the downy apex of her thighs. Her muscles tensed, and out of reflex she reached out for him, sliding her fingers into his night-black hair as he nuzzled her there with his hands and face. The powerful, taut line of his shoulders stretched the seams of his dark coat to the breaking point as he wrapped his arms around the backs of her thighs and raised her body slightly up to him. As his lips buried in the soft golden curls, her fingers twisted in surprised denial. He stopped and looked up at her, hungry desire burning brightly in his eyes.

"Let me," he muttered roughly.

Then, before she could think to deny him, he began to move with agonizing slowness across the curls, nuzzling, opening her with his mouth and penetrating her like hot fireflame. She sobbed with the sudden pleasure, a stirring of purest, rawest sensation that erased all fear and doubt. Suddenly she was pressing his head against her, opening her legs farther, inviting him deeper, closer, until his tongue was plunging in and out of her, making her delirious with need, until every nerve of her body seemed to center there where his mouth worked its feverish magic, driving her mad and wanton. Oh, God! It was indecent, what he was doing to her. But she was powerless to prevent it.

And she didn't care. She was lost. Her blood was on fire and her skin was aflame with a searing hotness that was internal and all-consuming, driving her beyond desire to a desperate, aching need that seemed boundless. She threw her head back, letting her pale hair spill nearly to the floor, her back arching, pressing her body against him as he searched out her every secret and worshiped it with his mouth and tongue, dipping and driving and tasting, out and in and out until she was panting and whimpering aloud, and cursing him too for bringing her to this pleasure precipice that was certain torment.

Then he was moving up, standing tall above her again, his face dark with shadow and damp, his moist mouth curling up at the ends in pleasure. "Do you want it so badly, *ma chère?*" he whispered.

"Yes," she responded hoarsely, urgently. She knew the madness now that drove them, all the others, to beg him for more. Angrily she repeated, "Yes."

With a shift of his shoulders, the black coat slid in a whisper off his arms and dropped to the floor by her clothes. She reached with her hands and twisted them into his shirtfront, wrenched, shearing it of its buttons from his throat to his trousers. She shoved the galluses from his shoulders, then dropped her hands to his waistband, fumbled urgently at the buttons down the fly. Each gave with reluctance, for the strain of him pushing out from beneath made the material taut. Finally it gave and she shoved it back, releasing the aroused virile beauty of his male body into her hands. The impossibility of his joining with her flashed through her mind. He was beautiful and magnificent and beyond anything she had ever imagined a man could be. He was made to be worshiped, a perfect god, pagan and dark.

He reached for her hands, raised them to his chest with its dark hair that felt crisp against her fingers. The wide shoulders tapered to a narrow waist, and as he shifted in and out of a lance of sunlight from the window, she was awash with the warmth of his body, the clean male and starched-linen smell of him that overpowered her senses and made her tremble with anticipation.

Wrapping his dark fingers around her pale wrists, he shifted her hands down over his flat stomach until her fingers brushed the crisp thatch of hair at his thighs, and within it, the burgeoning shaft of his maleness. Her fingers closed around him and he groaned, low and deep and primitive, in his throat. His skin began to glisten with a sheen of sweat as he watched her hands work their own special magic on his body, arousing him as he had her, until his hips were sliding forward and back in the same rhythm as her hands. His own hands clenched, and as his head fell back, his chest rose with a groan that sounded wild and painful in the silent room. For a brief space of time she was acutely aware of nothing but her ability to please him, to drive him to the brink on which she had earlier balanced so precariously. She grew heady with the knowledge of it, and as his pleasure intensified, she became aware of her own rising passion, even greater, more demanding than before.

Slowly she dropped to her knees and took him in her mouth, imitating with her tongue the same slow, teasing swirls and caresses with which he had tormented her earlier. She felt his body tense; it jerked and throbbed and swelled until he was groaning, "God . . . oh, God, Mercy . . . Mercy, damn you damn you damn—"

He moved away suddenly, caught her roughly beneath her arms with his hands, and lifted her, high and against him, shoving her backward until meeting the wall which shook from the impact. Wrapping her hands around his flexing, trembling shoulders, she lifted her hips with the help of his hands on her buttocks, and before she could open her mouth to cry out in surprise, he was driving in one burning, stretching thrust deep inside her, filling her to the point of blissful, mind-shattering ecstasy.

"Mine," he declared roughly-hoarsely-passionately-angrily into the hair at her temple. "Mine, by God, you're mine!"

Then the beat began, rhythmic and fluent, until the world was a spinning, roaring wonder that was expanding beyond her control. Until they ceased to be him and her and became simply them—one. It was an uncontrollable thing, like the swift current of a river driven by its own power toward its ultimate goal. Wrapping his arms around her, he swung around, holding her tightly against him, then dropped with her onto the sagging bed. He pressed heavily upon her and she turned her face aside, breathing in the scent of his aroused flesh, experienced the sweet-salty taste of him on her lips. For a moment she was blinded to everything but his mussed black hair curling around his nape and shoulders and the collar of his shirt. Then a beam of sunlight, swirling with dust, streamed over the curve of his back and into her eyes as he rose on his elbows above her.

They arched together in the same moment, she lifting to his thrust. His eyes, like passion burning, locked on hers as they moved, together and apart until the shocks of his body against hers drove her mindless, until he was forced to capture her wrists in his hands and press them down into the bed or she might surely have hurt him. And still he drove and twisted and drove until she was panting and writhing and frantic for the surcease.

"Say it," he said, hips moving and grinding. "You're mine. Say you're mine and no other's and you never will be."

"Yes," she wept. "Yes!"

"Forever, Mercy. Promise me forever, no matter what. No matter what!"

"Yes!" She screamed it. Then, with an abandonment that bordered on frenzy, he rode her to the climax, his head down so his black hair brushed her face and the sweat from his brow dropped like tears down her throat to collect near her shoulder; down so he watched their bodies meet and part and meet, the beat accelerating until she closed her eyes and let the cry tear from her throat like the culmination of the maddening passion that ripped through their bodies in the same instant. She bowed against him, suspended, expanding while he came in a hot liquid torrent inside her, branding her, throbbing inside her with the same beat of his words: "Yes. Yes. Yes." Then, flinging his dark head back, he cried out to the ceiling, "God, yes!"

16

There was a silver cobweb fluttering from the ceiling above her. Mercy stared at it a long moment, feeling her body relax little by little. She could have slept. The fire in her body that had been consuming her by degrees the past days had settled into a warm, glowing ember of contentment. A smile of comprehension touched her mouth.

"Who are you?" she whispered.

D'Abanville raised his head from her shoulder. His breathing had slowed; passion's flush still colored his face, and the hair about his temples was damp. His body softened inside her as he smiled and smoothed her hair from her face. He let the long blond skeins flow through his fingers before saying, "Does it really matter, *ma chère?*"

Mercy rolled her head to one side, closed her eyes. His body was heavy on hers, filling hers still. Their hearts beat together as the shadows in the room cooled their sweating bodies. She took a breath and released it.

"No," she finally said. "It doesn't matter."

They said nothing more as he slid his body out of hers, off hers, and helped her to sit up. As he turned away from her and hitched up his trousers, she felt, suddenly, very naked, and much chagrined. Covering her breasts with her arms, she waited as he scooped up their clothing and handed hers to her. He slapped the dirt and dust from his coat and from the knees of his trousers before looking about the floor at his scattering of buttons. He laughed and the sound eased the tension. When his eyes came back to hers, they were twinkling.

"Mercy, Miss Mercy, you never cease to amaze me.

However do I walk back into Greystone with my clothes
in tatters?''

''Very carefully,'' she told him, frowning and grinning
a little too. She was surprised that D'Abanville seemed
as ill-at-ease as she felt.

He began tucking his shirt into this trousers. Then he
walked to the door and looked out, giving her the opportunity to slip back into her clothes before he faced her
again. When she was finished, she looked up to find him
watching her, as she so often had, his eyes warm and his
mouth smiling as if he could somehow look into her mind
and heart and know what she was feeling. That look said
he understood. Then he held out his hand to her, took
her hand in his, and they walked together back to the
house, silent again, but comfortably so.

As they reached the place where the pathway branched,
one way leading to the back entrance of Greystone, the
other to the front, D'Abanville stopped and caught her
arm. He said nothing, yet in his eyes she read his meaning. A slow smile was curling his mouth and he looked
at her in a shining, hot way.

''I shall take the back entrance,'' she told him.

She turned to go, but he caught her once again. He
kissed her in full view of anyone who might have been
peering at them from some window of the house or from
behind some bush or tree. With the late-afternoon sun
beating down on their heads and shoulders, he smothered
her mouth with his again and again. She tasted and
smelled her own scent on him, and found it highly arousing, felt the familiar stirring of her senses deep inside,
where he had been earlier.

It was with some effort that she at last pulled away.
Her legs felt too weak to move, and in the core of her
body, under her ribs, there was a fluttering that felt both
exhilarating and unbearable. She could not move, but
stood with her face turned up to his, basking in his presence, knowing she should turn now and go, but unable
to, unwilling to let the moment pass, wanting it to last
forever. She gazed straight into his dark blue eyes, chal-
lenging, taunting him with this strange new power she
had over him, until, all at once, he swept her up in his
arms again, drawing her close to his hard body, his hand

dragging down the front of her gown until he could fill his hand with her exposed breast. Then he tore his mouth from hers and bent his dark head to take the love-swollen tip of her breast into his mouth with a hunger that made her whimper aloud.

Finally, and with a curse, he pushed her away, righted her dress. Breathing hard, his face full of the old danger and darkness that had enthralled and excited her since the beginning, he glared down into her face as if torn between a desire to murder and a desire to throw her to the ground and make love to her in the parterre of sweet williams by the path. He did neither; she did not give him the chance. Instead she turned and, with her skirt lifted slightly in her hands, ran toward the house. She did not look back, but threw open the door and swept through the kitchen, barely noticing the help as they turned to gaze at her in curiosity. She ran all the way to her room, threw open her door and slammed it, spun round and round in the center of the room, her arms outstretched and her hair flying like clouds behind her. She had expected guilt, shame, self-condemnation. But she felt none of those things. Now. Perhaps tonight, or tomorrow, or the next day, but not now. She felt free at last, and happy. Happy for the first time in months, perhaps in years.

She brushed out her hair, then plaited it, bathed, and changed her dress. She hurried from her room, breathless and anxious to see *him* again. How would they seem now in each other's presence? With George Balfour—her pace slowed—with George Balfour the humiliation of having to face him again had been as bitter as bile in the back of her throat. She had felt tainted, dirty, and swamped by remorse. Used. A fool. But not now. Whatever had happened between her and D'Abanville could in no way be compared with what she had experienced with Balfour. Whatever had taken place in that carriage house had been meant to happen. It was more than sex. Much more. She had been a part of him, as he was a part of her. Two halves joined to make a whole. Together. Body and soul. Complete.

She took the stairs as quickly as possible, then started for his office. She heard the voices then and stopped, turned back for the vestibule, where she found several dignified-looking men standing, as well as Roger and Miriam. D'Abanville stood among them, his coat buttoned to hide his disheveled state; his dark hair was tousled and falling nearly to his eyes. He stared down at the paper in his hands. Even from the distance she could see his hands were shaking.

"Her majesty sends regrets and trusts that you will understand that, considering the controversy surrounding the investigation and yourself, to continue with plans for your performance at the lord mayor's celebration would be an unpopular decision. If, however, this investigation is closed before then, and you are not found to be guilty of course, her majesty may very well reconsider the decision and reinstate your performance."

There was a long silence as D'Abanville continued to stare down at the paper.

"I hope you understand," the man said more softly. "Another time, perhaps."

D'Abanville nodded without looking up.

"It is a good day to you, then, sir," the man said. He tipped his head informally to Roger and Miriam and looked briefly toward Mercy before turning with his companions and leaving the house. Silence and emptiness welled up around them as the door closed with a dull bang.

Finally Miriam moved. She seemed to Mercy to have aged a decade since their talk that morning. Her face looked pale and her mouth pinched with anger. She walked up to D'Abanville and hesitantly placed her hand on his arm.

"You've survived greater disappointments," she told him.

"No." He shook his head, his eyes still on the letter, its royal emblem somehow a blasphemy as it caught the light and glistened. "I have survived no disappointment greater than this."

"But you will."

He closed his eyes.

"You will," she repeated more forcefully. "What is it you believe? That each hurdle in life that you successfully and righteously scale will take you one step closer to the Divine Wisdom?''

"But I'm tired," he whispered. "God, I'm so . . .'' His voice trailed off. Crushing the paper suddenly in his fist, he flung it across the room. "Chesterton did this. He and his goddamn bloodhounds. He's ruined me.''

"Don't do this," Miriam pleaded. Her worried eyes shifted to Mercy, then back to D'Abanville.

Roger moved closer, his eyes bright and wide behind his spectacles. "He's right," he said. "Chesterton set out to ruin him —''

"Shut up!'' Miriam turned on Roger and screamed, "Just shut your mouth. He doesn't need to hear this now.'' She turned back to D'Abanville, took his face in her hands. "It's going to work out. I promise you—''

"Stop it!'' He grabbed her hands and shoved her away so suddenly she almost stumbled. "Leave me alone. Just leave me the hell alone for once in your wretched life. *Leave me alone!*'' he roared.

Then with the litheness of an animal he spun and stormed by Mercy as if she were nothing more substantial than a shadow on the wall. The happiness she had floated upon moments before shattered like glass breaking as reality reared its ugly head and reminded her who and what he was, or could be.

No, no, she wouldn't, couldn't think it. Those doubts were buried. She had buried them the night before, put them from her mind; she had chosen to trust him, to believe in him.

". . . we should get him out of London as soon as possible,'' Roger was saying. "Have you seen the crowds outside the gate? They are growing by the hour. And once this hits the papers, we may well be faced with a riot.''

Mercy shook her head. "He can't.''

They turned and looked at her.

"He can't leave,'' she told them. "Commissioner Warren told him that he's not to leave London.''

Miriam shook her head. "This has to be stopped.''

"The only thing that will stop this investigation is their finding the killer.'' Roger removed his glasses and cleaned them with the tail of his coat. "It doesn't look good for him, Miri, you must confess. You remember that girl in Paris—''

''Oh, for God's sake, Roger, the tart was after money. Had he really attacked her, she would have gone to the police.'' Miriam looked again at Mercy. ''The silly bitch made up the whole ugly affair.''

Mercy was almost afraid to ask: ''What did he do?''

''Beat her up,'' Roger replied. ''She showed up at my door looking as if she had been run through a mill. Demanded an exorbitant amount of money from us or she was going straight to the authorities and report him.''

''D'Abanville had never seen the slut before in his life,'' Miriam argued.

''Then why did you pay her?'' Roger asked. Replacing his glasses on his nose, he stared at Miriam and waited. ''Don't deny that you did. I saw her later and she told me you gave her every franc she'd demanded.''

Looking very tired suddenly, Miriam said, ''I couldn't take the chance that she might hurt him, that he might possibly have . . .''

''Has it occurred to you that just possibly you have protected him for too long?'' Roger asked.

''But you don't know him like I do!'' Miriam cried.

''No. I daresay I don't.'' Squaring his shoulders, Roger glanced at Mercy one last time before quitting the room.

Then Miriam looked up at Mercy with a desperation that made Mercy's knees grow weak. Forcing herself to turn, Mercy ran back to her room.

Lying wide-eyed in the dark, Mercy went over and over again the events that had taken place from the day she arrived at Greystone to the moment she had forgotten every ideal and sense of propriety she had ever held precious and succumbed to the madness and magic that were Dominick D'Abanville. Just like all the others. No different. Why had she believed it would be any different for her than for all the others? He had expressed no devotion, no promise, not the slightest hint of love.

He *cared* for her.

That was all.

He cared for them all.

Or did he?

Covering her face with her hands, she thought of praying, then reminded herself that it wouldn't help. There was no one there to listen to her now, any more than there had been before. She must reconcile herself to the fact that she had fallen in love with an image of what, out of desperation, she had wanted D'Abanville to be. He was a performer. An artist of illusion. The best in the world! And she had fallen for it. All of it. Damn damn damn.

She rang for her bath. Micah arrived a half-hour later with a brass tub full of steaming scented water, fresh tea, and a plate of crumpets still hot from the oven. Mercy had dozed and did not hear him as he entered. He must have stared at her for several minutes before she became aware of his presence. Sleepily awakening, she looked up into his blue eyes, and for a moment thought she was back in the carriage house. She warmed under the intense gaze, and reaching for his hand, brought it to her face, cupped it to her cheek while his fingers gently stroked the tender lobe of her ear. Not until he pulled his hand away did she rouse enough to realize what she had done.

"Micah, I'm sorry," Mercy said. "I was sleeping and thought . . . Well, never mind what I thought," she added under her breath. Sliding from the bed, she looked past him to the water and food, smiled in gratitude. But when she looked back at Micah, she found his face somber.

"You're worried about Dominick," she said.

He turned away and for a moment Mercy found herself staring at the broad line of his back and the soft black hair that curled so becomingly over his shirt collar. She understood now why she had, for a moment upon awakening, mistaken him for D'Abanville. There were certain aspects of their appearance that were uncannily similar.

"I'm certain everything will be fine," she said. As he nodded and looked back at her, she was stricken with an uneasiness. As he continued to stare at her long and hard, she noted that in those blue eyes she did not see the emptiness of a child's innocence and ignorance, but a knowledge of something dark and almost frightening.

With some hesitation Mercy asked, "Is something wrong?"

He did not respond.

"Micah, do you know something?" Her eyes still trained on his, she moved slowly to the dresser and picked up her purse. She rummaged inside for a pencil and a piece of paper and held both up to him. "Can you tell me what is bothering you?"

He stared at her hand as if afraid to move.

She walked to him. "Perhaps I can help if you tell me." Lifting his hand and pressing the pencil and paper into it, she encouraged him with a smile. "Go on," she told him. "I swear I won't tell anyone else."

His hand closed on hers for a moment and the grip was almost painful. Then he took the paper and pencil from her, considered it for some time before turning for the dresser, where he labored over writing the message. He did not return it to her, but left it on the dresser and backed away, nervously rubbing his hands up and down the outside of his thighs before deciding to turn without looking at Mercy again and leave the room. She hurried to the dresser, retrieved the paper, and held it up to the light. It took a moment for her eyes to adjust to the child-like scrawl; her heart stopped beating as she read: "leev graston r di."

Mercy was still shaking when she arrived at D'Abanville's office door a half-hour later. Micah's message had been cryptic. But what did it mean? After bathing and dressing, she had searched for him, determined to learn his meaning, but had been unable to find him. Did he believe that she was in danger from Dominick? What else could he mean? But the two men seemed so close. Surely if he knew D'Abanville to be a killer, the camaraderie between them would be far less evident, if it existed at all. Mercy decided she would draw no more conclusions until she spoke with Micah on the matter. Perhaps it was only his child's mind that made him imagine the danger. Whatever, she could not allow all the old doubts to re-surface. What had happened earlier between her and Dominick had been a turning point. No going back. To do so would bring regrets. She was tired of regrets. She ached to feel like a woman in love; to compare what had taken place between her and Dominick to the awful, humiliating fiasco with George Balfour would taint something beautiful ugly. She simply would not allow that.

Mercy had not really expected to find Dominick in his office, so she was surprised when he responded to her knock. She opened the door.

He was sitting in the leather wing armchair behind his desk, one hand loosely clasped around a glass, the other about a bottle of brandy. The bottle was nearly empty. Malphas perched on his right shoulder.

"Ah, Miss Dansing," he slurred. "Come in. Come in." He wiggled one finger at her as he held up his glass. "We were just discussing you."

"We?"

"Malphas and I."

She closed the door and walked to his desk, her blue-and-green striped skirt whushing on the Persian carpet. She looked from D'Abanville to the bird. The bird stared back, its beak open, as if smiling.

"He thinks you don't like him," D'Abanville said.

"Does he?"

"Aye. Don't you, bird?"

Malphas lifted each foot alternately, as if he were marching in place. D'Abanville lifted his glass to the bird and the bird drank deeply, staggered a little, and roosted again on his shoulder.

"He doesn't talk much when he's drunk," Dominick said.

A quick smile touched Mercy's lips.

D'Abanville grinned, but it was a grin that did nothing to brighten his face. Mercy thought that he did not look much like the Great D'Abanville. His features belonged to a stranger's. There were lines she had never seen on either side of his mouth. His dark blue eyes looked bruised. She had thought about what to say to him the last hour, but now she found the words difficult to speak. He was hurting so badly . . .

Looking away from her and at his stacks of papers and books, D'Abanville said, "I was warned that eventually this sort of thing would happen, that it would take all of my will and concentration to rise above it. He told me, 'It makes no difference that infants and morons are the only people to believe the tricks are real, you are there

to amaze them, to entertain them, to make them let go—
however briefly—of reality and to experience the true joys
of miracles. Make them feel like children again, and they
will love you.' "

He brought his eyes back to Mercy's. "He believed
that until the day he died a pauper, buried in an un-
marked grave in Paris. I should have realized then, but I
was too young to understand that it's not in man's nature
to see the good in anything. They are the ones who killed
him with their doubts and disbeliefs and prejudices. They
broke his heart, and when that wasn't enough, they broke
him mentally. The very ones he'd made laugh as children
were the ones who grew up to call him warlock and Lucifer the Devil and to scorn their own children for believing in him. Tell me, Miss Dansing, where is it written
that just because a boy turns eighteen he can no longer
believe in magic without thinking it something twisted
and evil? What is it in ourselves that wants to find nothing but the dark side in any man's nature, and when unable to find it, we invent something with our minds that
is a thousand times more frightening than the reality?"

The bird on his shoulder roused and with a snap of its
blue-black wings flew to its perch. Dominick lifted the
glass again, held it slightly up before him, and stared at
the prisms of yellow candle light refracting off its delicate
curves.

"After all he did for them, not one of those sorry sons
of bitches came to his funeral. They won't come to mine
either, I wager." His hands tightened on the glass.

Mercy kept silent, sensing the building of tension, of
words he longed to let go but kept tethered by some fraying thread of denial. She looked from his eyes to the glass
and back to his mouth which was taut and dangerous.

"Do you know what he would say if he were here now,
Miss Dansing? Forgive them their ignorance. They don't
understand and they never will."

"Who?" she asked softly. "Your father?"

He laid his head back against the chair and closed his
eyes. In the quiet room the only sound was the ticking of
some distant clock.

"There are always the children," Mercy went on.
"They need you."

"Do they?" His eyes opened a fraction. "Do you?"

The question caught her off guard.

"Never mind." The words were thick. His head snapped up and he quaffed the brandy in one violent motion. "It's business as usual, then, I assume. That's why you came here, isn't it? Or did you think to offer me your resignation?"

She was too stunned to answer.

Leaving his chair and standing, fingers outstretched to the desktop for support, he raised one black eyebrow and smiled unpleasantly. "I won't stop you. You are free to go if you want. Damn the contract. It wasn't binding anyway. Go on and get out . . . I said to get out!"

She stepped backward, confused and unbalanced by the sudden rising of vicious anger she saw on his face. She turned for the open door, stumbling a little on one edge of the rug.

The door slammed in her face.

Mercy froze, her knees feeling as if they would buckle beneath her. D'Abanville moved up behind her. He caught her arm cruelly. All her old fears began swirling around in her head like leaves in a whirlwind.

"Mercy," came his ragged voice, "don't go."

She closed her eyes and stood rigid, refusing to answer, refusing to believe that the door had closed by itself; reality seemed to hang by some tenuous surreal thread just beyond her reach.

"Don't leave me now," he whispered. "I'll give you anything if you'll stay. More money—anything." He pulled her backward until his body was pressed against hers and his breath was falling hot and brandy-sweet against one side of her face. His fingers brushed her cheek lightly as he said, "Stay with me. I swear to you, you have nothing to fear from me. I would rather slice my own wrists before harming you in any way."

He turned her around. She closed her eyes, afraid to see him, her biggest fear of him bringing her senses to a heightened fever pitch, the same fear that brought her, night after night, upright in her bed, weeping.

"Look at me," he told her. "You're right about the children. There will always be the children."

She looked at him. He looked normal—no devil with

horns and cloven feet. Only a man. Dispirited. Disillusioned. A mirror image of herself short weeks ago.

He caught her hand, and opening the door, pulled her into the hallway. They hurried down the corridor to the room where his performance props were stored. She stared at the large glass case dominating the center of the room, then at the assortment of trunks about the walls, and finally at the floor. The gray metal box was gone.

"Stand there." He pointed to a place on the floor.

She didn't move.

He turned back to her so quickly she had no time to respond. Grabbing her arm, he pushed her to the place he had indicated before.

"There," he said more forcefully. "If we are to continue to work as a team, Mercy, you must learn to follow my directives. It is imperative that you do so, or your life could be endangered."

leev graston r di.

Her face went white. D'Abanville noticed. His lips thinned and a slight tic agitated a muscle in his cheek as he watched her. When she made no further move, he turned away, appeared to be at a loss what to do with his hands before grabbing up a paper cone and spinning around to face Mercy again.

"Hold this," he said.

He thrust the cone into her hands before picking up a cup full of cold coffee from a box and turning it over the cone. Mercy could feel the paper begin to disintegrate in her fingers, but before she could utter a word, D'Abanville rattled off what sounded like a hodgepodge of foreign phrases, passed his hand over the soggy cone, then grabbed it from her fingers. The liquid inside landed in a large brown splotch on the front of his shirt and dribbled onto his shoes.

Mercy almost laughed, believing the blunder had been his way of making light of the unhappy situation in which they had found themselves. Then, seeing the look, first disbelief, then anger, and finally a fear that turned his face into a mask as white as chalk, she realized the seriousness of what was happening.

"Right," he said, staring at the stain on his shirt, shoes, and floor. When he reached for another cone,

Mercy noticed his hands had begun to shake worse than they had when receiving the queen's letter.

He went through the routine again, more slowly this time, each movement deliberated before he did it. The outcome was the same, only instead of coffee staining his shirt, it was tea and tea leaves that made an ocher-colored mess over the front of his fawn-leather breeches. His face turned whiter, if that were possible.

"Dominick," she began carefully, "I think you ought to sit down."

He stared down at the tea and coffee several more seconds before raising his bloodshot eyes back to hers.

"Do you think so?" he asked softly. When she nodded, he said, "Will you tell me how my sitting down is going to remedy this situation?"

"What is the situation?"

"The liquid was to have disappeared, of course."

"I see." She stared down at the dark puddles. "I see. Perhaps if you practice—"

"Practice!"

Mercy jumped back, startled by his shout.

"Practice!" he repeated as angrily. Crushing the wet cone in his fist, he said, "An idiot can perform that feat, Miss Dansing. It is the first feat we are taught during our apprenticeship, and I have successfully performed it five thousand times."

"I beg your pardon. Then perhaps your cones are defective."

He stared at her in a daze, as if she had spoken in some language foreign to him. Then his dark head fell back and he began to laugh, an awful sound full of anger and desperation. He whirled suddenly toward the glass case, circled it like a fox might a hare, his eyes a little wild, his teeth chewing his lower lip in mad concentration.

She stepped toward him, and doing her best to drive the nervousness from her voice, asked, "What are you doing?"

"I was saving the best for her royal highness, but her royal highness sends regrets."

Mercy shook her head. "But it isn't safe. Miriam said it would be . . . ." She started to shake. Mercy backed to the door, her eyes trained on his face, on his hands which were reaching for a box of matches to one side. Whirling, she ran out of the room, up the hallway, her breath tearing through her chest and throat in short spurts of panic. She flew through the vestibule, sliding on the slick white marble and banging her knee on the floor. She must have cried out; she couldn't be certain, but suddenly Roger and Miriam were running into the room, and behind them Micah.

"Stop him!" she cried. "The case—the glass case—he's going to try it!"

Micah dashed by her, nearly toppling Miriam where she stood frozen by the stairs. Mercy followed, barely hearing Roger crying out her name. It seemed an eternity since she had run from the room—why hadn't anything happened? She saw Micah enter the room; then there were hands on her shoulders, pulling her back, and Roger was saying, "You can't go in there—you can't go in there." He was pulling her roughly around toward him, fighting her, his face not looking like Roger's at all, but—

The explosion drove her forward, hot wind and debris wrapping around her with a thunderous groan of wood and glass. Miriam's distant screams were lost with the impact that sent Mercy into Roger and both of them to the floor. For a moment she lay facedown on the carpet, paralyzed, confused. Then reality returned, and horror, as Roger groaned and squirmed beneath her.

Mercy raised her head slowly. There was pain in the back of her head, and a deafness in her ears that was almost unbearable. Something wet and warm ran down her face as she struggled to sit up. Gradually her senses returned. The air smelled charred and acrid, and as if she were sitting at the end of a long tunnel, the sound of crying echoed to her.

Instinct set in then, for the shock had still not left her. Mercy stumbled over the smoking wreckage of what used to be Greystone's east wing toward Miriam's cries. As the smoke cleared, she saw the woman rocking back and forth and weeping. "Someone help him. He's dying. Oh, God, he's dying!"

Mercy ran, tripped, fell hard against a pile of smoldering refuse, burning her dress, her hands. There was someone there beneath the timbers. She fell to her knees and shoved away the wood and mortar and slivers of glass that were everywhere. She knew before turning the body over that it was dead. There was blood, so much blood.

Micah.

She heard a groan then, and with a new surge of hope dug furiously through the wreckage. "He's alive!" she cried to Miriam. "Dominick's alive!"

It seemed as if she had been watching the entire horrible act being played out over and over. No one moved fast enough. It seemed she was forced to scream each directive at the gaping, somnolent servants a dozen times before they responded. Even Roger appeared to drag his feet in coming to D'Abanville's aid. She would tell herself later that it had only been her imagination that they seemed not in the least bit concerned that their employer lay bleeding to death beneath the rubble. In the end it was Miriam's hysterical raging and threats of violence to their persons that spurred them to help load Dominick into the coach. Miriam cradled his head in her lap while Mercy did her best to bind his cuts and abrasions as they traveled to St. Bartholomew Hospital.

They were met at the door by the hospital official on duty. As luck would have it, it was the administrator who had come to Greystone just days before requesting funds to purchase beds for the hospital's new wing. He stood at the open door of the coach and stared down at D'Abanville like a man who has just seen a not-so-pretty portion of his life flash before his eyes.

"Dear God, what has happened?" Gladstone asked.

"An explosion at Greystone," Miriam replied.

"He needs treatment immediately," Mercy said. "He is losing a great deal of blood. If you will direct us to the nearest bed . . . ?"

Gladstone did not move.

"Sir, we are wasting valuable time. If he is not treated soon, the shock alone will kill him."

Closing his eyes, Gladstone turned his face away. He shook his head. "I'm sorry. We cannot take him here."

Mercy blinked, trying to bring her mind into focus. Surely she had heard him wrong. The logical part of her mind would not allow her to accept his meaning. "I don't think I understand," she told him.

"You must understand, madam; considering all the controversy—"

"Controversy!"

"We rely totally on donations—"

"I am well aware of that. The man you are allowing to bleed to death on the floor of this coach happens to be one of your largest contributors. Do not tell me what your hospital relies on!"

"I'm sorry. I cannot do it. Were he discovered to be here, as surely he would be, we would have a riot on our hands. We are not equipped to deal with that sort of problem, young lady. You must understand!"

"I understand only that you are refusing to allow him the use of one of the very beds he paid for, sir, and I will hold you personally responsible should he not survive this."

Mercy shoved him out of the door and called up to the driver, "London Hospital. Quickly!"

If they could be fortunate in anything, Mercy surmised that they had been extremely fortunate that the awful accident had taken place at night. The streets were virtually empty, enabling them to cross town to London Hospital in minutes instead of hours.

By the time they arrived at the hospital, Dominick had begun to rouse, to groan slightly and open his eyes. Miriam did her best to soothe him, but Mercy suspected the woman was in a mild case of shock herself. Occasionally she would touch Miriam's hand, and found it cold and trembling with nerves.

The administrators did not hesitate to receive D'Abanville. Mercy watched helplessly, as did Miriam, as both doctors and nurses hefted him down the corridor on a stretcher, where they disappeared into the emergency quarters. With some reluctance they took a place on the benches running down each wall of the corridor. Huddled between the East End wretches who had found whatever ailment they could to get a warm, dry place to sleep for the night, they waited for the next two hours for word on D'Abanville's condition.

Miriam was the first to speak. After an hour's intolerable wait she suddenly blurted, "Damn them all!" loudly enough to awaken many of their dozing companions. "I told him time and again that this was the sort of thing that would happen, yet he continued to shovel his money out to them as if it were nothing more than horse manure. I told him that they wouldn't lift one hand to him if he needed them. But it was that damnable faith, that damnable belief in the basic goodness of human beings. Jesus Christ, the man should have been a priest."

She crossed her arms and stared down the hallway a long while. Then: "What the hell is taking them so long? You'd think they'd have the decency to come tell us something." Miriam turned back to Mercy. A little of the old fire had returned to Miriam's eyes, but her face was still pale. She seemed to see Mercy for the first time sitting there huddled against the wall. "God, sweetheart, you're a mess." Pulling a handkerchief out of her skirt pocket, she sat down again by Mercy, took Mercy's face in one hand, and began trying to wipe a smudge of blood from her forehead. "You did well," she said. "Extremely well. I was proud of you. You took over just like D'Abanville would have expected you to. He likes his women strong. He respects that in you. He told me so just last night. Give me your hands. Jesus, the blood."

"Micah is dead," Mercy said softly, looking at her hands. Odd how she had put that from her mind during the crisis. Now she felt like weeping, but the tears wouldn't come. Not yet. She was still too numb.

"I know. Listen, we won't say anything to Dom about it. Not just yet. For whatever reason, he was terribly fond of Micah. Oh, he was a strange one, was Micah, but he was good. Simple but good. Always gave me the creeps a bit, but I figured that was because of his speech impediment. Christ, can you image having your tongue cut out?"

"What?" Mercy stared at Miriam, stunned.

"Didn't you know? Must have happened some years back. Old Lady Casimire told me about it when Roger and I were negotiating the purchase of Greystone. Micah was one of the ones who resided on Greystone when she occupied the place. Seems he was born at Greystone and lived there his entire life. Rarely even left the grounds. Roger didn't like Micah, but he was pleasant enough. God, I can't believe he's dead.''

Miriam turned and pressed her back flat against the wall. So did Mercy. They stared at the row of miserably clad men and women across from them as they huddled together for warmth and comfort. At some time, Mercy wasn't sure when, Miriam reached over, took her hand, and gripped it.

An hour later they were approached by a doctor. He looked from Mercy to Miriam and asked, "Is one of you Mercy Dansing?''

It took some doing, but Mercy found her legs and stood up.

"D'Abanville has been asking for you,'' the man said.

"Is he all right?'' Miriam asked.

"There were several deep lacerations and a light degree of burning on his hands and face. He'll survive. By the way, who is Micah?''

Mercy looked around at Miriam, her heart leaping with the awful dread.

The doctor said, "He has been calling for Micah.''

"He was killed in the explosion,'' Mercy responded.

The doctor made no further reply, but turned down the hall, Mercy following before turning once to look back at Miriam. Miriam stood in the center of the corridor alone and lonely, and not for the first time Mercy experienced a stab of sympathy for the woman.

It seemed they were both in love with the same man.

17

Standing in the doorway of the hospital ward, Mercy recalled the first time she had entered such an institution. The smells of sickness, the cries of pain had haunted her for a week after. The helplessness, the calling out for compassion and having no one there to offer even a single kind word of understanding had driven her to return again and again to hold their hands, to mop their feverish brows and whisper words of encouragement. She had eventually grown accustomed to the wretchedness of it all. But nothing could ever have prepared her for confronting the man she loved in such a situation. Seeing Dominick stretched out on the bloody bed in the semidark room broke her heart, made her grow faint and desperate, and a little mad.

Walking to his bed, she tried very hard to control the hysteria she felt. She did not know what to expect. The doctor had mentioned lacerations. Burns. From her distance she noted bandages about his hands, about his forehead.

She stepped up to his bedside and looked cautiously into his face. Dark as the room was, she could tell very little. There were sutured cuts about his cheek and chin, and one eye was swollen nearly closed. She gently took his hand.

"Sir," she said, "I am here."

His head turned a little. He seemed to stare at some point beyond her.

"Mercy?"

"Yes."

He did not say anything for a long while. Then she heard him swallow.

"Where is Micah?"

"Sir, I think you should rest now—"

"Where is Micah?"

"The doctor said—"

"Is he dead?"

"Please . . ."

"Is he dead?"

Bending closer, Mercy gently touched his face.

"He is," he whispered. "Isn't he? Mercy?"

"Yes." She began to weep.

He turned his face away. His shoulders began to shake, a silent grief that frightened Mercy with its immensity. She didn't know what to do. She had often seen men cry with pain or fever, but never out of grief. There was no balm or draft of medication to take away the suffering. She could only hold him.

He wept like a child in the darkness, aloud, then quietly, resignedly, then angrily, until the medication the doctor had given him for his pain began to take hold and drag him down into its sweet oblivion. Only then did Mercy rest her head on his shoulder, close her eyes, and finally drift into sleep.

She knew it was morning without opening her eyes. She could hear the stirring of patients and nurses in the room. A smell of food teased her nostrils, then the stench of disinfectant and disease. It took her a moment to realize that she still lay with her head on D'Abanville's shoulder. He was unmoving but for the shallow rising and falling of his chest beneath her hand. She opened her eyes and stared sleepily at his bandaged chest and his fingers that lapped loosely over hers. She heard his heart beat steadily beneath her ear.

"Miss Dansing."

Mercy slowly lifted her head and looked up at Inspector Chesterton.

"How is he?" he asked.

"Why?" The word was a rasp in her dry throat. "If he is still alive, do you propose to kill him?"

"Nonsense."

"Is it? You have helped to destroy all that he is, all he worked to attain."

"I have an obligation to her majesty and the people of London to stop the perpetrator of these heinous crimes."

"But he is not your killer."

"How do you know?"

"I know him. No gentler or kinder man have I ever known." She stood and walked around the bed, her eyes never leaving Chesterton. He remained at D'Abanville's bedside, his face troubled as he watched Dominick sleep. "Why did you come here?" she asked him.

"I stopped by Greystone this morning and learned of the accident."

"Have you come to arrest him?"

His head came around. He stared at Mercy for some time without speaking. Finally he said, "There were investigators at Greystone for the *Times* and the *Star*. Obviously word is out about the explosion. It may be safer for him at the Yard."

"You mean to lock him up, then."

Chesterton reached into his macintosh, withdrew a rolled-up broadsheet, and placed it in her hands. "In case you are unaware, her majesty has received a petition signed by some four thousand women of Whitechapel. There are vigilance committees, headed by George Lusk, who are determined to stop the killings as well. The people are rioting."

Mercy stared down at the broadsheet. Printed there was the letter to the queen:

> To Our Most Gracious Sovereign Lady, Queen Victoria.
>
> Madam: We, the women of East London, feel horror at the dreadful sins that have been lately committed in our midst, and grief because of the shame that has befallen our neighborhood.
>
> By the facts which have come out in the inquests, we have learnt much of the lives of those of our sisters who have lost a firm hold on goodness and who are living sad and degraded lives.
>
> While each woman of us will do all she can to make men feel with horror the sins of impurity which cause such wicked lives to be led, we also beg that your majesty will call on your servants in authority

and bid them put the law which already exists in motion to close bad houses within whose walls such wickedness is done and men and women ruined in body and soul.

We are, madam, your loyal and humble servants.

Chesterton said, "Many are calling for the commissioner's resignation, as you well know."

"I understand your desperation," she replied quietly. Looking up into his face again, she said, "But what right does that give you to destroy another man so completely and irrevocably when you have no more proof to justify your suspicions than the fact that he was once Miss Russell's lover? Or because he was seen speaking to Mrs. Kinsdale at a charity ball? This is nothing more on your part than a witch-hunt, Inspector. Because of what he is, you immediately think of him as something evil, to be destroyed."

"There is an evil walking the London streets, madam."

"I repeat. You have no proof he is Miss Russell's killer or Jack the Ripper."

"He has shown me no proof that he is not. Not one alibi has he provided me during this entire investigation. When I question him on his whereabouts at the time of a murder, he simply tells me he was 'alone.'" Clasping his hands together behind his back, he squared his shoulders and regarded Mercy with something of his old arrogance. "Contrary to what you believe, I do not enjoy this. If I am wrong about D'Abanville, I will do what I can to rectify any damage I may have caused his reputation. But I honestly do not feel that I am wrong. D'Abanville is tied to the East End in some manner—"

"What proof do you have of that?" Mercy demanded more loudly, angrily.

They both looked down at D'Abanville. He slept still. In the light of day Mercy could make out his blistered skin and the angry red lacerations on his face. Then Chesterton caught her arm and moved her slightly further from the bed.

"I have had him followed, Miss Dansing. That is my proof. On two separate occasions—evenings—Lawton followed him to Whitechapel. On the first occurrence, D'Abanville, when reaching Buck's Row, disappeared. On the second occasion, Lawton, with the assistance of four other policemen, followed him into Whitechapel, only to have him vanish under their noses. One moment he was there. The next he was gone.''

"What are you trying to say?" she demanded.

"It is a foregone conclusion that whoever is killing the women of Whitechapel knows his way around Whitechapel. Every street and blind alley in the East End. He knows them well enough to escape the police who have been recently only mere minutes behind him. We feel that when the first of the last two victims was found, he might well have been standing in the shadows watching.''

Chesterton paced to the end of the bed and stopped. Mercy joined him as, lowering his voice and staring with determined concentration at the floor, he began to speak again.

"In daytime traffic it is a ten-minute walk from Berner Street, the place the first victim of the recent double murder was found, to Mitre Square. That is without shortcuts. In my estimations when Jack killed victim number one, he had forty-five minutes to strike up an acquaintance with the second victim, to lure her into a dark corner of Mitre Square, cut her throat, and perform extensive mutilations before the victim was found by police." As if suddenly remembering his company, he looked up at Mercy and frowned. "I do beg your pardon, Miss Dansing.''

Staring at the ceiling then, he said, "You must realize how Jack's timing is honed to perfection. Mitre Square is lined on two sides by a warehouse belonging to Messrs. Kearley and Tonge, tea importers, and is patrolled every fifteen minutes by a policeman. A night watchman was on duty in the tea warehouse at the time of the murder as well. The Ripper ran an even greater risk of discovery because Mitre Square serves as a shortcut for people going to Bishopsgate. After one o'clock on a Saturday night there were certain to be stragglers from the nearby pubs cutting across it on their way home. Not only that, but there are three entrances to the square—leading from Mi-

tre Street, from Duke Street, and from St. James Place—
which tripled the Ripper's chances of being caught red-
handed by a pedestrian or the police. But he was not,
Miss Dansing. He was neither seen nor heard. How does
a man appear in a square with a woman who never makes
a sound while he murders her, butchers her, then simply
disappears again into thin air, unless . . . we can attrib-
ute the murder to a . . . supernatural force.''

Mercy looked at Chesterton, surprised, uncertain if she
had heard him correctly.

He seemed somewhat chagrined and embarrassed at
the statement. Still, he did not take it back, just pressed
his lips together and rocked up and down on the balls of
his feet.

''I cannot believe what I am hearing,'' she whispered.
''I should laugh if it were not so frightening, Inspector.''

''Scoff if you must, Miss Dansing. But what other explanation can there be for a fiend who appears and disappears right beneath the noses of the best police force
in the entire world, committing some of the most notorious murders in London's history?'' Raising one eyebrow at her continued astonishment, he asked, ''Are you
aware of Mitre Square's history? No? Then allow me to
enlighten you. The latest Ripper victim was found at exactly the same spot where, in 1530 a woman was murdered by a mad monk name Brother Martin. In those days
Mitre Square was the site of the Priory of the Holy Trinity. Brother Martin, coming upon a woman at prayer before the high altar, seized her by the throat. The knife
descended with lightning rapidity, as I understand it, and
pools of blood deluged the altar steps. With a demon's
fury the monk then threw down the corpse and trod it
out of recognition. Brother Martin then plunged the knife
into his own heart. Naturally Mitre Square has remained
unhallowed ground, and just as naturally we can assume
that the Ripper murder was in fulfillment of some ancient
curse.''

''Oh, please . . .'' Mercy turned away. She covered
her face with her hands, feeling tired suddenly, and sore.
It occurred to her that she had never even bothered to see
to her own scrapes and bruises, so desperate had she
been over D'Abanville's welfare.

"I beseech you, Miss Dansing, do not take this information lightly," came Chesterton's voice behind her. "I am a man who relies on his instincts, and my instincts tell me that the man lying there is not who—or what—he appears to be."

She turned to face him. "I think I know him better than you, sir. His philanthropy to the sick and homeless is beyond reproach. I can supply you with all the verifiable information anyone could possibly need to prove that he is as good and generous a man as he appears."

"And I wager that I will soon be able to offer you proof that his entire existence is that of a fraud."

"I fear you are confusing his profession with the man himself," she said hotly.

"They are one and the same, Miss Dansing. One and the same. I expect to hear from my man in Paris any day now. And when I do, I highly suspect we may both be in for an unfortunate surprise."

"Until then, just leave him alone, Inspector. Leave me alone as well."

He stared at her hard for seconds longer. Then he tipped his head in dismissal. Turning on his heel, he quit the room.

Mercy waited until Chesterton had disappeared completely from sight before turning back to the bed. Dominick's eyes were open and watching her. For a moment he did not look like D'Abanville. His eyes were cold, lifeless, and though she reminded herself that such a glazed appearance in the eye was not unusual when the patient was sedated with morphine, she could not help but shudder. She sensed that he had somehow overheard her conversation with Chesterton. Overheard and, more important, understood.

It was not long after Chesterton's departure that Mercy was joined by Miriam and Roger. They convinced her to return to Greystone and rest. Mercy looked forward to a bath and a change of clothes. It seemed like an eternity since the night before, when she had bathed and spoken to Micah. Now he was dead. The final realization drove home painfully. Still, it was with some hesitation that she left the hospital.

Greystone's coach was parked next to the curb. The driver stood some distance away, talking quietly with a group of men. Dockworkers, by the look of them. They scattered when they saw Mercy approaching.

"Take me home," she told him. But as she reached for the door of the coach, she stopped and looked back. "On second thought, take me to Lady Casimire's on Park Lane. You know the address, I think."

He did not move.

"Should I repeat myself?" she asked.

"What'll you be goin' there for?"

"To tell her of the mishap. To inform her of Micah's death."

"Why should she care?"

"Perhaps she won't. That is not for you to determine."

"You're gettin' mighty uppity, ain't you, considerin' what you are."

"Which is what?" she demanded, her tone sharp with irritation.

"D'Abanville's whore."

She rocked a little with surprise. Turning to face him fully, her anger burning her cheeks like fire, she stated as rationally as possible, "As D'Abanville's assistant, whore or not, I have superiority over you. And considering I will see Lady Casimire with or without your driving me, it would behoove you to do as I say."

He gave her an insolent smile before turning to board the driver's seat. Mercy climbed into the coach and slammed the door, too tired and numb and sad to dwell on the driver's recalcitrance.

The idea of seeing Lady Casimire had not been as spur-of-the-moment as Mercy had first imagined. Resting her head back on the seat and closing her eyes, she realized that she had been dreaming of the dowager before awaking to find Chesterton at D'Abanville's bedside. Lady Casimire seemed to be Micah's only tie to the world outside of Greystone. Out of respect for him, Lady Casimire deserved to be informed of his death.

Because of the daytime traffic, the passage of Mercy's coach to Park Lane took the better part of an hour. She slept the entire journey and awakened only as the driver opened the door to let her out. He did not offer his hand

and she did not expect him to. Whatever animosity had lain unspoken between them in the past was now out in the open. Mercy did not question it but, in some way, understood it. In his eyes she was no more than an employee. No different from him, yet she was allowed a more privileged existence. It seemed there was a hierarchy even among the lower classes.

The plump, pink-cheeked maid who answered the door looked just as Mercy might have expected: scrubbed clean, not a hair out of place, her black muslin dress with snow-white apron spotlessly clean and stiff with starch. She gazed at Mercy in surprise and curiosity as Mercy asked to see Lady Casimire.

"Have you a card?" the servant inquired in a trained monotone.

"Do I look as if I would carry a card?" she responded with strained patience. "Tell her Mercy Dansing from Greystone is here to see her. I think she will remember me."

Mercy waited five minutes for the servant to return. She was shown down a hallway lined with portraits, all distinguished men wearing long white wigs and black robes. She was led through a morning room whose every table was laden with fresh cut flowers, then out through French doors into the back garden of the town house. Though not overly large, and boxed in by a towering red brick wall on three sides, it was a pleasant place. Well-suited and comfortable for a woman of Lady Casimire's advanced age.

Left alone at the foot of a white-gravel path, Mercy gazed about the shrubbery and blooming rosebushes a full minute before discovering the dowager. With her exceedingly broad-brimmed straw hat tied by a pink silk scarf beneath her chin, Lady Casimire ambled about her flowers with a pair of snippers, clipping away any browning rose blooms and the occasional weed that dared intrude on the perfection of her ladyship's handiwork.

Mercy made her way through the maze and stopped behind her.

"Miss Dansing," the dowager said without turning. "I have been thinking of you lately."

"I have come with sad news, m'lady."

Lady Casimire continued clipping, her face hidden by her hat.

"There was an accident, an explosion, at Greystone last evening. D'Abanville was injured, but Micah, the gardener, was killed."

She turned partially toward Mercy and Mercy glimpsed a portion of her aged white face. "Killed," the lady said.

"Yes."

Lady Casimire pondered the news a long moment. Finally she turned slightly and met Mercy's eyes with her own sharp perusal. "How very tragic. You look like hell yourself, my dear."

"I have just come from the hospital."

"London Hospital?"

Mercy nodded.

Less than steadily Lady Casimire rounded and walked to the shade of a spreading horse-chestnut tree that dominated the east corner of the garden. There were a wrought-iron table and chairs, a china tea service with two cups. She sat down in one of the chairs and spread her fine morning-tea gown evenly over her frail knees. Then she tugged off her gloves.

"Sit down, Miss Dansing."

Mercy sat.

"Would you care for tea?"

"Yes, thank you."

Lady Casimire poured them each a cup of the black steaming brew. She laced it with milk and sugar and placed it into Mercy's hands. She sipped at her own before saying, "And how was our Mr. D'Abanville this morning?"

"Resting. But I did not come here to discuss Dominick. I thought you would want to know about Micah."

"Whatever gave you that impression?"

"I was under the assumption that you felt somewhat responsible for Greystone's work force, considering the deal you struck with D'Abanville concerning their continuing employment at the estate."

Raising her face, Lady Casimire looked directly at Mercy for the first time. "My dear, I do not know what you are talking about."

"The agreement you made with D'Abanville that he

would not release any of the servants who had faithfully kept up the estate through the years."

"No such agreement was made," she responded.

Mercy frowned, confused. "Perhaps I misunderstood Roger."

"Mr. Forbes himself suggested the continuation of employment. I told him I could not care less if he took them on or not. I was too happy to be rid of the lot of them. I was glad to wash my hands of Greystone as well. It is D'Abanville's headache now, and good riddance."

Mercy placed her cup on the table and stood. "In that case, m'lady, I will not trouble you any longer. I was under the mistaken assumption that you would be upset by Micah's death."

"You are a testy little thing, Miss Dansing."

"I have just seen two men I know and care deeply for killed or very nearly killed. I have spent the entire night in London Hospital's indigent ward because St. Bartholomew turned D'Abanville away when he was bleeding to death in my arms. I have a right to be testy, m'lady."

"Sit down and drink your tea." Lady Casimire pointed one blue-veined finger toward Mercy's teacup. "Sit down," she said again. Mercy did so, and the dowager smiled. "I am sorry to hear about Micah's death. Tell me: did D'Abanville take it hard?"

"Very. Why do you ask?"

"Curiosity. I have heard from others that the two were very close."

A tree branch high overhead creaked in the wind.

Having finished her tea, Lady Casimire sat back in her chair, clasped her hands in her lap, and stared out over her garden. "Micah's mother was the servant who died at Greystone."

"Your lady's maid? The one who fell down the stairs?"

Her shrewd eyes shifted to Mercy's. "I will tell you something that I have never told another person. The young woman did not die immediately. I was first to her. She begged me to take care of her children, and I promised I would. Then she died in my arms. I admit to having been haunted since by her passing. I did not care for the children as promised. I had no children of my own, you see. Perhaps I was embittered by that, but I was not

comfortable around hers. I wanted no reminders . . .''
She smiled a little with some memory, and her harsh
features softened. "She was a rare breed. Faithful to the
end, was Colleen. I might have learned something from
her about loyalty, had I chosen to. But I didn't. I am too
old now to worry over it.''

"You mentioned children. Then there were others besides Micah. Where are they? Perhaps they should be
notified.''

"I cannot tell you because I don't know. I have not
seen them since they were taken from Greystone by their
aunt. Would you like more tea, Miss Dansing?''

Mercy shook her head. She waited as Lady Casimire
prepared herself a second cup of tea, then pursued, "Why
did Micah not leave Greystone with his aunt?''

"Colleen had two sisters, one of whom continued to
work at Greystone after Colleen's death. She agreed to
care for one of the children but insisted the others were
to be turned over to her sister. She chose to keep Micah.
Because of his . . . problem. She died some ten years
ago, as I recall.''

They sat in silence while the leaves overhead rattled in
the breeze. Finally Lady Casimire released a sigh and
looked at Mercy. "I shall take care of burial arrangements if you so desire.''

"I should think Dominick would prefer to do that. But
I will tell him of your generosity. I'm certain he will be
grateful.''

"I doubt it.'' Lady Casimire stared into her cup.

Mercy stood and the lady looked up.

"You will give him my condolences, Miss Dansing?''

"Yes.''

"You will tell him . . . I'm sorry. Exactly that. I'm
sorry. Please remember.''

"Yes,'' she repeated.

She turned to go, but stopped again as the dowager
added, "Take my advice and get out of Greystone as soon
as you can, my dear. Will you do that?''

Mercy looked around, and though the shadow of her
hat brim hid Lady Casimire's eyes, her mouth looked
pinched with age and worry.

"It is a wretched place,'' the dowager said.

"I will stay as long as he needs me," Mercy responded.

Lady Casimire smiled a little sadly. "Of course you shall, my dear. I never thought otherwise."

Less than an hour later Mercy stood in the rubble of what had once been D'Abanville's workroom and looked out through the crumbled, scorched ruins of the wall to the courtyard. Nothing had been disturbed since the explosion. Dominick's props lay strewn like broken toys beneath fallen timbers and bricks. Even as she watched, one of several paper cones was dislodged by the wind and went tumbling end over end into the distance.

She did not hear Stan McMillian approach until he spoke.

"Miss Dansing, are you all right?"

She turned to face him. "No," she said. "I don't think I am. Micah is dead."

"I know. I came by earlier to see you, and Roger told me. How is D'Abanville?"

"Grieving."

They stood silent as the wind whipped up ashes around Mercy's feet and scattered them over her skirt hems. Then McMillian looked at the parcel in his hand and said, "I thought you should see this. It is the next two entries in Mary Casimire's diary. I realize that you have other things on your mind now, but there is something about the entries that I find rather disturbing in light of what has been happening."

Mercy took one last look around her, then carefully walked back through the wreckage to McMillian. Standing in the hallway did nothing to lessen the impact of the effect of the destruction. If anything, it was intensified. All four walls had been blown outward, including the very wall that McMillian and his men had been repairing just days before. It had been a miracle that D'Abanville wasn't killed. It occurred to Mercy now that only one thing could have saved him. Micah. Micah had taken the full force of the explosion himself.

McMillian caught her arm and led her back up the corridor, stopping at Mary Casimire's bedroom. Opening his case, he withdrew several sheets of paper. "I think you should read this," he said.

She took the papers, entered Mary's room, and sat down in the rocking chair beside the window. Mercy rubbed her eyes a moment, then read the entry for yesterday's date, one hundred years ago:

4 October, 1788.

We made love for the first time today, Peter and I, in the carriage house. We could no longer deny our desire, nor fight it. I am glad it happened. I am only sorry we waited so long. I do love him so, regardless of what Richard says about it. Since the moment I first saw Peter, I felt as if we were destined to be together. I fully understand what love means now. It is loving regardless of the consequences, perhaps because of the consequences. I want to shout out to all of London that we are lovers, but I dare not. I can do nothing now to threaten what we have. Soon we will leave Greystone and return to Peter's home in Paris, but until then we must do nothing to raise my brother's suspicions. I fear Richard more every day. He looks at me in a lustful manner that is unnatural, and he invites his friends to do the same. They are always here now, coming and going throughout the day and all hours of the night. I was awakened again last night by my nightmares and heard their voices somewhere in the distance. I fear it was from that tower. I'm certain of it. There were women too, and the sounds were too horrible to describe. I rang for the help but no one came. I became frightened and went to Mama's room. She slept like a dead woman and it was all I could do to awaken her. From her bedroom window we looked out over the courtyard to the tower. I dare not repeat what I thought I saw. It would distress mama, and I know it could only be my imagination, some remnant of my nightmares.

5 October, 1788

My darling Peter was nearly killed today by what my brother claims was a stray bullet meant for a buck. Had Peter not stumbled at that precise moment, the bullet would have buried in his back instead of his shoulder. Richard claims it was an accident, but I don't think so. Perhaps now I can convince Peter that we should leave this place as soon as possible. I'm certain Richard realizes that I suspect him of trying to kill Peter. I have caught him staring at me numerous times, but all he does is smile as if he cares not a whit that I think of him as a murderer. I know in my heart that if we remain here something dreadful is going to happen. But I cannot leave without Mama and Papa, and Papa cannot be moved because of his health. Mama's health has begun failing as well. I have no one to turn to but Peter. He has promised me that somehow he will find a way to remove us all, myself, Mama, and Paper, from this house before the week is up. Now the only relief I can find from my fears is in his arms. I live for the moment when we are free of Greystone and that dreadful tower, and my brother. I must hold on until then. I must!

Mercy stared out the window.

McMillian moved up behind her. "Well," he said. "What do you think?"

She looked once more at the paper in her lap. Her eyes returned again and again to yesterday's date and the first line of Mary's entry: *We made love for the first time today, Peter and I, in the carriage house.*

McMillian said, "As you pointed out yesterday, Mary spoke of the killings, and of Richard's knowing one of the young women who was murdered. Last night as I lay in bed the thought occurred to me: perhaps Richard was somehow involved with those killings as well. It is plausible, I think, considering he later murdered the entire Casimire family."

"What point are you trying to make, Mr. Mc-Millian?"

"It does seem as if history is repeating itself."

"That is called coincidence, sir."

"Perhaps. However, I must admit to having become somewhat fascinated, as you are, by the diary and Mary

Casimire's dilemma. Knowing that she was murdered makes the reading of these final pages a grim task. I feel frustrated by knowing the murder is about to take place, and helpless that there is no way to stop it. Which brings me to you, my dear. I would feel better if you left Greystone, I think.''

"That is impossible."

"If you are in need of some place to stay—"

"D'Abanville needs me."

"He has Roger and Miriam."

"No."

"I cannot help but feel—"

"Please." She turned to face him. "I cannot leave him now. Not until he's recovered and this terrible investigation is ended. Then perhaps we'll both leave. He's mentioned Paris . . ." Mercy did her best to smile. "I appreciate your concern, however, and I hope you'll keep me informed about further developments with the diary. I feel as if I have grown to know Mary. If she were alive today, I know we would be close friends.''

"Perhaps I'll speak to Lady Casimire. She may know more about her husband's family than she has been willing to admit.''

Mercy left the chair and walked with him to the door. "This house has become quite an obsession with you, Mr. McMillian. Do you always become so entranced by the histories of the houses you restore?''

"No, I don't. But then, not all houses have such a long history of tragedy, Miss Dansing. Give D'Abanville my regards when you see him.''

His round face solemn and distressed, McMillian watched Mercy another long minute before walking up the hall. He paused one last time and looked back, once at her, then at the destruction farther down the hall. He then left the house.

Mercy requested a bath be sent to her room. In the meantime she searched the library for some material that would hopefully divert her mind from the terrible occurrences of the last two days. She picked up several books at random and returned to her room. The bath had been delivered. A fire had been started in the stove, and water put on to boil. She prepared her pot of tea, left it to steep before stripping off her soiled clothes and throwing them in a heap beside her bed. She then poured her cup of tea, climbed with it into the tub, and sank up to her shoulders in the scented water. She drank her tea, then reached for the books she had placed by the bath.

Dictionary of the Occult.

Mercy yawned and opened the book. She gazed disinterestedly at the listings, her mind still reliving the last terrible hours. Unable to concentrate she was about to toss the book aside when "BLACK MAGIC" caught her attention. Her eyes skimmed the lengthy definition. Then stopped.

> Connected strongly with black magic are unusual sexual practices, ranging from the deliberate defloration of innocent virgins to sexual activities between evil and mischievous spirits and sleeping humans. (*See* Incubus.)

She flipped through the pages.

> INCUBUS—A spirit which assumes the likeness of a man in order to have sexual intercourse with a human female, a function often performed as the woman sleeps and the reality of which is covered by the woman's belief that she was having an erotic dream.

Mercy threw the book to the floor. It landed open and the breeze through the open window fluttered the pages back and forth like a fan.

Cupping water in her hands, Mercy splashed her face, then wished she hadn't. The water felt oily and cold. She glanced toward the book, then away. She wouldn't allow herself to think it. Magic and the occult and theosophy, men who disappeared and appeared at the snap of a finger, mad monks who searched out women and killed them with knives—these were all products of someone's over imaginative mind.

She stumbled from the tub, wrapped herself tightly in her towel, and stood shivering in the middle of the floor.

Sleep. That's all she could think of, all her body craved. Yet as she stared toward the bed, some thread of reasoning rebelled.

"Not now," she said aloud. She backed from the bed, tripping over the book, kicked it aside angrily. The towel slid to the floor as she walked to the fire. She wasn't cold any longer, but hot. Her skin felt on fire.

Mercy picked up the broadsheet the servant had apparently brought with the bath. Tried to concentrate on the words that swam dizzily around on the page. She could not seem to focus. Her eyes kept closing by themselves. So tired. She hadn't realized how exhausted she was until now. Sleep would help. Just a short nap, then she would return to the hospital.

She paced.

She poured more tea and tried to drink it. Having grown cold, it seemed thick and bitter, and no matter how much sugar she added to it, nothing seemed to help.

She looked again at the broadsheet.

> Has anyone seen him? Can you tell us where he is? If you meet him you must take away his knife. Then give him to the ladies. They'll spoil his pretty fiz. And I wouldn't give you tuppence for his life.

Mercy turned the paper over.

> Richard Mansfield withdrew his spine-chilling *Jekyll and Hyde* from the Lyceum after a run of ten weeks. Before closing, the actor will give a benefit performance to raise funds for a night shelter for the homeless poor in the East End. Mr. Mansfield has determined to abandon the creepy drama, evidently beloved in America, in favor of wholesome comedy. The murderous Hyde will peer round the drawing-room windows and leap at his victims' throats for the last time during the forthcoming week. Experience has taught this clever young actor that there is no taste in London just now for horror on the stage. There is quite sufficient to make us shudder inside our own doors.

Mercy watched the paper slide from her fingers and float to the floor. The dark was closing in. She wondered how it had gotten so late so quickly.

Her head felt leaden. And it hurt.

She tried to stand. She felt slightly nauseated and tried to remember the last time she had eaten. Yesterday. Just before all hell had broken loose. Before Chesterton had shown up with his ridiculous notion that D'Abanville was Abby Russell's killer, and Mrs. Kinsdale's, that he was Jack the Ripper. Before the carriage house. *We made love for the first time today, Peter and I, in the carriage house.*

Coincidence.

She pushed from the chair and fixed her eyes on the bed. Rest. She needed rest. Just a short nap. And then . . .

18

Mercy opened her eyes and looked up into Miriam's tired but smiling face.

"I was beginning to think you would never awaken. You must have been exhausted," Miriam told her.

"A nap," Mercy finally managed.

"A nap? Do you realize how long you've slept, Miss Dansing? You left the hospital exactly twenty-four hours ago."

"That's not possible." Mercy tried to raise her head and was swept with a wave of nausea.

"Not to worry. You were exhausted, so we let you sleep. But I thought you would want to know. We are burying Micah this afternoon."

Confused, Mercy closed her eyes. "How is Dominick?"

"Home."

Mercy looked at her in surprise.

"We brought him home last evening. Roger didn't agree, insisted the hospital keep him overnight, but I thought he would rest better here. And he did. So did I. I slept like a dead woman throughout the night. I didn't realize how exhausted I was."

Miriam left the bed and walked to the window. She stared out several minutes before saying, "Look at that damnable tower. It wasn't even shaken by the explosion. Dominick insists on staying there, for whatever reason. So he can be alone, I suppose. To dwell on his problems." Her eyes came back to Mercy. "Perhaps you can convince him otherwise. He will listen to you."

"I have seen no evidence of that."

"He will now, I think, considering everything that has

336

happened. I'm worried about him, Mercy. I have never seen him so . . . despondent.'' Her voice became bitter as she added, ''He doesn't listen to me any longer. Not that he ever really did, you understand.''

''I'll do what I can, Miriam. But Dominick doesn't strike me as the sort of man who can be manipulated. I suspect he resents such interference.''

Miriam smiled with one side of her mouth as she turned her head to look at Mercy. A sickly yellow light poured through the window onto the side of her face. Mercy thought it was a little like staring at a theater mask of tragedy and comedy.

''Seems you have learned a lot about the Great D'Abanville already,'' Miriam said. ''It has taken you a month to learn what took me five years to realize. Dominick likes to control. Everything. There are no exceptions, Miss Dansing. I smothered him. He did not need a mother, he needed a partner. Yet I'm sure you will agree that it is impossible to know him and not desire to take care of him. He is like a child in some ways. You *want* to nurture him. I told him once that he should take himself a male lover if woman's natural instincts bothered him so much.'' She threw her head back in laughter as Mercy frowned. ''Don't act so shocked, my dear. It is done regularly in Paris. Not that I believe he ever did, mind you. I've seen young men who were . . . turned, who could be as clinging and suffocating as I ever was. Dominick always had enough admirers hanging about his heels without intentionally adding any more.''

Miriam closed her eyes briefly. When she opened them again her anger had returned. ''I suppose he doesn't have to contend with them any longer, thanks to Chesterton. There has to be some way to stop Chesterton's crusade to destroy Dominick, Mercy. If we don't stop him . . .''

Miriam glanced about the room as if by doing so she would free her mind of its distressing thoughts. Then she walked to the door. ''Stan McMillian was by earlier.'' She pointed to the dresser. ''He left you a sealed package and said it was imperative that you read it as soon as possible.''

Mercy waited until Miriam had left the room before attempting to leave the bed. She felt the aches and pains of her ordeal now. Her head hurt abominably, as it had when she imbibed too much champagne the night of D'Abanville's Liverpool performance.

She made it as far as the rocking chair before collapsing. Dear God, what was happening to her? The last thing she remembered was trying to rise from the rocker. Yet she had, at some time, dressed in her nightgown, climbed into the bed, and slept undisturbed for nearly twenty-four hours.

Or had she?

She looked toward the window. There had been dreams, remote as they seemed now. Or were they dreams? Of course they were. Still, the image of herself standing at the window looking down into Greystone's courtyard seemed so real. And there was another image—someone standing in the garden looking up, beckoning her down with a lift of his hand. He had been surrounded by people whose animallike faces had been lit by torches and . . .

No, I must have dreamed it, she said to herself. For that was where reality ended and the nightmares began.

Leaving her chair, Mercy rushed to the ewer and poured water into the basin, splashed her face, hoping the shock of the cold water would hasten away the disturbing flash of memory, dream-images, of herself standing, nude, in a circle of onlookers, hearing over and over again . . . What was it?

Aman . . . Amani . . . Amanita . . .

She slowly raised one leg and stared at the sole of her foot. Dirt. Caked and dried. Flashes of her dream bombarded her again, the cold wetness of the ground on her bare feet as she walked toward the gathering, the feel of the night wind on her naked body, the dull flutter of the torch flames as they were whipped by the wind. Her heart throbbing in her throat, Mercy continued to stare down at her feet and tried to reason why they were dirty if she had not left her bed during the night. The idea that she might have been sleepwalking disturbed her. She had never been a sleepwalker; there had to be some other explanation.

Frantically she attempted to retrace her movements from the day before. It all seemed a lifetime ago, almost as if the disaster had never happened. But it had happened. Micah was dead and D'Abanville had spent a very long, grueling night in London Hospital. She had then visited Lady Casimire, returned to Greystone, where she had relaxed in a steaming hot bath before tumbling headlong into some oblivion that was black as empty space. Except for the dream. And the words: Aman . . . Amani . . . Amanita . . .

Deciding there was no time to dwell on the strange occurrence now, she hurriedly dressed, brushed out her hair, and joined Miriam in the vestibule. Miriam was busily attempting to assign the servants the chore of cleaning up the debris from the explosion. The servants did not appear enthralled with the duty. D'Abanville's driver was among them. He smirked and winked insolently at Mercy as she entered the room. His appearance and manner reminding her of Oliver, Mercy shuddered and looked away.

As they all turned and shuffled out of the vestibule to their assigned tasks, Miriam shook her head. "God, they are a sorry lot. It's no wonder Lady Casimire left them to rot in this miserable house."

Roger entered the room then. "We've an hour before the funeral," he said. "Someone should get Dominick."

They looked at Mercy.

Dominick did not respond to her knock. As Mercy shoved open the door, the first sight to greet her was Malphas strutting up and down his perch with his wings outspread. He then flew across the room to light on the back of D'Abanville's head. D'Abanville raised his head off the pillow and swung his fist at the bird.

"Stupid bird," he said.

"Abracadabra!" Malphas screeched.

"Disappear," Dominick snapped. Then he looked around and saw Mercy.

"I assume you mean the bird," she said.

Wincing, he rolled his feet from the bed, sat up. He managed a smile that looked painful. She walked to him, wrapped her arms around his shoulders, and pressed his head gently against her breasts. She stroked his hair.

"I don't understand how it happened," came his muffled words. "It shouldn't have happened."

She took his face tenderly in her hands and tipped it up. "I'm sorry Micah died," she told him. "But I'm glad you did not."

He didn't move. Then his hands came up and closed, cold and hard, upon her wrists. "It shouldn't have happened," he repeated, and this time his eyes looked a little mad. "It should never have happened."

They buried Micah with little ceremony at Thrawl Street Cemetery. Dominick stood at the head of the grave and read from a book that was not the Bible. Mercy stood between Roger and Miriam, listening to the words rise and fall with the wind, felt the sting of dirt as it whipped against her ankles and shifted through the flowers on the coffin. There were flowers from the Greystone servants, who were scattered in groups about the grave, flowers from Stan McMillian, Lady Casimire, and, of course, D'Abanville. The cloying sweet fragrances of the arrangements made Mercy ill, and even before the reading was ended she turned and left the site, stood with her back to the grave and looked out through the distant gates of the cemetery to the busy London street. That was when she noticed the stately coach parked some distance away and the small figure of a woman, dressed in black, whose hat and veil covered her face entirely. Lady Casimire.

It was all over in ten minutes. Roger and Miriam boarded one coach. Believing D'Abanville still wished to be alone, Mercy was about to join them, as she had on her journey to the cemetery. He caught her arm, however, and directed her toward his own coach. That was when he saw Lady Casimire.

He stopped.

As the grip on her arm became tighter, Mercy glanced down at his hand and bit her lip. He then pushed her toward the coach.

"Get in," he said.

She obeyed him. He then boarded and took his place across from her. He did not look at her. Neither did he look at Lady Casimire as their coach rolled by hers.

Mercy caught a glimpse of the woman's frail white hand
lifted in greeting as they passed. Then she was gone.

They rode in silence to Greystone. Mercy had thought
earlier that she had smelled liquor on D'Abanville's
breath. Now she was certain of it. The coach smelled of
brandy and flowers and cold fresh earth. It was suffocating.

The crowd outside Greystone's gates parted in silence
as they passed. Then someone called out, "Hang him!"
Another cried, "Murderer!" A stone hit the coach, then
another before the gates could be closed behind them and
secured. D'Abanville only lowered his head a little,
looked at his hands that were loosely linked between his
knees. Then his eyes came back to Mercy's, and they
burned.

Mercy, Miriam, and Roger met in the parlor. D'Abanville did not join them.

Mercy took her place by the fire and warmed her chilled
hands in the heat while Miriam walked to the window.
"Look at him," she said. "He just stands there alone.
Do you realize what this has done to him? He has lost
everything now. That bastard Chesterton has done this."

"He did not kill Micah," Mercy said.

"As good as. Had Dom been in his right mind, the
accident would never have happened. He knew the dangers, was always careful about charging his powder, cau-
tious to the point of fanaticism about it." She shook her
head. "He frightens me when he's like this."

"Have you seen the newspapers?" Roger asked.
"Seems there has been a great deal of response to the
reward notice in the *Gazette*. The CID is questioning
numerous witnesses who have come forth with information about the Ripper."

"No doubt Chesterton will be here soon to humiliate
Dominick further."

Roger looked at Miriam directly. "You are right that
the inspector must be stopped. But how?" He left his
chair and walked to the decanters of sherry and brandy
on the table against the wall. "I don't know about you
ladies, but I need a drink. This entire ugly affair is beginning to grate on my nerves. Just last night the men
whom I stationed on watch around the perimeter of the

estate caught three different intruders attempting to sneak over the walls." He peered at Mercy over the top of his glasses. "One of them was carrying a wooden stake and a hammer. He actually believes Dominick is a vampire; intended to drive that damnable piece of wood through his heart if he got the opportunity."

Miriam turned from the window, her face even whiter, her eyes on the decanter as Roger poured himself a drink. As he moved to restopper it, she said, "Perhaps . . . just a small one, Roger. Please." She glanced at Mercy and her smile was thin and forced. "Under the circumstances, I think Dom will understand."

Mercy excused herself and started for her room. She felt tired and ill, and disturbed still by her behavior last night. She dreaded the confrontation between Chesterton and Dominick that she knew would come very soon. At this moment she didn't feel much like coping with it. She only wanted to sleep, but even that distressed her. She was not even safe in her dreams. In truth, it seemed her dreams and reality were becoming more and more difficult to tell apart.

There was a group of servants standing at the foot of the stairs. They watched as she approached.

"Yer lookin' right peaked, Miss Dansin'," one of them said.

Mercy recognized her as the maid who generally brought her her meals.

"Is anythin' wrong?" the servant asked.

"My head is aching," she said.

"I've got just the remedy for that—a cup of jasmine tea."

"I don't care for jasmine tea," Mercy responded.

"Oh, y'll like this. Me own granny concocted it. 'It's a sure cure for aught that ails ya,' she used to say."

Mercy did not feel like debating the issue, so she smiled her thanks, passed through the watchful group, and started up the stairs. She looked back once and found them still staring at her, unsmiling.

One of the young women stepped forward then and said, "It were a real tragedy about Micah, don't you think?"

"Certainly."

" 'Course, he always did have a way of buttin' in where he shouldn't. That's what happens, I s'pose, to people who go about mindin' other people's business."

Frowning, Mercy left the girl at the foot of the stairs and returned to her room, closing the door behind her. She felt relieved to be alone at last to contemplate her feelings.

Leaning back against the door, she looked directly at her image in the mirror. The servants were right. She was looking less and less like Mercy Dansing every day. There were dark blue smudges under her eyes. Her cheeks appeared even more gaunt than they had upon her arrival to Greystone. She could not seem to think cohesively any longer, and that was what frightened her most. Gone were all the aspirations that had driven her just short weeks ago. She never thought of the wretches she had left back in the East End, never shook a fist in the face of society for ignoring the poor's plight, never imagined walking down Park Lane waving a red flag for socialism. She never daydreamed about the Nightingale School of Nursing. Never even imagined returning to Huntingdon. The only sharp memory that remained was of D'Abanville. He obsessed her every waking thought, every stirring of emotion. At some point she had turned into Abigail Russell and Miriam and all the others before them. He owned her now—body and soul—like some dark angel of heaven or hell. For that's what loving him was: heaven and hell, sublime and agonizing too. Even now, as she remembered the carriage house, her body took on that slow hot fire that brought color, the only color, to her face. And she realized in one stunning instant that D'Abanville was the only thing that could make her feel alive. Truly alive. Without him she would be . . . lost.

Mercy walked to the dresser. That was when she noticed Stan McMillian's letter. She picked it up, studied it a long moment, hesitant. She opened it. Attached to several papers similar to those he had delivered to her before was a note from McMillian himself:

Miss Dansing:

I called earlier today and was told by some surly servant that you were unwell and sleeping. I find this most distressing. Upon reading the following transcript, you will—I hope—understand why. Enclosed you will find the next entry from Mary Casimire's diary. I trust you will find it as disturbing as I did. I am off this very evening to speak with Lady Casimire.

Regards
S.M.

5 October, 1788.

I am ill. I feel as if my life's blood is being very slowly drained from me. Mama too is weak. All she does is sleep. Greystone has become like a mortuary. Bleak. Still. Death is waiting around each corner. Sometimes I fantasize that I see him, Death. Often these last days I have thought I would welcome him. It would be an end to the horrible dreams that rack my endless nights. An end to my fear of Richard and his companions. But Peter continues to give me hope. He is my strength, my courage. He has promised: he will save me from Greystone if it is the last thing he ever does. I will hold on to that faith. Forever, if I must.

Mercy walked to the window. Clouds were piling up on the horizon like great gray walls, blocking out the sunlight, ushering in a premature dusk. She shivered in the breeze, not because it was cold, as it had been at the cemetery. It wasn't cold, but threatening.

The clouds moved directly overhead, twisting and coiling around the top of the towerhouse. Miriam had been right. The damnable tower stood like some battle-weary relic of the past, defying all forces. As Mercy looked more deeply into the ceiling of purple clouds, a great wall of sheet lightning split the sky, shocking her eyes into temporary blindness. Closing her eyes she waited for the thunder. But it didn't come. There was only silence, and when she opened her eyes again there was only the red. The same red that had stopped the entire city of London that hot August afternoon, the same red that had driven the people a little mad.

Then the chimes. Soft. Distant. She sensed that he was

near and her heart began its rapid throbbing of expectation.

She turned. D'Abanville stood just inside the room, his back to the closed door.

"I didn't hear you knock," she said.

"I didn't knock."

"What do you want?"

"You." He raised his hand to her. "Come here."

She could not take her eyes from his hand. It seemed to be reaching for her over a long, long distance. Beckoning her from beyond some threshold from which, should she cross it now, she would never return. The allure of it frightened her. Yet even as she thought to deny it, she felt the awakening of her body, as she always did in his presence, the warm stirring of her senses. She knew the magic, had experienced it. Yet there was something about him, some change, that frightened her, threw up those doors of resistance that began crumbling piece by piece to the wayside as soon as he smiled. Chesterton's words of warning, his suspicions, kept rushing back to remind her that she did not know this man. She knew nothing about him.

"I've missed you," he said.

She backed away, feeling the wind through the open window rake her back and billow her hair around her shoulders. She felt numb and wondered if this were simply another one of her odd dreams, her fantasies that were becoming more real every day. Then her eyes were drawn to the floor, to the book she had thrown down—how long ago? *Dictionary of the Occult*. It lay open, and even as she watched, the stirring of the air in the room riffled the pages.

She forced her eyes from the book, back to his face. His beautiful face, full of light and dark. He moved toward her slowly, and as he neared her, she could see his suffering, his disappointments, his anger and pain etched deeply into the flesh around his eyes and mouth. As he lifted his hand to stroke her face, she did not move, but caught her breath in anticipation, nestled her cheek into his palm like a love-hungry child. She was no longer strong enough to fight it. She did not want to. Like Mary Casimire, she was tired of the struggle. If he was Death, she welcomed him. Ached for him to put an end to this madness that had gripped her since coming to London. It seemed she had been but one step ahead of the Grim Reaper the last months, running faster and faster toward a fate she could no longer control, had never controlled. She knew that now. Before her stood eternity. Her past. Her present. Her future. Her existence was somehow entwined with his, and she could not escape it. She no longer wanted to.

She turned her face up to his.

He kissed the hollow at the base of her neck. He opened her gown, slid his dark fingers over the white flesh of her breast and closed them over her hardened nipple. She made a soft moan of longing deep in her throat. Her body shivered as his hot tongue dipped in her ear once, twice, teeth gently nipping her sensitive lobe while his breath whirled inside her head.

His hands crept up, skimming her throat, cradling her face as he gently turned her. He backed her toward the bed, and she went willingly, defenseless against his magic, against the tide of desire that rose up inside her to drive rationality from her mind.

They stopped at the bed. He dropped his hands to the opening of her blouse, twisted his fingers into it, and sheared it of its buttons, as she had his in the carriage house. He released her skirt and it fell to the floor. Her pantalets followed with as little effort. Only her chemise remained clinging to her damp skin. He took it too, then, and rent it apart so it fell like so much debris to the floor. Then he went to one knee and, with the tips of his fingers, rolled the gossamer stockings down her legs to her ankles and removed her shoes. He stood. She stood before him, naked and unashamed while the heat of his perusal swept her body like a wave of red fire.

He removed his shirt, his shoes, his trousers. His body was bruised and blistered, yet the shaft of him was erect and desirous, throbbing with the same passion's blood that turned her own body into a caldron of yearning.

"Lie down," he said in that hypnotizing voice that brooked no refusal.

She did, throwing her arms wide and her legs even wider. As in her dreams, they felt shackled to the bed.

She could not move, but waited, her senses straining for the first touch of his mouth, his fingers on her quivering, damp flesh.

When it came, she could not control her cry of surprise. As if she had been scored by the very flames that had burned his flesh two nights before, she writhed and twisted as he buried his face into the soft, sensitive skin of her lower belly, then lower and lower until her body shuddered with shock and acceptance of what he was doing, what he had done before. Her legs thrashed helplessly and he caught them over his shoulders, held them in place, fingers digging into the pale skin of her thighs while his lips and mouth and teeth drove her toward delirium.

She tried to cry out, but there was only a moaning, a madness that made her thrust her hips up, then down, then up with a wantonness she had once experienced only in the secret confines of her mind. His tongue repeatedly thrust, then drew away, then thrust, delving deeper with each soft, moist penetration, until she became mindless, until every nerve had centered there where his tousled head moved with feverish motion against her secret aching flesh.

Then he left her, stood at the foot of the bed as he had in her dreams, his body stretching, arcing toward her like some pagan god of lust. She slid back on the bed as he raised his hand, and for one spellbinding moment light seemed to dance on his fingertips. Raising her arms above her head, she gripped the cold smooth rail of her bed and looked him in the eye.

"I want you inside me," she said roughly. "Deep inside me. Now. *Now!*"

He moved over her and pressed her legs wide apart with his knees, then slid his hands beneath her buttocks, lifting her body up, then away, until she was rolling her head from side to side and pleading. Only then did he sink deep into passion's blood-red heart, into the center of her, stretching and burning. Slightly behind him the mirror reflected his rise and fall against her, the smooth curve of his back and the dancing muscles of his shoulders.

Their bodies were hot and growing hotter. His chest

heaved, and now his breaths came in pants each time their bodies met. As she clung to the bed, the cold iron biting painfully into her sweating palms, she was reminded that this was no dream. His hands were on her waist, her hips, her breasts, as he lowered his sweat-moistened head to hers and took her mouth with his, his tongue mimicking the thrust and draw of his body inside her. He groaned, and it occurred to Mercy that he was experiencing pain. Not just the ache for assuagement that she was experiencing, but a brutal, piercing pain of the flesh. His blistered skin was angry and hot, and the stinging bite of his own sweat was like salt in his wounds.

And yet he wanted her, with a fierceness, a possessiveness, that made her lose all control. She released her grip on the bed and reached out for him, twisted her fingers into his curling damp hair and dragged his face back to hers. She sucked his lips and tongue and raised her legs high up over his back until he was moaning, "Damn you, damn you," into her mouth, until consciousness turned into oblivion. Throwing her head back, she cried, "Oh God oh God oh God," as she was swept by an instant of purest sensation, of transcendent expansion, a universe of dancing light that, for a moment, lifted her beyond the infinite.

Still he moved, and as her world righted itself she looked up into his face. It seemed too exquisite to be human, just as what had happened, was happening, between them seemed too savage to be love. Yet it was love. She knew it. It was all too right between them to be anything but love.

Then his dark head was thrown back and his body stiffened. He lunged one last time, throbbed again and again, filling her to overflowing with his seed. And as he eased his body down onto hers, he cupped his hands under her buttocks and raised her hips, letting her take and keep all of him deep inside her.

"My love," he sighed. "Oh, my love."

Mercy awakened some hours later, stared at the ceiling, listening to the silence. The rain had stopped momentarily but the storm still hovered over the house, brightening the room in erratic light every few seconds.

The soft click of the door closing brought her out of her dreamy state. She reached for Dominick. He was gone.

Mercy sat up in bed, shivering from the damp air that swirled through the window. She stared at the door, ears straining for the sound of footsteps. There!

As quickly as possible she left the bed, ran to the door, and looked out. The sparsely lit hallway was empty. She rushed back for her clothes, pulled them on with haste, disliking the clammy feel of them. Without donning her stockings, she shoved her feet into her shoes, ran to the door, out into the hall, to the stairs, hesitating as she looked down the curving balustrade. It was a little like looking down a black well.

She took one step, then another, plunging deeper into the dark. Down and down she went, until, reaching the floor, she hurried up the hallway to the vestibule. The front door had recently been opened. She could smell the damp wind that had rushed into the room.

Mercy threw open the door and paused under the porte-cochere as she searched down the drive. Then, picking up her skirts, she ran as fast as she could until she was certain she could call out without being heard from the house.

"Dominick!"

Lightning turned the world into daylight. D'Abanville looked around, his face like ice-blue marble.

"Are you insane?" she demanded.

"Go back to the house," came the quiet command.

The dogs at his side lowered their heads and growled.

"Not until you tell me what you are about to do."

"That is none of your business."

"It is," she shouted. "I care for you!"

"Then just leave me alone, Mercy. I have to do what I came to London to do."

"Which is?"

A silence ensued, as heavy as the clouds overhead.

"You wouldn't understand," he finally said.

"I might."

Blackness poured in on them again. For a minute D'Abanville was lost in the shadows.

"Please!" she called out. "This can only make matters worse. Don't you care what Chesterton thinks? What all of London thinks?''

Silence.

Mercy moved forward, strained her eyes to see through the darkness. She saw him then, walking down the drive, his black cape billowing about his legs. She began to run.

''Damn you!'' she cried, and for an instant she thought of Miriam and her obsession with protecting him, with loving him. Mercy saw the same obsession in herself now, felt mad with it as she shouted, ''I won't let you do this! I won't!''

She grabbed for him, her fingertips brushing the wet wool of his cape, but nothing else. He whirled to face her, stood tall above her, his countenance an odd mixture of confusion, fear, and determination. He might have touched her face, or perhaps it was only the wind that momentarily caressed her cheek.

''My love,'' came his whisper, ''have faith. I beg you, have faith.''

''Faith!'' she cried. ''Do not ask me to have faith; there is nothing left of faith inside me!'' He stepped away, and before Mercy could reach for him again, a crack of fire not unlike the lightning jolted her off her feet and threw her to the ground. When she lifted her head, he was no longer there.

Disappeared. . . .

19

Mercy jumped in her sleep, then opened her eyes while her heart beat so painfully in her chest she almost cried out. Surely it had all been a dream. Just another terrible dream that, like the others, seemed vividly real.

No dream. Neither his lovemaking nor his vanishing in sulfurous smoke had been an illusion.

"Miss Dansing," came a voice outside the door. "Miss Dansing, are you all right?"

"Who is there?"

"It's the maid, miss. There is someone to see you downstairs. A Detective Lawton. He says to hurry."

Mercy rolled from the bed, looked down the long length of her skirt, finding it crushed into wrinkles and the soles of her shoes crusted with mud. She didn't bother to brush out her hair, but splashed her face with water, dried it, then hurried to follow the servant down to the vestibule. Lawton stood in his rigidly correct manner just inside the door, his hat tucked under his arm, his free hand shoved into his coat pocket. When he saw Mercy, his face melted a little in relief, then in consternation.

He clicked his heels and bowed in greeting. "Miss Dansing. I am sorry to have disturbed you so early."

"What do you want?"

"I should like to speak with you privately. Perhaps outside?" Opening the door, he waited for her to pass out of the house before joining her. He did not stop, but took her arm gently and ushered her toward his coach.

Taken off guard, Mercy stared at his hand and said, "What are you doing?"

"Remain steady," he said. "Please get into the coach."

351

"Why?"

"Please, Miss Dansing."

"Are you arresting me?"

"Indeed not."

"Then why—"

"Chesterton wishes to see you."

"Well, then, tell Chesterton he can come here."

"He cannot do that. Now, get into the coach." He lifted her and put her in the coach. He had not even settled onto his seat before the vehicle lurched away. He fell with a huff into the leather cushions.

"I demand to know the meaning of this," Mercy said. "If the intent is not to arrest me—"

"Chesterton has information regarding D'Abanville he thinks you should know."

"Information?" Mercy's heart beat loudly in her ears, drowning out the clip-clop of the horses' hooves on the granite sets. She stared at Lawton, waiting for him to speak. "Well? What is it?"

"I don't know."

"What do you mean you don't know? Didn't he tell you?"

"No. He was . . . unable to."

"Sir!" she nearly cried. "You are speaking in riddles. Why was he not—"

"He was nearly killed this morning."

Mercy braced herself against the back of the seat and stared unblinking into Lawton's eyes.

"Actually, it was just before dawn. He was returning home, and as he unlocked his door, some fiend came up behind him and . . . stabbed him in the back. A neighbor heard him cry out or he might have lain there and bled to death."

Mercy closed her eyes. For a moment consciousness swirled in and out of her brain like wisps of smoke.

"Miss Dansing . . ." Lawton changed to the seat beside her, took her hand, patted it gently before briskly rubbing her wrists. "Please, Miss Dansing, it has been a very long morning and I do not think I can deal with a swooning woman. Pray do not swoon."

"I will do my best," she responded in a small voice. "Tell me. How is Chesterton?"

"He was barely conscious when I saw him last. In truth, I fear it was only his determination to see you that kept him awake."

Mercy turned to look at Lawton directly. He seemed very young in the dim coach, much younger than Chesterton. His eyes looked a little frightened. "You say you do not know what he learned about D'Abanville."

"Only that the inspector's investigator arrived in London from Paris just after midnight. He sent word immediately to Chesterton and they met and discussed the matter until just before dawn."

"And Chesterton told you nothing?"

"He only asked for you. He said I was to get you to the hospital by any means possible without alerting the others."

"Then I assume that whatever information he gleaned from this man is not good."

"I could not say. You must understand, he was in a great deal of pain. Had the knife entered another inch to the right, he would likely be dead."

"He does not know who attacked him?"

"Of course he has his suspicions."

"Of course. It is not too difficult to determine whom he suspects."

"Who else would want him dead?"

Mercy turned her head and looked out the window. A numbness had come over her since pleading with D'Abanville the night before not to leave Greystone. There was no denying to herself now that he was walking London's streets. But beyond that, she refused to acknowledge the doubts that twisted like nightmares in the shuttered recesses of her mind. Time after time she had battled them back, only to have them rear up again and again, stronger and more frightening every time, until she had begun to question her own sanity.

Faith. She had denied to herself that she even believed in the term any longer. Yet there it was. Fighting an invisible war with her disillusionment. What would she become if he let her down? He had become something to believe in, despite the controversy surrounding him. Perhaps because of it. When the world had turned a blind eye on her in the blackest time of her life, he had taken

up her hand, had given her hope, friendship. Had asked
only that she return the favor with a little show of . . .
faith.

The hour was yet early. The streets were mostly deserted but for the occasional vendors and gutter cleaners,
who were wading through ankle-deep torrents of rainwater. A little desperately they glanced toward the sky,
knowing that another day of slack business because of
the deluge would mean another day of empty stomachs.
If they were unable to work, they would be unable to buy
food. For a ha'penny they could buy a ha'penny meal at
the soup kitchen, a meal consisting of a crust of bread
and a broth thickened with meat. But they would have to
sell many a sprig of cress for that. And no one would be
buying cress on such a miserably wet day. Mercy knew
that with winter just around the corner the people's despair was only just beginning. George Balfour had once
told her that fifty-five percent of all East End children
died before they were five years of age. It was mostly the
winter's cold and its diseases that killed them.

They took the back alley to London Hospital, taking
no chances that they would be seen by any passersby.
They entered the infirmary through the back door. It was
a route with which Mercy was well-acquainted. She had
taken it every morning that she volunteered to work at
London Hospital.

The crew from some local workhouse had already finished their chores and had taken their places around the
tables provided by the hospital to feed the men. Heaped
high on a platter in the center table were pieces of bread,
chunks of grease and fat pork, the burnt skin from roasted
joints, and bones—everything the patients of the hospital
had left on their plates, had handled with their disease-
infested fingers and mouths. But the starving men gathered around the table cared little. Better to chance
catching an illness than slowly starving, most agreed. So
they ate ravenously of the swill, and when they could eat
no more, wrapped as much as they could in handker-
chiefs and stuffed them into their shirts.

After passing through the kitchen, Mercy and Lawton
arrived at the same emergency area D'Abanville had been

brought to only days ago. Chesterton was there, his face pale as the sheet beneath him.

Lawton bent over him and whispered, "Sir, I have brought Miss Dansing."

His eyelids fluttered.

Lawton repeated, "Sir, I have returned."

"Lawton?"

"Yes, sir."

"Ah. Good man. You have brought her, I assume?"

"Indeed I have."

"No trouble?"

"None, sir. I think we were not noticed leaving."

"Good. Bring her here."

Lawton caught Mercy's arm. She refused, stared into his face before looking past him to Chesterton. "Please," she said. "Let me go. I don't want any part of this. I don't want to know!"

Chesterton raised his hand.

"No!" She shook her head, and for the first time realized she had begun to cry.

"Miss Dansing." Chesterton's voice was thready. "Quickly. I do not know how much longer I can hold on."

She felt herself moved toward the invalid man. His hand came out and gripped her wrist in a surprisingly hard manner considering his condition.

"Young woman," he said, "I have not suffered here in misery for the last hour, refusing medication from my doctor, only to be told that because of some idiotic infatuation you hold for D'Abanville you will not hear me out. If you do not cease struggling this minute, I will see that Lawton arrests you for accessory to murder."

Weeping, she said, "Please, you do not realize what you are asking of me. I love him. He saved my life. He gave me the strength to go on living; he gave me hope, dammit, and I will not let you destroy that! Please, please don't ask this of me!"

"Miss Dansing, listen to me. Do not let mere gratitude get in the way of logic. Do not misinterpret your gratitude for love."

"Don't. Please, don't!"

With great effort he caught the front of her dress and

pulled her down, so closely his sour breath filled her nostrils and the tears from her eyes fell on his face and ran down his cheeks. So closely her nose bumped his and her hair surrounded them both like a silver blanket and puddled on the dingy yellow sheets beside his head.

"Miss Dansing, I fear my patience is at an end. Another moment and I . . . another moment and I may lose consciousness altogether. I tell you this only for your sake. I know you are innocent in all of this, and I find your unwavering loyalty most commendable. But . . ."

He moistened his lips with his tongue. Briefly his eyes rolled back in his head before he pulled himself together and gripped her more tightly, determinedly. He clenched his teeth with pain before saying, "Do you remember our last conversation . . . in this . . . in this very hospital?"

She nodded.

"I told you then . . . something about Dominick D'Abanville was not . . . was not right. Strange."

"Please. I don't want to know. What good could come of telling me?"

"Must be aware . . . get out of Greystone immediately. Don't go back. Miss Dansing . . . my man from Paris has learned . . . Dominick D'Abanville . . . is dead."

Mercy stared into Chesterton's eyes, unbreathing.

"Did you understand me?"

"I don't believe you," she whispered at last.

"True. D—D'Abanville is dead. Died fifteen years ago. Buried at . . . Montmartre Cemetery, north Paris."

Mercy closed her eyes. Shook her head. "Another Dominick D'Abanville," she said.

"Magician. Death records prove . . ."

Chesterton's eyes rolled closed. His hands released her dress and wrist and fell limply to his chest. But Mercy remained as if she were still shackled by his bone-wrenching grip and the macabre message his lips had last whispered. "I don't believe you," she said into his still face. "That is not possible."

Lawton moved up behind her, took her shoulders in his hands, and lifted her off Chesterton. "He's lost consciousness," he said.

"He's lying," she said. "This is all some sort of vicious trick just to frighten me into leaving D'Abanville. He's lying."

"I would not know, Miss Dansing. He did not pass on the information to me. I can assure you, however, that the inspector's source in Paris is more than reliable. Chesterton is genuinely concerned for you, and in light of what happened to him this morning—"

"You don't think Dominick did this? Do you have proof? Did anyone see him . . . Well? Did they?"

Her voice had risen to a hysterical pitch. Lawton looked about disconcertedly, lacking the polished, seemingly uncrackable veneer of his superior. His cheeks dotted with color, he glared at Mercy and said, "Can you provide us with proof that he did not leave Greystone in the early hours of morning?"

She covered her face with her hands, her heart like a bleeding wound in her chest.

"Miss Dansing, did D'Abanville leave Greystone this morning?" He gripped her shoulders and shook her. "Miss Dansing!"

"Yes!" She screamed it.

The confession ripped through Mercy like a knife. She began to shake uncontrollably. "What have I done?" she said. "Oh, God, what have I done?"

"You are going to help us stop Jack the Ripper," Lawton said kindly.

"But he is not Jack the Ripper. And he did not kill Abigail Russell or anyone else. I don't care what Chesterton said. I know there has to be some explanation—"

"He will be given that opportunity at the station. I promise you that D'Abanville will be given a fair trial—"

"Fair! The people of this city will murder him before he ever sees the inside of a judge's chamber—dear God, before you can get him so far as Greystone's gates if they think he is the Ripper." Twisting from Lawton's grip, Mercy backed away. "I want to go home. I want to go home now, Inspector."

"I think that would not be wise."

"You have gone after him already. Haven't you?"

Lawton stared at her a moment longer before squaring

his shoulders, taking on the same cool exterior as Chesterton.

"You bloody bastards," she hissed. "Take me home now or I will tell all of London that you kidnapped me from Greystone and tortured me into lying about D'Abanville's whereabouts this morning simply so you could at last have a scapegoat for your own inabilities to stop the Ripper."

"You wouldn't," he said, stunned.

"Give it a chance," she said. Lowering her head and looking perhaps a little mad, she clenched her fists and walked toward him so he was backing up the aisle. "I see you ain't dealt too much wi' East End riffraff, boyo. We can sing a mighty pretty song when we want. And considerin' that her majesty has recently opened an eye to our mistreated lot—"

"All right," he said. He fingered his tie before taking one last look toward Chesterton. "I'll no doubt answer for this. Well . . . get on with you," he said.

Mercy shoved by him and ran for the coach.

Mercy's worst fears were realized as they turned onto Buckingham Street. Greystone's gates were thrown wide. People crowded the entrance, craning to see over and around others. Lawton called out to the driver to do his best to get the coach through the crowd, but when they found that was impossible, Mercy threw open the door and jumped to the street despite Lawton's frantic pleas that she stop.

She elbowed her way through the mass at the gate. By the time she reached the first bend of the drive, the shouting of the crowd had become a roar.

"It's Jack the Ripper!"

"Lynch him!"

There came the sound of glass shattering and the piercing whistles of the police as they did their best to warn the hysterical crowds away. Finally Mercy reached the police barricade. Shoulder to shoulder, they stood against the heaving masses, their faces straining from their efforts to keep them back. But with each surge of the frenzied multitude, they lost another foot, then two.

In that moment Greystone's front door was thrown

open. A swarm of blue-coated policemen exited, and among them, D'Abanville. He looked around only once. As if he knew that she stood there, his eyes found Mercy's. The barricade gave way in that moment and the crowd rushed like a tidal wave over the police, carrying Mercy with it. She caught a glimpse of Dominick diving toward the coach, of the police lifting their clubs to fight back the onrushers.

"Get him!" the people shouted.

"Kill him!"

"Lynch him now!"

With a sob Mercy ran toward the police, pushing and shoving her way past the frantic crowd. She cried out Dominick's name as the mob surged over the men who were trying so valiantly to protect D'Abanville. Then someone shoved Mercy from behind. Only the terror of falling beneath the maddened crowd kept her from tumbling completely to the ground. She grabbed for anything that would offer support, nearly dragging a man down with her. Someone set her roughly back on her feet. Finding her balance, she ran on, elbowing her way around and sometimes under and over the moving bodies.

Dominick and the police seemed frozen amid the mayhem. They were so close and yet so far from the cab.

The chant of "Lynch him" had risen to an ear-splitting pitch. Mercy knew that should these people break through that last protective body of policemen, there would not be enough of D'Abanville left to hang. Even though there was no hope of his hearing her, she cried out his name over and over. Where was his magic now? she thought frantically. Why did he not use it to vanish from this melee before they reached him and killed him?

Time after time she hit and kicked and clawed her way one step closer, dodging the indiscriminate swing of some club or fist. Once she didn't duck fast enough and was stunned by a blow to her cheek. For a terrifying moment the mad world went dark and confusing, full of mind-splitting pain that made her cry out with even greater fear. Then someone stumbled into her back, jolting her to awareness again, and once more she struggled toward the police, angrier and more determined to reach D'Abanville than before.

To her own dismay and frustration, it was the police who kept her from him. As she finally arrived at the human barricade, an overzealous policeman drove his stick like a battering ram into her shoulder. D'Abanville saw, and for the first time since he had left the house his face became maddened, his eyes crazed as he helplessly watched her reel away into some man who tossed her aside.

Suddenly there were arms closing around her, holding her, struggling to drag her back toward the house. Mercy tried her best to jerk away but was only shoved more forcefully into her captor's arms by some man who, in his exuberance to crash through the police defenses, lost his balance and fell backward into Mercy. She twisted around and looked up into the familiar features of Greystone's driver.

"Let me go!" she screamed. She drove her fist into his shoulder. He winced, but set his jaw more determinedly and dragged her on toward Greystone's open front door. Police were stationed there as well, forcing back any persons who thought to trespass beyond that threshold. Beyond them stood Roger, his face white with worry, his eyes wide with fright behind his lenses. They widened even further when he saw Mercy.

With one more surge the driver pulled her through the last of the crowd, beyond the police, and into the house. She fell to the hard floor at Roger's feet, weeping and pounding the white marble with her fist. Roger dropped to his knees beside her, wrapped his arm about her shoulders.

"There, there," he said. "Miss Dansing, try to control yourself."

Throwing back her head so her hair flew wildly about her shoulders, she shouted, "How could you do this? How could you allow them to come here and take him like this when they have no proof—"

"But they have!" he said sternly. "Have you not seen the morning broadsheets? They have a witness who said she was accosted by D'Abanville the night Stride and Eddowes were murdered. She identified him by the sketch in the *Gazette*."

"She is a liar!" Mercy struggled to her feet. "Surely

that is not what has driven these people to such madness!''

Shaking his head, Roger withdrew the rolled-up broadsheet from his pocket. He opened it and Mercy stared down at the sketch of D'Abanville, his black cape whirling about his knees, his eyes staring in a hypnotizing manner into a supine woman's eyes. Behind his back he held a long-bladed knife. Beneath was the quote:

"He accosted me just down from Mitre Square. Come up behind me in a dark alley, grabbed me about me throat, and says, 'I'll cut off yer head if you scream.' I was bloody terrified."

Beneath the quote were details of the Stride inquest.

Mercy closed her eyes, threw the paper to the floor. She looked frantically about the vestibule. ''Where is Miriam?'' she demanded.

''D'Abanville's office,'' Roger replied. ''But I warn you, she will do you little good, Miss Dansing . . .''

Mercy ran down the corridor, no more than glanced toward the distant destruction before throwing open the door of D'Abanville's office. Miriam sat in his chair, her head on his desk, her hair spilling wildly over stacks of papers. Malphas fluttered his wings and danced up and down on the back of the chair.

''Watch out!'' the bird screamed, ''Here comes trouble. Heads up, y' old lush, and face the music! Miri's a lush! Abracadabra! Miri's a—''

Miriam threw an empty decanter as hard as she could at the bird. It shattered against the wall, missing Malphas by several feet.

Mercy stopped at the desk, her heart sinking as Miriam turned her swollen, red-rimmed eyes up to hers.

''Oh, God,'' Miriam whimpered. ''They've taken him.''

''Where does Dominick keep all of his charity records?''

Miriam blinked at her stupidly.

Mercy began shoving the papers aside, searching for the ledger she had happened upon before. She found it beneath Miriam's elbow. ''Are there others?'' she demanded.

Not waiting for an answer, Mercy rushed around the

desk, pulled open drawers, and dragged out files labeled: "Hospitals," "Orphanages (London, Liverpool, Leeds, Paris, Stockholm)," and "Misc. Charities." Her arms overburdened, she slammed the drawer closed with her knee.

She ran from the room, back to the vestibule, just as Lawton stepped through the front doorway. His eyes widened with relief.

"Drive me to wherever D'Abanville has been taken," she demanded. When he opened his mouth to argue, she turned on him, scattering papers around their feet. "I beg you. I think you owe us that much, Inspector."

He stared at her hard for a moment, then pointed to her papers and books and asked, "What is all of this?"

"Character witnesses."

Seconds passed. Finally he nodded, helped her with her load, and escorted her back through the dwindling crowd to his cab. After they were under way, he removed his hat and mopped his brow with his coat sleeve. "This is madness," he said. "Lunacy. These people have lost all reason."

"They can hardly be blamed, when all they read are newspapers describing each gory detail of the murders."

He glanced at the files. "Do you honestly believe those will help?"

"It is his only defense. If, for whatever reason, he will not speak up in behalf of his innocence, then I must do it for him."

They traveled without much difficulty for the first mile. At Commercial Street, however, their progress slowed to a virtual snail's crawl. Already word had reached the streets of D'Abanville's arrest. Voices could be heard screaming over and over, "It's the Ripper!" "They've caught the Ripper!" Men, women, and children ran past the cab toward the police station. Groups of men wielding clubs stormed their way through the onlookers who had already gathered outside the police barricade, their baritone voices repeating "Lynch him!" until the entire crowd took up the chant.

After proceeding as far as they could by cab, Mercy and Lawton took to the streets. They were carried along by the crowd, pushed and shoved and elbowed until coming to the barricade, three officers deep, that surrounded the entire station. Lawton flashed his credentials in the policemen's faces before catching Mercy's arm and dragging her with him. That was when she heard her name being called.

"Miss Dansing! I say, Miss Dansing!"

She looked back over her shoulder. Stan McMillian was doing his best to fight his way toward her.

His face red and sweating, his coat torn in places, he waved at her frantically and called out, "I must see you. It is imperative that we . . ." He disappeared in the throng, appeared again slightly further back, as if he were a helpless piece of driftwood caught in an undertow.

His arm came up again and he waved a parcel above his head. " . . . must see this!" he cried. "I must speak with you as soon as possible . . . Casimire . . . imperative . . ."

Swallowed again by the crowd, he tried one last time to reach Mercy, throwing his bulky weight forward, stretching his arm out to her. Mercy reached for the packet. It brushed her fingers. He tried again and she gripped it just as the police gave her a shove through the barricade. She stumbled and might have fallen had Lawton not extended his hand and caught her, righted her, and, taking her under his arm, dragged her the last distance to the door of the station.

They found little relief inside the Commercial Street station. At every window and door the officers stood ready, their faces grim, their brows sweating from the strain of waiting. Outside, the chanting had grown into a roar that shook the very walls of the building.

"It's like Bloody Sunday all over again," someone said. "Who would have thought it?"

"I'll be damned glad when the blokes from Leman Station arrive. If that crowd grows any rowdier—"

A crash of glass somewhere in the distance cut off the officer in mid-sentence. He, along with a companion, hurried toward the disturbance, while Mercy stood like a statue, her papers and files clutched to her bosom and her eyes on Lawton.

"A fair trial," she said hoarsely. "That *is* what you said."

He did not respond.

Shifting her files, she told him, "I want to see Dominick."

"That will have to be authorized. You will, of course, have to be searched for weapons."

"Will you get me authorization?"

"It may take some time. The fact that Chesterton is the officer in charge of D'Abanville's particular case—"

"But Chesterton is not here."

"Which means someone else will have to give his approval. I suspect, considering the charges that will be brought against D'Abanville—"

"Which are?"

"Six counts of murder and one of attempted murder against an officer."

Mercy swallowed and looked away.

Lawton placed a gentle hand on her shoulder. "Commissioner Warren will have to be consulted. I imagine, lass, that he will question you at length as well."

"How soon can I see him?"

"I'm not certain he has arrived yet from the Thames Street station. I suggest that you make yourself as comfortable as possible. It is likely to be a rather lengthy wait."

He showed her down a short hallway and into an office furnished with little more than a table and several chairs. He left and returned with a cup of coffee, which he placed on the table in front of her. Mercy refused to return his look, but stared instead at the steam that rose from the hot beverage. Eventually he left the room.

Mercy sat frozen on the edge of her chair, breathing too fast, her head whirling and ringing with terror. She felt numb with fear. She felt ill. Her stomach churned in a way that was not unfamiliar. She had felt the same when she had first come to London. Then again, even that fear had not been so all-consuming. So irrational. She understood now how people could commit some heinous crime in a fit of passion. The hysteria tasted metallic in the back of her mouth and it was all she could do to swallow it back.

This was a nightmare. Another horrible nightmare from which she would awaken at any minute. But no.

This was all too real, too painful to be anything but reality.

She thought of Dominick shut up in some tiny room with bars, a thousand people outside these thin walls crying out for his blood. And here she sat, clinging to her beliefs of his innocence as if her own life were somehow in the balance.

An hour passed. Then another. Several times she walked down the hall, making herself visible to Lawton on the off chance that he had forgotten her. Noon came, and with it a visit from Lawton. He tossed her an apple and placed a meat pie on the table. He pulled another apple out of his pocket, perched on the corner of the table, and smiled.

"Thought you'd like to know. Chesterton is going to be fine. The wound was not overly deep; should be back on the street in a fortnight."

Mercy studied her apple.

"Not hungry, lass?"

"Not overly."

"Would it help your appetite to know D'Abanville is secured from the mob?"

She shook her head.

"Would it help to know that Warren has arrived?"

Her head came up. For a moment she thought she read sympathy in Lawton's eyes, and the idea flashed through her mind that had Lawton been in charge of Abigail Russell's case, D'Abanville might never had been a suspect. At least, not for very long.

"Do you think he is guilty?" she asked.

"Do you?"

"Certainly not. You know my thoughts on that, sir."

"Never a doubt?"

She hesitated.

"There," he said. "So you see where we stand. If we doubt a man is guilty, so must we doubt that he is innocent. There is no certainty of innocence or guilt as long as doubt exists. Had Chesterton not doubted D'Abanville's guilt, he would have arrested him long ago."

"*Have* you arrested him?" she asked.

"No formal charges have been made. That will be left up to the commissioner now."

"I want to talk to him."

"He is aware of that."

"Then he is avoiding me."

Lawton bit into his apple, savored it a moment before swallowing. "He is a very busy man, Miss Dansing. Since his arrival two hours ago—"

Mercy came out of her chair. "Two hours! I have been sitting here two hours—"

"As I was saying: since his arrival, he has addressed four different committees, all demanding his resignation. Since the double murder there has been a meeting of some thousand people at Victoria Park demanding his resignation, as well as the home secretary's. Since Colonel Fraser posted a reward, we have had a trail of beggars through these doors that would rival Union's soup kitchen on a free day. It has been our duty to interview all of these civic-minded souls and decide whether or not they are telling the truth. That is not to mention the dozen or so men we have brought into the station each day on suspicion of being the Ripper. That, of course, is not including the men, and occasional women, who stumble in drunkenly, waving knives and screaming that they are Jack the Ripper."

He bit into his apple again and licked his lips. "Then, of course, there are the papers. The *Times*. The *Star*, whose circulation, because of Jack, has topped three hundred thousand. *Punch*. Not to mention W. T. Stead and his fine *Pall Mall Gazette*. Let us not forget Harmsworth's *Answers to Correspondents* and Newnes's *Tit-Bits* either. They seem to know more about the killings than we do. If we have anyone to blame for this lunacy, other than Jack himself, of course, it is the papers. Warren must deal with this every day. Then, certainly, there are the frequent letters from Lord Salisbury on behalf of her majesty—"

A man walked to the door. He glanced at Mercy before addressing Lawton. "Our witness has arrived," he said.

As Lawton left his seat, Mercy caught his arm.

"Of the many witnesses we have interviewed," he explained, "she is the only one who could give us information we deem reliable."

"Such as?"

"That he approached her, grabbed her, pointed a knife at her throat, and threatened her with bodily harm if she didn't . . . perform certain acts of what she termed 'perversion.' Then, as she was forced to carry out these acts, he terrified her with how he hated whores and he would wipe the—with due respect to your sensibilities—unmentionable scum from the earth if it was the last thing he ever did. She also gave a very detailed description of his appearance—"

"She could have gotten that much from the papers!" Mercy argued hotly.

"Down to the color of his eyes? There was certain information we purposefully did not disclose in the *Police Gazette,* including that, his height, his very slight accent. She relayed each with as much accuracy as you might have, Miss Dancing. Now she is to be questioned by the commissioner himself. If he feels she is telling the truth, he will then press charges against D'Abanville."

She stood stock-still as Lawton walked to the door. She thought she might faint.

"This might take a while," came his voice. "You may as well make yourself comfortable."

Mercy listened to his footsteps toll in the hallway like a death knell. Her eyes went blurry, and closing them, she said, "Dear God in heaven, if I ever needed you, I need you now, not for me, but for him. I do not ask you for myself, as I have in the past, but for a man who we both know is innocent of this horrible crime. I beg you, do not let me down again."

She wiped her tears away with the back of her hand, tossed the apple in the trash, then left the room.

20

Mercy walked down the hallway. She could feel the men watching her, but as she turned her head to meet their inquisitive stares, they looked away. Someone commented on the weather, that another storm was boiling to the west and would reach them by nightfall. Someone else responded that he hoped the rain would drive away the crowds, while yet another person remarked that nothing short of a lynching would drive away the crowd. They all looked at Mercy again.

There was an office door open. A dozen men pressed toward the door, some standing on tiptoes as they listened to the conversation going on within. Mercy stopped and listened hard, recognizing Commissioner Warren's weary voice.

"No charges have been made so far. The suspects were brought in for questioning only . . ."

Mercy walked on, determined to find Dominick.

She had come to the end of the hallway, was about to turn and retrace her steps, when she glanced into what at first appeared to be a deserted office. On second inspection she noticed a woman sitting with her back toward the door, her blond hair streaked with brown spilling like matted straw to the tops of her shoulders. Mercy stopped and stared. There was something familiar about that hair, the gray ulster she wore, and the hat with paper flowers tossed on the table beside her.

The woman, as if sensing that she was being watched, turned partially toward the door. Her eyes widened when she saw Mercy.

Mercy, her eyes riveted to Liza Baxter's startled features, shoved open the door and stepped into the room.

"You," she said in a whisper. *"You* are Warren's witness."

Liza gave a toss of her head and smirked. "So wot?"

"So what? So what that you are the biggest fabricater in London?" Mercy walked very slowly across the room as Liza left her chair to face her directly. Standing toe to toe with Oliver's slattern, Mercy took hold of the girl's shoulders and hissed, "Ollie has put you up to this, hasn't he?"

"Get yer bloody hands off me afore I scream for the bleedin' Peelers."

"He has. Dear God, of course he has. The bastard would have killed our own mother for that much reward."

"Is that any way to be talkin' about yer dear brother after he got y' that fine position—"

"Tell me the truth!" Mercy shook the girl hard.

Liza shoved her away, over a chair and onto the table. Mercy kicked the chair aside as she stood up. "You filthy little whore," she said. "I will wring the truth from you if it is the last thing I ever do."

"Whore!" Liza laughed. "I'd be talkin'. Y' think we don't know wot's been goin' on up t' that fine big house between you and that bloody hocus-pocus man? The truth is, sweetheart, yer lover-boy is Jack the Ripper."

"Liar!"

"Come up to me on the streets, he did. Stuck a big sharp knife to me throat and made me do naughty. Would y' like to hear all about it?"

"How much is he paying you?"

"Don't know wot y' mean."

"What cut of the reward money will Ollie give you for this?"

Liza perched on the chair arm and studied her chewed fingernails. "He's a right handsome bloke, I must confess. Didn't much mind doin' wot he asked me t' do."

"I am going to prove that you are lying," Mercy said. "I will find witnessess—there are dozens of them—who will testify that you have not spoken one true word since the day you were born."

"They've checked out my story," Liza pointed out. Standing now, her hands planted on her scrawny hips, she glared at Mercy and said, "I weren't this far from him that night." She held up two fingers for emphasis. "I were the only witness who could testify that he had blue eyes, that he stood this high, and he talked in a Frenchy sort of way. Now, how do you explain that?"

Mercy allowed her a cold smile and stalked her again. "Because Ollie has been this close to him." She held up her fingers. "Ollie has looked up into his blue eyes and has heard his voice very distinctly. He gave you that information. Didn't he?"

Liza's mouth screwed to one side as she backed away.

"Didn't he?" Mercy demanded more loudly.

"No."

"You are lying, Liza Baxter."

"Y'd best stay away from me, Mercy. Y' know how Ollie gets when someone upsets one of his girls."

"I am going to prove you are lying."

Liza backed around the table.

"I'm going to make you a liar before all of London. You will be a laughingstock before all of London."

"Get away from me afore I scream."

"Go ahead. The sooner we end this, the better."

"Yer bloody crazy."

"And getting crazier by the minute. I will venture to say that within the next minute or so I will be totally out of my mind and therefore will be unaccountable for any mayhem I might perpetrate against you in that moment."

"You little witch." Liza sneered. "I ain't half-afraid of you."

"We shall see about that."

"Miss Dansing!"

Hands outstretched toward Liza's hair, Mercy froze at the sound of Lawton's voice. She looked around.

Lawton and several others stood just inside the doorway, their gazes locked on Mercy. "Miss Dansing," he repeated slowly, "I trust you will reconsider."

Liza hurried across the room to stand beside Lawton. "Oh, sir," she said as pitifully as possible, "you come just in time, sir. This woman come sailin' at me like a banshee, threatenin' me with bodily harm if I testified against her boyfriend. I were so afraid, sir. So afraid."

"Indeed." Forcing his eyes from Mercy's, he raised

one brow and looked down his nose at Liza. "Are you ready to speak with the commissioner now or are you too racked by your distress?"

"Oh, no, sir. The sooner, the better, sir, for us all, eh?"

He nodded once toward one of his companions. Then Liza was escorted from the room.

Mercy, her hands pressed together to keep them from shaking, moved to the table and leaned against it. Her spurt of fury having left her, she did her best to swallow back the realization that she had come very close to discrediting herself in Lawton's eyes.

"I could have you arrested for this," he stated calmly, not unlike Chesterton. Indeed, he might have been Chesterton standing there in such a rigid and disapproving manner. The sight made Mercy's blood turn cold.

"I'm sorry," she said. "But you must let me explain."

"Must I?"

Her knuckles dug into the table until they hurt. "That woman is lying. She is a prostitute and works for my . . . for my brother. I am certain that he put her up to this. He knows Dominick. I heard Oliver threaten Dominick. Oliver would do anything—anything—for money, and he would force his girls to do anything for money."

"And are you one of his 'girls' as well, Miss Dansing?"

"No!" She covered her mouth with one hand until she felt certain she could speak again clearly. "The information you withheld from the *Gazette* would not be a secret to anyone who knew D'Abanville personally. It would be easy enough for Oliver to fill her in on those particular details. It is only fair that the commissioner know what sort of woman Liza Baxter is and where she might have attained that information."

Lawton continued to stare at her in silence.

Mercy closed her eyes and said, "Please."

Seconds ticked by, an eternity, as Mercy waited.

"Very well," he finally answered.

A shaky sob escaped her.

"But I must caution you, Miss Dansing; another display like I just witnessed and you will find yourself in serious trouble, not only with me, but with Scotland Yard.''

''I will remember.''

He stepped out of the office and looked back. ''After you, Miss Dansing.''

She forced herself to move around the table, tried to bring her mind into sharper focus as she left the room and walked at Lawton's side down the dim corridor. There were men still gathered outside the commissioner's door, some with their stiff blue collars buttoned all the way to their chins and their military-style hats pulled low over their eyes.

Lawton left her in the corridor while he spoke with Commissioner Warren. She was afraid. Terrified. D'Abanville's life depended on her being levelheaded, but her mind, exhausted, confused, was anything but rational. She felt a little mad, standing alone and watched in the corridor. Judged. She knew what they saw when they looked. D'Abanville's whore. Barely better than Liza Baxter in their eyes, though they tried to hide it by looking away. The idea made her cheeks burn, brought a tightness to her throat that she tried to swallow before Warren called her. Then it occurred to her that she really shouldn't care what they thought of her. It was D'Abanville whom she cared about. It didn't matter if her name was smeared from one end of Britain to the other as long as his name was cleared. *He* was at least innocent of his crimes. She knew it in her heart. She would prove it.

''Miss Dansing, you may come in.''

The officers parted, allowing her to pass. Commissioner Warren sat behind a desk stacked high with papers. His face looked thinner; the sputtering, flickering electric light dangling from a thin wire above his head gave his skin a jaundiced color that made him look ill.

He rose from his chair to greet her. ''Miss Dansing, we meet again.''

Mercy did her best to ignore Liza, who had backed to the wall, her face flushed an angry red. ''Sir,'' Mercy said. ''Thank you for seeing me.''

''What would you like to say on behalf of Mr. D'Abanville's innocence?''

''That Liza Baxter is lying if she told you that she

knows D'Abanville from some incident near Mitre Square.''

"I ain't," Liza replied. "I told 'em exactly wot he done."

"She works for my brother—rather, my half-brother. He has met D'Abanville, in fact had a confrontation with him just after my going to Greystone. It is my heartfelt belief that Oliver schooled her in this information in order to receive the reward offered by Colonel Fraser."

"Yer bloody off yer rocker," Liza spat. "You'd say anything t' protect yer pretty piece. I seen 'im, I tell you. 'Twas just after midnight when he grabbed me." She took two long strides so she stood toe to toe with Mercy again. "He were this close. Closer, if y' know wot I mean. Couldn't get no closer'n wot we was. He was like a bloody bull. Weren't no stoppin' wot he wanted t' do. We girls got special ways to satisfy the men, keepin' it neat and quick and safe, if y' know wot I mean. We ain't got time to dally on our backs with every bloke who tosses us a penny in a night. So's we take 'em up against the wall, like, between our thighs. You know, hold his piece with our thighs so he gets it over with quick and we don't worry over no babies. But this man won't have it. Wants it proper and then some, he tells me. Wot was I to do when he had a knife to me throat? That's when I looked up into them blue eyes, and I tell you, I felt as if I was lookin' into Satan's face. Hypnotized me. I know he did, or I wouldn't ever have done all them naughties, regardless of the knife."

"No," the commissioner said dryly, "I'm certain you wouldn't."

Liza grinned. "When I seen that *Gazette* and that picture of D'Abanville, I counted my lucky stars that I didn't end up like them others. I shiver to think on it, I do."

Commissioner Warren rubbed a hand over his eyes before addressing Mercy again. "Can you verify beyond any shadow of a doubt that D'Abanville did not leave Greystone that night?"

They all waited as Mercy struggled with her conscience. All it would take was for her to say that he had spent the entire night in her bed, so why could she not say it? If she believed in his innocence so devoutly, why could she not simply lie to save him?

She closed her eyes, shaking with a sense of defeat. She saw in her mind the picture Liza had so vividly drawn, and deep inside she felt that ugly sense of doubt struggle one last time for dominance. The memory of Chesterton's disclosure that morning drove sharply through her, staggering her reason, fraying that tender thread of faith . . .

"Miss Dansing, the last thing we want to do is to arrest an innocent man. God knows, I am in enough deep water as it is, but if Miss Baxter is telling the truth . . ."

God . . . oh, God, she thought, what am I going to do?

The light above the commissioner's head sputtered and dimmed to a tiny flickering spark, throwing the room into virtual darkness.

"Dammit," Warren muttered. "That is the third time since morning that blasted light has faulted. Someone fetch me a lantern so we might get on with this miserable business."

"I fear it is the storm moving in," came a man's voice from the shadows. For a moment he glanced down into Mercy's face as he moved by her, brushing her in his expediency to assist the commissioner. "I beg your pardon," he said.

The image that flashed across her mind's eye in that instant was like a bolt of lightning. Mercy grabbed the officer, pulling him back on his heels.

"Don't touch that light," she said. "Not yet." She shoved him toward Liza until they were face-to-face. She then reached up and grabbed the light-pull, gave it a yank so it went off completely. Only the dim light from the corridor lit the room.

"Miss Dansing," the commissioner said. "What is the meaning of this?"

Mercy spun back to Liza and the officer. "Tell us, Liza, what color are the officer's eyes?"

Silence.

"Quickly. What color are his eyes?"

"Bloody hell," Liza responded. "How am I supposed to know in this light?"

"I wager it is lighter in here than it was at midnight six nights ago. If you cannot determine the color of this gentleman's eyes, I find it highly suspicious that you were able to see D'Abanville's eyes distinctly enough to note their color."

"We was under a streetlamp."

"Oh? I assumed you were in darkness. That's what you were quoted as saying, 'He came up behind me in the dark.'"

"The Peeler's eyes are brown," Liza snapped.

Commissioner Warren reached up and tugged on the light-pull. With a click the harsh yellow light poured over them all. The officer turned his eyes on the commissioner, then on Mercy. His eyes were green.

"I'm tellin' you," Liza said, "the man who accosted me that night was that bloody magician."

Her gaze steadfast on Warren, Mercy said, "I wager if D'Abanville was lined up with a number of other men similar in height and coloring, she would not know him. I have seen the *Gazette* and am almost positive the sketch of Dominick looks enough like many other men that you can hardly tell them apart. If she truly saw D'Abanville in person, then she would know him. If she didn't . . ."

They all looked at Liza, who glared at Mercy, her lips pulled back in a grimace of anger. "I'll show you." She sneered. "Bring on Jack. I'll point 'im out and make *you* look like the imbecile Ollie always said you were."

"I am more than willing to take that chance." Mercy continued to stare at Commissioner Warren. "Will you do it?" she asked.

He appeared somewhat disconcerted by the sudden turn of events. Lawton stepped forward then and said, "With all due respect, sir . . . in all fairness, sir, I feel it would behoove us to consider all possibilities."

"Oh?" he responded. "Young man, do you realize that this could be the very man who attempted to murder your superior this morning? What do you suppose Chesterton would think?"

"With all due respect, sir, knowing Inspector Chesterton as I do, I feel he would wish it to be proven beyond any shadow of a . . ." He glanced at Mercy. ". . . beyond *any* doubt, sir, that this man is guilty. After all, we are all aware of the public's reaction, should charges be pressed against him.''

"I hardly need any reminders of that." The commissioner stood erect, shoulders back and chin squared as he regarded Mercy. "Very well, young woman. But I must warn you: should Miss Baxter be unable to identify the gentleman in question, that will by no means cause the investigation surrounding him to be dropped. There is his link to Miss Russell and Mrs. Kinsdale, not to mention the very fact that you yourself disclosed to Mr. Lawton that D'Abanville was not in residence at Greystone last evening.''

Mercy turned and glared up at Lawton before saying to the commissioner, "Will you at least allow me to see him now?''

"Certainly. Lawton will take you to the prisoner." As a pair of officers stepped toward her, he waved them away with one hand. "I don't think a search is necessary.''

She waited for Lawton in the hallway for several minutes before he joined her. It gave her time to collect her thoughts. Facing D'Abanville had never been easy, but in this sort of circumstance she suspected it would be even harder.

She walked to the nearest window overlooking the street, noted that the crowd had thinned somewhat. The chanting had subsided. Only an occasional cry of "Lynch him!'' or "Murderer!'' rang out.

Lawton joined her then, and they moved out of the hallway, through a door, where they ascended a steep flight of stairs. Arriving at the second floor, they were met by an officer who unlocked the first of several doors they were to pass through on their way to D'Abanville's cell.

It seemed they walked forever through the dark corridor. The sounds and smells were frightening. Mercy did not dare look for fear of what she might see. But what frightened her most was that D'Abanville had been placed among these wretches.

He was in the last cell, alone. The others around him were empty. She stared hard through the iron bars, attempting to find him in the shadows.

Lawton said, "I will wait just there. Call me when you are ready to leave."

"Will you let me inside?" she asked softly.

"I'm sorry. I cannot do that." He reached for the ladder-back chair to one side of the cell door and placed it before her. He then left them alone.

It was a long moment before she could force herself to look again inside the cell. The idea had suddenly occurred to her that perhaps this was a humiliation to him.

She raised her head and met his eyes.

"Hello," he said.

She tried to smile. Her eyes and throat burned too badly; she could not do it. She gripped the cold iron bars in her hands and swallowed.

"Mercy," he said, "you shouldn't be here."

She pressed her face hard between two bars as she tried to see him better. He sat in a chair leaned back on two legs. A faint light from a narrow window overhead cut his face into light and dark ribbons. He was smiling.

She began to cry.

His chair dropped to the floor. He stood against her, or as close as he could, his hands cradling her face, smoothing her hair. She pressed as close as possible, craving his nearness, feeling desperate as the metal dug into her flesh, a cold reminder.

He made a painful sound in his throat as he touched her face. "Ah, damn. Don't cry. Mercy, don't cry. It's going to work out. You have to believe that it's going to be fine."

"Not as long as you continue to cloak yourself in this secrecy! Why won't you tell them who you are?"

"It shouldn't matter," he said more sharply. "Why should it matter where I came from or what I do? All that should matter is that I am innocent of these crimes."

"But I have a right to know!" she insisted. "I love you!"

He walked away from her, dissolved a moment into the shadows before moving in and out of a shaft of light. Then he looked at her again and his eyes looked green and angry in the dingy yellow sunbeams.

"Then love me for the man I am now and forget about the past. The past shouldn't matter."

Mercy watched him a moment longer, her frustration growing. "I am trying to help you," she told him. Then, closing her eyes, she said, "Chesterton told me this morning that Dominick D'Abanville is . . . is dead. If you do not tell me now who you are, I will walk away from this place and we will never see one another again."

She listened, hearing her heart throb in her ears, feeling the metal cut into her face as she pressed closer, waiting for a sound.

Silence.

Silence.

Silence.

"Damn you to hell," she hissed without looking at him. But as she moved to turn away, he was suddenly up against the bars, reaching, his hand grasping her arm and pulling her back around. He buried his hands in her hair, and though her eyes were closed, she knew he was staring at her. She could not resist raising her eyes to his.

"Mercy, don't do this. Don't do this to me. I need you too badly now. Ah, God, if you walked out on me now . . ." He pressed his face against the bars, trying to kiss her. She raised her fingers and lightly placed them against his mouth.

"Who are you?" she asked tenuously.

He closed his eyes. A drop of sweat glistened on his temple before sliding down the side of his face. "No one. Anyone. Just someone who hoped he could make a difference. Just one more fool like a million other fools who imagined that he had been put on this stinking earth for some reason grander than just existing. That he would somehow reach out and touch some soul with just enough magic to make a difference in his life. I wanted to speak and be heard. I wanted to be seen instead of being looked through as if I didn't exist." He grinned, and for a moment he looked like the D'Abanville she had met when she first came to Greystone. Mischievous. Mysterious. As always, mesmerizing. "Seems I got a little more than I bargained for," he said.

He strained his body into the bars; their fingers interlaced and gripped with painful intensity. She thought she heard his heart pounding in the quiet, and she realized: he is afraid.

"It will all work out," she heard herself saying.

Distant doors opened. Footsteps rang down the corridor.

Mercy looked to his eyes. "Have faith. If you have taught me anything, it is that you must never give up. The night may seem dark, but there is always tomorrow."

He could not seem to move away, but gripped her more tightly. When he spoke again, his voice was rough and deep and urgent. "I love you," he said.

Hearing the words now was painful for Mercy. She had longed to hear them for so long . . .

"Marry me when this is over," he whispered. "We'll go to Paris and forget. Tell me you'll wait, Mercy. No matter what happens, wait for me and never give up. Swear it!"

"I swear!" she promised him.

Lawton stood with several policemen and Commissioner Warren. They all looked at Mercy as she turned to face them.

One of the officers stepped forward and unlocked the cell door. It was a moment before D'Abanville stepped out. He tried to put on his coat but could not seem to lift his arms.

Lawton took Dominick's coat and stepped around him. "Allow me, sir," he said. He then slid the coat up onto D'Abanville's shoulders.

They walked in a silent group down the stairs. Upon arriving at Warren's office, D'Abanville was separated from the others and shown down the hall into another room. Lawton then caught Mercy's arm and ushered her into a large dim chamber. She was shown to the rear of the room, where several people waited. One of them was Liza Baxter. Leaving Mercy, Lawton took a place to Liza's right. Commissioner Warren stood at Liza's left. He then nodded to the officer at the door.

Six men filed in, all in dark suits, all of a similar height and of similar coloring. They lined up against the white wall, facing the spectators.

Commissioner Warren glanced at Liza and said, "Very well, madam, you may now point out the gentleman who accosted you the morning of 30 September."

"It ain't fair," she said. "I ought to be allowed to see the *Gazette* again—"

"Don't be ridiculous. If you know the man as well as you claim, you should be able to pick him out. Have a go."

"It's too bloody dark."

"Imagine it is midnight, Miss Baxter."

"He weren't standing this far away."

With a sigh of exasperation, he called out, "Turn on the lights."

An officer went down the row of men, turning on lights above their heads. The commissioner walked Liza forward several feet.

"Better, Miss Baxter?"

She cocked her head at the commissioner, then looked back at Mercy. "Right," Liza said. "Now, let's see . . ."

The minutes dragged by. The heat from the lights soon made the room uncomfortably warm. The men along the wall began sweating and fidgeting in impatience.

"Miss Baxter," Warren implored her, "you told me that you could identify this man blindfolded."

"Right," she said. "Have 'em all drop their breeches and I can."

Someone coughed and cleared his throat.

Liza snickered.

"My patience is growing thin, young woman."

Liza walked forward again. An officer put out his arm to stop her. She paced back and forth, looked hard into each man's face until Warren was grinding his teeth.

"I've got 'im," Liza finally announced.

Mercy's knees turned weak.

"Then by all means, Miss Baxter, point him out."

Mercy turned her back to the proceedings, faced the wall. She could not watch.

"That's 'im," came Liza's declaration. "I'd know 'im anywhere."

"You are absolutely certain, beyond any shadow of a doubt, that that is the man who accosted you the night of 30 September? The man whose likeness you saw in the *Gazette*?"

"I'd know 'im even without seein' his likeness in the

Gazette. I'm tellin' ya, that's yer man. That's bloody Jack the Ripper.''

A long silence ensued.

Mercy prayed.

''Very well. Let everyone present bear witness to the fact that she has pointed out this man.'' Warren walked to the far side of the room. ''Everyone but this man may be excused.''

Mercy listened to the men file out of the room. Still, she could not force herself to turn.

Someone caught her arm. She looked up into Lawton's eyes. They told her nothing, and her panic increased.

''Miss Dansing,'' the commissioner called out, ''would you care to join us?''

''Miss Dansing,'' Lawton urged her.

Mercy turned and froze.

Commissioner Warren took a cigar from his coat pocket and looked down at a smirking Liza. ''Miss Baxter, allow me to introduce the gentleman you have pointed out as Jack the Ripper—John Michael Irons, vicar of St. Mary Woolnoth Church.''

21

By the time Mercy left the room the officers had taken D'Abanville away. She followed Lawton and the commissioner to his office, where he stood behind his desk and shook his head in apparent disbelief.

"Christ," he said. "Now what?"

Mercy stepped forward. "Perhaps now you will listen to me." She left the room and hurried to the office where she had earlier waited, gathered up her files, and returned to Warren's office and placed them on his desk.

"As briefly as possible, Miss Dansing," he said, "tell me what this is."

As briefly as possible, she told him.

Warren thumbed through the material and shook his head. "This is not evidence. There is nothing here that proves his innocence. You have shown me nothing here that explains why he is walking London's streets after dark or where he was at four o'clock this morning as one of my top investigators was being knifed in the back." He looked at Mercy again. "I'm sorry, Miss Dansing. I fear I have no choice but to continue to hold D'Abanville." He gathered up the files and placed them back in her arms. He repeated, "I'm sorry."

A knock at the door interrupted. A young man stepped into the office and addressed the commissioner. Warren excused himself and left the room. Lawton followed. Alone, Mercy sank into a chair, feeling the last of her hope slipping through her fingers as easily as the papers scattering in her lap. McMillian's envelope, which she had forgotten, was among them. She stared at it, then flipped it open and slid the numerous papers out just enough to read the message:

Miss Dansing: It is imperative that we speak before you return to Greystone. Do not return there until we have discussed the enclosed transcript of Mary Casimire's diary—her final entry. Meet me at four o'clock at the Baltic Coffeehouse. S.M.

Mercy half-closed her eyes, her defeat numbing the impact and importance of McMillian's words. She didn't care about Mary Casimire's diary now, nor about McMillian's obsession with a crumbling house. Besides, the hour must be very nearly four now. She was already late.

She flipped the note down and glanced at the diary entry:

7 October, 1788. It is very nearly midnight. I know now what is going on. I am going to die tonight unless Peter arrives in time.

Mercy dropped the paper. Not intentionally, but almost as if a shiver had rushed through her in that moment, breaking her concentration. Her fingers shook. The chill seemed to creep up her arm and center deeply in her chest. For a moment she thought: This is what it feels like to be dead.

She forced herself to stand and walk to the doorway. She asked an officer for the time, thinking remotely that if she hurried to the Baltic Coffeehouse . . .

"Six-ten," the officer replied.

Surprised, she looked toward the nearest window. Darkness, with a smattering of lights, greeted her. Where had the day flown? Soon she would have to return to Greystone . . .

Mercy turned the thought aside and did her best to concentrate on the excited talk now rippling up and down the corridors of the station:

"Do you think the commissioner will believe her?"

"If she's his mistress, she would certainly have the motive."

"She looks crazy enough."

Lawton stepped out of an office and looked at Mercy.

His face was white. He said, "Someone has just confessed to the attempted murder of Inspector Chesterton."

Before Mercy could respond, Lawton nudged open the door.

Miriam turned in her chair to face Mercy.

Commissioner Warren stared down at the bloodied knife before placing it in the care of one of his officers. "Deliver that at once to Dr. Brown," he said. Then, to Mercy and Miriam, he explained, "Dr. Brown is the surgeon of the City of London police. He was also in charge of the postmortem on Catherine Eddowes—"

"Wait just one minute," Miriam interrupted, coming out of her chair. She wobbled a little unsteadily, and Mercy reached out and offered her a hand. "I confessed to stabbing Chesterton, not to being Jack the Ripper." Miriam tried to laugh. "That's as asinine as accusing D'Abanville."

"We would be highly remiss in our investigation if we did not suspect that your weapon might have also been the weapon used on the other victims."

Miriam glanced uneasily at Mercy.

"Of course," Warren continued, "there is the possibility that you are doing this to protect your lover."

"He is not my lover," Miriam said. "He hasn't been in over a year."

"Yet you would kill for him."

"I . . . love him. I won't deny that."

"Well." The commissioner looked from Miriam to Mercy. "Isn't this cozy?"

Miriam leaned slightly over his desk and said, "I stabbed Chesterton. I arrived at his house about midnight. He was leaving. I waited until he returned at four, and when he arrived I calmly walked up behind him and jabbed him. I meant to kill the malicious son of a bitch. He has destroyed my friend."

Mercy closed her eyes in disbelief.

As angrily, the commissioner also leaned over his desk and looked Miriam in the eye. "Madam, I trust you are sober enough to realize what you are confessing. There will be a certain prison sentence for the attempt on Chesterton. If we also prove you were somehow behind the murders of Abby Russell—''

''Now, just stop right there!'' Her voice now panicked, Miriam said, ''I didn't confess to killing that silly bitch!''

Mercy grabbed Miriam's arm. ''Please, Miriam, take care what you say!''

Her face white as the walls around them, Miriam stared back at Mercy. ''Jesus God, I never—''

''Nothing more,'' Mercy stressed.

Miriam dropped into her chair, and Warren looked at Mercy. He said, ''I suggest you give her some coffee. She will need to be as sober as possible when we question her.''

He left the office. Soon two cups of coffee were delivered. Only then did Miriam look at Mercy and speak.

''Well, isn't this a fine kettle of fish? I come in here to confess to jabbing a Peeler and find myself facing murder charges. The next thing you know, they'll be calling me Jill the Ripper.''

''Where is Roger?'' Mercy asked.

''He'll be along.'' Sipping her coffee, Miriam looked at Mercy a little sheepishly and smiled. ''Have you seen him?''

''Yes.''

''How is he?''

''Holding up.''

''He always does.'' She drank again. ''When I look back on all the times I thought I was taking care of him, I realize it was the other way around. He sat back quietly and allowed me to hover because he knew I needed to hover. It made me feel necessary.''

Mercy said, ''He is very tolerant.''

''Devout,'' Miriam amended. ''He's going to climb that road to Divine Wisdom if it kills him.'' She laughed and shook her head. ''If half the religious sects in the world were as faithful to the causes of 'endurance of personal injustices, a brave declaration of principles, and a valiant defense of those who are unjustly attacked,' we wouldn't be wallowing in this swill of iniquity now. Jeez, he should be canonized, and they want to crucify him.''

''It will all work out,'' Mercy stated firmly, believing.

''Good God. Another one.'' Miriam threw back her

head and laughed. "He'll have you believing next that your souls have traveled through a million lifetimes together and that you have come together again because fate decreed it."

Mercy laughed. "Nothing so strong as that." She stared down into her coffee before admitting quietly, "He has asked me to marry him."

A long silence followed. Then Miriam spoke.

"That's good. He's never done that before, asked a woman to marry him. You should take that as proof that he loves you very much. Just like I told you. Did you accept?"

Mercy nodded.

Another silence. Then, "Well."

They did not speak again for over an hour. Occasionally Miriam would leave her chair and pace the room. She broke down and cried once, buried her face in her hands and repeated over and over again, "You old fool, you damned stupid old fool." Mercy considered asking her again if what she had confessed was the truth, or if she was only trying to protect D'Abanville again. But she didn't want to know. As much as she hated to admit it to herself, and although she felt very sorry for Miriam, she *wanted* it to be the truth. Miriam's guilt would bring D'Abanville one step closer to freedom.

It was nearly eight o'clock when Lawton slipped into the room. He whispered to Mercy, "Dr. Brown has arrived. He is with the commissioner now."

Mercy looked at Miriam. Sitting in Warren's chair with her head resting on the desk, she appeared to be asleep. Mercy left the room with Lawton and followed him down the hall, and although she was not invited into the office, she stood at the door with Lawton and listened.

"It is my opinion that the knife the suspect used on your inspector—if that *is* the knife she used on the inspector—is not the knife that has been used to kill the women in Whitechapel. As I mentioned at the inquest, I believe the instrument used to murder those women must have been a strong knife, at least six inches long, very sharp, pointed at the top, and about an inch in width. It may have been a clasp knife, a butcher knife, or a surgeon's knife. I am almost positive it was a straight knife.

As you can see, this knife you hold in your hand, although in appearance it seems sturdy enough and is, in fact, long enough in the blade, it is very lightweight and its width is much too great. Neither is it sharp enough to have performed those types of mutilations.''

"Could it have been used on the Russell or Kinsdale woman?"

A moment of silent consideration passed. Mercy held her breath.

"As you know, Commissioner, it has been my own and Dr. Sequeira's opinion that these killings were not in any way tied to the Whitechapel murders. Although in Miss Russell's case there were a few ghastly similarities, there were even more dissimilarities. Her wounds were random and not so calculated. The knife wound in her throat commenced on the right side, whereas Jack begins on the left. You know of my opinion—that Jack is left-handed. Now, in Mrs. Kinsdale's killing . . .'' Dr. Brown shook his head. "We have already stricken the possibility that she was murdered by Jack. The wound was from a very large dog.''

"But the possibility exists that this knife may have been the weapon used on Miss Russell.''

"Very possibly.''

"And do you think a woman could have inflicted that sort of damage on Miss Russell?''

"I do not. As the investigation has shown, Miss Russell struggled with her assailant. The bruises about her jawline and face could have been made only by someone gripping her from behind with his hand over her mouth, probably attempting to keep her from calling out.''

"Then he would be a big man.''

"Much taller than Miss Russell.'' Dr. Brown looked up at Mercy, and beyond her, to Lawton. He studied them a moment. "Taller even than this gentleman is in comparison to the young lady.''

Warren looked directly at Mercy and said, "How can you tell, Doctor?''

"From the bruises on Miss Russell's face. The pressure was exerted upward. Had the killer been shorter, the pressure would have been more balanced, or even down.

No Miss Russell was dragged back and up, probably against the killer's shoulder or chest.''

"Then he would have to be as tall as six feet.''

"Or over. Beyond any shadow of a doubt.''

While Mercy stood in the hallway outside Warren's office, Inspector Lawton arrested Miriam for attempted murder of a law-enforcement official. Pale and trembling, Miriam meekly allowed him to lead her out of the office. Upon seeing Mercy, she stopped and managed to smile.

"Won't he just die when he sees me?'' Miriam said, meaning Dominick.

Mercy nodded.

"Shall I give him a message from you, sweetheart?''

"No.'' Then, "Yes. Tell him I'm waiting still.''

"And that you love him.''

"Yes.'' Mercy smiled.

Miriam turned away, then stopped again and looked back at Mercy. "By the way, I never got around to saying thank you.''

"For what?''

"Dom told me what you did for me back in Liverpool. You know, talking him into taking me back, giving me another chance after that fit I threw at the hotel. Knowing how you felt about him even then, it was a pretty risky thing to do. Guess you figured the best woman would win him in the end, huh?'' When Mercy did not respond, Miriam smiled, tossed her head with a bit of her old fire, and said to Lawton, "Well, what the devil are you waiting for?''

He took hold of her arm and they disappeared around the corner.

Mercy stood in the hallway staring after them and feeling . . . lost.

"Miss Dansing.'' A hand touched her shoulder. "Mercy. My dear, are you all right?''

She turned very slowly to face Roger.

He adjusted his glasses and for a moment his eyes looked as if they were floating on invisible waves. "You look exhausted.''

"I am,'' she said.

"The coach is just outside. I'll drive you home. You can get a decent night's sleep and return first thing in the morning."

"I don't want to leave."

"But you must. God knows what tomorrow may bring. Besides, I've already spoken to Commissioner Warren. He tells me that you won't be allowed to see D'Abanville again tonight."

She looked at him a moment longer, unable to tell him, to understand herself why the idea of returning to Greystone tonight disturbed her. She had had little time to think about it the last two hours, but now even the simplest thought of the house brought a subtle rise of panic into her throat.

"Perhaps," she said, "I will go see Mr. McMillian."

"This late? Come, come, Miss Dansing, look at yourself. I would be remiss in my duties if I allowed you to do anything but return home with me. You will do Dominick little good through these next grueling days if you are unwell or too tired to function." He took her arm and smiled warmly. "Think how wonderful a nice hot bath will feel, followed by a cup of tea."

"I am very hungry," she said, feeling her stomach ache with the mention of tea.

"Then by all means, let us be off. There is a dreadful storm moving in, but if we hurry we may make it to Greystone before it hits."

Too tired to argue, she returned to Warren's office and gathered up the files. She had decided, while sitting with Miriam, that she could write to the officers in charge of these charitable organizations and convince them to testify on Dominick's character and philanthropy, if the need arose. Perhaps she would pen a few letters tonight and post them tomorrow.

Upon leaving the station, Mercy was struck by the silence. The streets were empty. Perhaps the coming storm had spooked the rioters away, or perhaps they had simply tired of their murderous quest. Whatever the reason for their departure, Mercy was relieved.

As they started for the coach, a rumble of thunder erupted overhead. A blast of wind struck with a force that made Mercy stop and look up. For an instant a flash of Greystone came and went through her mind's eye, and she shivered, unnerved again by the idea of returning there without Dominick.

Having walked ahead, Roger stopped and turned. "Are you coming?"

She looked up at the driver. He held the leads tightly as the nervous animals pranced in place; he did not seem to notice Mercy.

"Hurry!" Roger called. He opened the coach door and Mercy climbed inside, sinking onto the burgundy seat. After boarding, Roger closed the door and dropped into the seat across from her. His face looked ashen in the shadows.

He regarded Mercy in silence the entire journey to Greystone. As they turned onto Buckingham Street, Mercy noted with relief that there was no trace of the crowds that had haunted Greystone these last troubled weeks. Only a single boy stood near the gates, his arms full of papers as he cried out: "Murder! Paper! Jack—the—Ripper—caught! Paper! Whitechapel! Paper! Got—him—at—last! Paper! Murder! Ripper! Paper! Got—him—at—last!"

As the gates swung closed behind the coach, Mercy could no longer hear him. Only the wind moaned, stirring the trees so they rattled and sighed around her. A shadow darted past, and as Mercy leaned more closely to the window to see what it might be, the dog stopped and turned its giant head around so it stared at her with slanted eyes, its repulsive tongue hanging from one side of its panting mouth. For a moment it seemed to be laughing at her, as if saying: At last. At last.

Sitting back in her seat, her heart racing, Mercy closed her eyes.

"Is something wrong, Miss Dansing?" Roger asked.

She did not respond. She could not. She continued to shrink into the seat and fight back the irrational terror that became more intense the closer to the house the coach drew. McMillian's words came racing back to her—*do not return to Greystone*—over and over again, and over and over again she continued to turn the words away until the warnings swirled in her head, making her feel she was on the verge of losing her mind.

Finally the coach stopped. The door was opened. The driver smiled up at her and said, ''You're home.''

The driver and Roger waited for her to move. At last she slid toward the door and stepped to the ground.

Roger walked by her to the door, stared back at her briefly before entering the house. Mercy sensed that the driver stood near; then he moved up behind her, very close. She could almost feel him brush her back. Had she leaned against him, she thought, the top of her head would not reach his chin. It occurred to her that he was as tall as D'Abanville. No, she thought. He is taller.

She followed D'Abanville's manager into the house, stopped just inside the door. Greystone's entire staff appeared to be assembled in the vestibule, some Mercy had never seen before. They all regarded her in return.

''We're glad yer back, Miss Dansin','' someone remarked.

''Aye,'' another said. ''Welcome home.''

The servant who normally attended her stepped forward, smiling. ''You look exhausted. I've drawn y' a hot bath. There's tea brewin' on the stove. Is there aught else you'd like sent up?''

Mercy shook her head.

The girl walked to her. ''I'll help y' with them things,'' she said, referring to Mercy's files.

Mercy stepped away, clutching them to her. ''I need these,'' she said more sharply than she had intended. ''There are letters to be addressed from these files. I intend to prove to all of you that your employer is innocent of these terrible charges that Chesterton has brought against him.''

No one responded.

''Don't you care that D'Abanville has been falsely accused?'' she demanded angrily.

''Of course they do,'' Roger said. ''Now, please, my dear. It has been a distressing day for us all.''

The servant reached for Mercy's files. ''I'll carry 'em up for ya,'' she said, smiling again. This time Mercy released them reluctantly and left the vestibule for her room.

Any other time and she might have felt relief on entering the familiar chamber. Now she felt nothing of comfort in the threadbare room. Not in the warm light of the fire, or the glowing lamps, or the tub of steaming water that waited in the middle of the rugless floor. All the old nightmares rushed from every shadowed corner until she felt as if the weight of her fear was suddenly heaped upon her, crushing the life from her slowly and deliberately.

"I'll place yer files here," the servant said.

Mercy looked around as they were dropped on the bed. That was when she noticed the boxes. "What are they?" she asked.

"Yer dresses were delivered this mornin' from Madame Cartier. I suppose y' won't be needin' 'em now, though, considerin' . . ."

"What is that?" Mercy pointed to the white garment placed neatly over the foot of the bed.

"A gown," the girl said.

"I don't recall being fitted for such a gown."

The servant picked it up. The gossamer material flowed as lightly as a feather over her hands. "It was a gift from D'Abanville, Madame Cartier said."

Mercy turned away, unable to look at the gown.

"Y'll wear it tonight, won't you? It would make 'im feel worlds better if he thought y' liked it. Y' could tell 'im tomorrow when y' see 'im that y' wore it—"

"Thank you," Mercy interrupted. Without looking back at the servant, she walked to the stove. "If you don't mind, I'd like to be alone now."

"Certainly, miss. Have a good sleep, miss."

Mercy waited for the girl to leave. It seemed an abnormally long time before she heard the door click shut. Only then did she allow herself to breathe.

She decided that she would not think about the day's occurrences. To dwell on them would serve no purpose. Her mind must be clear to formulate her plan, to deal with each anticipated hurdle they would face tomorrow and the day after that.

Mercy walked to the window and looked out. Dark silence and emptiness welled back at her, and again she was stricken with an overpowering sense of aloneness. Every friend she had in the world, few as they were, had been taken from her. Micah. Miriam. D'Abanville. Then she thought of Stan McMillian again. She hurried to the bed, where she rummaged through the files, at last locating his letter. Still, she could not force herself to open it, but dropped it back on the bed and backed away. The room suddenly felt small and hot; she thought she would suffocate for lack of air. Perhaps a walk . . .

She hurried to the door and threw it open. Coming face-to-face with Roger, she stopped abruptly, swallowing back her cry of surprise.

"Is something wrong?" he asked.

"I am going for a walk," she said.

"But that is not possible."

"Why not?"

"The coming storm, of course. It is just above us. Besides, the dogs are loose. It just wouldn't be safe."

Mercy backed into the room.

Roger smiled in a kindly manner. "My dear, you look exhausted. Please try to get some rest. I promise you, we will return to the station just as soon as it is daylight."

She closed the door and pressed her ear hard against it. She could not hear if he left, but some sense told her he hadn't. What was he doing there, guarding her door as if she were a prisoner?

This is ridiculous, she told herself. There was no reason why she should fear Roger, or even Greystone, for that matter. She had allowed people's silly superstitions to affect her logic.

Taking a deep steadying breath, she began to undress slowly. She hummed to herself, doing her best to keep her mind on other things—D'Abanville, Miriam, Chesterton. She glanced back at the door, thinking she heard the knob turn. She stared hard at the yellowed ivory orb, but it did not move.

Thunder rumbled and the glass in the window rattled like dice in a jar.

Tap tap tap

She briefly closed her eyes against the frightening memory, then walked to the stove and poured her tea. Steam rose to her face, smelling sweet and pungent. She carried it with her to the bath, sank into the fragrant water, and sipped the tea slowly, hearing the continuous thunder, watching the erratic display of light flicker outside the window.

Little by little she felt herself relax. She placed the empty cup aside, slid down into the water, and laid her head back against the rim of the tub, closing her eyes.

Long silent seconds ticked by.

Mercy jumped, startled. For a moment she had drifted. She raised her head and stared at the water. Little threads of perfumed oil coiled around her, twisting, writhing with the water's movement. And the water felt cold. Icy cold. Numbing her arms and legs so she could hardly move them. How long had she slept?

She moved from the tub, dried off before the stove, hoping its heat would warm her. It didn't. She shook from the inside out.

Her head had begun to ache, a pressure forcing its way out against her temples. Dropping the towel, she pressed her palms against the sides of her head, imagining at any minute that her skull would begin disintegrating piece by piece; she could not think. A lethargy was dragging her down until it seemed an eternity between each deliberate breath, between each hesitant beat of her heart.

She felt horribly thirsty. She poured herself more tea, gulped it down, barely feeling the blistering heat as it slid like hot treacle down the back of her throat.

Sleep. That's all she needed. Roger was right. She was exhausted.

She looked toward the bed. It seemed lost in the shadows, dark and cold. She could not shake the notion that should she retire there, she might never get up. There was nothing comforting there, only memories of nightmares and D'Abanville's loving. The mere thought of D'Abanville made her ache with the bitter loneliness of knowing he was so far away. Had it been only last night that he had come to her room, pressed his body into hers, so deeply inside hers that she had seemed to exist no longer, to become only him, to feel each throb of his heart as if it were her own, to know the deliriousness of soaring so close to shining limits and then spiraling over into oblivion, lost and mad and dying?

Mercy walked to the bed and picked up the gown. She put it on. White lace and satin and ribbons floated like wisps of clouds to her ankles. Looking in the mirror, she thought she looked a little like some virginal bride on her wedding night.

She gathered up the files and moved closer to the fire, sat down in the chair, doing her best to ignore the pain in her head that seemed to pulsate with her heartbeat. She stared down at McMillian's letter, refusing to acknowledge it. With trembling fingers she picked it up, glanced toward the fire in the stove. Toss it in, her mind told her. Just toss it in and be done with his idiotic superstitions. Whatever had happened to Mary Casimire had nothing to do with her. Whatever evil had plagued London one hundred years ago had nothing to do with what was happening at Greystone now.

Mercy eased the envelope into the fire, gripping it with the tips of her fingers as she watched the orange flames lick hungrily about the fine paper. As a gray stream of oily smoke began to rise from the paper, Mercy jerked it back, slapped at the charred edges of the envelope, sending bits of ash floating to the floor.

It seemed that the decision had been made. Very carefully she opened the envelope and withdrew the letter.

> Miss Dansing: It is imperative that we speak before you return to Greystone. Do not return there until we have discussed the enclosed transcript of Mary Casimire's diary—her final entry. Meet me at four o'clock at the Baltic Coffeehouse.
>
> S.M.

She laid her head back against the rocker and closed her eyes. That was when she heard—or felt—the slow throb in the still air. As if the walls around her had come alive, as if the house were alive, breathing in and out, its heart slowly pounding out a rhythm that was seductive and alluring enough to make her smile. Until she heard the words again in her mind.

Aman . . . Amani . . . Amanita . . .

Or was it in her mind?

Raising her head, Mercy forced open her eyes, expecting the sounds to vanish. They did, and she relaxed, thought again of tossing McMillian's letter into the fire,

reached to do so, determined to put an end to this idiotic
superstition. Then it came again, the throb, the words,
so very faint, yet slamming with a force on her ear, making her heart jump and her skin grow hot with fear. Every
sense expanded, probed the rising, howling wind,
searching for the source of the song.

She dropped the files to the floor and pushed herself
from the chair. The room took a slow rotation around her
until she felt as if she were being gradually sucked into
the eye of a whirlpool. Into her mind swept so great a
fear that it verged on panic. She could not breathe and
ran to the window, clawed at it impotently until manag-
ing to shove it open. Anticipating a lashing from the
wind, she found only stillness. And quiet. No wind, no
thunder. Only the constant lightning that flashed as
brightly as daylight every few seconds over the house.
Just as on the night of D'Abanville's ball, the first night
she had spent at Greystone, the air felt charged with expectation. The fine hairs on her arms stood up and her
skin tingled. She found herself straining toward the silence, her heart racing, waiting for the music, the chimes.
Of course he would come. She needed him. Of course
he would come. Why rot in that miserable cell when he
was innocent? When with one snap of his fingers he could
disappear from that dark, cramped room and return to
her. He was magic. He could do it. He could if she prayed
hard enough. If she believed—*if she really believed!*

Then the music did come, but it wasn't the chimes. As
Mercy stared out over the garden's dark expanse, lights
appeared, orange and flickering and glowing, in the vicinity of the old carriage house. They formed a sort of
line and moved toward the house, and as they neared,
she could see that there were people carrying them. Or
were they?

Mercy closed her eyes and backed from the window.
She was dreaming again. That's all it was. Any moment
she would wake up and . . .

Having returned to her chair, she dropped into it. She
could hear them now, chanting. Numbly she thought:
This is not a dream. It never was. Whoever they are, they
are coming for me, as they came for Mary Casimire.

She picked up McMillian's letter from the floor, clumsily dragged the papers into her lap, vaguely aware that, little by little, her body seemed to be dying. There was no feeling now in her fingers beyond a numb tingling, as if they were frozen. Her eyelids felt heavy, so heavy, and though she knew she should be trying to escape whatever fate awaited her outside this house, she could only imagine how peaceful it would be to lie down and drift into that sweet black oblivion that had beckoned her each night since she arrived at Greystone.

7 October, 1788.

It is very nearly midnight. I know now what is going on. I know that I am going to die tonight unless Peter arrives in time. I saw them. Before this evil they have been feeding me took control of my senses, I crept up to the top of that dreadful tower and I watched them, writhing together like animals. I know now why the servants ignore my calls, because they are up there as well, drunk with lust and God knows what else. Perhaps the same potion they have been feeding me so my mind is racked by nightmares and my body by unnatural desires. Oh, God, they are coming for me. I hear them now shambling down the corridor. Where is Peter? He promised me. He would come if he could. I know they have harmed him. And Mama and Papa too. They are coming. I hear them outside my door and there is nothing I can do to stop them. Where is Peter? Where is Pet—

The paper fluttered toward the floor, rising momentarily in the heat from the stove, then settling in a pool of yellow firelight near Mercy's feet. Her head back against the rocker, she stared toward the door of her room, unable to lift her head, unable to see beyond the curtain of darkness that was very slowly closing around her. Like Mary, she knew they were there, waiting for her to slip over the edge . . . and then what? She tried to remember how Mary had died. Had it been simply the drugs or . . . ? Who was doing this? And then it occurred to her. Roger. Of course it was Roger. He had brought her to Greystone. He had kept her from running into that room with Micah because . . . Dear God, *Roger* had sabotaged D'Abanville's prop in order to get rid of him. Had she entered that room, she might have died with Micah and all their plans for her would have been for nothing.

What were their plans?

She tried to rise from the chair. Hopeless. Whatever drug they had been feeding her had taken its full effect. Each breath was an effort. All the old nightmares waited just beyond the dark—waiting to become reality—and she knew if she calmly slipped over the precipice now, she would never return. She understood it all now. *They* had killed Abby Russell and Amanda Kinsdale and tried to frame D'Abanville.

With the thought of Dominick came a final rush of determination. Very slowly she pushed herself from her chair and slid to the floor, where she reached for the transcript of Mary's diary. She would hide it. Someday someone would find it, as she had Mary's diary, and then, perhaps, this lunacy would end.

She crawled on her hands and knees to the dresser, cursing with angry tears as the gown caught beneath her legs and dragged her down each time she moved. Finally reaching the dresser, she tugged weakly on the bottom drawer, one inch, then two, slid the papers inside, then shoved it closed. She could hear them coming now, up the hall. The chanting was louder. She could hear it also through her window, see the fiery red glow like sunrise turn the windowpanes the color of blood. Lying on her back, she stared at the ceiling, allowing her mind and body to drift on some calm cloud of acceptance that was beyond fear, beyond pain. And for a moment—just for a moment—she thought she heard the chimes, beautiful and haunting and so full of love. D'Abanville.

Closing her eyes, she thought: Our Father, who art in heaven . . .

22

As if rising from a deep black pool of water, Mercy struggled to the surface of consciousness, hearing the cries and shrieks like no human sound she had ever heard before. Shadows loomed over her, frightening, indistinguishable. Rough hands grabbed her arms, her hair, her legs, wrenching, dragging her off the floor until she seemed to be soaring high in the air and then falling into some abyss of confusion that was occupied only by vague, twisted shapes too horrifying to be real. Surely, surely this was all a nightmare!

A cry rang out, obliterating the mayhem for a short moment. Then she realized it was herself, weeping, and she could not stop it.

Again she was lifted high in the air; someone held her feet, someone else gripped her shoulders. They moved down a corridor lit by burning torches, deeper into the darkness, down, down the spiraling staircase. She remembered that pitch-black well, and at the bottom . . .

She screamed and the shrieking grew louder, jubilant. Dear God, dear God, what were they doing to her? Where were they taking her? Who were these frenetic creatures with the bodies of men and faces like animals? She struggled to awaken, to shake that deathlike lethargy that stole the breath from her lungs and the strength from her limbs. She could not fight them, she could only weep, then pray, then scream out: *Dominick!* and *God help me!*

A bolt was thrown and a door swung open. Dense and black, the darkness swallowed her. Again she was rising, up, up, hands, wicked hands, monsters' hands gripping her flesh, exaggerating the pain in her head and the nausea that rolled in waves through her stomach. Then a wind hit her face like a blast from a furnace. Forcing open her eyes, she stared up into the boiling, churning stormclouds, and for a moment she thought she was free, free of the monsters and of that wretched house.

Then the screams erupted again, louder this time, and closer, piercing the midnight heat with maniacal laughter that drowned out even Mercy's cries. Around her the bodies moved, gyrating and twisting, together and apart, lascivious and horrible with naked forms painted gold by the torchlight. Overhead, the sky rumbled and flashed, threatening the revelers with lances of lightning that ripped like spears toward the earth.

She was lowered and placed flat on something cold and hard. Though they did not bind her, she could not move. As in her dreams, she felt bound to whatever rocklike bed was beneath her. She could only stare toward the furious sky and feel the rising wind tear at her hair and gown and body.

Then there was silence. Deafening silence more frightening than all the inhuman sounds that she had heard before. She watched the roiling sky waiting for some dark vengeful angel to come swooping out of heaven with a spear of lightning in both hands and announce with a voice as shattering as thunder that this was her punishment for surviving Sultan Street. But no angel came either to punish or to save her. Only the wind, the darkness, and anticipation washed over her. Someone was coming . . . He was already here.

He emerged from the shadows to her right. Tall and slender, beautiful and terrifying to behold, he watched her from within his satyr's mask with eyes that glittered with torch fire. She knew those eyes. Oh, dear God . . .

Stepping up onto the marble slab, his legs spread, his manhood erect and evil-looking in the flickering firelight, he raised his hands and beckoned someone from the shadows. And the chanting began, the same as she had heard in what she had once believed were her dreams.

"Aman . . . Amani . . . Amanita."

Someone raised her head. Someone else pressed a cup to her lips. "Drink," came the familiar voice. "Please, miss, drink it up and it won't seem so bad. You won't ever know—''

Mercy tried to turn her face away, but the hands holding her head gripped more tightly.

''Drink, my dear,'' came Roger's voice. ''We would not want to anger the prince. It will seem much less painful if—''

''No!'' She struggled and the voice over her boomed: ''Idiots! Why wasn't she already drugged?''

''She were,'' the servant insisted. ''We slipped it in her tea, as we always did. She must not've drank it all—''

''Silence!'' the satyr demanded angrily. Towering over Mercy, he stared down at her and began to laugh. Then he waved the servant and Roger away with a lift of his hand. ''So be it!'' he said. ''I'll have her awake and aware and enjoy her all the more for it.''

The chanting began again, and the dancing. Music from pipes continued to rise in pitch until Mercy thought she could no longer endure it. She longed to raise her hands and press them to her ears to shut out the sound. She closed her eyes, telling herself over and over that this was all a dream, just another terrible nightmare. Yet when she looked up again, he was there, leering at her from behind his mask, his eyes slits of yellow fire and lust.

With no warning he dropped onto her. She screamed, struggled to raise her arms, cursing the drugs that had paralyzed her. His body writhed against hers; his hands moved over her, stroking and probing, while his laughter echoed, hauntingly familiar, in her mind.

Louder and louder the music played, and the chanting around her became more like a prayer. ''Master of Darkness, Prince of All Dead—''

Gritting her teeth, she closed her eyes and put all of her concentration into raising her hand, as she had in her dreams. And as if she had suddenly broken the invisible ties that had bound her to the slab of marble, she reached out for the mask and tore it from his face.

''Bastard!'' she screamed into Oliver's startled eyes. ''How you could defile our own father—''

"My father is Bune," he hissed. "My mother is Hecate!"

"Hail, Hecate!" the followers called.

Oliver rolled from her line of vision and Mercy did her best to rise. Little by little she managed to lift her shoulders, to drag herself to the edge of the marble slab. Then he was back, his mask in place. Something glimmered in his clasp, and in horror she watched as he raised the long-bladed knife above his head and began advancing step by step up the altar.

Around her the cries grew frenetic and the gyrating increased. "Hail, Hecate!" they chanted. "Hail, Bune, Prince of All Dead—"

The sky exploded then in a burst of blinding light. Mercy fell back on the marble, covered her ears against the deafening crack that far surpassed thunder in magnitude. Oliver tumbled backward and the revelers screamed out in alarm as fire and smoke rose up from the floor and engulfed the sky, a shimmering white heat rising, rising toward heaven. And within it stood a man, tall and dark, with eyes as bright and blue as the fire that danced at his feet.

The screams that arose from the worshipers were of fear and not elation. They fell to the floor and trembled as D'Abanville raised his hand toward Oliver. For a moment light danced on his fingertips, and as Oliver sprang to his feet and charged with his knife at the smoky illusion, fire erupted again, engulfing Mercy's brother with smoke and light and knocking Oliver onto his back.

Mercy rolled again to the edge of the altar. Forms were running blindly through the billowing smoke and flames, and as the sky opened once more and blasted the trembling earth with another spear of lightning, their terrified screams seemed to multiply a thousandfold.

Through the smoke she saw Dominick and Oliver come together, two powers unleashed that appeared to bring the cacophony from the sky to an ear-shattering pitch. For a moment the surrounding flames reflected in the upraised knife in her brother's hands, and she screamed, stumbled to her feet, then collapsed to her knees. Beneath her the tower trembled and cracked sharply like wood splintering to a thousand ancient pieces. Mercy closed her eyes, unable to breathe, unable to see anything but the uplifted knife in her brother's hand over and over in her frantic mind.

There were hands on her then, hard hands, lifting her from the rubble, and for a moment she thought Oliver was back.

"No!" she screamed, and drove her fist through the dense smoke, connecting with someone's shoulder.

"Miss Dansing!" came the familiar voice. "Miss Dansing, it is John Lawton!"

Mercy cried aloud in relief as Lawton lifted her in his arms. Then he was carrying her through the fire and smoke, away from the altar, away from Oliver and D'Abanville. "Help him!" she tried to call out, but the smoke choked the words to little more than a hoarse whisper. She struggled to loose herself of Lawton's grip, but too soon she was being handed down through a hole in the floor, into another pair of waiting arms.

"The tower is going!" Stan McMillian called up to Lawton. His arms around Mercy, McMillian whirled toward D'Abanville's bedroom door while the walls crumbled to the floor, and the floor swayed underfoot like a boat in water.

"You can't leave him!" Mercy rasped. "Dominick is up there; you can't just leave him!"

They burst through the door of the tower, McMillian almost stumbling over the debris of the earlier explosion. Lawton followed. Suddenly there were dozens of policemen around them, helping them beyond the smoke and the flames that were racing as fast as they up the corridor of the house.

The night wind hit them with gale force as they exited the house. McMillian continued running down the drive, cradling Mercy in his arms until she refused to go any farther, twisting from his grip and making him stumble and fall with her to the ground. Behind them the roar from the wind and sky mounted like a cyclone that shook the very ground where they lay.

Joined by Lawton and the others, they looked back at the house, watched the tower shimmer yellow and red against the ink-black clouds. Then the sky lit one last time in a blinding sheet of light that consumed the tower in brilliance. Mercy covered her face and wept into her hands while the world trembled under the force of the final impact. Then there was only the darkness . . . and a gentle wind that soughed through the trees like the sighing of angels.

The breeze stirred the limbs of the chestnut tree. Mercy pulled her shawl more tightly about her shoulders as she looked cautiously toward her guests. "You have news," she said.

McMillian glanced at Chesterton, who sat relaxed in the wrought-iron chair, his arm in a sling. They both looked at Mercy.

"We have retrieved the last remains from the rubble. D'Abanville was not among them."

A slight smile touched her mouth. She looked away, toward Lady Casimire's rose garden. "I had faith that he would not be found there, and he wasn't. He is gone, sir. You will not find him."

"And where do you think he has gone?" Chesterton asked.

She looked at him as a sudden wind whipped her hair around her face. "To wherever he came from, I suppose."

"And that is?"

She looked away.

Chesterton left his chair and spoke quietly to McMillian, but not so softly that Mercy could not hear him.

"I fear this ordeal has driven her quite mad," he said. "We both know there is no possible way D'Abanville could have survived the destruction of that tower." Looking back at Mercy, Chesterton asked, "Are you certain you have not seen him, Miss Dansing?"

"Of course she is, Inspector." Lady Casimire dropped her pruning shears on the table and sat down. "What do you want with him anyway? You know now that Roger and Oliver were behind the Russell and Kinsdale killings. The survivors of that holocaust confessed that it was all a plan to rid Greystone of D'Abanville so they could carry out their ritual. You cannot possibly still believe that the man you know as Dominick

D'Abanville is in any way responsible for the East End murders. It is my understanding that Commissioner Warren has ordered the investigation surrounding him to be dropped.''

"So he has," he replied. "I cannot help my curiosity, however. For my own peace of mind, I would like to know who he really is.''

"But I told you. His name is Peter Reed, and he is the son of Colleen Reed, who was once my lady's maid. His reason for returning to Whitechapel is simple. He was searching for his aunt, who abandoned him and his twin sister at London Hospital and never returned.''

"Why did he simply not tell us that?''

"I think he felt he would be cleared of these charges without his having to reveal his past to the public. Perhaps he was concerned that his audience, once learning he was an East End orphan, would find him less acceptable.''

"Conjecture." Chesterton raised one eyebrow and peered out over the rose garden. "The truth is, you don't really know anything about the man who called himself Dominick D'Abanville. Who he is. Where he came from before arriving in Paris. You assume he is Peter Reed, but without his corroboration, you will never know for certain. The only thing certain about this entire case is that he is missing. That he managed to escape Commercial Street police station without any of fifty officers seeing him leave. He vanished without a trace, my lady. And for that you have no explanation whatsoever.''

"Must there always be an explanation, my dear Inspector Chesterton? I think if that young man left us with anything, it is the belief that without a little faith in miracles, what dreary, hopeless lives we would all lead.''

There was a softening in his countenance as he looked again at Mercy. As her eyes met his, a shadow of a smile crossed his mouth. "Perhaps you are right." He pulled his shoulders back, and with a grimace of pain said, "I'll be off, then. A good day to you, ladies. And, Miss Dansing, I hope you have a pleasant sojourn to Paris. I understand it is nice there this time of year.''

"It seems you have been working overtime again, Inspector," Mercy stated.

"So it seems. . . . I wish you the best of luck in your search, my dear."

"Thank you."

"I will see you out," McMillian said.

Mercy watched the men as they walked through the rose garden, gravel crunching underfoot as the sun poured down on their shoulders. And she smiled.

EPILOGUE

Paris, 22 October, 1888

"I suspected all along that he was Peter Reed," Lady Casimire had said. "Even before I came to Greystone to meet him. I was certain of it the moment he turned those blue eyes full of anger and hate down to mine. It was the same look he gave me as a child when he and his sister Charlotte were turned over to his aunt in the East End. That look has haunted me for the last twenty-five years of my life. It will continue to haunt me until I am certain he is at peace. Find him, my dear. For both of our sakes."

Mercy stared at the ill-painted door before rapping softly. A moment passed before it opened. A man's aged face with wide dark eyes peered up at her and smiled. "Monsieur Lavoisier?" Mercy asked.

"Oui."

"I am Mercy Dansing. We have an appointment . . . ?"

He opened the door and waved her in.

Mercy stepped into the dim apartment. She glanced about, noting the yellowed and cracking posters on the walls announcing "Lavoisier the Magnificent!" She looked then toward a darkened doorway at the rear of the room. A curtain of red glass beads hung there, swaying slightly.

"Sit down," he told her, pointing to an overstuffed chair near the window.

Mercy looked toward the dark doorway once more before sitting in the chair. She stared for a moment out the window. There was a pond close by. Dark-haired children squealed in laughter as a breeze caught the tiny sails of their toy boats and propelled them along the shore.

"You have come concerning Dominick D'Abanville?" came the curious voice.

"Yes." Mercy looked back at her host.

"There has certainly been a great deal of interest recently in my old friend."

"D'Abanville is dead?" Mercy asked.

"Yes, yes," he said. "Just as I told the investigator from London. He died many years ago."

"Are you aware that there is another man who is passing himself off as Dominick D'Abanville?"

He smiled and shrugged his shoulders. "It is the nature of the business, I think."

"You have no idea who that man might really be?"

"Mademoiselle, why should I know such a thing?"

"Did your old friend not have a family? A son, perhaps, to whom to pass on his secrets?"

"D'Abanville was never married, Mademoiselle Dansing."

Mercy left the chair and strolled casually about the small chamber. Each corner was stacked high with dusty books and papers. She pretended to study a chart of the universe tacked to the wall, while her eyes were drawn once again to the dark doorway. There was a stirring of air there that made her senses warm and her heartbeat quicken. She listened hard for the message.

"I was saying," came Lavoisier's voice, "my old friend never married."

Mercy said without turning, "Perhaps he adopted."

No response.

She turned and smiled at the old man, who smiled in return.

"Perhaps," she continued, "during one of his charitable performances in London, he came across a young boy who he thought showed promise of becoming a protégé for his magic. Perhaps he brought the boy back to Paris and taught him all he knew. Perhaps, because the young man was so grateful to D'Abanville, he took his identity when D'Abanville died and carried that name to new heights throughout the world, something the old man dreamed of doing but never managed to accomplish."

The old man chuckled and clasped his gnarled hands

together in his lap. "A nice fairy tale. Go on," he coaxed her.

Mercy walked closer to the doorway. "After achieving his goal, however, the young man decided he must face his past and return to London. I think he might have felt a great deal of guilt because he had escaped the poverty in which so many still lingered. I imagine he might have tried to give all his money away to the impoverished. Perhaps he might even have searched for the aunt who had left him and his sister on the steps of London Hospital's charity ward."

"A rather grim story," Lavoisier commented with a shake of his head. "Does it end well, I hope?"

"That, I think, would depend on the young D'Abanville . . . if he existed."

"Indeed."

Mercy walked to the room's front entrance before looking back at her smiling host. "I am staying one more night at the Etoile Hotel across from the Arc de Triomphe. In the morning I shall pay my respects to Monsieur D'Abanville at Montmartre Cemetery, then I return to London."

"A pity, mademoiselle."

"I agree," she said. "I like Paris very much, but there seems to be nothing here for me, whereas back in London there is an eligible young inspector who has taken a fancy to me, I think. I daresay he might even propose as soon as I return."

"How wonderful for you." Lavoisier smiled again.

"Good-bye," she said.

"*Adieu,*" he responded.

Mercy stepped out the door, onto the walk, and did not look back until she had crossed the street. She watched Lavoisier's apartment for some time before hailing a cab and returning to her hotel.

Perhaps she had only imagined his being there, hiding behind those glass beads, listening to every word she said. But Mercy didn't think so.

Looking up through the dawn fog, she called to the cab driver, "Montmartre Cemetery, please!"

Climbing aboard the cab, she closed the door and sank

back into the seat, hugging herself against the cold and damp that reminded her so much of London. She hadn't lied to Lavoisier. She intended to return to London this afternoon if her hunch didn't pay off. After searching every cabaret in Paris for the last two weeks in search of anyone who might have seen Peter Reed, she had finally decided to call on the magician, knowing from Chesterton that Lavoisier had been the old D'Abanville's closest friend.

Upon arriving at the cemetery, she paid the driver and watched as the cab disappeared through the fog, back toward Paris. She stared at the ivy-covered archway overhead before forcing her feet to move her through the gates and up the pathway. She climbed the hill forever, it seemed, until her bruised legs began to tremble from the strain. Over and over again she told herself that he would be here. If Peter Reed loved her as much as she hoped he did, he would not allow her to return to London without seeing her first.

Fog shifted about the towering marble monuments like drifts of gray snow. Mercy searched for long minutes before locating the simple statuary. Standing over the grave, she looked out over the twinkling lights of Paris and waited, listening, before reading the inscription written on the marble slab at her feet.

> Do not stand at my grave and weep;
> I am not there. I do not sleep.
> I am a thousand winds that blow;
> I am the diamond glints on snow.
> I am the sunlight on ripened grain;
> I am the gentle autumn's rain.
> When you awaken in the morning's hush,
> I am the swift uplifting rush
> Of quiet birds in circled flight.
> I am the soft star that shines at night.
> Do not stand at my grave and cry.
> I am not there; I did not die.

He was here. She could feel him. It was in the gentle sweep of air over her face, warm like a breath against her temple. Turning, she fixed her eyes on the pathway, hearing the music, the chimes, swirl in the cavalcade of fog over the hilltop. The wind sang in harmony through the trees, shifted the dreary clouds into the vague image of a man in the distance. The image came closer, until she was certain she could reach out and touch it, if she dared.

If she dared . . .

"Hello," he said.

She closed her eyes, letting the magic of his voice enfold her, warm her, and make her shiver. She smiled and looked at him again. "I've missed you," she said.

The wind stirred, smelling strangely of roses. The clouds parted and a shaft of morning sunlight poured over his features. His blue eyes twinkled as he held out his hand. "Come here," he said.

Mercy placed her hand in his. They turned and walked back toward Paris.